Praise for the work of Leonard B. Scott

CHARLIE MIKE

"One of the finest novels yet written about the Vietnam War."
—*The Washington Post*

THE LAST RUN

"It's more *Charlie Mike*, but better. . . . The kind of book that leaves you wanting more."
—*Atlanta Journal & Constitution*

THE IRON MEN

"Superbly written . . . A very fine and fast-paced story, a sweeping and generational tale of murder and retribution, set against the headline events of the last half century."
—NELSON DEMILLE

FORGED IN HONOR

"This story is better than *Rambo* in any of his incarnations and flows smoother than many high-adventure yarns . . . [with] battles so spectacular that those who love adventure and great war scenes will jump for joy at reading this well-plotted novel."
—*Ocala Star Banner*

By Leonard B. Scott
Published by Ballantine Books:

SOLEMN DUTY

Leonard B. Scott

BALLANTINE BOOKS • NEW YORK

Copyright © 1997 by Leonard B. Scott

All rights reserved under International and Pan-American Copyright Conventions. Published in the United States by Ballantine Books, a divison of Random House, Inc., New York, and simultaneously in Canada by Random House of Canada Limited, Toronto.

http://www.randomhouse.com

Library of Congress Catalog Card Number: 96-95383

ISBN 0-345-41997-9

Manufactured in the United States of America

First Edition: May 1997

10 9 8 7 6 5 4 3 2 1

Solemn Duty
is dedicated to those who serve our country

PART I
1972

CHAPTER 1

May 9, 1972, Camp 147, Cambodia

Captain Robert Anderson stood outside the sandbagged command bunker rigid with anger. Minutes before, a radio message from his operational commander, Lieutenant Colonel Richard Stroud, had ordered Anderson and his ten-man team to turn over responsibility for Camp 147 to their Cambodian Special Forces counterparts and be ready for chopper extraction within the hour.

Sick to his stomach, Anderson lowered his head. There must have been some kind of mistake. *My God, how do I face them?* he asked himself. Only six months earlier he had ordered the helicopter pilots to circle over the village so the rest of the team could acquaint themselves with the lay of the land. For Anderson, the Special Forces A-team commander, the aerial view had only confirmed what he'd already known after being briefed by Colonel Stroud. The Cambodian village designated 147 was strategically perfect. Located only a kilometer from the border of South Vietnam and flanked by rugged mountains, the hamlet was situated on a small hill in the neck of a bottle-shaped valley. If a large North Vietnamese Army force wanted to strike quickly into South Vietnam, it would have to use the bottle-shaped valley as an invasion route. Stroud assigned Anderson to turn Hamlet 147 into a cork by training the indigenous population and fortifying the village.

Anderson shook his head to clear the memories of the past

and looked out over the camp. That was a mistake; the rectangular fort depressed him even more. It had once been a beautiful village, with tall stands of green bamboo lining the paths that led up the hill to magnificent, elevated, thatched houses made from sayo and yellow bamboo. But all that was gone; he had seen to it. To clear fields of fire, the bamboo had been cut down and replaced with iron pickets and miles of barbed wire and concertina forming three concentric perimeter fences. The villagers' beautiful elevated houses next fell victim to his plans. They had been torn down because their thatch roofs would have made them fire traps should the new fort be attacked. The farmers' homes were replaced with sweltering tin-roofed huts surrounded by six-foot walls made from stacked sandbags. Nothing remained that remotely reminded him of the serenely beautiful village. Where children had once played, there now were dug-in mortar positions and machine-gun bunkers. Interconnecting trenches and fighting positions crisscrossed the once grassy slopes where water buffalo had grazed; and where the women had dried rice, there were supply and ammunition bunkers. *Yeah, I accomplished the mission,* Anderson thought. *I turned this once peaceful village into a Southeast Asia version of Fort Apache.*

"Sir?"

Anderson turned and faced his best friend and operations sergeant, Staff Sergeant Jerry Rhodes. "What is it?" Anderson snapped, hoping the sergeant would get the hint and leave him alone.

Rhodes frowned. "Christ, sir, it ain't like we're hangin' 'em out to dry. We'll only be thirty klicks away, and we'll have a battalion-size strike force on call to reinforce 'em if they get into trouble. Plus, sir, don't forget the air support. Our counterparts can hold things down until we get here. Hell, this is just a temporary thing. That fuckin' Stroud has another wild hair up his ass is all. You'll make him see the light once we get back."

Anderson nodded in silence. Kicking a stone with his boot, he motioned toward the bunker entrance. "Have Shark find

Lieutenant Tram and tell him to see me. And make sure the rest of the team talks to their counterparts before we go. I want this handoff to go right. Understood?"

Rhodes stepped closer and put his hand on his friend's shoulder. "Look, Bob, you're lettin' this get to ya. Hell, none of us like it any better than you do. It's another Stroud fuck-up. Sooner or later the higher-ups are gonna catch on he's a loose cannon. In the meantime ya best get hold of yourself. Lieutenant Tram is bringing the chief up so you can tell him the bad news. Ya sure as hell don't want to be showin' him that long face of yours. He'll read ya like a book, and then things really *will* be fucked up."

Anderson's jaw tightened at being told to get his emotions under control. What really angered him was knowing that the sergeant was right. He lowered his head. "It doesn't make me feel any better, Jerry, but I'll do my part with the chief. Now let me stew awhile in peace."

Allowing himself a small smile of victory, the sergeant turned and walked back into the bunker. Alone again, Anderson looked out over the fort, feeling no pride in what he and his men had accomplished. *The mission is complete, but at what cost? What have I done?* he wondered. Then he saw Frenchy, the chief's twelve-year-old grandson, walking toward the bunker. The small boy was wearing his usual infectious smile and ridiculously large fatigues. Waves of guilt washed over Robert. *Christ, I don't even remember his real name. Wasn't it enough that I destroyed their village, their rice paddies, their lives? Did I have to change them, too?*

A minute later the small boy bounded up, came to attention and saluted. "Cap-tian Ro-bert, Frenchy, ports!"

Anderson forced a smile as he returned a salute. "And what's my chief scout have to *re*-port?"

The boy grinned and pointed to a distant bunker. "Sar-geant Louie say bunk-er sayen fini."

"So seven is finished, is it?"

"Yes sir, A-O-kay, fini," the boy said, bobbing his head.

Anderson fought back his emotions as he regarded the beaming almond-skinned boy who had stolen his and the team's hearts from day one. Not quite four feet tall, Frenchy was different from the other villagers in that he was half French. The chief had explained that the boy's mother worked for a rubber plantation years ago, as a cook, and became involved with a French engineer. The Frenchman left her and his new son soon after the boy was born. Shamed, the boy's mother brought the boy to the village to live with her parents, then left for Phnom Penh to begin a new life. She had never returned.

Anderson looked at the small boy, feeling his heart breaking. As usual, Frenchy's fatigue pockets bulged with cans of C-rations, and around his thin waist was the ever-present frayed web belt from which hung an old metal canteen and a battered K-bar sheath knife that reached almost to his knees. A sweat-stained, faded green beret that Anderson had given him as a present covered the boy's brown hair. And, of course, he wore his usual broad smile.

"Cap-tain Ro-bert, what wrong?" the boy asked, pointing at his own eyes. "You not see Scout Frenchy?"

Anderson put his hand on the boy's shoulder. "I'm sad, Frenchy, because I have to leave you and the village. The team and I have been ordered to Pleiku for a while. On, now, don't give me that look. You know I wouldn't leave you for very long. It's just that—"

He stopped in mid-sentence, feeling the presence of another. He turned and faced the boy's gray-haired grandfather, whose face was like cracked brown leather. He was followed by Anderson's counterpart, Cambodian Special Forces Lieutenant Quan Tram.

Anderson brought his steepled hands up to his chest and bowed. The elderly chief returned the greeting and spoke to Lieutenant Tram, who interpreted.

"Captain, the old one says he heard you and the team were going to Pleiku. He wants to know how long you will be away."

"Tell Po I'm sorry he heard the news from others. I wanted

him to hear it from me. Tell him not to worry, we will return very soon. It's a mistake of some kind."

Dressed in shorts and a dirty fatigue shirt, the old man nodded as if very tired and spoke with obvious sadness.

"Captain, old one says his heart will be heavy until you return. He thinks the enemy will come soon. He says scouts and patrols have seen their trail runners. He says the trail runners are like the small winds that come before a big storm."

"Tell the chief to remember that my team and I gave our word of honor and the honor of our nation that we would stand with the people of the village and defeat the nonbelievers. Tell him when his scouts see the enemy approach that he is to report to you, Tram. Remind him that you will call us on the radio in Pleiku and we'll come immediately in helicopters with a battalion of strike force soldiers. Tell him planes and helicopter gunships will come, too, and help stop the nonbelievers."

After listening to the translation, the chief looked out over what had once been his village with a somber expression. Finally he spoke, almost in a whisper.

Tram stepped closer to Anderson and translated quietly. "Captain, the old one says war is no good. He says he prays to the enlightened one that when the battle comes and the nonbelievers are defeated, the war will end forever. It is time for peace."

Anderson swallowed a dry lump in his throat before speaking. "Tell him, I too pray for the war's end. I have learned to love his people as he does. I want more than anything for his people to live in peace."

Po listened to the translation then reached into his fatigue pocket and took out a small brass cross that gleamed in the sunlight. Stepping closer to Anderson, the old man reached up and pulled the dog tag chain from beneath Anderson's shirt and attached the cross to the chain. Lifting the cross, he touched it to Anderson's lips, and with his other hand he placed it over the captain's heart.

"Old one say you have become son to him, Captain Robert.

He says go to Pleiku with knowledge he and his people are here, in your heart forever. He made the cross for you from shell casings. He says he made it so your God will keep you safe."

Anderson's eyes welled as he patted the old man's hand. "Tram, tell him I will always carry him and his people in my heart and will always wear the cross he has given me. Tell him I will be back very soon . . . we will fight for peace together."

The ten men of Anderson's team stood bent slightly forward under the weight of their heavy rucksacks. Like their leader, they stood solemnly as the people of the village watched them prepare to leave. Robert Anderson faced his counterpart Lieutenant Tram and raised his hand in a salute. "My friend, I turn over command of 147 to you. I wish you Buddha's blessings."

With tears in his eyes, Tram returned the salute. "I accept command, my friend. I shall miss you."

Hearing the choppers approaching, Anderson turned to walk to the landing pad, but saw Frenchy standing at attention only a few feet away. He forced a smile and saluted. "Chief Scout, I want you to give your new commander all the support you have given me."

The boy saluted with the wrong hand. "O-kay Cap-tain Robert. You come back t-t time o-kay? Scout Frenchy wait for you. All people wait. You come back t-t time o-kay."

Anderson's eyes were watering and he only managed to nod and say, "Okay." He motioned his men toward the pad and looked over his shoulder at the throng of villagers. Sick at heart, he tried to lift his hand to wave but couldn't find the strength. The wind from the landing Huey suddenly tore at his clothes and he whispered, "I'm sorry."

May 12

As the sun began to sink behind the mountains, the silence of the forest was broken by the sound of a small frightened boy's tortured breathing as he ran down a hard-packed clay trail. Barefoot and wearing too-big U.S. Army fatigues, Frenchy had been sent ahead of the others in the patrol with the horrible news. He veered off the track, slid down an embankment, leaped over a small stream, and fought his way up the slippery bank where low-hanging branches and vines tore at his face and caught his shirt. The boy spun, kicked, and fought until he broke their tenacious grasp, then continued running as fast as he could. Seconds later he crossed a rise and in the distance finally saw his village looming ahead in the twilight. Although his pounding heart felt as if it would burst through his chest, he pumped his legs even harder. Bursting out of the tree line, the boy jumped onto a rice dike and raced across dry, fallow rice paddies. Ignoring the pain in his chest, he followed the twisting serpentine path that led through the barbed-wire perimeter fences. Finally, through the obstacles, he screamed as he made the final sprint toward the command bunker. "The nonbelievers are coming! They are coming!"

Pleiku

In the underground tactical operations center the radio operator tossed down the handset and quickly picked up the field phone. Seconds later he had the duty officer on the line. "Captain Anderson? . . . Sir, Lieutenant Tram just radioed in from Camp 147. He reports at least a battalion-size NVA force has crossed the river and is headed toward 147. He requests immediate air support and the strike battalion."

Anderson made himself speak calmly although his insides felt like a bowl of Jell-O. "Tell him we're on the way, then call the aviation battalion and have them scramble the gunships and slicks. I'll notify my team and the strike battalion. We'll all be ready for pickup in twenty minutes at the airfield. Contact the Air Force forward air controller and have him get fast movers there as soon as possible. Got it?"

"Yes, sir. Will do. Out."

Anderson recradled the handset and spun around, yelling at the men playing poker behind him. "The NVA are moving in on 147! Sergeant Rhodes, notify the strike-battalion commander to saddle up his boys!"

Rucksacks on their backs, and holding CAR-15s, the team approached the tarmac where the five hundred men of the strike force stood waiting in full combat gear. Anderson searched the early evening sky for the choppers and was about to ask for the radio handset to find out what was holding them up when a sergeant approached and saluted. "Sir, Colonel Stroud wants to see you immediately. He's in the TOC."

"I don't have time to bullshit with the colonel," Anderson snapped. "The birds will be here any second."

"Sir, you'd better talk to him—I don't think the lift birds are coming. I heard that he canceled them."

"What?"

Tall, sandy-haired, and wearing glasses, Lieutenant Colonel Richard Stroud stood studying a wall map in the tactical operations center when Anderson stormed in and confronted him. "Sir, what the hell is going on? Where are the slicks?"

Stroud slowly cocked up an eyebrow. "Captain, surely I don't have to remind you who's in operational command here. *You* do not have the authority to mount an operation without my say so. And you most certainly don't have the authority to authorize the use of aviation assets or the calling out of the strike battalion. You were out of line, Captain."

"Out of line?" Anderson repeated incredulously. "One forty-seven is going to be attacked! As duty officer I ordered what was necessary so we could respond as quickly as possible."

"Captain, I'm well-aware you were responsible for the training of the indigenous population of 147, but *one* sighting report from an inexperienced Cambodian officer does *not* justify mounting an operation. May I remind you I have six other camps under my operational control, and each is just as important as 147. Confirmation of the report is necessary; there are procedures that must be followed and priorities that must be considered."

Anderson closed his eyes for a moment to try and control his seething anger. He took in a breath, let it out slowly and spoke, trying not to sound condescending. "Sir, Lieutenant Tram is anything but 'inexperienced.' He has been in the program for four years. He was a college professor and taught English at Phnom Penh University before he enlisted in our program. He rose through the ranks, sir, and has been in more action than all our teams have seen put together. He's been wounded three times and he's been awarded more medals for bravery than Audie Murphy. When *he* says the NVA are approaching and that he needs support, I believe him. Time is critical, sir. We must have the fighter bombers hit the lead NVA units before they have time to deploy and organize for the assault."

Stroud smugly held out a handwritten report from the radio operator. "Look for yourself, Captain. Lieutenant Tram reported his scouts saw a single battalion of North Vietnamese regulars. One forty-seven has over three hundred defenders. A single battalion of NVA is almost the same strength . . . hardly a threat to an entrenched force I should think."

Shaking with frustration, Anderson ignored the report and pointed at the map. "That's right, sir, he reported a battalion. Their *lead* battalion. The terrain restricts the enemy's movement until they reach the valley. If the NVA are moving in battalion-size strength, you can bet more battalions are following the first. This is it, sir. This is what we've been waiting for. We've got the enemy in strength, and in the open. We can annihilate them."

The other operations staff officers and NCOs had stopped work and were watching, holding their breath. Stroud felt their eyes on him. He raised his chin and motioned Anderson toward the planning room. "I think we should discuss this matter in private."

"Discuss what?" Anderson blurted. "There's nothing to discuss! Every second we delay reduces the chances of getting the strike force there in time, and the Air Force's chances of hitting them before they deploy. I need those slicks, sir. I need them now!"

Stroud began to respond but was stopped by an excited voice coming over the nearest radio speaker box. "Papa Zulu Three, this is Camp One-four-seven. We are being hit by mortar and rockets. Where is the air support? Over."

"You need any more confirmation, sir? That's Lieutenant Tram's voice."

The colonel visibly tightened and he barked loudly, "Everybody out! Clear the TOC! Not you, Anderson. You stay. Everybody else out, now!"

The radio operator lifted the handset as if confused. "Sir, what do I tell Lieutenant Tram?"

"Turn the radio off and follow my orders. Get out!" Stroud hollered.

Oh God, God, please don't let this happen, Anderson said to himself as the officers and sergeants hurried to the door. He had known since first meeting the colonel half a year ago that high command could not have picked anyone more ill-suited for the position. Not Special Forces or even airborne qualified, Stroud was a Military Intelligence officer who had never commanded troops at any level, nor had he ever served in a line unit. He'd been the regional commanding general's intelligence staff officer and yes-man. Though extremely intelligent, Stroud had no idea what was going on in the field and made no effort to find out. Not once in the six months since his arrival had he visited a field site or camp. Behind his back everybody called him Dugout Dicky.

Stroud pushed his glasses farther up on his nose in a quick motion and snarled, "Anderson, that display of hostility toward me in front of my subordinates is going to cost you. Don't bet on a promotion anytime soon."

Anderson looked his superior in the eyes and spoke, trying

to keep himself under control. "The *birds*, sir, I don't give a shit about promotion, I care only about getting the birds and those fast movers. I promised the people of 147 I'd be there. I made that promise because it was a part of *your* script. My word and the word of our nation is at stake here, to say nothing of the lives of those people. You have to get me those birds, sir. I beg you."

Stroud glanced at the wall map and slowly shook his head. "It's impossible. I couldn't get you slicks even if I wanted. The political situation won't allow it. The administration's new policy of turning everything over to the South Vietnamese government and getting our boys home has escalated into something none of us was prepared for. Orders have been sent to all regional field commands instructing that no further tactical operations by U.S. forces will be conducted that place American servicemen's lives at risk."

Anderson's knees suddenly felt like rubber and his stomach seemed to have descended down to his testicles, but he wasn't about to give up. "There have to be exceptions, sir. This situation certainly warrants one."

Stroud took off his glasses and walked to his desk. Sitting down, he looked up at the visibly shaken officer. "You're not listening, Anderson. It's over. We're pulling out of this God-forsaken country. We're turning over operations to the South Vietnamese. It's their war now."

"What about the Cambodians? Jesus Christ, sir, we armed and trained them; we promised them our support! We can't back out and let them die!"

"A bit theatrical aren't you, Captain? If Lieutenant Tram is as experienced as you say, then 147 has a good chance of beating off the attack."

Anderson's jaw muscles rippled as he stepped closer to the desk. "They can't hold without air support. You have to authorize at least two dozen sorties of fast movers to give Tram and the villagers a fighting chance."

The colonel sighed and leaned back in his chair. "Afraid not.

The Air Force won't fly missions unless they're protecting U.S. forces. One forty-seven is on it's own."

"Do you realize what you're saying? You're condemning those people to die. They think we're coming, they're going to fight in the belief we'll stand by our word!"

"Anderson, our past president promised the American people we would win the war, and now we've got over fifty thousand dead servicemen and we're no closer to winning than when we started. The South Vietnamese government promised their people they would win the war, and they've lost well over half a million lives. In war, promises are made with the best of intentions but things change, promises get broken. Look, I know it's tough to swallow, but as I said before, it's over. Stand down your team and pack your gear. Tomorrow I want you and your team on the first bird to Nha Trang. Your job here is finished."

Anderson stared at the colonel accusingly. "You knew this was going to happen, didn't you? You knew and yet you didn't say a word to me. Why? Tell me, Colonel! Why didn't you tell me and the other team leaders? Was it because you knew we would have never agreed to train and arm the people. Was that it?"

Stroud put his glasses back on but avoided Anderson's stare. "Every North Vietnamese soldier that the defenders of 147 kill or wound is one less soldier for the South Vietnamese government to contend with. Sacrifices must be made, Captain Anderson. Yes, I knew some time ago these changes would occur, but neither my mission nor the general's mission changed. General Gradd and I discussed the matter in some detail and we both felt—although it was a very difficult decision for both of us—that you and the other team commanders should not be informed. As you alluded to, we both knew how attached your teams became to your indigenous villagers. To be quite frank, we did consider that you and the others might dissuade your people from becoming our early warning trip wires."

Anderson nodded as if understanding. "I see," he said quietly, then he exploded. Lunging across the desk, he grabbed the colonel by his fatigue shirt lapels, yanked him out of the chair and slammed him on the desktop. Leaning over, he hissed in Stroud's face, "You're going to murder the people of my village, you sonofabitch! You used me and you used them. 'Early warning trip wires'? No sir, they are *people*, decent, hard-working, loving people who believed in us. You remember that when you look in the mirror for the rest of your miserable life. God damn you to hell!"

Releasing his grip, Anderson backed away and marched out the door into the darkness. He only made it four steps before he sank to his knees in anguished pain. Closing his tear-filled eyes, he saw the faces of the people he had grown to love. *Forgive me, please forgive me!*

Frenchy sat on the ground beside his wounded grandfather, who lay looking up at the eerie swaying yellow light high above in the smoke-filled sky. Around them the ground shook with teeth-rattling explosions and the air seemed alive with green and red tracers that zipped overhead, singing their songs of death. The parachute flare finally faded and fizzled out, leaving the camp defenders blinded in darkness. The machine gun's chattering and the screams of the wounded and dying seemed louder in the dark, the frightened boy thought as he squeezed his grandfather's hand for reassurance. Then he heard the familiar popping noise, and high above, another flare burst into life, once again bathing the fort in golden light. Leaning over, the boy checked the old man's wounds and saw to his horror that despite his best efforts to stop it, the strange, black frothy blood was still oozing from the thumb-size hole in his grandfather's breast. The old man's eyes rolled slowly to his grandson and he spoke thickly. "Go . . . go to your grandmother in the bunker, little one. See to her and the others. They will be afraid."

His hand trembling, the old man felt his chest for the gold chain, found it and tried to bring it to his mouth but was too weak. The boy reached out, lifted his grandfather's battered

ivory Buddha and gently placed it between the old man's
trembling gray lips. Immediately the fear in his grandfather's
eyes was gone and he began mumbling his prayers. The boy
watched with hope, but the light of life in his grandfather's eyes
dulled, and like the flare, dimmed and slowly extinguished.

Knowing he was safely in Buddha's arms, Frenchy patted
his grandfather's hand one last time, picked up the rifle the old
man had carried, and stood. Bright, rapid flashes of blue-
orange light from the portals of the remaining bunkers told him
they were not yet defeated. He felt pride knowing they were
still holding on after so many hours of constant battle, but he
knew all too well that time was running out. Once again he
looked up, as he had countless times before in the past hours,
praying to the enlightened one to see or hear approaching helicopters. But the hissing flares danced alone in the night sky.
Where are you Cap-tain Ro-bert? Where are you?

A bullet zinged so close by his ear that he felt the hot wind of
its passing. Lifting his chain, he placed his Buddha in his mouth
and started walking toward the lower bunker, where the women
and children were taking refuge. A rocket swished past, leaving
a spiraling trail of white smoke, but he didn't notice because his
eyes were searching the ground so he would not step on the
dead. The light of the flares had given everything the same
unearthly golden hue and cast strange, ghostly dark shadows.
The dead, some with torn or shattered limbs and others with
even more ghastly killing wounds, lay like golden monuments,
silent and still, serene in death. Gripping the heavy rifle tighter,
the boy continued on, stepping over the moaning wounded and
past those still alive, who fired their weapons, reloaded and fired
again. Walking down the smoking bullet-plowed slope, he had
to jump several trenches, and he could see at the base of the hill
yet more golden bodies hanging limp in the wire, their eyes and
mouths blackened like demons. Then the light began fading
from gold to orange-brown then death-black. He stood frozen in
place, afraid to move in the darkness. Only his eyes moved, left
then right at each muzzle flash of a weapon being fired. Gun

smoke mixed with the smell of turned earth and the coppery sweet odor of blood filled his nostrils, making him feel dizzy.

Suddenly, a flare popped overhead and he was bathed once again in the golden yellow light. Clutching the rifle, he again began walking down the slope until he heard men shouting to his right. As he crouched, yelling, running men came through huge gaps in the wire. Red tracers from the bunkers' machine guns cut some of them down but many kept coming up the slope. One of them threw something inside the portal of a machine gun position. A moment later the earth seemed to erupt beneath his feet. He fell, and an instant later a white-hot wind passed over in a rush, then clods of dirt rained down around him, followed by a choking cloud of dust.

Forcing himself back to his feet, Frenchy coughed and gagged as he staggered down the slope and finally broke out of the suffocating cloud. The bunker where his grandmother and the rest of the village families had sought refuge was just ahead. He thanked Buddha, but seeing two men running toward the same bunker, froze in horror. He raised the heavy rifle and pulled the trigger just as the American sergeant had taught him. One of the running men grunted and pitched backward. The boy swung the barrel but the remaining man had jumped into the trench leading to the bunker's entrance.

Screaming, Frenchy ran to the lip of the entrenchment with his rifle ready. He stopped in horror, seeing that the bunker door had already been opened by the attacker and that he was tossing something inside. He heard the women and children cry out as he pulled the trigger again and again. The golden man's head snapped back, hair, brain tissue, and skull fragments splattered against the sandbags. Although Frenchy saw the man fall, he kept pulling the trigger, thinking that if he kept killing him, the frantic, chilling screams coming from the bunker would end. And they did—suddenly the bunker disappeared in a brilliant flash of searing light. Frenchy's silent scream of horror and pain was frozen in his throat as he was thrown skyward by the thunderous blast.

CHAPTER 2

May 20, Central Highlands, Republic of South Vietnam

The sun was just rising over the mountains as Sergeant First Class Carl Hanson lifted his canteen cup to his lips. Shutting his eyes, he savored the bitter taste of the C-ration instant coffee and told himself he was now ready to face the day. He opened his eyes and growled, "Pockets, get me Tanner. He's checkin' the perimeter for me."

Whining, the radio operator slowly got to his feet. "Aw, Pappy, it ain't light 'nough yet to go out there. Damn cherries will blow me away sure as shit."

"Move your ass or I'll blow you away right here," the grizzled sergeant replied with a menacing glare.

Minutes later the RTO returned with a short, broad-shouldered, twenty-year-old staff sergeant badly in need of a bath and shave.

Hanson motioned to the ground beside him. "Take a load off and let's talk."

Sergeant Eli Tanner took off his battered helmet, set it on the ground, and sat on top of it. Hanson handed the squad leader his canteen cup with a grin. "Ranger, I'm leavin' today on the resupply bird. I done beat the odds and made it da fuck outta Nam. My time's up."

Eli Tanner took a sip of coffee and lowered the metal cup with a smile. "Congratulations, Pappy. I'm gonna miss ya."

18

"You're the only fuckin one gonna miss me. Look at em, will ya? Ya ever seen a collection of so many shitbirds in one platoon? Christ a'mighty, none of 'em could hold a candle to the men I had last tour. This bunch of pot-smokin', bead-wearin' hippies ain't worth spit."

Eli shrugged and ran his hand through his short brown hair. "Not their fault, Pappy. The war's windin' down, and they know it. None of them wanna be the last trooper killed in da Nam. Cut 'em some slack, they've done everything you asked."

"Yeah, and fuckin' bitched every fuckin' second doin' it, too. Well, it ain't my problem anymore. It's yours. I'm recommendin' to the L-tee he make ya the platoon sergeant."

Eli took another sip of coffee and shook his head. "You'll be wastin' your time. The L-tee will never let it happen."

"Bullshit. He's dumber than a box of rocks but he ain't stupid. You're the only Ranger-qualified staff sergeant he's got, and you've got the most experience. He'll make the right decision . . . I'll talk to him and make sure it happens."

"Pappy, the L-tee doesn't like me, pure and simple. Since the day I told him he ought to tape his grenade pins, he's treated me like an ugly stepchild. Anyway, Collins has me in time of grade."

"Yeah, and Collins still can't find his ass with both hands. Christ a'mighty that shitbird still can't read a map, and he's the biggest pothead in the platoon. Ain't no way the L-tee gonna let that shitbird take over for me. Now look, Ranger, loosen up and listen to Pappy. The word is this operation is the last. They only sent the company up here to make sure these mountains ain't crawling with regulars before the ARVNs take over our base camp. Once this walk in the sun is over, the battalion is gonna stand down. Lookee here, what I'm tellin' ya is this: Do it by the book. Keep your security well out and keep the shit-birds on their toes. There's dink regulars up here—Fouk says so and we've both seen the signs. I figure they know we're pullin' out so they're kicked back, just waitin' for us to leave . . . but they ain't gonna pass up a sure thing. If the platoon lollygags and forgets everything I taught 'em, them regulars gonna kick their ass. You gotta keep the scouts out for early warnin' and keep the boys ready to rock and roll. The gooks ain't gonna mess with a unit that's got its shit together."

Tanner motioned across the perimeter, where the lieutenant was pouring water from his canteen into his helmet to shave. "You best explain all that to him. I've tried tellin' him we've been followed since we landed up here. He thinks I'm paranoid or somethin'."

Hanson rolled his eyes and shook his head. "What'd'ya expect, he was the battalion fuckin S-one weenie—pushed paper, for Christ's sake! I heard the colonel felt he owed him and sent him to the company to get his career ticket punched as a rifle platoon leader. That dumb sonofabitch can't lead shit. Tryin' to talk sense inta him is like tryin' to push a wet noodle up a wildcat's ass. Watch him, Tanner, he's dangerous 'cause he thinks he knows what he's doin'. As platoon sergeant, you do what I said and get these shitbirds back to base camp all in one piece."

"Hell, Pappy, the way you're talkin', a person might think you cared about us shitbirds after all."

The old sergeant mumbled and pulled his canteen cup from Tanner's hand. "Get out of here, Tanner. You're as bad as the rest of 'em. Go check on the shitbirds and make sure they're securing the area for the resupply bird. I'm goin' back to the world, Tan. I'm goin' and ain't gonna lose no sleep worryin' about the likes of your lousy ass."

Tanner knew better. He stood and put on his helmet. He gave Pappy Hanson a light pat on the shoulder and smiled as he walked away. "Yep, sure gonna miss your little pep talks, Pappy."

The yellow smoke swirled crazily as the resupply helicopter landed in the small clearing surrounded by massive sayo and teak trees. Sergeant First Class Hanson lowered his head, letting his helmet buffer the strong rotor wash as the second squad ran toward the shaking bird to unload boxes of C-rations and other supplies.

Lieutenant Duane Billings stepped up beside the old sergeant and offered his hand. "Sergeant, I know we've had our differences, but I wish you a safe journey back to the States."

Hanson hesitated a moment before taking the officer's hand, but knew he had to try one more time. "Sir, you gotta reconsider your decision. Make Sergeant Tanner your platoon sergeant—he's young, but in all my years I ain't seen no better leader."

"Like I told you before, I'll take it under advisement, Sergeant. You'd better get on, the bird's almost unloaded."

Hanson knew his words had been wasted again. He hefted his rucksack to his shoulder and glanced to his right, where Eli was standing, his rifle at the ready, watching the tree line. *I was wrong, the hardheaded asshole is dumb* and *stupid.*

As if he heard the unspoken words, Eli turned just as his platoon sergeant climbed up into the Huey. Eli smiled and lifted his hand with a thumbs-up.

Overcome with guilt at leaving his men, Hanson couldn't make himself return the young sergeant's smile. The rotor wash increased and the slick began to rise. Hanson kept his tearing eyes locked on the young sergeant and finally found the strength to lift his hand and give a return thumbs-up. *Good luck, Ranger, God knows you're gonna need it.*

"Squad leaders report to me," Lieutenant Billings barked.

Three young sergeants approached their platoon leader, who sat on his rucksack holding a manila envelope he'd received in the resupply. The officer lifted the envelope with a grin. "It's good news, guys. Once we arrive back in base camp, we'll begin standing down and turn the camp over to the South Vietnamese Army. Looks like the war is over for us and we're all going home early."

The three sergeants exchanged grins and pats on the back as the officer took a map from his fatigue pocket and spread it out on the ground. He motioned toward Staff Sergeant Collins.

"Andy, I'm making you my platoon sergeant, you've got the most time in grade. Have Specialist Washington take your position as squad leader. All right, everybody look at the map. As you all know, three days ago the company was airlifted to this mountain plateau. The mission was to look for North Vietnamese regulars that might have moved into these high ridges to establish rocket-firing positions. Seeing no signs of recent activity, the company commander decided it would be faster to check out the area if each platoon worked independently and took a ridge to follow all the way back to base camp. Right now, first platoon is about two klicks to the north of us following this ridge, and third platoon is a klick to the south, on this one. I've looked at the map and have decided it would be better if we backtracked two klicks and took this bigger trail that leads to the valley. The terrain is easier and it'll be a much faster hump for us. I figure we'll make it to the valley by tomorrow and be in base camp by nightfall the following day. We'll depart at—"

"Ya don't wanna do that, L-tee," Eli Tanner said, shaking his head.

Not happy at being interrupted, especially when he was on a roll, Billings snapped, "Really? What is it I don't want to do?"

Eli motioned to the map. "Sir, like I told ya before, we've been followed since we landed. Fouk says it's trail watchers keeping track of us. Going back on the same trail is askin' for trouble. It's a Ranger rule too, sir, when in enemy territory ya never go back the way ya came."

"Are you finished?" Billings asked sarcastically. "I thought once I got rid of Hanson I could run this platoon without someone always questioning my orders. Did he tell you to hassle me just for old times' sake?"

Eli kept his gaze steady into the officer's eyes, letting him know he wasn't intimidated.

Sergeant Dan Murphy, the second squad leader, bobbed his head. "Sir, I learned that rule about not going back the way ya came in NCO school. Tanner's right, we'd be askin' for trouble."

"Great! Now I've got two of you that think you can run things," Billings said, throwing up his hands. "Forget it, this isn't a damn democracy where everybody votes. First squad will lead, followed by your squad, Murphy. Tanner, your squad will be last; maybe you'll find some of those *trail watchers*. We'll move out in an hour. Any questions?"

Eli rose and put on his helmet. "Yes, sir, but it's not a question. It's a suggestion. I think you'd better have Fouk take point. If there's trouble, he'll smell it."

Billings's eyes narrowed. "I don't want or need any more suggestions or advice from you, Sergeant Tanner. Anyway, I don't trust him. I heard he defected from the North Vietnamese Army some years ago."

"No, sir, that's not true, he's Cambodian. He worked with the Special Forces for four years and is considered to be the best scout in the battalion."

"I don't care what he knows; I don't trust him, plus I can't understand a damn thing he says. He stays with your squad. That's it, no more talk. The faster we get out of these mountains, the sooner we'll be going home. Return to your squads and prepare to move out."

Eli was oiling his rifle bolt when a smiling young black specialist walked up holding a white envelope. "Dig it, Tan man, I got accepted for school, man."

Eli grinned and set the rifle down. "Let me see it, Cotton; you can't read. . . . Well, I'll be damned, it says right here you were accepted, all right. But hell, man, Tuskegee is in Alabama. Your mama gonna let ya get that far from her?"

Cotton Pierce slapped at Eli's shoulder. "Shiii-it, Tan man, what you givin' a brother Columbus, Georgia, boy the hassle for? My mama let me come to da Nam, man. She be proud of her war hero, I be profilin' soon, walkin' with books, not this fuckin' ruck, man. And I be sleepin' in a bed, not on the ground, eatin' regular hots and no more C's. Women be wantin' to hear old Cotton tell em' war stories and shit. I be snoopin' and poopin', lookin' for me some good times, not gooks. . . . Yeah, man, this Georgia boy gonna be what's happenin' on campus."

Eli handed the letter back. "I'm proud of you, Cotton. I mean it, man."

Cotton motioned to the open letter by Eli's ruck. "Who writin' you, man? The draft board? Send 'em a gook ear and say you done did the time."

"Naw, it's from my brother Jerome."

"Yeah, I remember your brother, man. For a white boy he sure could play football. I thought he got drafted by the Falcons, man."

"He did, but got cut. That's what the letter was about. He's going into the Justice Department—can you believe this—he's goin' to the FBI academy."

"Jerome Tanner, a G-man? Man, now that's a trip. Your bro and you was nothin' but trouble, man. Was it Jerome the one who got busted for sellin' moonshine to us niggers, or you, man? Can't remember."

"Me, dummy. Jerome was too smart."

Cotton grinned. "Yeah, that's right, your daddy told my daddy you was facin' time. Got out of it, though, didn't ya, Tan man? Slick-ass white boy skated. This nigger be doin' time for that shit."

Eli shrugged. "I'm doin' the time now, aren't I?"

"Yeah, you done paid, slicky boy. Soon you goin' ta be back in Columbus. You goin' to school, man, or you gonna be a lifer?"

"A lifer? Do I look that stupid?"

"Hey, all white boys look the same to me. Are ya? Goin' to school, man, or go work for your old man?"

"School," Eli said, picking up his rifle again. "I'm going to apply to Georgia U. and see what happens. Hey, this hump ain't goin' to be a cakewalk, so keep your eyes open. I want us Columbus boys to make it back in one piece."

Cotton lifted his rifle and puffed out his chest. "Man, you talkin' to the best team leader in the first squad. I be a snoopin' poopin' fool. No sweat, man. You third squad shitbirds be watchin' your own ass. I got the first covered, man."

Eli raised an eyebrow. "You take it easy, Cotton, serious shit now, I mean it."

Cotton's smile dissolved and he nodded. "I'll be careful, Tan man. You do the same, man. See ya when we laager and we'll split my mama's brownies she sent me. I gots a care package in the pony along with my acceptance. We be chowin' down on Georgia *pe*cans, man, can you dig it? See ya."

Eli smiled. "Yeah, man, I can dig it. See ya," he said as he stood. Lifting his rucksack to his shoulder, he barked to his squad, "Saddle up third, time to ride."

Soaked in sweat, Sergeant Dan Murphy stopped alongside the trail, letting the rest of his squad pass by. He waited for only a few seconds and saw the Cambodian scout approaching, followed by his friend and fellow squad leader. Waiting until Eli Tanner was within a few feet, Murphy stepped back on the trail and joined him. "I don't like this worth a shit, Tan. We're movin' too fast and the L-tee doesn't have the point team out far enough."

Eli hunched his shoulders to relieve the weight of his heavy rucksack. "What'ya expect? He's in a hurry to get back to base camp. Just keep your boys on their toes. Remember, when we humped this trail yesterday it widened about two hundred yards up, where we saw those house-size boulders. He'll have to stop and send the point team out to check them out before we move on."

Murphy wiped sweat from his brow with the frayed end of an olive-drab towel that hung around his neck. "Ya gotta try and talk sense into him, Tan man. I got a feeling about this, a bad feeling. It's too damn quiet, and you've seen the same prints I have. What's Fouk saying?"

"He says they're here, all right. He says we're dinky dau, crazy, for backtrackin'. Look at him, he's walkin' like a cat on a hot tin roof. You'd better get back to your squad. I'm sure we'll be stoppin' in just a second or two, and I'll go up and try and talk to him again."

"I'll go with ya, Tan. I'm not lettin' him get us killed 'cause he's in a hurry. See ya in a bit."

Tanner nodded silently as Murphy increased his pace to catch up to his men.

A full minute passed and the hand signal for halting had still not been passed back. Not liking what he was feeling, Eli slowed his steps. He kept telling himself the L-tee was surely going to stop the platoon and send the point team ahead to check out the danger area. His friend Cotton was good and would check the area with his fire team. The place was strewn with huge boulders and aboveground tree roots, some taller than a man. The trail twisted and turned through the maze, and just about any point on it was a perfect ambush position. *Surely he's going to halt. Surely . . . surely. Shit.*

Eli raised his hand, signaling the squad to freeze. Just ten feet ahead of him, Fouk was crouched down, looking off to his left front as if he saw something that wasn't right. Eli tensed as the small Cambodian slowly moved his hand to his fatigue shirt and pulled out his gold neck chain. Keeping his distant stare, Fouk felt down the chain to the small Buddha and brought it up to his mouth.

Eli spun around; they were in serious trouble. Fouk only placed the Buddha in his mouth when he thought he was in danger of dying.

"Gun up," Eli whispered to the two men a few feet behind him. Both came forward in a run, the first holding an M-60 machine gun, the second carrying additional belts of linked ammunition.

Making a quick survey of the ground, Eli pointed and whispered, "Set up there by the base of that tree. Link two belts and, when I tell ya, hose that area to your left front and keep it comin'." He quickly motioned the four remaining men of his squad up and pointed to where he wanted them to go. He whispered as they got down into their positions. "Put weapons on

semi and get out your frags. If they rush, use your frags first."
Taking in a breath and pushing his rifle's selector switch to
semi, he looked down the trail, hoping Murphy's squad had
halted. *Shit!* They were still moving, following the first squad.
Breaking the foreboding silence, he yelled, "*Murphy*, get your
men down! Dink ambush! They're to your—"

To his left and front the forest seemed to explode in an earsplitting, single *crack* that immediately turned into a sustained
roar of gunfire. He dove to the ground knowing his warning was
too late. The distinct loud cracking sounds of the NVA weapons
were those of Chinese-made RPD machine guns and AK-47s.
Shit! He rolled out of his rucksack and barked to his gun team.

"Not yet, wait for their assault team to show themselves.
Keep steady, boys . . . stead-deee. Grimes, keep watching our
rear. Everybody get frags ready to toss. Stead-dee."

Then Tanner saw them. Like ghouls, they seemed to rise out
of the ground only thirty yards away. It looked as if the forest
was rushing toward, for they were all wearing camouflaged net
capes and helmet nets stuffed with leaves and ferns. Despite
the fact that his heart was pounding so loud he could hear it
over their hollering and gunfire, Eli felt hope. Their assault
force was made up of close to fifteen men, and they were
headed toward the other two squads on the trail. It was going to
be the NVA's turn to be surprised.

"*Now!*" he yelled to his men, and immediately five
grenades sailed toward the attackers and the M-60 rattled,
spewing out a red stream of death.

Tanner tossed a second grenade, threw himself to the ground
and picked up his rifle. Peering from beneath his helmet toward
the killing ground, he could see the red tracers from the M-60
disappearing into contorting bodies that twisted, spun, and fell
in heaps. Then the grenades began exploding in earsplitting
cracks, throwing out white-hot shrapnel that immediately tore
and ripped through flesh and bone. Stunned, the surviving
attackers ceased their yelling and their charge.

Knowing he had to take the offense while the enemy were

still dazed, Tanner rose and yelled for his men to fire. He brought his M-16 up, aimed, and squeezed the trigger. His target looked as if he had hit an invisible wall; with a look of shock he fell backward. Tanner swung the barrel, aligned his sights on another and squeezed again. The small Vietnamese soldier was knocked off his feet and rolled on the ground in agony. Eli didn't see him rolling; he had another already in his sights. He fired, and the man dropped his rifle as if it were red-hot then fell face first to the ground. Red tracers from the machine gun whizzed through his next target before he had a chance to fire. He looked for another but none were left standing. His men had finished off the others. Dropping to a knee, he quickly changed magazines and felt a wave of relief, hearing the familiar popping of M-16s coming from the trail where the two squads had been ambushed. *Some of them made it! Thank you Lord, thank you!* He rose up and was about to order his men forward to help the other squads when he heard a frantic scream from Grimes, who had been watching the trail behind them.

"More are comin' up the trail!" A long burst from the trooper caused Tanner to spin around. *Oh shit!*

Gun smoke lay like a heavy mist on the forest floor as Eli Tanner walked slowly, checking the small perimeter. Only seven men in the platoon were still able to fire their weapons, and like himself, three of them were wounded. He winced as he bent over and patted Dan Murphy's back. "Steady, Murph. Gunships are on the way. How's the shoulder?"

The sergeant shook his bare head. "Hurts like hell . . . but I can still shoot. Any word on the third platoon?"

Bone tired, Eli sank to his knees. "Pockets says they're about a klick away. Hang on, buddy, we'll be out of this in an hour or so."

Murphy looked up at the kneeling soldier, then took the towel from around his own neck. "You're still leakin', Tan. Better take my drive-on and wrap that neck wound of yours. Another quarter inch to the right and you'd be history. It hurt?"

"It did, kinda numb now. Murph, they're gonna hit us again. Fouk crawled out and heard 'em. Looks like it was a company, and there's still a platoon of 'em left. They think we're done for. We got claymores out during the lull so it looks like we got a chance. I've shifted the guys over to my side of the perimeter, where Fouk says they'll hit us. You're gonna be alone here, man. Keep your eyes open and holler if you see somethin'."

Murphy was silent for a moment then nodded once. "I've got it, Tan . . . take care, huh."

Tanner patted his friend's back, and using his rifle as a crutch, he slowly rose and walked back to the center of the perimeter, where the badly wounded lay in rows. He stopped by the platoon medic, who was knotting a tourniquet on a trooper's leg. Eli could see the medic's efforts were wasted, the soldier's ash-gray face a sure sign that he'd already lost too much blood.

Finished tying the knot, the black medic wiped his bloody hands on his shirt, glanced up, then moved to his next patient. "Tan, it's bad, man. I'm outta everything. I got seven down, and six of 'em is critical. Cotton died just a minute ago. When's the fuckin' Third Herd gettin' here?"

Tanner quickly shifted his eyes to the last man lying on the ground covered by a poncho. He began to move toward the body but the medic grabbed his leg. "Tan, he's dead, man. What about the third platoon?"

Tanner hardened his heart; there wasn't time to grieve now. He quickly wiped his eyes, then tried to speak calmly. "Pockets is talkin' to them on the horn, they're movin' as fast as they can." He leaned over, touched the soldier's shoulder and whispered, "They're gonna be hittin' us again."

"Oh Jesus, Tan. We can't hold them this time."

"Stead-dee. We crawled out and got claymores from the rucks and set 'em up, and we've got gunships comin'. We'll hold. You just keep the wounded down when the shit hits the fan."

Standing back erect, Tanner slowly turned, looking over his small perimeter, nestled between two huge teaks. After stopping the attack to their rear, he'd had his men move up the trail to join the other survivors. It had been far worse than he thought. The entire first squad had been killed or wounded. Sergeant Collins and the lieutenant were dead, and Murphy's squad was badly torn up. Pockets, the radio operator, survived, but he'd been hit in the legs. Tanner had found the slight depression between the two trees and ordered his men to move the wounded into it and establish a defensive position. Walking over to the west side of the depression, the young sergeant kneeled down by Pockets, who was sitting up, supported by two rucksacks.

"You gonna be able to keep on the horn?" he asked softly.

The young soldier raised the handset to show he still had the strength. "I ain't dyin' here, Tan. I been humpin' this twenty-five-pound motherfuckin' radio for four months and now, it's payback time; it's gonna save my ass. I gave the map coordinates ya gave me to the gunships. They say they'll be here in less than five minutes. I saw Fouk crawl back in—the gooks gonna attack us again?"

"Yeah, looks like it. Stay on the horn and be ready to pop a smoke for the guns. Tell 'em we'll need it in close. Maybe if the guns get here the dinks won't try and—"

Green tracers whizzed over Tanner's head. He fell to the ground and frantically crawled to the claymore clackers that would detonate two deadly directional mines set up fifty feet away. Bullets chewed up the ground around the depression's rim as Tanner grasped the two plastic devices and talked to himself to try and remain calm. *Those are machine guns firing, Tanner. They want to keep everybody's head down while an assault force moves in close for the kill. Wait, Tanner, wait till the machine guns lift their fire, then it'll be time. Wait, wait. wait.*

Suddenly, the fire lifted and he heard shouting. Rising, he saw them rushing forward. *Oh God! Two attacking waves!* He ducked down, closed his eyes in prayer and pushed the clacker handles down. Although he thought he was ready, the horrific explosion still caused him to groan in pain from the shear violence of the ear-shattering roar. Covered in dust and leaves from the back blast, Tanner rose with his M-16 in his hands. Deafened by the explosion, he felt strangely all alone and very small. A black-brown cloud to his front was lifting, revealing what the mines' hundreds of ball bearings had done. Torn, darkened bodies lay in grotesque positions, but out of the smoke more men suddenly appeared, running straight for him. Screaming in anger and frustration, he fired from the hip at the closest man, only three feet away, hit him in the face, spun, fired, spun again, and shot another and another.

Suddenly he was reeling back from a powerful unseen blow to his chest. Everything became blurry and he felt himself falling backward. He blinked to clear his vision and could see the green forest canopy high above him, but his eyelids became so heavy he couldn't hold them open any longer. He knew he was on his back but had not felt himself hit the ground. *Got to get up, got to try and stop them. Oh Jesus, I can't move, there's something on my chest pushing down. It's pushing down harder. It hurts so damn bad! No, gotta fight through it, gotta try. I gotta try.*

Eli Tanner's eyelids fluttered and his hand twitched but he could not make his body respond. Knowing it was the end, he let his body relax and he accepted the cold, silent darkness that had come for him.

64th Evac Hospital, An Khe, Central Highlands

The ward nurse was seated in her cubicle updating patient records when a figure passed by her open door. Frowning, she got up and marched to the door. "Hold it right there, Sergeant. I thought I told you to stay in bed."

Dressed in a light green hospital gown, Sergeant Dan Murphy slowed his steps and spoke over his shoulder. "Aw hell, Cap'n, I can't sleep till I know for sure he's gonna make it. Has he come to yet?"

The captain strode forward quickly, catching up to the persistent patient. He'd been driving her crazy since he and the others had been admitted late that afternoon. "Sergeant, I told you I'd tell you when he became conscious, now get your butt back to your bed."

Murphy stopped in front of the patient he was seeking, and had to grab the bed rail to keep from sinking to the floor. One look at his friend's pale face told him it didn't look good. He reached out and patted Eli Tanner's hand. "You stopped them, Tan. I wanted you to know, you stopped 'em cold."

Seeing tears trickle down the sergeant's face, the nurse lost her frown and stepped closer. "Your friend will make it, Sergeant. It will take time, but he'll be going home."

Murphy kept his eyes on Eli Tanner. "They're sending me on to Japan, ma'am. Will ya tell him for me and the other guys that everybody made it . . . except Fouk. He was our Cambodian scout, ma'am. When they attacked, Tan here charged right into them and Fouk followed him."

Murphy turned and held out his hand toward the nurse. "Ma'am, give him this for me." He opened his hand and a thick gold chain with a gold-encased ivory Buddha fell into her open palm. "It was Fouk's, ma'am. Tan should have it. None of us cared for Fouk very much . . . he was different, ya know. But not Tan. He liked the little dude . . . they were close."

"I'll make sure he gets it, Sergeant. Tell me something, if you can. What makes a man like your friend charge into certain death?"

Murphy looked back into Eli Tanner's face and shook his head. "I'm not sure, ma'am . . . love, I guess. It's hard to explain. We all got real close over the past months . . . tryin' to keep alive and all. Ya know everything about everybody. Ya kind of become brothers. Ya do all ya can to keep your brothers alive."

"I'll walk you back to your bed, Sergeant."

Murphy patted his friend's hand one last time and whispered, "Thanks, Tan."

PART II
PRESENT DAY

CHAPTER 3

June 1, Junction City, Kansas

The deputy police chief brought his cruiser to a smooth stop in front of a yellow-tape barrier. Holding a cup of coffee, he stepped out of his car and approached the two patrol officers. "What we got, boys?"

The taller officer motioned toward a small rusted trailer house. "Old codger popped himself with a .22. Neighbor found him this morning when he was pickin' up his paper. Looks like the old man didn't wanna make a mess in the trailer, he kneeled down over there by that cottonwood, and *bam*. One in the temple."

"Ya find a note?" the deputy asked as he walked toward the body.

"Not yet, we're still lookin'. The damn trailer is a pigsty. The old man was a juicer."

The deputy leaned over the body to get a better look at the pistol and wound. He nodded to himself, seeing the weapon still in the man's hand. Standing erect, he took a sip of coffee and raised an eyebrow toward the tall officer. "I make him to be in his late fifties . . . only a few years older than me. Watch it when ya call him an 'old man.' He got a name?"

"Sorry, Barry. I guess the effects of all that Jack Daniel's aged him some. We found a driver's license and retired-military ID in his wallet. His name is James D. Hollis. What'd'ya make of the gold chain in his mouth?"

Shrugging his shoulders, the deputy casually leaned over the body for another look. He wasn't about to admit he hadn't noticed the chain the first time. "Looks like whatever the chain is holdin' is in his mouth. Here, take my cup, will ya? And give me your pen."

"Aw hell, Barry, use your own. I only have this one and I gotta write the report."

Sighing heavily, the deputy took out his own pen, wrapped it around the loose chain by the dead man's jaw and gave it a light tug. "A cross, just what I thought," the deputy said, backing up and retrieving his coffee cup from the patrolman. "The way I got it figured is, this sinner wanted us to know he'd found religion. Easier for the family. Soon as the coroner gets here, bag him. No sense in getting the crime scene boys involved. It's a suicide clear and simple."

"Barry, Mr. Hollis's .22 wasn't registered. We called in and checked."

The deputy shrugged again. "You two know how many unregistered guns there are in this town? Take it from me, boys, you don't wanna read anything more inta this than what you see. Hollis was drinkin' up his retirement check for a reason. Look at the trailer, his clothes, that beat-up pickup. How depressed would *you* get knowin' this was goin' to be how you lived for the rest of your life? I've seen this before . . . guys retire after twenty or thirty years and they find out they're in another world . . . the civilian world where nobody gives a shit. The Army was their life. When it's gone, their life ends. They think they're too old to start over, and most of 'em are right."

The tall officer lowered his head. "We'll write it up, Barry. Sure a sad way to go, all alone and all. Maybe if he'd found religion sooner?"

The deputy tossed the last of his coffee into the dirt yard and spoke over his shoulder as he walked toward his car. "With that cross in his mouth, maybe he didn't think he was alone."

Atlanta, Georgia

Seated at a small table in his paneled office, Don Farrel, Special Agent in Charge of the Atlanta office, shook his head. "I don't like this, Stew. Are you saying I don't have a choice, I *have* to take him?"

Sitting across the table from Farrel, Steward Goddard, the Bureau's assistant director of personnel, ignored the question as he unsnapped his attaché case and took out a file. "Don, I flew here to explain all this to you personally. None of us like it, but we're in a situation. As you know, last week Burton took over as the superintendent of the schoolhouse in Quantico. The first day on the job he calls the director and demands the removal of one of his academy instructors. Burton says he'll resign unless the guy is gone in forty-eight hours."

Farrel's eyes began to narrow, knowing where the conversation was going. "Let me guess. The director backed him up, and now you've got to put this agent somewhere. Why here, Stew? If the guy's a foul-up, I certainly don't want him."

Goddard pushed the file across the table. "He's no foul-up. You'll recognize the name as soon as you open the file."

Farrel opened the jacket, read the name, and looked up at his supervisor with a glare. "No way, Stew. Not him. I won't do it."

Goddard sighed as he took a cigar from his jacket pocket. "Like I said, we're in a situation. Burton overreacted, and the director made a mistake in agreeing to stand by Burton's decision. You and I both know you can't remove an agent without cause, especially this one. The deputy director was left with cleaning up the mess, and he passed the job to me. We couldn't let this thing get blown out of proportion, and most importantly, we had to clean up the mess before the press found out. We made a deal with the agent to get him to leave quietly. He got his choice of assignments, and he chose this office, Don, so he would be close to his home."

"Bullshit! This is pure bullshit, Steward! What the hell am I going to do with him? He's the most hated agent in the Bureau, and you expect me to take him?"

Goddard rolled the cigar in his hands, showing no expression. "It wasn't his fault that he was given the task of running the internal investigation of the Ruby Ridge fiasco. He wrote a report that many of us disagreed with, but it was his call."

"He leaked that report to the press, and you know damn well if they hadn't spread it all over the papers, the congressional hearings would have never taken place. We still haven't recovered from that exposure."

"He was cleared of leaking the report, Don. Do me a favor and just look at his file. It's very impressive. He served in the Army and went to their Airborne and Ranger courses before going to Vietnam. In the war, he saw a lot of action, he even received the Distinguished Service Cross, the second highest award for valor. He was wounded very badly during a battle, but recovered fully after a year and got out of the Army. He used his GI Bill to attend Georgia University, then joined us after graduation. Because of his Ranger experience, he was assigned to the special tactical unit. Just look at his file and you'll see he's had tough jobs and done them all well."

Farrel opened the folder and turned to the summary page of assignments. As soon as he began reading he started shaking his head.

"He's had nothing but special ops assignments. Jesus, Stew, he's not one of us. He's specialized and an independent. No wonder the bastard wrote the report the way he did. He didn't grow up in the system. He never learned to respect it."

Goddard raised an eyebrow. "This isn't personal, is it? I know you didn't get along with his brother when *he* was in charge of this office."

"Look, Stew, Jerome retired four years ago and I never met his damn brother. I knew he had one in the Bureau but I didn't know the details of his career. As the honcho of this office, I'm worried about my other agents. They all know about this guy, and like me, most of them don't believe he didn't leak the report. I don't need any more problems, and you're talking about forcefeeding me another big one."

Steward lowered his head a moment, as if in thought, before looking into his friend's eyes. "Let me give it to you straight. What I say doesn't go out of this room. The agent has already been promised he would be assigned to the Atlanta office. But I can promise you this, he will be here just under a year when he receives a letter from Bureau informing him that due to reductions in our budget, personnel cuts are necessary. He will be told that a board of his peers has selected him for early retirement but that he will receive his full benefits. What I'm saying, Don, is—we're going to get rid of him, the right way. It's the way Burton should have handled it, but the damn hot-head didn't have the patience. As you know, Burton was named in the agent's investigation as one of those who tried to cover up the Ruby Ridge affair. Burton had been on the fast track, now he's sidetracked to a dead-end position. Don't you make the same mistake. You're already in a bit of trouble over the E.O. complaint filed against you by Agent Sutton. I'm telling you as a friend, don't make me tell the deputy director you don't want to cooperate."

Red-faced, Farrel restrained himself from slamming his fist on the table. Instead he took in a deep breath and lowered his chin. "I'll cooperate, Stew. Do you have any suggestions as to what I should do with him?"

"As a matter of fact, I do. You're not going to like it, but it will help you with your other problem, Agent Sutton. Assign him to your resident office in Columbus to work with the Army at Fort Benning."

Farrel's eyes widened in disbelief. "Are you nuts? That makes the problem worse. I just sent that whining bitch, Sutton, to Columbus a month ago to get her out of my hair. This guy is senior and would bump her down from running the office."

"Tell her it's only temporary and that within three months

you'll assign her back to Atlanta to work in your white collar crime division."

This time Farrel couldn't control himself. He slammed the table with the palm of his hand. "Goddamn you, Stew! That means I'd be giving in to the bitch."

"Don, listen to me. The equal opportunity complaint she filed against you is no little thing. Face it—you blew it when you yelled at her and said the things you did. You don't have much choice in this one, either."

"Stew, that prissy bitch pranced in here the first day she came to work and told me, *told me*, damnit, that I was treating her unfairly by assigning her to Columbus. She didn't *suggest* I reconsider her assignment or even *ask* me to reconsider, the bitch stood right there in front of my desk and *demanded* that I change her assignment to white collar. She was lucky I didn't throw her tight little ass out of my office instead of just giving her a piece of my mind."

"Calling her a 'goddamn female squirt' was not smart. If you had left out female, you would have been all right. But what really got you in trouble was your last line. What was it . . . 'You damn women libber agents are ruining the Bureau'? What were you thinking, saying something like that to her?"

"I'm tellin' you, Stew, if you'd seen the look she gave me when she came in, you'd have done the same thing. She burned holes in me with those damn green eyes of hers. And the way she talked, Jesus, it grated every nerve in my body to listen to her tell me I was making the decision because of her sex. I lost it. I admit it. She got to me. I've been in the Bureau for twenty-four years, and that little bitch with no more than four years under her belt comes in and accuses me of violating her rights. And now, now you're sittin' there tellin' me I've got to give in and put her in White Collar?"

"Afraid so, Don. That is, if you don't want to retire sooner than you thought. You should have looked at her file more closely before talking to her. . . . All the warning signs were there."

"What are you talking about?"

"See, that proves my point. Had you read her file, you would have known her background and been more careful. She went to college on a scholarship provided by the state of Virginia. . . . Her father had been a detective in the Virginia State Bureau of Investigation. He was killed in the line of duty when she was ten, and the state started a college fund for her. She got married when she was a sophomore at college, dropped out and worked to help her husband pay the bills for school. She lost a baby two years later, and when the hubby graduated from law school, he dumped her. Like I said Don, the warning signs were there . . . all you had to do was read between the lines. The husband dumped her. . . . How do you think she felt about men in general after that? And hell, if that didn't tell you something, all you had to do was read what organizations she belonged to when she went back to school. She was a Gloria Steinem clone, for Christ's sake. Look, Don, I'm sitting on the E.O. complaint at the present. If you bring her up and do as I suggested, I'll consider the matter resolved. If you don't, I'm letting you know now it won't be brushed under the carpet. They'll go after you."

Farrel sank back in his chair and picked up the file before him. "It's a sad goddamn day for the Bureau, Stew. I have to take this asshole, Special Agent Eli Tanner, the son of a bitch who's tarnished all our shields. And now it looks like I have to give in to Special Agent Ashley Sutton. She better be damn glad she wears a skirt or she'd be lookin' for work in the fast food business. They're both trouble, Stew."

Knowing his job was done, Goddard closed his attaché case, stood, and walked toward the door. Stopping, he looked over his shoulder. "Look on the bright side, Don. At least for a while they'll both be together in the one place where nothing ever happens. Fort Benning isn't exactly New York. Maybe they'll drive each other nuts."

* * *

It took ten long minutes before Don Farrel felt calm enough to press his intercom. "Maggie, call our Columbus office and get Agent Sutton on the line for me, please."

"Sir, Agent Sutton is here in the building. I saw her a few minutes ago down in Supply. She drove up from Columbus to pick up the new computer software and other equipment for their office."

"Okay, find her and have her come and see me, please."

"Will do, sir."

Five minutes later Farrel's intercom buzzed and his secretary's voice came over the speaker. "Sir, Agent Sutton is here."

Taking a breath for strength, Farrel pressed the button. "Send her in, please."

He leaned back in his high-backed leather chair and told himself to stay in control. Only a couple of seconds passed before the door opened and she strode in. He still couldn't believe that the first time he'd seen her he had actually thought she was cute. Thirty-three years old, strawberry-blond, only five-three or -four and maybe 115 pounds, she looked like one of those retired ice skater types on TV who did the commentary on the young ones, always looked good and never seemed to sweat. She even wore an ice skater's wedge hair style. Some men would have considered her attractive overall just because she had a drop dead figure, but he knew better: she was flawed inside and out. Her radiant green eyes were a little too close together, and when they turned cold, watch out. He knew from experience those glossy emeralds could freeze your balls off. Her nose had a slight upturn like a ski jump, and when she got angry her nostrils flared in and out like a maddened bull. *Christ, and I thought the bitch was cute?*

Farrel did not get up. He motioned to a chair beside his desk. "Have a seat, Agent Sutton."

She didn't move. "Thank you, sir, but I'd prefer to stand."

"As you wish. Agent Sutton, I've just been informed we're getting another agent assigned to us. He reports for duty in one week. I'm telling you this because his sudden assignment affects you. As we both know, we did not have a very pleasant meeting a month ago when you reported for duty. I accept responsibility that it was partially my fault. After some thought on the matter, I realized I was out of line. Agent Sutton, I now apologize to you and assure you that I have the utmost respect for all agents of your gender. My words were inappropriate and I hope you will accept my apology."

Ashley Sutton dipped her chin, saying nothing. She knew there was some kind of catch. She took in a breath and held it as her boss continued.

"Because the conversation became heated and got out of hand, I didn't have the opportunity to explain why I assigned you to Columbus. Again that was partially my fault. I was fully aware that you are a computer expert and that your expertise and past experience were in white-collar crime. But you must understand that I have others assigned who are just as qualified as you. I could not and would not reassign one of those agents just because you came on board and wanted to be assigned to a division with no vacancies. I made what I felt was the right decision at the time, and I still feel it was correct; however, things have changed. I am now giving you notice that you will be coming to Atlanta in three months and will be assigned to the white-collar division, just as you desired."

Ashley slowly exhaled. Her complaint had paid off. The bastard was rolling.

Farrel saw the gloating look in her green eyes and told himself he could get through this. Tonight he'd have two more martinis than usual and chalk this up as a learning experience. Clearing his throat, he tapped a file laying on his desk. "The agent I mentioned will be taking your place as the resident Agent in Charge of the Columbus office. He's a senior agent with a military background, so the transition should be very smooth. I now ask a favor of you. The agent is not aware of his assignment to Columbus, and as it happens, he is on leave and visiting his brother there. I have here a photocopy of his file that I'm going to give you so you'll know more about your replacement. On the first page you'll find his leave address. I would appreciate it if you would please drop by and see him and give him this envelope. In it are his assignment instructions and all the necessary paperwork for him to fill out to bring him on board. He can come to Atlanta at his convenience once he's established, and I'll give him the usual welcoming spiel. Assist him any way you can in finding suitable housing and in getting him acquainted with the community. You two can work out the handing off of your case loads and the details of the transition. Well, that's it, Agent Sutton. Do you have any questions?"

Ashley Sutton was going to say no and leave, but something about all this didn't sound right to her. It was too easy. "Sir, what is the agent's name?" She asked to stall for time and try to figure out the catch.

"Tanner, Eli J. Tanner. Here's his file, and the envelope I'd like you to give him," Farrel said, holding out his hand. He looked into her eyes to see if she showed any sign of recognition of his name. He was relieved; he didn't want to have to explain the circumstances to her and listen to her bitch.

She stepped forward and took the documents. "Sir, isn't it unusual for Agent Tanner to be moved so quickly?"

Farrel forced a smile. "It happens sometimes. By the way, just so you know: Agent Tanner's brother was the SAC of this office before he retired four years ago. His name is Jerome Tanner. You might have met him while you've been in Columbus? I hear he's doing quite well—he runs a private investigation and security business in town."

"No sir, I haven't met him. Being there only a month, I haven't had an opportunity to meet hardly anyone but the local police and Benning's Military Police and CID people. Sir, there is one more question. I'm in charge until I leave, correct?"

Farrel braced himself. "No, Agent Sutton, Agent Tanner is senior to you. He takes full responsibility once he starts work."

She shocked him when she smiled. "Just checking." She said, "It will be too late to see Agent Tanner by the time I get back, sir. I'll see him first thing in the morning and inform him. And, sir, thank you."

Farrel relaxed; she was no longer showing her she-wolf side. He returned a smile and rose from his chair. "Now that this has all been resolved, I would hope that you would withdraw the E.O. complaint. It would certainly make things better for both of us."

Ashley kept her smile. "No, sir, not until you apologize in writing to me. For the record, sir. At your convenience, of course. A faxed copy sent to the office will do just fine. Good day, sir."

He waited until she was out the door before muttering aloud, "Damn women libbers to hell."

CHAPTER 4

3:30 P.M. Saturday, June 2, Green Island
Country Club, Columbus, Georgia

The two sweat-soaked men sank into their chairs and took long pulls from bottles of Gatorade. The bigger of the two men lowered his bottle and looked tiredly at his younger brother. "Elly, I'm goin' to kill her for this. This was her idea, you know, playin' together would be fun, she said. Look at me, I'm dyin', it's at least a hundred degrees on this damn court and we've been playin' for over two hours. Fun? She thinks this is fun?"

Carrying towels, a smiling, attractive middle-age woman walked up behind the two men. "Watch it, buster, I heard that. You two look great. Keep playin' like you are and you'll be the tournament doubles champions."

Jerome Tanner gave his wife his best scowl. "I'm dyin' here, and you're thinkin' of trophies? You signed us up because you thought I needed the exercise and this would be fun. We were *supposed* to lose in the first round then sit around and drink beer. That was the plan. Remember?"

She tossed her husband a towel and motioned to his partner. "How was I supposed to know Eli kept his game up?" Shifting her gaze to her brother-in-law, she grinned. "Hang in there, Eli. Carry this ol'-timer through this match and you two will be the champs."

Eli Tanner gave his brother a glance and shook his head. "I

think he's had it, Millie. He can't hang with the big boys anymore."

Jerome tossed his towel down, gripped his racket and stood up. "Can't hang, huh? Come on, Elly, I'm goin' to show this woman who's been carryin' who."

Eli stood and gave his sister-in-law a wink before following his brother onto the court.

The tennis ball seemed to hang in the air as Jerome backed up and jumped for an overhead slam. He swung with all his might but hit only air. The ball hit the court a foot behind him. He thought all was lost but out of the corner of his eye saw his brother coming at a full run. The sweet sound of the ball hitting Eli's racket strings gave Jerome hope again. He looked up and smiled, seeing the ball drop over the net into the alley where neither of their opponents had a chance for a return.

The small crowd applauded politely and the court judge spoke into his microphone. "Tanner and Tanner win game, set, match, for the championship."

Jerome spun around and threw his arm around his brother's shoulder. "You're somethin' in the clutch, Elly. But next time what'd'ya say we win in two sets and not three? I'm gettin' too old for this shit."

Millie bounded up to the two men, giving each a kiss on the cheek. "My my my, aren't you two splendid? The Tanner boys sure showed 'em."

"Beer, woman. Me and Elly need beer, not compliments," Jerome said with a grin.

Millie's smile wilted. "You can have one, honey, but Eli, you've got the finals single's match to play. I'm so sorry. I had no idea you two would win all your matches. Please forgive me for signing you up for singles, too."

Eli leaned over and kissed her cheek. "Don't be sorry, Millie, I'm on a roll. Come on, let's get this old-timer a beer and let me get off my feet for a while."

The threesome had just made it to the steps leading up to the clubhouse when Eli felt a tap on his shoulder. He turned and faced a tall, handsome man he judged to be in his late thirties. Blond and tanned, the man smiled, but Eli knew it was insincere because the stranger's eyes were measuring him. "Hi, I'm Rod Perkins. We play right here on court one in fifteen minutes."

"Fifteen minutes?" Jerome growled. "No way, Rod, we just got through playing. Eli needs at least an hour break."

Blondy raised a bushy golden eyebrow. "The time for the match is posted, Jerome. Your brother can always default if he's too tired to play."

Millie poked her finger into the blond man's chest. "Rod, if both players agree to a later time, it's okay, and you know it. Quit being a jerk and give Eli an hour."

"Sorry, Millie, but I have other things to do. I promise I'll make it quick, and not too humiliating."

"You pompous ass!" Millie barked. "I'm going to talk to the tournament committee and we'll see what they have to—"

Eli patted his sister-in-law's shoulder. "It's all right, Millie. I'll play him in fifteen minutes." His eyes settled on Perkins and turned frigid. "After all, this *gentleman* has said he has things to do and he'd make it quick. Isn't that what you said, sir, 'quick and not too humiliating'?"

Perkins felt the effect of the icy stare and realized he'd better say nothing more. He just nodded. Eli stepped closer, keeping his hold on the man's eyes. "Get somebody to warm you up. I won't need it. I'll be back in exactly fifteen minutes."

In the clubhouse, Eli put on a dry shirt and accepted another bottle of Gatorade from Millie. "Nice folks ya'll have in the club," he said with a mocking grin.

Jerome handed his brother a pair of dry socks. "Rod's a lawyer, what'd'ya expect. He moved here a couple of years ago from New York. We put up with him 'cause his wife is a local and active in everything—a real class act."

"She married a Yankee, Jerome. What kind of class is that?" Millie said, making a face.

"She's still class in my book, okay? Look, little brother, he's good. I wish I could tell ya he had a weakness, but he doesn't. He's won the singles event for the last two years. He's a baseline player, so don't look for him to come to the net. He's got a strong forehand and a sizzlin' two-handed backhand, and he was serious when he said he'd try and make it quick."

"We'll see about that." Eli stood up.

Millie groaned and shook her head, seeing the ball pass just beyond Eli's reach for the winner. "It's going to be worse than I thought. Rod's won four straight games."

Jerome smiled. "Don't count Elly out just yet. I think he's been feeling him out. He's had three easy put-aways, but instead put the shots deep in the corners to make Rod run. I think we're about to see Elly drop the hammer on him."

"Hon, Eli is good, but he's exhausted, there's no way."

"Watch and see."

A small woman wearing a stylish light cotton dress and flowered straw hat walked down the steps from the clubhouse toward the stadium court looking for a man she thought she knew all too well. It was all there in the file. Although Agent Ashley Sutton didn't know what Eli Tanner looked like, she knew his type. He was definitely a Rambo. His record reflected a man who had volunteered and successfully completed the Army's and FBI's toughest training courses. He'd jumped out of perfectly good airplanes, eaten snakes, been shot in Vietnam, and shot twice during assignments with Bureau's special tactical units. It was clear he was a man who loved to be in harm's way but didn't know when to duck. He would be tall, heavily muscled, have a crew cut, and be square-jawed. He would be like the jocks at school or the muscle-bound idiots at the Y who spent more time looking at themselves in the mirrors than pumping iron. He'd have that confident strut of all the tactical team agents. And he would most assuredly think he was God's gift to women.

Stopping on the landing, she began her visual search of the small crowd that was intently watching the tennis match. She'd called the number on his leave form, but got an answering machine in his brother's home. The message said the Tanners could be contacted at the country club. The receptionist at the club desk had told her she didn't know Eli Tanner but that a Mr. Jerome Tanner was a member of the club and she thought he would be watching the singles competition finals on court one.

Ashley finished searching the spectator's faces on the far side of the court and stepped down to continue her search among the chairs on her side of the court. Seeing the two together would clinch it, she thought. It didn't take a rocket scientist to figure out Jerome Tanner had used his influence with his old cronies to have his younger brother assigned to the resident office. It was the only explanation for the sudden move. The "good ol' boy" network had worked its voodoo magic again. Despite the rules, the secret society of the "good ol' boys" always managed to make end runs around the system.

The collective gasp of the spectators broke her train of thought and she looked toward the court. A very tall, handsome blond man was running toward an obviously well-placed ball. With surprising power, the blond hit the sphere like a bullet toward the opposite court in what looked like a clear winner. But his opponent, a short, well-built man positioned close to the net, lunged and hit the ball back to the opposite side of the court. Again the blond put on a burst of speed and managed to get his racket on the ball, but it was a weaker return. The short man attacked with a vicious overhead slam and put the ball into the opposite corner for a winner. The sedate crowd came alive with loud applause.

Ashley smiled to herself. She liked to see hard work pay off, and it was clear the sweaty, short player, who was obviously older than his opponent, was trying very hard. His looks reminded her of Steve McQueen in his prime; he had that lithe, rangy look of a big-game cat—not a lion or leopard, but more

like a cheetah. He was probably five-eight—perhaps -nine—
and like a cheetah, had a thick chest, narrow waist, and heavily
muscled legs. She should have used the pause in play to search
the crowd for Mr. Macho Rambo, but there was something
about the cheetah that intrigued her. He had a definite presence
about him. Perhaps it was the unusual premature gray hair that
contrasted so starkly with his tanned face. No, that wasn't
it, she thought. It undeniably had something to do with his
looks, but it was much more, it was his elegance. Yes, she
thought, the word was unusual to describe a man, but it
matched him perfectly. It was the way he held his head and
moved with no wasted motion, and the way his eyes were
always steady and focused. He was a man who was in complete control of himself, she thought. Turning, she spoke to the
elderly woman seated beside her. "Excuse me, do you know
the score?"

The woman motioned to the tall player. "Rod Perkins is up
four to two in the first set."

"Thank you," Ashley said, feeling angry at herself. Hearing
herself speak had been like being hit with cold water. She
hadn't come to watch a tennis match. She had a job to do, and
that was find Rambo, give him the envelope, and tell him he'd
been assigned to the resident position. As if he didn't know
already, she thought. His good ol' boy brother and he would
act surprised for her benefit, but they knew. The sound of the
blond hitting his serve drew her attention involuntarily back to
the court. The ball was just a blur, but the cheetah pounced on
it with a blistering forehand that swished by the shocked blond
before he could even get his racket back. An attractive middle-
age woman five chairs down and a row back rose up and
shouted, *"Yes!"*

The crowd applauded again, this time even more loudly.
The onlookers began shifting toward the edge of their seats; the
momentum of the match had changed. Ashley, too, felt the
intangible air of excitement building, and despite her good
intentions, found her eyes glued to the tall player as he hit

another blinding serve to the cheetah's back hand. Cheetah chipped the ball back, barely clearing the net and the blond had to sprint to try to return it. In a dead run, he just got to the ball and popped it up, but the cheetah was waiting and smashed it in an overhead that hit the alley line.

The blond shouted, "Out!"

The crowd murmured and the attractive woman stood and hollered, "No way! It was on the line!"

The court judge seated in the elevated chair leaned over his mike. "The ball was in, Mr. Perkins. The score is thirty, love."

The crowd erupted in applause, and the blond tossed down his racket and shouted angrily, "That was out, damnit! Are you blind?"

Again the judge leaned over the mike and spoke in a monotone. "Thirty love, continue play, please, Mr. Perkins."

Ashley forced herself to look over her shoulder and begin to search the intense faces. She heard the sound of the serve, but didn't flinch; she had her control back, she told herself. A pinging sound told her the cheetah had returned the blast, but again she kept up the search. The crowd applauded and the voice of the attractive woman five chairs down called, *"yes!"*

Where are you, Agent Tanner? Ashley asked herself. *Come on, I know you're here somewhere sitting by that good ol' boy brother of yours. You're forty-seven-years old and Jerome is at least fifty. Where are you, damnit?*

"Forty, love," the court judge said.

Unable to concentrate, Ashley spun around just as the blond served another bullet, but the cheetah attacked the yellow blur and smacked it back toward his opponent. Too surprised even to move, the ball hit the blond's right shin with a resounding smack.

The crowd erupted in applause and the attractive woman rose again, her raised fist clenched. "Thataway, baby!"

The elderly woman seated beside Ashley chuckled and leaned over. "Millie sure is enjoying this. I must say I am, too. Her brother-in-law is quite good, isn't he?"

Ashley nodded and glanced at the woman, who was still standing. "The way she was yelling, I thought she was his wife."

"No, that's just Millie, she's a dear girl who doesn't particularly care for Rod. He's a northerner you know?"

"No, I didn't realize, but I certainly should have guessed it."

Ashley tried to contain a smile. *I'm definitely in the Old South,* she thought as she looked back toward the players, who were taking their break before changing sides. The cheetah, toweling off his racket grip, smiled at his sister-in-law. Ashley couldn't help but smile, too. It was an easy smile, as if he did it a lot. It was a good smile for a man, genuine and natural, like that of a small boy.

A man rose up beside the woman and barked toward the cheetah, "You need another dry shirt?"

The cheetah shook his head and grinned as he motioned toward his feet. "I just need a pair of younger legs."

Ashley smiled again. She liked the way the cheetah didn't take himself too seriously. His attitude was a stark contrast to Blondy on the other side of the court. He had on his game face and was staring at the cheetah as if he wanted to tear his throat out. *Get a life, Blondy,* Ashley thought. *Cheetah may lose the match, but he's got you beat in the game of life. . . . Okay, that's it! I'm getting back to business now. It's time to find Agent Tanner and carry out my mission.*

Ashley was about to turn and begin her search again when the court judge spoke into the mike. "Score is Mr. Perkins, four, and Mr. Tanner, three. It is Mr. Tanner's serve."

Ashley's face paled as she abruptly swung her head toward the court in disbelief. *No, it can't be. I must have heard wrong.* Twisting in her seat, she touched the elderly woman's arm. "Excuse me, but what did the judge say the older player's name was?"

"Tanner, dear. Eli Tanner. Millie introduced me to him this morning before he and Jerome played doubles in the second round. Such a gentleman. He's in the FBI, just like Jerome was. The heat getting to you dear? Your face is so flushed."

Not sure what he was supposed to do, the waiter stood at the side of the crowded table holding a tray of drinks. Millie saw his dilemma and quickly picked up the two first-place trophies to make room. Setting down the tray, the waiter motioned toward the bar. "Dr. Fielding sends his congratulations to all the victors."

Jerome waved toward the balding man seated on a bar stool. "Thanks for the drinks, Harry. Pull up a chair and join us."

The doctor smiled and slid off the stool. "I'm sure I'll hear all about how you single-handedly won the finals in doubles."

A woman in an expensive warm-up seated beside Jerome rolled her eyes. "You're right, Harry. Jerome was just telling us for the *fifth* time how he carried Eli in that third set."

Jerome stood and made an overhead smash motion. "Tell her, Harry, I do it all the time. I faked the miss to get John and Colin out of position."

Harry shrugged as he brought up a chair. "If you faked that miss you ought to get an Academy Award." His gaze settled on Eli. "Young man, you played well despite your brother's valiant attempt to lose. However, I must tell you that I especially enjoyed your singles match with Rod. Coming back and winning the first set when you were four down was something to see. I'm afraid you took the heart out of Rod after that. I don't recall Rod's winning a single point in the second set."

Eli dipped his chin. "Thank you, sir, but I'm paying the price. I can't get up from this chair."

"As your brother's physician, I offer you a bit of advice. Beer. Drink beer until you can't feel anything. Tonight I guarantee you'll be able to sleep, and when you wake up tomorrow, your head will hurt so bad you won't even notice the aches, pains, and soreness of the match."

Directly behind their table, Ashley Sutton sat alone on a plaid couch facing a television. Hearing the outburst of raucous

laughter from those around the table, she cringed. *Pa-lease.*
Will they ever stop with the jokes and the gloating? She'd been
waiting for her chance to deliver the envelope, but as yet had
been unsuccessful. After the match, the Tanners and the other
players had retired to the clubhouse for the awards presenta-
tion, dinner, and the retelling of war stories. The women
doubles champions were especially loud, and one of them, a
buxom redhead wearing a very short tennis skirt, was falling
all over herself trying to get Special Agent Eli Tanner to notice
her. It was sickening, Ashley thought as she nursed her second
gin and tonic and pretended to watch the Braves game. She had
by then gotten over her shock at her mental image of Agent
Tanner being so far off base. Well, not that far off, she thought.
He might not look like Rambo, but she knew behind that
impish smile there was still a conniving good ol' boy and
macho man of the worst kind.

At the victory table, the partner of the redheaded vixen stood
and pointed at her gold Rolex. "Sorry, fellow winners, but I've
got to get home to hubby; it's getting late. It's been fun."

Others stood, saying they hadn't realized it was so late, and
in less than a minute only the Tanners and the determined redhead remained. Millie eyed the vixen with suspicion and
leaned over to her. "Barb, why don't you and I go and freshen
our faces."

"Do you think I'm in need of repair?" the woman drawled as
she wiggled her painted eyebrows at Eli.

He smiled. "Miss Barbara, I fear I'm not qualified to comment on such matters. I believe, however, that Millie would
like your company. My mother always said a lady should
never walk alone."

"And your mama was right," the redhead said, getting to her
feet. "Now don't run off on me while we're gone. I want to talk
to you about playing mixed doubles next time you come and
visit. We'll make a perfect team."

Jerome waited until the two women were out of earshot
before shaking his head. "Watch her Elly, she's got *playing* in

mind, but it isn't tennis. She was divorced last year and is on the hunt."

Eli sighed and picked up his mug of beer. "I couldn't *play* if I wanted to." He shifted his gaze to his brother and sank back in his chair. "We've been playin' tennis for two days straight and haven't had much time to talk about the move. I have to tell ya, Jer, it looks like I'm washed up—they're putting me out to pasture with this assignment."

Jerome lowered his head. "You knew that when you wrote the report on Ruby Ridge. They can forgive a lot of things, but in their minds you broke the code. Disloyalty to the boo is the one thing they won't stand for. How long do you think you have?"

"A year at the most. The Atlanta office posting is just window dressing to make it look good. They'll make it as miserable for me as they can. The good news is, at least they gave me Atlanta for the torture. It'll make it easier having you and Millie just ninety miles away."

Jerome put his arm over his brother's shoulder. "Screw 'em, Elly, retire now and come work for me. I've got offices opening in Marietta, Selma, and Macon. You'll oversee the whole kit and caboodle and give Millie and me a chance to finally do some traveling."

Eli patted his brother's hand. "Thanks, Jer, but I'm going to stick it out so I can receive full retirement benefits. Keep the offer open, though. I'd like nothing better than to work with you. . . . We had fun today, didn't we? It really was like the old days."

Jerome squeezed Eli's neck. "Yeah, it was a day to remember. I just wish Dad could have seen us. He would have been happy to see his hard work pay off."

Jerome lowered his head a moment before looking up. "Elly, I'm gettin' old. It's damn hard to admit, but I am. I can't move like I used to. My mind thinks I can, but my body says, 'Screw you.' It was good winning again. Thanks."

Eli shut his eyes a moment, savoring the feel of his brother being close. It's been too many years, he thought. Opening his eyes, he patted Jerome's hand again. "Brother, they say things always happen for the best. After today I believe that saying. I was feeling pretty low when I got here, but now, being with you and Millie, I'm feelin' a whole lot better about the move. I'm not going to let the bastards get me down. They don't know it, but they just threw Br'er Rabbit into the briar patch."

Millie walked up with her usual smile. "Who's Br'er Rabbit?"

"Men-talk, hon. Where's Barb?" Jerome asked.

Millie raised an eyebrow. "We had a little talk in the women's room. I explained to her Eli wasn't available."

"You're kiddin', right?" Eli said. He sat up. "I really liked Barb. Well, at least parts of her looked interesting. She said we'd make a perfect team in mixed doubles."

"Forget it, Bub, that's your hormones talking. She's not your type. It just so happens I have a friend who—"

Jerome sighed. "Aw hell, hon, ya promised you wouldn't try and fix him up."

"It's a woman's thing, okay? Now cool it. Cynthia is a sweet girl who—"

"Has a great personality," Jerome finished, elbowing his brother in the ribs. "And she makes her own clothes and doesn't eat much and—"

"That's enough, Jerome Tanner, or you'll be lookin' for a gal with a great personality who'll wash your dirty socks and put up with your snoring. Are you two ready to go?"

Jerome raised his hand from the table. "Almost, but I think there's someone who wants to talk to me before we leave." He looked over his shoulder directly at Ashley Sutton. "Is that right, miss? You did want to speak to me, didn't you?"

Shocked, Ashley stammered, "Well, uh, no, sir, actually I wanted to speak to your brother."

Jerome stood and pulled his chair out farther. "Then come on over, Agent Sutton, and sit right here beside him."

Caught off guard, Ashley put on a plastic smile, got up and walked toward the table.

Jerome raised an eyebrow as she sat down. "Just so you know I'm not psychic, Linda at the reception desk told me who you were and that you had asked about me. She said you showed your boo ID and said it was business."

Ashley winced. "I'm sorry about that but they weren't going to let me into the club without a member to sign me in. I didn't want to disturb you. It really is business. I have something to give Agent Tanner."

Shifting in her chair, she faced Eli. "Agent Tanner, I'm sorry I didn't introduce myself sooner, but with your victory and the party, I didn't think it a good time to hand you your assignment instructions."

Reaching into her purse, she took out the envelope. "Agent Tanner, I'm Agent Ashley Sutton. The Special Agent in Charge of the Atlanta office asked that I give you this. Congratulations, you will be replacing me as the resident agent heading up the office here in Columbus."

Eli stared at the envelope. Jerome slapped his brother's back with one hand and took the envelope with the other. "You're in the briar patch, Elly! Hot damn!"

Ashley nodded to herself, seeing Eli's reaction. He's good, very good, she thought. A great performance. He really looks like he's surprised—yeah, right.

Millie kissed Eli's cheek and gave him a hug. "Now, I'll have time to find you the right woman. This is wonderful, Eli! We've got to celebrate! Come on, let's go to the house and break open a bottle of champagne. Ashley, you must come and tell us all how this happened. My God, assigned right here in town. This is going to be great!"

Ashley began to make an excuse and make a fast exit, but Millie already held her arm and was gently pulling her up from the chair. "We haven't been properly introduced. I'm Millie, the big guy's live-in housekeeper and, when he's nice, wife. I haven't seen you before, have I?"

"I don't believe so, Mrs. Tanner, I just moved to Columbus a month ago and—"

"Hold it, you two," Jerome said. He motioned to Eli, who was grimacing. "I think we've got a problem here."

Eli spoke through clenched teeth. "I—I can't get up."

"Cramps," Jerome said. "Take a couple of deep breaths and try to relax. Hon, go get the car and bring it up to the door. Ashley and I will help him to his feet and get him to the entrance."

Millie looked worriedly at her brother-in-law, who was in obvious pain. "Anything I can do for you, Eli?"

Jerome rolled his eyes. "Yeah, get Barb back; she'd probably love to work on his cramps. Go on, hon, get the car. Ashley, you get his right arm and I'll get his left. Good. On one, lift. One . . . "

Millie poured Ashley a cup of coffee and glanced toward the room where Eli was sprawled on the couch. "I gave him some muscle relaxers, I hope it helps."

"He was in a lot of pain. I'm surprised he didn't show it more," Ashley said.

"He's a Tanner. Oh, just listen to me! That's bull. My Jerome is the biggest baby I know when he's sick or hurt. Eli is different. He knows pain a lot more than the rest of us. The Vietnam War did that to him. He came back different. Not in a bad way, you understand, just different. He went through hell during his therapy, broke my heart seeing him like that, but he made it."

"Does he have children?" Ashley asked.

Millie gave her guest a questioning stare. "How did you know he'd been married?"

"His file. The SAC gave me a copy to read so I would know about him."

"It's just more pain that he had to endure," Millie said, pouring herself a cup of coffee. "Yes, he has a son, but he hasn't seen him in almost ten years. It's a long story you probably don't want to hear."

"No, please, Millie. How come he hasn't seen him?"

Sitting down at the kitchen table, Millie shook her head. "You have to understand, Eli is a very dedicated agent—almost to a fault. His wife, Kathy, wanted him to quit the Bureau and get a job where he could spend more time with the family. Eli loved the boo ... he couldn't give it up. Kathy pretty much gave up on him ... started messing around with a doctor. Eli found out and confronted the doctor, who made the error of telling Eli he wasn't good enough for Kathy. Eli kind of lost it. . . . The doctor required twenty stitches and about two months of drinking his meals through straws while his rewired jaw healed. Of course there were charges filed against Eli, but because of the circumstances, he got off lightly ... but he wasn't so lucky during the divorce proceedings. With the help of the doctor, Kathy got herself a high roller lawyer who used the assault as a means of keeping Eli from even having visitation rights. It was sickening. The lawyer called Eli dangerous, violent, and other horrible things that just weren't true. The judge, a friend of the lawyer, ruled in Kathy's favor. Eli was not allowed to see his son or to communicate with him in any way except by letter."

Millie sighed and leaned back in her chair. "It almost killed Eli. It took a long time for him to accept the decision ... and I still don't think he really has. He's just learned to cover it up for our benefit."

"I would have thought a man like Eli would have remarried."

"Ashley, the divorce and separation from his son changed him in a way even the war couldn't. It killed something inside him—relationships with women come very hard for him. He's had a couple of close calls over the years but it never seems to work out. Jerome and I are still hoping. We want to see him happy."

Ashley saw her opening and took it. "Your husband was lucky he still had connections and could get Eli assigned here in Columbus. It must be nice knowing he'll be right here in town."

Chuckling as if knowing an inside joke, Millie slowly shook her head side to side. "Jerome pull strings? That's almost funny. When he retired from the boo he was bitter, frustrated, sick and tired of the political wrangling. He didn't want anything to do with them ever again. To this day he has never spoken to any of his former superiors. Don't get me wrong, the boo was good to us; it's just that the higher you rise, the more political the job becomes. For years it was fun. But when Jerome made SAC of the Atlanta office, it got ugly. I'm sorry, I shouldn't be telling you all this; you probably love the boo, and it's not fair for me to paint such a bleak picture of what lies ahead for you. I'm sure you enjoy your work very much."

"I—I must be honest with you Millie. I thought your husband had influenced his brother's assignment. I assumed it was just another good ol' boy deal. It was the only explanation of why Eli had been moved so quickly. It's very unusual."

Millie studied her guest's face a moment before leaning over and patting her hand. "I'm afraid you couldn't have been more wrong. I think Eli got the Columbus assignment because of a deal of some kind having to do with him writing that report on Ruby Ridge. You would know more about that than I would."

Ashley quickly shook her head. "No, I don't know. I mean I know the Bureau got a black eye from what happened, but I didn't know Eli was involved."

Millie stared at her cup. "Eli's investigation report told the truth. He wrote about the shoot-to-kill orders from Washington and how the higher-ups tried to cover their tracks. Needless to say, he got into hot water. If it weren't for the congressional hearings, he would have been forced out of the boo. Instead he was treated like a hero outside the boo for his courage for standing up and telling it like it was; inside the boo he was hated by those who hadn't wanted their dirty laundry exposed to the public. He was assigned to the academy as a special weapons instructor so they could keep tabs on him. Recently, Calvin Burton was made the superintendent of the school, and he was one of those Eli pointed a finger at in his report. I think you can guess the rest. The big surprise is them giving Eli the resident position. It's a good deal for him, and we didn't think that was possible."

"Millie, to be honest with you, the resident position is not as good as you think. It's a dead-end job away from the big action in Atlanta. To be assigned here is not exactly moving up the ladder of success."

"You're here," Millie said with a searching stare.

Ashley nodded without making eye contact. "Yes, because I'm a 'female' agent who won't be one of the boys. I got tired of the bigotry and decided I wouldn't take it anymore when I got to Atlanta. Sure enough, the Atlanta SAC was like the rest of them—he assumed I wasn't qualified and that I needed field experience so I could be like the guys. As I said, I had made up my mind to fight this time. I fought back with an E.O. complaint. It worked and I'll be going back to Atlanta, but I'm probably marked as a troublemaker."

Millie smiled without humor. "Sounds like you're finding out a lot sooner than we did how political things are. If I were you, I wouldn't worry about it. If the SAC is moving you back to Atlanta, it means he's seen the light. From one female to another, I'm proud of you—hang in there, the boo needs you. Come on, let's go join the guys and see how Eli is faring."

Walking into the great room, they saw Eli on the couch and Jerome in an overstuffed rocking chair, both men sound asleep. They retraced their steps to the kitchen. Millie patted Ashley's back. "Sorry about this. They aren't making a very good impression, I fear."

"They deserve the rest. I need to get back to the hotel and get some rest anyway. Thank you for inviting me over, Millie. And thank you for straightening me out about Eli."

"Hotel? Are you still in a hotel after a whole month living here?"

"I rented an apartment, but I found termites a couple of days ago. They sprayed this morning, and I had to move out for a few days."

Millie nodded in understanding and walked the agent toward the kitchen door. "Ashley, I'll call you and we'll go see if we can find Eli a decent place to live. If we don't, he'll rent a trailer or something worse—he lives kind of simply, if you know what I mean. I'm going to make it my mission to get Eli back into the real world; a nice place is a start. Next I'll be finding him a suitable lady friend."

Ashley forced a smile. She knew all too well how he lived; he lived the way she did, alone, with only the job. But not anymore, she thought. Eli now had Millie and Jerome to help him find more than the Bureau. Grasping the door handle, Ashley faced her hostess and lied. "I'd love to help you find him a place. Good night, Millie."

Not waiting for a response, Ashley opened the door and walked into the darkness.

5:00 A.M. San Antonio, Texas

Simon Hernandez held a fiberglass expandable pole and skim net as he walked down the steps leading to the river walk. The pole and net were the only tools he required for skimming the canal from the Crockett to the Houston street bridges. Stuffed in his belt were five black plastic garbage bags he would fill with floating beer cans, paper, condoms, and anything else that floated in the city's number-one tourist attraction. Simon liked the job because he worked alone and nobody hassled him. And he liked being important. He knew if the canal was not cleaned of the trash, it would turn into a sewer within a week. Knowing the rich tourists continued to come because of him, he took pride in his work.

Reaching the walkway, he turned right to walk under the bridge toward Crockett, but something was wrong. The usually well-lighted passage was dark. He stopped to let his eyes adjust. The neon pedestrian light attached to the underside of the bridge had to be broken or the bulb was out. He made a mental note to inform his supervisor about the light, then continued on. But he saw something strange only a few feet away. At first he thought it was a half-full garbage bag. He stepped closer and froze.

The police officer's flashlight beam settled on the corpse, and Simon Hernandez crossed himself as he spoke. "I tell you de gringo *aqui*."

"Si, stand back but don't go anywhere," the officer said as he and his partner stepped closer to investigate.

"Got a weapon here. Twenty-two, by the look of it, there in his right hand."

"Has he got a pulse?"

"With that hole in his head? You kiddin', a pulse? Give me a break, will ya? He's about as dead as they come. Helluva place to do yourself. Hey, look at this, he's got part of his neck chain in his mouth."

"The dude was loco, man. He was tryin' to eat gold. Call it in and let's get the party started. Got to get the body out and the mess cleaned up before light. Wouldn't want the *turistas* upset."

Standing in the darkness, Simon Hernandez lowered his head to say a prayer for the dead man's lost soul. Finished, he looked up at the dark sky and said another prayer, but this one was a prayer of thanks. He was thankful the dead man had not fallen into his canal. He would have been too big to skim out.

CHAPTER 5

6:30 A.M. Monday, June 4, Columbus, Georgia

In her bed, asleep, in the Columbus airport Sheraton, Ashley Sutton was awakened by knocking on her door. Lifting one eyelid, she looked at the digital clock on the nightstand and groaned. Turning over, she barked toward the door. "Go away, come back and clean the room in a couple of hours!"

Closing her eyes, she settled back on the pillow. Then she heard knocking again. *Why can't they hire maids who speak English! Damn!* Angrily throwing off her covers, she got up, put on her robe, marched straight toward the door and swung it open. "I said I didn't need my room—oh God."

Standing two feet away was Eli Tanner, dressed in tan chinos and faded jean shirt. His smile drooped. "I got you up, huh? Sorry, I thought you'd be getting ready to go to work."

Still frozen holding the door, Ashley closed her eyes, hoping his appearance was a bad dream. *I'm standing here in my bare feet holding the door, and my robe is open exposing to the whole world that I wear Mickey Mouse pajamas, my hair must look like God knows what, and I'm not wearing makeup. Tell me this isn't happening.* She opened her eyes. "Oh God."

Knowing he'd made a very bad mistake, Eli averted his eyes from her and motioned down the hall. "Uh . . . I can see it's not a good time. I'll go have some breakfast in the hotel café and read the paper. Maybe later we can talk. . . . I'm real sorry about this."

Afraid her morning breath might knock him down, she mechanically nodded, stepped back and shut the door. "Oh God."

Eli shook his head and walked down the carpeted hallway. *Real good, Tanner—first you crash and burn on the couch and don't say a word to her, and now you wake her up. Real good.*

Eli was reading the sports page when he heard the chair across from him being pulled back. He lowered the paper and cautiously smiled. "Am I forgiven?"

Ashley sat down, busying herself with putting away her purse so she wouldn't have to look at him. "Forgiven," she said and quickly picked up a plastic menu card to hide her red face.

"The special is good," Eli offered, knowing she'd lied.

The waiter approached and Ashley handed him the menu. "Wheat toast, no butter, and coffee, please."

"We have an excellent breakfast buffet, ma'am. It includes—"

"Wheat toast, no butter, and coffee, please," Ashley repeated a little more loudly.

"Would you like orange juice with that, ma'am?"

Ashley looked up at the waiter with a glare that made him take a step back. "Uh . . . I'll get that coffee right away, ma'am."

Eli quickly turned his head away and coughed to cover up an involuntary chuckle.

She lifted an eyebrow and spoke menacingly. "What's so funny, Agent Tanner?"

Eli coughed again. "Eh, nothing, I was just—" He couldn't help it, he laughed aloud, tried to stop himself, but the laugh came out in a sputter.

"I was right about you. You *are* a bastard," she said, keeping her glare on him.

He tried to speak but began laughing again. She didn't move a muscle or blink as she kept her burning gaze on him. Regaining control of himself, he said, "I'm sorry, but if you could have seen your face when you opened the door this morning. And the look you just gave that waiter was—"

"I'm not a morning person, Agent Tanner, okay? Why are you here and how did you know where I was? At least you could have called first."

Eli frowned as if pained. "I felt bad about us not having a chance to talk the other night. Passing out on the couch was not very gentlemanly. Millie told me you were staying in a hotel, so I did some calling. And I'm sorry, I didn't know you weren't a morning person. I'll remember next time."

Ashley broke her glare from him and rearranged the salt and pepper shakers to keep her hands busy. "You're feeling better, I see, over the soreness?"

Eli lifted his arms in a stretching motion. "I'm pretty stiff, but movin' around seems to help." He looked into her eyes. "Why did you think I'd be a bastard?"

"Because you're a man, Agent Tanner," she said, with no hint of a smile. "I thought you had used your brother's influence to get assigned to Atlanta. Millie dispelled that notion Saturday night, so you're halfway off the hook. But only halfway because you didn't call me before coming up to my room. You're still suspect."

"Would it help to tell you I liked your Mickey Mouse PJs?"

Again her eyes narrowed. "I appreciate a sense of humor, Agent Tanner, but not at my expense."

Eli sighed and extended his hand. "Let's start over, okay? Hi, I'm Eli Tanner."

She reached over the table and took his hand. "Hello, I'm agent Ashley Sutton."

Smiling, Eli leaned back and motioned to himself. "Please call me Eli."

Ashley nodded. "And you can address me as Agent Sutton, Agent Tanner. I, for one, believe familiarity between agents is unprofessional."

Eli let out a long sigh. It was really dumb of him to think she was different from the others. Obviously, just like the rest of them, she thought of him as a traitor to the Bureau. He dipped his chin and spoke softy. "Very well, Agent Sutton. I will try and be more professional. It's obvious you've read my file and know who I am, but I don't know *your* background. I could sit here and do the twenty-question thing, or you could just give a quick rundown on yourself."

The waiter approached and poured coffee into Ashley's cup while keeping as much distance from her as he possibly could. "Your toast should be right out, ma'am," he said meekly, then quickly walked away.

Ashley picked up her cup, took a sip, then looked at Eli. "I was born and raised in Richmond, Virginia. I'm thirty-three years old. I was married then divorced. I went to school at UVA, graduated, and was accepted by the Bureau in ninety-two. After graduating from the academy, I was assigned to Seattle. I'm a computer analyst and my specialty field is white-collar crime. I was assigned to the Atlanta office a month ago and the SAC assigned me here. Need any more info, Agent Tanner?"

Eli shook his head. "Nope, thanks. Now let me clarify something about me. I'm going to say this only once. You can believe it or not, it doesn't make any difference to me. I did *not* leak my investigation report to the press or anybody else."

She lowered her cup. "Millie told me about the investigation report. I guess I should have remembered your name, but to tell you the truth, I didn't follow the controversy the way most of the Bureau did. I thought you did the right thing, and to me that was that. So what, that you showed the Bureau wasn't pristine? All of us in it know that."

Feeling better, Eli again leaned back in his chair. "If you don't mind, I'd like to discuss me starting work as soon as possible."

"I thought you were on leave," Ashley said.

"I am, but I gotta get out of the house. Millie is drivin' me nuts with her matchmaking. Tonight she's got one of her divorced friends coming over for dinner. I need an excuse to skip it. Would it be possible if we stayed late this evening at the office and went over the case files?"

Ashley's eyes began to narrow. "You came to my room at six o'clock in the morning and woke me up so I could get you out of a dinner date?"

"Whoa there, Agent Sutton. I didn't even think about the caseload thing until just a few seconds ago. It's not the date . . . I just really *need* to get back to work. I've been tossed out of one job like a rancid piece of meat, and I need to get involved in something that makes me feel whole again. I need a chance to start over. I hoped you would understand."

Ashley was angry at herself. Thankfully, the waiter arrived with the toast, and she immediately took a bite so she wouldn't have to apologize to him again. Misjudging him was getting old. Finishing off one half slice, she picked up another and looked at him. "Why don't you come with me to Fort Benning this morning? I'll introduce you to the Military Police and CID people you'll be working with. After that we'll go to the office and I'll show you around and we'll discuss my caseload . . . and yes, it will take some time and probably extend into the dinner hour. Happy?"

"Yes, very."

She was about to take a bite of her toast but stopped and eyed him again. "And Agent Tanner, if you tell a soul about my Mickey Mouse pajamas, I will shoot you dead. Are we communicating here?"

Eli smiled. "Perfectly, Agent Sutton."

Walking out the hotel front doors, Ashley glanced at her fellow agent. "Your car or mine?"

"Yours. I drive a pickup and it's full of my things. I guess I ought to tell you now so you know. I'm a terrible driver. I do all right on interstates, but in towns I'm really bad. I get tunnel vision or something."

Ashley sighed and faced him. "Anything else I should know about you?"

"I don't have any taste buds, burned them out in Nam with all the hot sauce I put on my C-rations. . . . I hate being in water, nearly drowned once, and I loathe hospitals. . . . Let's see . . . nope, that's about it. How about you, I mean other than not being a morning person?"

"No, I don't have anything to divulge to you. Come on, that blue dodge van is ours, it's rigged special."

Eli grinned as he approached the vehicle. "A boo ride, no less."

She pressed the entry remote on her key chain, the van beeped and the door locks sprang up with a single resounding click. "What is this 'boo' business?" Ashley asked. "Millie used the word, too. I've never heard the Bureau referred to that way before."

Eli climbed in the passenger side and fastened his seat belt. "Jerome's son, Jason—when he was little he couldn't say Bureau, instead he said 'boo.' He'd say, 'My daddy works in the boo.' We all picked it up. Now it's kind of a family thing."

"I like it," Ashley said as she motioned toward the dash. "Open the glove compartment and you'll find a fax machine. Between us in this big armrest is a minicomputer. The phone is here, below the radio. You've got everything you need to communicate with our office, GBI, Atlanta, or the Bureau. Neat, huh? Oh . . . I didn't even ask, you do know computers, don't you?"

Eli opened the armrest and studied the small gray computer. "When I was in Quantico they wouldn't let me do much, so I took the time to take classes on these things. The modem is built in on this model, right?"

"I'll be, Rambo has become a wirehead."

"What's that supposed to mean?" Eli asked.

"Nothing, I'm just impressed, Agent Tanner. I would have thought your type wouldn't even know what a modem was."

"Tell me, Agent Sutton, what 'type' am I?"

"The special ops guerrilla-type, of course. I read your file, Agent Tanner, remember? I know you. Well, I thought I did.

These little surprises of knowing computers and actually admitting you're a poor driver don't fit the mold, however. It gives me hope."

Eli gave her a quizzical look. "Hope for what?"

"The hope that you're not an ass like the rest of them."

Eli sighed. "Agent Sutton, you can stop hoping. I am an ass, or at least most people in the boo think so."

Ashley slipped the shift to reverse and gave him a side glance. "I never have cared what other people think, Agent Tanner. And I don't think you have, either. We'll just have to wait and see, won't we?"

As the van passed through Fort Benning, Eli saw familiar training sites and buildings that transported him to a time when he'd been a young soldier training on the post. The three huge orange and white jump towers, the landmarks of the fort, especially brought back good memories. The United States Army Airborne School had been a tough course, but one he'd enjoyed. Like many young soldiers in those days, he had never flown in an airplane before. He got his chance at the Airborne school, but didn't have much time to enjoy the flights. After being airborne for only ten minutes and attaining an altitude of only 1,150 feet, he and the rest of the scared students were ordered to jump out. Eli closed his eyes for a moment, remembering that day. He'd never been so frightened in all his life as he stood in the open door of that aircraft looking down at the distant earth. The 150-knot wind tore at his fatigues, and everything in his being told him not to jump. Then the jumpmaster yelled, *"Go!"*

Eli smiled to himself. He had closed his eyes, prayed to God for forgiveness for being so foolish, then sprung into space. As he tumbled to earth, for three very long seconds he had known he was going to die. Then came the abrupt jerk of the chute's opening. Looking up, he witnessed the most beautiful sight he had ever seen, a fully open army-green-issue parachute. He'd done it, defied death and overcome his fear. It was a day he would never forget.

Feeling her passenger's silence, Ashley gave him a quick glance. "You weren't impressed with the CID people, were you?"

Eli broke away from his past and shook his head. "No, the opposite in fact. They seem very dedicated. They're awfully young, but the chief warrant officer knew his stuff."

"What about the Military Police crew?"

"The major was a pain, but the rest were okay. I think the major is a yes-man to his boss, who was too busy to see us. What's the story on Colonel Washinski, anyway?"

"I don't know, I've never met him. The major always tells me his boss is too busy to see me. Lydia, the captain who works for the major, has hinted to me the colonel is not particularly fond of federal agents."

As he looked out the window, Tanner said, "What 'type' does that make him?"

Ashley ignored the question and motioned ahead. "Where do I turn? Are you sure your old Army buddy will even be there?"

"Turn right at the intersection and head for that huge buff building. It's known—at least it *was* known—simply as Building Four when I trained here. It's the schoolhouse of the United States Infantry. I called him when we were visiting the MPs. He said he'd be waiting out front."

"How long has it been since you've seen him?"

"Ten years or so. I visited him once when he was stationed at Fort Bragg. We write each other now and then to stay in contact. Look, I'm sorry about asking you to change your schedule, but I promised I'd see him when I got to the post. It won't take long. They have a snack bar inside so you can get a Coke or something."

Ashley pulled the van into the drive in front of a building where a huge statue of a soldier stood waving his arm forward.

Eli motioned to the statue with a smile. "That's the famous infantry statue known as Follow Me. Impressive, huh?"

Ashley rolled her eyes. "I guess, if you like big men."

"There he is! Pull over."

Just ahead, a ruddy-faced soldier wearing camouflage fatigues was holding up his hand and beaming. Ashley pulled over, and immediately her passenger was out of the van. Seeing the two men unashamedly embrace and hug each other, she regretted her comment about the statue. She realized then that it meant something to men like them. Their tears and obvious affection for each other made it all too clear they had been through a lot together and were bound by more than mere friendship. She felt that, had her brother Josh lived, he would have been just like the two men.

Eli motioned toward the van, and the ruddy-faced man grinned as he approached Ashley's open window. "Hi, Agent Sutton. I'm Dan Murphy. The Tan man and me were in da Nam together. Park right over there where it says guest parking and come with us. We're all going up to my office."

"Sergeant, I don't want to be in the way. I'll just get a Coke or—"

"That's an order, Agent Sutton. Ain't no good tellin' war stories without somebody to impress. I promise we'll bore ya to tears, but at least you'll know more about the Tan man. Hell, one day he's goin' to be famous. When he dies, they're goin' to name a training area after him. We do that for our infantry heroes, ya know?"

Minutes later Ashley sat in a small office holding a can of Diet Coke as the sergeant major leaned over and patted Eli's shoulder. "Still can't believe you're goin' to be assigned here. That's great. I'll take ya fishin' on the river with a couple of vets, and we'll really do some tall tale tellin'."

Eli grinned. "Sounds great, Murph. What do you do, man? Last time you wrote, you were the Airborne school sergeant major. What are you doin' now?"

Murphy shrugged and leaned back in his chair. "I'm gettin'

ready to retire, that's what. I work for the post sergeant major inspectin' trainin', and do the ash and trash shit. Uh, excuse me, Agent Sutton."

Ashley smiled. "It's all right, Sergeant. I don't have virgin ears. My dad was a detective and my brother was in the Army."

Murphy nodded with embarrassment. "My wife says I got to cut down on my bad language if I expect to land me a job on the outside. I've been workin' on it. The hard part is the clothes. I've worn a uniform for well over twenty years, and now I have to start thinkin' about colored ties, dress shoes, and shi—stuff like that. I don't even know what's in style."

Eli took out a pen and a pad of paper from the sergeant's desk. "Call this number, Murph. My brother needs good men. The hours stink, but it pays good."

Murphy smiled. "Thanks, Tan man, but I've got me one lined up already. Wife don't know it yet but an old vet friend of mine that retired two years ago is sales manager for a bass boat company here in town. Can't beat the benefits—use of a boat and all the beer and fishing gear I'll ever need. Thanks for the thought, though. Hey, I wasn't kiddin' when I said they'd put your name on a training area sign. I put your name in, man. I got the write-up on your DSC and submitted it to the board that does that sh—stuff. All you gotta do is die and you'll be right up there with the rest of them guys who got the big ones. Four-inch letters no less. Can't ya just see it? 'Tanner Range, named in memory of Eli J. Tanner, Sergeant, Infantry. Received the DSC 1972.'"

Eli grinned. "You're kiddin', right? You wouldn't do that to me?"

"Hell, it's done, Tan man. You're a hero in my book. You saved my ass, didn't ya? I know the Budweiser people are sure glad you pulled me through. I've drank enough of their brew in the past twenty years to buy 'em a new plant."

Murphy shifted his gaze to Ashley. "You know all about this, right?"

Before she could speak, Eli stood. "Later, Murph. I just

stopped by to tell ya I'm goin' to be here in town. When I get settled, I want us to go fishin' and drink some of that Bud of yours. We gotta get goin'; I've already screwed up Agent Sutton's schedule enough."

The sergeant stood and hugged Eli again. "Goddamn, I'm glad to see you, Tan man. Sure, you two get goin'. I understand. But damn ya, call me when you get laagered in."

Letting Eli go, the sergeant put his hand out to Ashley as she got up. "Agent Sutton, it's a real pleasure meeting you. The offer of fishin' goes to you too. Anybody who can put up with this old vet deserves a Bud or two."

Once in the van and on the road leading off the post, Ashley broke their silence. "Tan man? And what is a DSC? You Army types speak an entirely different language."

Eli gave her a questioning look. "I thought you said your brother was in the Army? Didn't you learn any of the lingo from him?"

Ashley kept her eyes on the road. "I was eight when two officers came to the house while we were having Sunday dinner. They told Dad and Mom that Josh had been killed in action in a place called Hue. So no, Tanner, I never learned the lingo . . . I just remember they wore green suits."

"I'm sorry, Agent Sutton."

"No, don't be sorry, Tanner. It happens. You know that better than most. So? What is this Tan man business, and what's a DSC?"

Eli shrugged as he looked out the window. "Murph and some of the guys in my old unit called me that. And the DSC is just an award they give. It's nothing. Murph is something, isn't he?"

Ashley smiled despite knowing he was shutting her out of that part of his life. "I liked him a lot. He sure likes you. . . . No, that's not the right word—he *cares* a lot about you, I can tell. Do you have a lot of other veteran friends like him you stay in contact with?"

Eli closed his eyes for a moment, remembering the trail where all the dead and badly wounded from his platoon had lain that fateful day. He shook his head and spoke in a whisper. "No. I've lost contact with most of them."

She nodded in silence and left him with his memories.

Seated in a booth, Ashley pushed a plate of half-eaten ribs out of the way and picked up her briefcase. Taking out a handful of case files, she set them down and glanced toward the jukebox. "If that music gets any louder, I'm outta here and we'll have to discuss these in the office tomorrow. God, how can you stand that music?"

She picked up the first folder and opened it. "Okay, this is the most current one. Five missing M-16s from a weapons maintenance facility. The weapons were accounted for before going in. Four sergeants are the only possibles. Nobody else had access to the weapons."

She looked up from the file and saw her tablemate looking at her with a distant gaze. She wrinkled her brow. "Are you listening?"

Eli kept his look. "You don't like them, do you?"

"Who?"

"The Military Police, the CID—all of them. You don't like military people, do you?"

She tossed down the file. "Look, Tanner, we're discussing case files, not how I feel about the military. Let's get this over with and—"

"Why don't you like them?"

Lowering her head, she sighed then looked once again at him. "I told you I lost my only brother in Vietnam. I was young. I blamed the guys who brought the news. . . . It's dumb, I know, but it's something I can't help. I see those young kids in uniform and I see my brother . . . lambs . . . lambs for slaughter. Yeah, I probably keep my distance from them. I have to, it bothers me."

Eli broke his stare from her and picked up his bottle of beer.

He took a sip and leaned back in his chair. "I'm sorry about your brother . . . but please don't blame these young troopers for his death. They're like your brother was, they're trying to do their duty. They don't need your attitude . . . it's not fair to them."

Ashley's eyes narrowed into slits and she was about to lash out at him, but he raised his hand. "I'm not insulting you, Agent Sutton. I'm just stating a fact. I had to say it for their benefit. I was once one of them and had to put up with the same kind of look you gave them, the look of disdain. I'm asking that you think about it, that's all. Please leave it at that. I owe them."

Ashley stared at him a long moment then slowly lowered her eyes. "I . . . I will think about it. I didn't realize my feelings were so obvious. I didn't mean to—"

"You going to eat the rest of those ribs?" Eli motioned to her plate.

She knew he was trying to save her from more embarrassment, so she shook her head, accepting the ploy. "No, eat up. I'm done."

He scooted her plate closer. "You were an athlete, weren't you?" he asked as he picked up a rib. "You still look like one. . . . You must run or play racquetball. You have to do something to stay in as good shape as you're in."

"I played softball in high school, and when I went back to college in eighty-eight I found out I was still good enough to make the women's softball team. And no I'm not a lesbian, and yes I still run a couple of miles every day to stay in shape."

Eli took a bite and shook his rib bone at her. "I didn't ask if you were a lesbian, I'd never do that. I know you're not anyway."

"How do you know that? Maybe I'm lying."

"I know 'cause I know. It's this secret thing I have. It tells me."

It was obvious that he was trying to lighten the conversation. She canted her head. "Yeah, and what secret thing of yours tells you all this?"

"My gut. It knows good ribs and good beer, knows who's dirty, who's lying, and whether a person is gay or not. I trust my gut with my life."

She opened the first file again. "Well, tell your gut to listen while I bring you up to speed on these cases. I'm counting today as your first day of work. That means in eighty-nine more days I'm gone and leaving you and your gut to handle these. Is your gut listening?"

"He's full," Eli said, straight-faced.

"Tough. As I was saying, the first case is about five missing M-16s and . . ."

Eli nodded to himself, knowing it had been hard for her to hear the criticism, but she'd handled it pretty well and didn't take it personally. He thought she might even have a sense of humor hidden somewhere behind that professional mask she wore, if she ever loosened up.

CHAPTER 6

Tuesday, June 5, Columbus, Georgia

Ashley opened the office door and was surprised to find Eli sitting beside her desk, reading one of her case files.

He looked up and studied her face a moment before cautiously smiling. "Is it safe for me to talk, morning person? I told you I would remember."

She looked over to the secretary's empty desk. "I'm perfectly fine despite those ribs you fed me last night, Agent Tanner. I see our office assistant is late as usual."

Eli looked back at the report he'd been reading. "Nope, Regina was here when I got here. We were out of coffee for the machine so she went to get us a couple of cups."

Ashley snapped her eyes at him. "Agent Tanner, if Regina were a man, would you have sent him to fetch your coffee?"

He kept his eyes on the report. "Nope, she volunteered and I gave her the money." His eyes slowly rose to her. "Have you tried a cold shower when you get up? Maybe that would work."

The door swung open and a tall black woman stepped in. She was holding a cardboard carton holding two huge plastic cups of coffee. "Boss, I hope you like it with cream 'cause I didn't know and put it in anyway. I like cream. Oh, Agent Sutton. Good morning."

Still fuming over Eli's suggestion that she take a cold shower, Ashley spoke in a monotone. "Good morning, Ms. Washington."

The black woman set the carton down and handed him his cup. "I got Sweet'n Lows and NutraSweets and some sugar. I don't use sugar—watchin' my figure, ya know. Stirrin' stick here somewhere. I got the big ones 'cause they were on special, couldn't beat it. Wake us for sure, won't it?"

Eli had stood to accept the cup and looked around as if searching for something. "Thanks, Regina. Where do we keep the extra cups? I'll pour some of this into one for Agent Sutton. I think she needs it."

Ashley glared as the secretary pointed to a cabinet. "Second shelf. I best be checkin' the police reports from last night. I'll highlight any of interest, boss." She walked slowly, carefully holding her cup, and disappeared into a back room.

Ashley attacked immediately. "You two certainly seem to be getting along. In all the time I've been here, Ms. Washington has never volunteered to get *me* coffee."

"Mother instinct, Agent Sutton," Eli said as he walked toward the cabinet. "She's trying to make a good impression, don't take it personal."

"I don't *need* coffee, Tanner," Ashley growled. "And I most certainly don't need a cold shower."

Eli turned around. Without speaking he took up his old position in the chair and resumed reading the report.

A full two minutes passed before Ashley finally slapped the desk. "Okay, I'll take a half cup. Jesus, I hate the silent treatment."

After getting a cup and pouring her coffee, Eli pulled his chair closer to her desk. "Let me see if I've got this right. We're a three-agent office but Agent Doss is on loan to the Richmond office for a special task force, and Agent Watkins is in Atlanta working with the U.S. assistant attorney preparing for a trial?"

Ashley nodded. "Right, but as long as I've been here it's been just me. I know what you're thinking, but don't worry. Watkins should finish up in another two weeks and be back to work. You're not going to be stuck with just me."

Eli motioned to the files he had stacked on the floor. "Sure not much to do around here. We've got thirty active cases and none of them are major, mostly paperwork."

"As I told you last night when I went over them with you, that paperwork takes up most of my time, as it will yours. We've been lucky, we also handle graft, corruption, and bribery of local elected officials, but for some reason it's been slow. They've been good boys for a change. Are you worried you're going to get bored?"

Eli shrugged. "Not really, it's just I thought there would be more—"

"Action?"

"No, Agent Sutton, I was going to say *business*. 'Action' means a lot of things, none of them good. I'm not complaining—in fact, I'm pleasantly surprised. By the way, Millie asked me to ask you to call her."

"She upset you didn't make it to dinner last night and meet her friend?"

"Let's say she wasn't pleased. It's on again for tonight; Millie never gives up when she's on a mission . . . and I think I'm the mission. I was wondering if . . ."

"Don't even think about it, Tanner. I'm not giving you an excuse tonight. You'll just have to suffer through dinner with the lady Millie wants you to meet."

Eli sighed and pushed his chair back. "One more night of discussing caseloads wouldn't kill ya."

Ashley cocked an eyebrow. "I might have considered it if you had taken me someplace decent to eat. Bubba's Rib House was not exactly a four-star eatery. It might have qualified for a half star if we hadn't had to fight off the flies. And that music, how could you concentrate on what I was telling you with that loud country western crap twanging in your ears?"

Eli stared hard at her, but knew she was enjoying the verbal swordplay and was actually attempting to beat him at his own game. We'll see about that, he said to himself. "Agent Sutton, we have a problem. If you don't like barbecue ribs and country music, we're going to have a hard time getting along. It isn't crap. You're talking about real America when you talk about country music. Please be sensitive and remember that in the future."

"Right, Tanner, and I'll try and burp aloud like the locals next time, too."

He shook his head as if in disgust and picked up another case file.

Ashley smiled to herself. She gave him a side glance and saw that he was looking at her again. "What?" she snapped. "Have I still got barbecue sauce on my face or something?"

His eyes narrowed. "Why didn't ya tell me ya didn't like the place?"

"Just like a man, you didn't ask. You assumed I'd like what you liked."

"All ya had to do was say something."

"And all you had to do was ask."

He rolled his eyes and resumed reading the report.

Ashley leaned back in her chair, savoring her victory. This is fun, she thought.

"Shortstop, right?"

Ashley looked at him. "Did you speak to me?"

"You played shortstop for your team, right?" Eli asked.

"Yes, how did you know?"

He motioned to his stomach, smiled and went back to his reading.

Ashley took out a marker, walked to the calendar on the wall and placed an X through the fifth of June. She turned and mumbled aloud so he would hear. "Eighty-eight days and counting. It won't come soon enough."

7:30 P.M.

Jerome got his brother's attention and flicked his eyes to the door. Understanding the signal, Eli smiled at the woman sitting across from him. "If you'll please excuse me a moment, Miss Cynthia, I have to check in with my office. We're working a very important case."

"Dear me, and you just arrived, too," the attractive woman drawled.

Jerome quickly stood. "Ladies, if you'll excuse me a moment as well, I'm going out to check on the dog. Skunks have been coming around and I want to make sure the fence is locked."

Millie gave both men her best glare as they headed for the door. "I expect you both back soon," she said in a warning tone.

Once out of the dining room side door and safely out of earshot, Jerome shook his head. "Sorry, Elly. There are some things I can control, but Millie isn't one of them."

Eli put his arm over his brother's shoulder. "She means well. Cynthia isn't that bad. How was your day?"

"The usual. Three wives came in to have their husbands tailed. One said her Charley got a new-style haircut and she'd read in *Cosmo* it was a sure sign he had himself a girlfriend. Go figure, will ya? How was your day?"

"Okay. Found out I have a real winner in our secretary. She's smarter than a whip and knows the office work inside and out. She could run the place with no problem."

Jerome eyed his brother. "And Agent Sutton? How are you two gettin' along? Come on, don't give me that look. She's a tight-ass if I ever saw one. Sure she looks good, but she's got serious head problems. She a lesbo, you think?"

Eli shook his head as he allowed Jerome to step out into the garage. "Naw, she's really not that bad when she loosens up. 'Course, those moments seem pretty far apart at times."

Jerome smiled. "If she's not a lesbo, use your Tanner charm."

"I think I lost that when my hair turned gray. It's not a big thing, we're really gettin' along pretty well, considering. I don't know what in the hell she's talking about half the time.

She talks about policy this and regulation that, I think she can even quote the Constitution and the Bill of Rights. She's into rules and regulations."

"Inexperienced ones have to hang on to something, Elly. Plus she's older than most of her peers who came in the same time she did. . . . I'm sure that puts a little more pressure on her to do good. She's probably a little awed by you. Keep your cool, she'll be gone soon. Hey, John called today and says he and Colin want a rematch. You up to playing this Saturday?"

Eli smiled and patted his brother's shoulder. "It's begun, Jer. It's sinkin' in that I'm really here and this is goin' to be home. Hell yeah, tell 'em we'll play 'em again. We Tanner boys are together again and goin' to kick ass."

Jerome winked. "Play your cards right, ya might get lucky tonight. Cynthia is droolin', and she's loaded, Elly. Her ex had to give her half of his assets, which were very sizable. Rich and horny ain't a bad combination for a lonely guy like yourself."

"But can she cook?"

"Elly, you'd better listen to that rules lady—she's right, you are a sexist. Come on before Millie kicks both our asses for sneakin' out."

A mile and a half from the Tanner house, Ashley sat in her small apartment living room with the phone next to her ear. ". . . just moved back into the apartment today, Mom . . . No, I checked and haven't seen any termites, the bug people got them all . . . The new agent? He's not new, Mom, he's a senior agent, you know, like Dad was a senior detective . . . Yeah, we're getting along all right, I guess. He reminds me of Dad sometimes . . . How? I guess it's the way he walks and holds his head. He's got that confident walk like Dad had. And he has a good sense of humor just like Dad had . . . Me? Interested in him? Heavens no, Mother, he's an agent . . . Mom, I know I'm not getting any younger . . . Don't worry, I've met a couple of prospects that have asked me out. Don't worry about me, okay? I'm happy . . . Yes, I'm sure I'm happy. In less than

three months I'll be in Atlanta and things will even be better . . .
Mom, I have to go now, my beeper went off . . . Yes, of course,
I'll call again tomorrow. Love you. Good-bye."

Feeling guilty for having lied about the beeper, Ashley
placed the handset back into the cradle and slowly shook her
head. She rose from the couch and looked at the stacked boxes
along the far wall. *See,* there's *a reason to be happy. I don't
have much to pack. I still have boxes I didn't unpack from the
last move.*

She walked into the kitchen, opened the small freezer door
and took out a frozen burrito. Opening one end of the wrap-
ping, she placed the burrito in the microwave and set the timer.
Pushing the Start button, she turned, looked again into the
living room, and thought about unpacking. *You've been here a
month, you know? What would you do if somebody wanted to
come over and visit? Right, big chance of that happening. No,
leave it like it is. Who cares?*

The microwave's beeping broke her from her reverie. Minutes later she was on the couch, the TV tray on her lap holding
a paper plate and what was left of the burrito. Setting the tray
on the coffee table, she picked up the photo album, and put it
on her lap and began turning the pages. She stopped when she
found the picture she was looking for. A smile slowly came to
her. "Hi, Dad. I called Mom again today. She's hangin' in
there, Daddy. She really likes her job at the courthouse and
seems to be really enjoying life . . . Me? Come on, Daddy, it's
Button. Remember, I'm your tough little gal who never lets
anything bother her. I'm doin' real good. I . . . I miss you is all.
I just needed to see you again."

Ashley felt the tears coming and closed her eyes. "Why,
Daddy? Why did you go into that damn alley? Mom and I
needed you so much."

She opened her eyes, looked again at the smiling man and
nodded. "I know Daddy, it was your duty . . . you had to go in.
Yes, I remember what you told me when we heard that Josh
had died. You said Josh had died doing his duty for his

country. I thought it didn't matter, Dad. I'm sorry. I thought Josh had died alone without anyone caring but us. . . . I was wrong, Dad. I saw yesterday that soldiers do care for one another very much. . . . I know now, Dad. I wanted you to know I know."

Running her fingers over the picture one more time, Ashley slowly closed the album and took in a deep breath. Exhaling, she set the album aside and stood. "I think it's time I got this place in order," she said aloud. "It depresses me like this. Okay, first the boxes, then I'm putting up the curtains. I think it's time I gave up living like a bag lady. I'm a Sutton, damnit. We don't give up; we have a duty to go on. Time to get to work."

Two miles away, Cynthia leaned over in the plush leather seats of Jerome's Lincoln and patted Eli's hand. "Thank you for takin' me home, Eli. Would you like to come in for some coffee? It'll only take a minute."

Eli smiled and turned off the ignition, thinking it might be nice. He was starting over and this was one way to do it, have coffee and whatever else Cynthia wanted to share with him. She was a nice lady, a little too touchy-feely, but sweet, he thought as he got out of the car. I can do this, he told himself, taking her arm. Just let nature take its course. She'll keep the lights low and turn on soft music for starters, then walk into the kitchen and come back with wine, not coffee. Step three will be we'll talk awhile, and then step four comes and we'll start making out and things will heat up. Then comes step five, when I suggest we should get more comfortable, and that will be it; no more doubts what will happen after that. Yep, I can handle this. No sweat.

Cynthia unlocked the front door and quickly walked across the foyer and turned off the alarm. "Sorry, the house is just a mess. Just follow me back to the great room."

The house was a small mansion. In the foyer, a Tang horseman was looking unconcernedly across a Bukhara rug at two celadon vases. Eli followed her back to the great room, where she picked up a remote control and pointed it at a burl wood cabinet. Immediately Frank Sinatra's voice filled the room in surround sound.

Eli cringed. He knew there would be music, but Old Blue Eyes? Cynthia swayed her hips as she approached him. "Don't you just love him?"

Eli wanted to ask if she had any Garth Brooks or Clint Black tunes, or even that white guy that sounded black—Michael Bolder or Boston or something like that—but instead he smiled and said, "Yes, he's great."

Cynthia pressed her body against him. "I knew you would," she whispered and kissed his chin. She backed up slowly, giving him that look, and purred. "I'm going to change into something more comfortable. There's a bottle of wine just behind you. Why don't you pour us a glass . . . I'll be right back."

Eli was stunned. Where were steps two, three, and four? Shit, she was already at five and that was *his* step! He grabbed for the cell phone inside his jacket and punched the keys as fast as he could. He brought the phone to his ear and waited. Finally Jerome answered sleepily.

Eli whispered, "Call me in five minutes . . . I know it's late and you were asleep, damnit, call my cell phone number. It's on the refrigerator door under the Big Bird magnet . . . Yeah, I want you to get out of bed and walk *all the way* into the kitchen! Listen to me, you got me into this—well, Millie did—and you're gettin' me out. Shit, Jer, I've been in the house just a minute and she's already into the slippin' into the somethin' more comfortable stage . . . Look, just call me, five minutes damn you, 'bye."

Putting away the phone Eli hurried to the counter and picked up the corkscrew. Jesus, she'd had this planned for days, he thought. What's she going to come out in, her birthday suit?

To the tune of "Moon River," he opened the bottle and poured two crystal wineglasses half full. His wait and won-

dering were over. Cynthia appeared in a filmy see-through robe
that barely covered her thighs. He wasn't quite sure what it was
she wore under the robe, but it didn't have much material and
left absolutely nothing to his imagination. Cynthia obviously
went to a tanning booth because there were no tan lines anywhere, and he could almost see all of her where lines would have
showed. For a woman in her late forties, she looked terrific, he
thought.

She swayed back and forth as she came closer and lifted her
arms. "Dance with me."

In that, you want me to dance? He smiled and took her into
his arms. "You look super, Cynthia, you must work out a lot to
keep in such good shape?"

She winked. "Wait till I get you upstairs, honey, then you'll
see a workout."

So much for sweet Cynthia who talked about her flowers
while at the dinner table, he thought. I'm dancing with Lady
Godiva and Madonna all rolled into one.

"Moooon river, wider than a mile. I'm . . ." Cynthia sang,
pressing closer to him.

Eli sneaked a glance at his watch and wished he'd told
Jerome three minutes, not five.

At the end of the song he felt as if she'd become a second
skin. He might have actually enjoyed the belly rubbing, but
her perfume was too strong and made him feel nauseous. As
she stepped back, lifted an eyebrow and said, "Come on, let's
go upstairs," he knew it was not the perfume, or the music. It
was him. He wasn't ready for this, and wondered if he ever
would be.

He still played it right, kissed her lightly on the lips and
backed away slowly. "Let me get the wine for us," he said. He
picked up the two glasses and stepped forward, kissing her
again, and said, "You're wonderful."

They got all the way to the bedroom when his cell phone
beeped and he set the glasses on the nightstand. Taking his
phone out, he whispered to her, "It's probably nothing, but I

have to take it." He put the phone to his ear and said, "Special Agent Tanner . . . When? . . . How many were hurt? . . . I see, sure I'll be there in twenty minutes, get me a crime scene unit and contact the GBI. Right, out here."

He looked into Cynthia's disappointed but understanding eyes. "I'm truly sorry about this, but I have to go." He pulled her to him and kissed her passionately, liking the way she kissed, but finally backed away. "I'll call you tomorrow and tell you how things went," he said, then reached up and touched her face. Slowly, he let his hand drop and walked for the hallway.

He felt tremors of guilt quaking in his stomach, and the first eruption when he heard her say, "Be careful, Eli, I won't be able to sleep until you call."

He picked up his pace and held his breath until he shut the door and was outside. The sticky night air smelled of lilacs as he breathed in deeply and headed for the Lincoln. She deserved a helluva lot better than him, he thought as he slid in behind the wheel.

Fifteen minutes later he pulled into a roadhouse he'd spotted as he was driving her home. It was just what he needed.

The smell of smoke hit him first, then the loud twang of guitars. He walked on past the crowded tables and bellied up to the bar. A cute barmaid smiled. "What ya havin'?"

"Bud Light with a twist of lime, please, ma'am."

Eli turned, looked at all the people and didn't feel so lonely. He knew after a few beers the guilt would be gone, and tomorrow he'd call Cynthia and apologize. But he'd never go back to her place. His gut told him it wasn't right, and his gut never lied. Cynthia deserved someone who liked to dance to Old Blue Eyes.

CHAPTER 7

Wednesday, June 6

Ashley walked into the office and saw Eli seated behind Regina's desk, typing on her computer keypad.

She walked past him, put her purse on her desk and turned around, facing him. He kept on typing. She cleared her throat. He kept on typing. She sighed. "Good morning, Agent Tanner."

He nodded but kept typing as he spoke: "Good morning."

"What are you working on?" she asked.

"I'm doing the tutorial on Word Seven. It's not that different from WordPerfect, the one I used in Quantico. Actually, it's better—easier."

Ashley stepped closer. "Thank you. I ordered it for the office and just picked it up last week. So, how did dinner go? Was the lady nice?"

Eli stopped typing, pushed the chair back, picked up his coffee and walked to the worktable. "Dinner was fine. She was okay." He sat down and picked up a case file.

Ashley followed. "How did you two get along?"

"Fine."

Ashley nodded, seeing she was getting nowhere, and walked back to her desk. Regina entered from the back room holding a stack of printouts. "Boss, you was right as rain. The Puerto Rican is the dirty one. This sure 'nough proves it."

Eli lifted his eyes from the file and looked at her. "What do you think of Frank Sinatra, Regina?"

She shrugged. "I think he's old. Why?"

Eli looked back at the file. "Yeah, that's what I think, too. I like that white guy that sounds black, long hair, real popular, what's his name?"

"Michael Bolton?"

"That's him. He's still popular, isn't he?"

"To white folks he is. My sister don't like the man. Says he don't have soul, but I think the man is cool. Why you askin' about Frank, boss? You takin' up ballroom dancin' or somethin'?"

Eli shrugged. "A lady I met last night liked him a lot. I thought maybe his stuff was on the comeback and I was out of touch. I was just checkin'."

Regina grinned and stepped closer to him. "Well now, you meetin' ladies already? That's cool. How'd it go? You two click and dance to Frank?"

"Naw, I had to go . . . I was pooped."

"Didn't click, huh? That's all right, boss, hang in there. That right lady goin' to come along and ring your chimes for sure. You'll know when ya wanna dance and there ain't no music."

Ashley couldn't take it anymore and walked over to the table. "What was all that about a Puerto Rican being dirty?"

Regina motioned to the printouts she'd set out. "The boss had me get the bank records of the four sergeants involved in the loss of the M-16s on post. He was right. The dirty one showed up."

Ashley shifted her gaze to Eli. He picked up the case file beside him. "This is the one you told me about the night before last. The five missing weapons and four sergeants who were the only suspects?"

"Yes, I was scheduled to interview them this afternoon," Ashley said.

Eli handed her the printouts. "Sergeant José Gonzales is

your man. Look at his bank statements for the past four months and then look at the current one."

It took her several minutes to examine the records before she gave Eli a questioning stare. "So?"

"So, he hasn't made any withdrawals this month and hasn't written any checks. José and his wife are obviously paying for everything in cash. José is not too smart . . . he'll roll if we get the D.A. to agree to a reduction provided he names who he sold the weapons to. Ten years versus five in Leavenworth will sound good to him."

Ashley shrugged. "I had him anyway," she said and walked back to her desk.

Eli stood. "What'd'ya mean, ya had him?"

Ashley reached in a drawer and pulled out a notebook. She opened it and motioned to a page. "José's wife left for Puerto Rico two days after the weapons were reported missing. She paid cash for a first-class ticket, which was big bucks. I had him without the bank records, but thank you for getting them for me."

Eli's jaw muscles rippled. "When we discussed the case, you didn't tell me you checked out the wife, Agent Sutton."

"And you didn't tell me you were going to begin working the case, or I would have told you not to bother, Agent Tanner."

Eli counted mentally to three, drew in a deep breath and exhaled it slowly. He nodded. "You're right, my mistake. I should have asked you about the case before jumping in. I'll remember next time."

Ashley sat down and put away her notebook, not sure what to do; her victory was ruined by his admitting his mistake. She glanced at him, but he'd already picked up another case file. *Damn, now I'll have to show him I can accept victory graciously . . . except I've never done it before. Damn.* "Eh . . . Agent Tanner."

He looked at her, and she frowned. "My fault, too. I should

have given you all the information when we discussed the case. Okay?"

Eli smiled. "Okay."

Regina glanced at Ashley then Eli and shook her head. "Well, how 'bout me? Is anybody goin' to say, hey Regina, thanks for nothin'?"

Eli reached up and patted her arm. "Thanks for runnin' the printouts. I couldn't have made a fool of myself without ya."

Regina leaned over and whispered, "We'll get her next time, boss."

Millie Tanner walked into the empty living room and saw Ashley standing just outside the sliding glass doors on the balcony, staring out at the Chattahoochee River. She joined her, leaning on the balcony railing. "What'd'ya think?"

Ashley turned and looked back inside. "He'll like it because of this view."

Millie smiled. "That's what I think, too. Thanks for coming over during your lunch hour and taking a look. The rent isn't too bad for a two bedroom, and the kitchen is functional, though small, and the blue rugs aren't *too* ugly. Now I won't have to worry about him living in a damn trailer. Seven Brothers says his things should be here in another week. I don't even want to think about what he's got coming to furnish these rooms with. By the looks of that old pickup of his, I can imagine, though—Salvation Army rejects, I bet."

Ashley looked back at the tranquil river. "I bet it will surprise you. I'd think he'd want things that meant something to him. Won't be fancy, but they'll all have purpose and meaning."

Millie gave Ashley a side glance. "Don't get me wrong when I say this, but are you getting along all right with him? He's mellowed some with age, but his temper can get the best of him sometimes . . . that, and he usually says what's on his mind. It kinda puts women off when they get to know him."

Shrugging, Ashley took a step back from the railing. "We're

doing okay. I'm not the easiest person to get along with myself, but he seems to know when to stop pushing. He's . . . he's more sensitive than I would have thought. Kind of rare for guys in the boo. He's got a good sense of humor too . . . although most of the time it's at my expense. We're going to do fine for the next eighty-seven days . . . I think."

"That's right, you're leaving for Atlanta. I'd forgotten. You're going to miss out on me finding Miss Right for him. 'Course, the way the search is going, it might take ten years to find her. Do you know what he did the other night? Don't breathe a word of this, but that lug called Jerome from Cynthia's house and told Jerome to call him back on his cell phone in five minutes. After all my work, and he wants Jer to give him an excuse to leave. I don't know if I can face Cynthia again. She'll ask about him, and what do I say? See what he's done to me? He's getting me into trouble with my friends, and all I'm trying to do is help him."

"Maybe what you want for him isn't what he wants," Ashley said. "He's a big boy. I'm sure he can find places to meet a friend."

"I'll tell you, Ashley, I'm out of it, I don't know where singles go to meet people. You find any interesting places since you've been here?"

"I don't go out, Millie. I did a while back, but it was the same old thing—the lines got old very fast, and when I did find somebody interesting, sooner or later they turned out to be jerks. It burned me out and I gave up."

Millie gave her new friend a look of concern. "Come on, that's just temporary, right? I mean how can you stand being alone all the time?"

"You get used to it. . . . It's not as bad as most people think, you just don't think or worry about it and just accept that's the way it's going to be."

"No way, not you, Ashley. If you were overweight or homely then I might feel sorry for you, but I'm not buyin' you can't find a little happiness; you look great. You've got all the tools; looks to me like you just need to put them to work."

Ashley smiled and patted Millie's shoulder. "You and my dad would have gotten along great. He was like you—thought hard work could get you anything. He was right about most of it, but when it comes to relationships, I always seem to strike out. I got hit by the ball from my ex . . . he hurt me and I guess it's made me shy of the plate. I stay too far back in the box to do any good."

Millie smiled. "Then find yourself a slow pitcher. Whatever he throws can't hurt you, and you still make it to first base. My brother always told me ya can't score unless you're on base. And it sounds to me like you need to do some scoring. Come on, I'll buy you lunch. Together we're going to get you back in the game. I know a few bachelors your age that . . ."

Ashley followed Millie toward the door, glad to have found a friend. Millie's intentions were good, and that was enough. It was nice to talk to another woman about things other than work. She would probably allow Millie to set her up on a couple of dates, but Ashley knew it wouldn't help; the game didn't mean anything to her anymore.

12:03 A.M. Fort Smith, Arkansas

Amos Blevins looked up at the cloudless night and took in a deep breath of the fresh air. He felt something brush up against his leg and looked down with a frown. "Go on, damn ya, you wanted out to piss, didn't ya? Do it on old man Jenkins's lawn. He needs it fertilized anyway. Go on, I'm not goin' anywhere." Amos smiled as his terrier ran toward Jenkins's lawn. "Good boy."

"Sergeant Blevins."

"Christ!" Amos blurted, spinning around. "You scared the B-Jesus outta me. Who the hell are you?"

A man approached wearing black. "Do you not remember me, Sergeant?"

"That's close enough, buster. Don't come any closer or I'll floor ya."

"Look at me, Sergeant. Do you remember?"

"Goddamn you, I said stay where you are. It's too damn dark to see who you are. Get the fuck off my property right now or I'm callin' the cops."

The dark figure lifted his hand and Amos heard a strange buzzing noise at the same instant an excruciating pain lanced his chest. Immediately, it spread through his body. He tried to scream, but his throat muscles had contracted and he couldn't breathe. He sank to his knees as the man stepped up to the porch and leaned over him.

"How's his wife doing?" the detective asked.

The paramedic stepped off the porch holding a black case. "She's still in shock. Says there's no way he would shoot himself, though. Says he didn't even own a pistol."

The detective turned and panned his flashlight across the body on the driveway. "No sign of foul play. He must have kept his problems to himself."

"Pretty big problems, to put a pistol to his head and rearrange his brains, Detective," the medic said.

"Yeah, a helluva way to check out. Get away, dog! Damn it, Doug, I thought I told ya to catch that mutt and put him inside. Christ, damn dog keeps lickin' his face."

Another detective materialized out of the darkness. "Checked the house and didn't find a note. I asked the wife about the cross we found in his mouth. She said he wasn't a religious man and didn't wear one."

"Well, he's got one now. What do you think? This guy kill himself or not?"

"Nothing here to say different. No signs of a struggle, and the weapon *is* in his hand. The lab boys will tell us for sure once they run tests on his hand for residue. If he fired the weapon, then it looks to me like the case is closed."

"No note, a .22 from nowhere, and the cross . . . none of that bothers you?"

"Yeah, it bothers me, so does him doing it with his old lady in bed forty feet away. I can't get in the guy's head and tell ya why he decided to up and off himself. What ya want me to say?"

"Something brilliant, maybe? Shit, I don't like it. I'm callin' in the crime scene boys."

"Captain ain't goin' to let ya. It's almost one-thirty in the fuckin' mornin', and you goin' to wake him up and request he send out the C.S.? Good luck, Joe. You know what it costs in overtime to bring out C.S.? I don't know, either—but you can bet your ass the captain knows. And what are you going to tell him? The wife says he didn't own a pistol, but he shot himself with one. He didn't write a note, at least one we could find tonight. . . . Oh, and he had a cross in his mouth hangin' from a gold chain that the wife said he didn't own. Like we all don't hide shit from our wives?"

"Come on, Charley, this stinks and you know it."

"No, I don't know it. I do know there are no signs of a struggle, and the dead man has the pistol in his hand. I know that once he's bagged, tagged, and in the morgue, tomorrow the lab boys can check his right hand and they'll probably find residue, proving he pulled the trigger on himself. That's what I know. You asked, so I told ya."

The detective turned to the coroner, leaning on his station wagon at the curb. "Bag him, Bill. The lab boys will come over tomorrow and run a residue test. For now we're writing it up as a suicide."

CHAPTER 8

10:40 A.M. Saturday, Green Island
Country Club

Millie Tanner sat in a lawn chair overlooking court four, watching the doubles rematch between the Tanners and the opponents they played in the tournament. She reached down for her can of Pepsi and heard someone walk up behind her. She turned and had to raise her hand to block the sun to see who it was. She was surprised to see it was Ashley, and even more surprised by her outfit. Glistening with sweat, Ashley stood in nylon running shorts, tank top, and a pair of well-worn Nike shoes.

Millie smiled. "You're tryin' to make me feel guilty just sittin' here, aren't you?"

Ashley patted Millie's shoulder as she stepped up beside her. "I was just running by and saw them playing. . . . What's the score?"

Millie sighed and leaned back in her chair. "The Tanner boys are havin' fun but gettin' beat. It's a good match, but my poor hubby is havin' a bad day. Sit down and let me tell you the latest."

Ashley smiled. "The quest for a mate, right?"

Millie waved her down. "Last night I had my friend Paula over. She helped me cook some wonderful penne meal. I thought things were going great between her and Eli, but then she asks him what kind of wine he would like to have with his pasta. The idiot said he wanted a beer. She should have got him a beer, but no, Paula is a connoisseur of wine, you see, visited Napa Valley and all that. She starts in on how wonderful wine is and gives us all a ten minute lecture on aging, texture, taste, all that. She then asks him what kind of wine he wants again. He says he wants a beer again. Needless to say, it kinda went downhill from there. I had to drive her home."

Ashley laughed and patted Millie's arm. "Hang in there. Any of your friends a barmaid?"

"It's not funny, Ashley, I'm runnin' out of prospects fast. Plus I'm worried the word will get out about how set he is in his ways, then I *will* be lookin' for a barmaid. What are you doin' this afternoon?"

Ashley shrugged. "Thought I'd start organizing my things for the move . . . make lists, that sort of thing."

"You can do that tomorrow. I need a big favor. Come with me this afternoon to keep me company. Eli has invited Jer and me to go fishin' with him and his Army buddy, Dan Murphy. This Murphy person supposedly has a new fancy boat he wants Eli to see and try out. I don't want to be the only gal out on a darn boat on the Chattahoochee worryin' about snakes. Don't say no, 'cause you already told me you weren't doing anything important. I need you or I'll go crazy out there telling them how much *fun* I'm having."

Ashley laughed again. "Come on, it can't be that bad?"

"Good, I knew I could count on you."

"Millie, I didn't say I'd—"

"Bring some sunscreen along. I've got bug repellent. What kind of wine coolers you like?"

Ashley knew when she was fighting a losing battle. "Peach will be fine."

"Have you tried piña colada? They are *wonderful*. I'll bring some for you along with peach so you can . . ."

Dan Murphy grinned as he switched off the motor and let the sleek new bass boat glide into the inlet. "Jerome, is this class or what? Custom metallic silver flake paint, nonfading carpeted deck, four detachable, elevated, deep-cushioned, swiveling captain's chairs, two built-in coolers, fish hold, fish finder, trolling motor, AM, FM, stereo CD, CB, the works. This baby is the Cadillac of bass boats."

Jerome Tanner smiled as he ran his hand over the Naugahyde fake leather seats. "It's a beauty, Dan. I really like these elevated seats ... they even rock. What size motor does it have?"

Millie leaned over to Ashley and whispered, "Isn't this the tackiest thing you ever saw? If it had a wall, they would have hung one of those black-velvet paintings of Elvis. The fire-engine red carpeting is making me nauseous."

Ashley nodded. "This is definitely a bubba boat. Uh-oh, they're getting the fishing poles out ... they're going to make us actually fish."

Murphy walked across the carpeted deck and handed Millie and Ashley each a rod with reel. "Ladies, you all sit there in those two front elevated captain's chairs and toss your lines out over toward those submerged bushes. Bass hangin' out there this time a'day. Tan man, I got purple worms there in the tackle box. Will you rig up the ladies for me?"

Seated on a flotation cushion in the exact center of the boat, Eli forced a smile. "Sure thing, Murph, no sweat."

Murphy strode back to the rear of the boat and tossed Jerome a rod. "That's the newest model, Jerome, super light, with the best reel Zebco makes. Here, try one of these fluorescent spinners ... they're the hottest thing goin', fish just go crazy after 'em."

Minutes later everybody had lines out and Dan lifted his beer can as if in a toast. "Fishin' ain't fishin' without a little competition. Men against the ladies on who catches the most and biggest fish. Since we got three of us, we'll spot you ladies three fish. Fishermen rules, losers clean the catch."

Murphy glanced at Eli, still seated on his cushion in the

middle of the boat. "Hey, Tan man, move on out on the deck so you can see your line better."

Eli shook his head. "I'm fine, Murph, really. I think I felt a nibble already."

Jerome swiveled in his seat and shook his head. "Dan, Elly's scared to death of the water."

"No way, not the Tan man," Murphy said, tossing his line out again.

Millie set down her wine cooler and cast again. "It's true, Dan. Eli almost drowned just up the river a ways when he and Jerome were boys."

Eli kept his eyes on the tip of his pole. "I'm not *scared to death* ... I'm just not real comfortable around muddy water, you guys. I'm fine, everybody just fish and drop the subject. I'm fine ... really."

Ashley gave Eli a side glance. His neck muscles were taut as steel cable. Millie leaned over and whispered.

"He'll be okay after another beer or two. I'll keep my eye on—" She suddenly swung around and jerked her pole to the right, squealing, "I got one! I got one! I got one!"

Jerome stood and barked, "Keep your rod up! Give him some line!"

Dan grabbed for a fish net. "Keep him away from them branches!"

Ashley's rod suddenly jerked in her left hand. Dropping the peach cooler in her other hand, she grabbed the reel. "Oh! *Oh oh!* I ... I ... have something! Oh!"

The two women sat on the marina dock sipping wine coolers and watching the three men clean the catch along the shore.

Dan Murphy tossed the fish he'd just cleaned into the cooler and shook his head. "Tan man, this ain't good for my reputation."

Jerome tossed another fish into the cooler and stood. "That's all of them, Dan, let's face it. The fish liked the purple worms more than those spinners we were usin'."

Eli cleaned his hands in the water and stepped back from the shore. "I think the fish were attracted by their squealin' and hollerin' and dancin'. They were all male fish."

"Yeah," Murphy said. "Maybe I get me a tape made of them doing all that squealin' and play it on underwater speakers. . . . I think you're on to somethin', Tan."

Millie stood and put her hands on her hips. "You guys can knock off feelin' sorry for yourselves. Ashley and I will cook up a mess at the house soon as you all quit cryin' in your beer."

Murphy sighed and walked toward his boat. "Thanks for the offer, Millie, but I got to go home and get some rest. I got graveyard in the ops center tonight. Anyway, fish don't go down right when they been caught by the fairer sex." He turned with a smile and pointed his finger at her. "And don't be spreadin' it around ya'll beat us . . . See ya'll. Next time, fellers."

Eli and Jerome waved. "See ya, Dan."

Minutes later the cooler of fish was loaded in Eli's pickup and Jerome motioned to his Lincoln. "Come on, ladies, we'll head to the house and start the fire. Elly will take forever, the way he drives."

Ashley stepped up beside Eli. "You two go on, I'll ride with agent Bubba here to give him some company. Besides, I haven't been in anything so low-class as a pickup in years."

Eli handed her the keys. "You drive, agent Bubetta."

Minutes later they were on the road. Once he saw that she could handle the stick shift, Eli leaned back in his seat and smiled. "You had fun today, didn't you?"

"Yes, I did, Agent Tanner. I had more fun than you did, that's for sure, and I'm not just talking about beating you guys. The water thing really bothers you, doesn't it?"

"I thought I handled it okay. It's just been a while since I've been on the river, is all. I don't have any problems in pools . . . it's just muddy water that gets to me."

"What happened? How did you almost drown?"

Eli looked out the window and shook his head with a distant

stare. "I was fifteen and Jerome was home from college. . . . We went to the river with some old friends to gig snakes along the bank. We were in this old boat and—"

"Gig snakes? What does that mean?"

"You know, like giggin' frogs. You have this gig, a pronged-fork-lookin' thing on the end of a long stick. We'd paddle along close to the bank lookin' for snakes all curled up, sunnin' themselves. Then we paddle in nice and slow and stick them with our gigs. They put up a heck of a fight. I know it sounds cruel, but it was the way we made a few dollars. We sold the snakeskins to a leather shop in town and they'd make things out of them. Anyway, we were giggin' snakes, and I gigged this big monster. I'm not kiddin', its body was as thick as my arm and must have been six or seven feet long. It was everything I could do to hold on. When he finally quit fighting, I lifted the pole so Jerome could whack it on the head and kill it for sure when it suddenly starts squirmin' and twisting again. The pole snapped in two and that snake was in the boat with us. I was out of the boat in a heartbeat, did a back flip and started swimmin' as fast as I could. . . . Trouble was, I was swimmin' away from shore. I didn't even think about it until I got tired— and I got tired fast because I was scared and beating the hell out of the water.

"Then it happened. I got a cramp in my side and I couldn't kick. It felt like somebody poured molten lead down my throat and it settled low in my intestines. I tried to yell but swallowed water, and I remember thinkin' this was it. I was going to drown and Jerome was going to catch hell for it from Mama. I went under and there was nothing I could do. Then something hit me soft like on the side of the head. My hand came up and touched it and that's all I remember about it. Jerome didn't even know I was in trouble because he and the others were beating on the snake. When he finally did look for me, he said I was holding onto a log. It was a submerged branch of that log that hit me, I guess. Anyway, Jerome got to me, and between him and the other guys, they figured out how to do CPR enough to get me breathing again. I didn't *almost* drown, I did drown, but they brought me back . . . them and that old log that just happened to be floating south."

Ashley relaxed her tight grip on the steering wheel and let out a breath. "My God, Tanner, I've got goose bumps running up my arms just thinking about it."

Eli nodded. "Yeah, the thought of that snake in the boat does it to me, too."

"No, not the snake. The thought of you going under, ooooh, I'm getting them again. My God . . . do you know how you managed to surface and hold onto the log?"

"Nope . . . I guess it just wasn't supposed to be my time. My mom said that, and I've always believed it. I've had a few other close calls in my life, Agent Sutton, where I thought I was going under and staying for good, but each time I woke up still hangin' in there. I'm getting more careful in my old age. . . . I figure you only go under so many times in your life before you stay down, and I've maxed the limit."

She took her eyes off the road and looked at him. "Why in the world did you get on that boat today?"

"Because I have to face it and try to beat it . . . You helped me today. Watching you have such a good time took my mind off it. Thanks."

Ashley smiled and was about to respond when he raised his hand. "But, Agent Sutton, I really think you and Millie went a little overboard with the putdowns and sarcastic comments about us guys' fishing abilities. We could have used purple worms, too, you know, and then it would have been no contest."

Ashley shook her head. "Just when I thought there was hope for you, you go and blow it. Face it, Tanner, you just can't take it that we women won. Would you mind telling me why something like that bothers you men so much?"

"Yeah, I can, Agent Sutton. When you go to the river to fish, you're entering our world. It's our turf, our territory, our sacred ground. We're talking tradition here, Agent Sutton, tradition that says we males are the hunters and fishermen. It's about male pride, male honor, male—"

"Egos?" Ashley interjected.

"Yeah, that too, male egos. Just remember that next time, huh?"

"Are you finished, Tanner?"

"Yeah, I think I've pretty well answered your silly question."

She looked at him and smiled before turning back to the road. "Good try, Tanner. I know you like arguing with me, but not this time. I'm savoring my victory with sweet silence."

"I win, then, Sutton. You're conceding to me."

"Does your gut say I would concede anything to you?"

"Damn you . . . I should have never told about that."

Ashley looked at him for a second and smiled to herself. This was the happiest she'd been in years. Millie had been right, the game wasn't over for her after all. Eli Tanner was showing her the game could be fun again.

Jerome and Eli were standing by the grill, watching the fish fillets cooking. Jerome dipped a brush in melted butter and began painting a fillet. He glanced over his shoulder to make sure the women were out of earshot before he elbowed Eli. "That little gal turned out to be a winner after all. I like her."

Eli shrugged. "Yeah, she's all right. She's different when she's in the office, but today showed me there's hope for her."

Jerome cocked an eyebrow. "Aren't you even a little bit interested in her?"

"She's an agent, Jer."

"She wears a dress, Elly, that make's her a woman—or have you forgotten?"

"Give me a break. I like her, but it's strictly a professional *like*. She leaves in eighty-some days, remember?"

"She'll be ninety miles away, brother. I think maybe you should think about it."

Eli shook his head. "And I thought Millie was bad. Jesus,

Jer, listen to yourself. You're sounding like Ann Landers—worse, like Millie Tanner. Next you're goin' to tell me she's got a great personality."

"Well, she does!" Jerome blurted.

Millie walked up with a plate. "She does what?"

Eli turned very red and stammered, "Uh . . . we were talkin' about, uh . . . my secretary, Regina. She does great work."

Millie set the plate on the table by the grill and shook her head. "You can't lie to me, Eli. You're my hubby's brother, and that's the one thing you two have in common. So, who were you two talking about?"

Jerome glanced over his shoulder to see if Ashley was close by, and saw her seated by the pool. He looked at Millie with a guilty expression. "Aw hell, hon, I was just tellin' Eli he should take a little more interest in Ashley. I think she's a—"

Millie grinned and patted her husband's shoulder. "I love ya, big guy, but leave the matchmakin' to me. Now you two take those fish off the grill before they burn, then come on. I've got everything else ready." She turned and took a step, but halted and looked over her shoulder at Eli. "I hate to say this, but your older brother might actually be right." She began walking and shook her head, mumbling aloud, "I can't believe I just said that."

Ashley turned in to her apartment building's parking lot and eased the pickup alongside the curb. Looking at her passenger, she wrinkled her brow. "I'm supposed to say thanks for driving me home, but since I drove, I guess I'll just say see ya Monday morning."

Eli nodded. "Yep, see ya Monday mornin'. I'm glad you came today; you made it fun."

Ashley opened the door and got out, and Eli scooted over behind the wheel. She began to walk to the sidewalk but stopped herself and faced him. "You're lucky, Tanner, having a friend like Dan, and family like Millie and Jerome is really special."

Eli shifted to first gear and smiled. "I know . . . and guess what? They're your friends, too. We're both lucky." He eased off on the clutch and steered toward the road. Stopping at the lot exit, he glanced in the rearview mirror, but she was gone.

5:04 A.M. Sunday

Eli was stone dead to the world when he was shaken awake. He opened one eye. Holding a portable phone out toward him, Jerome was standing by the bed in his underwear.

"Wake up, damn ya," Jerome said. "Dan is on the line wantin' to talk to you. He sounds upset. If he's drunk, remind him it's five in the damn mornin', will ya?"

Eli took the phone and brought it to his ear. "Dan, it's Tan. What's up?"

"Christ, Tan man, I'm glad I got ya. Somethin' terrible has happened, man. My buddy, Jerry Rhodes, the post sergeant major, is dead. I'm on duty up here in the ops center and got the call five minutes ago. Shit, all hell is breakin' lose. The MPs say it's suicide, but that's horseshit. Jerry would never kill himself. Christ's sakes, I know him. Tan, he'd been just selected for sergeant major of the Army. We were close and he told me. The Secretary of the Army's office notified him a week ago but told him to say nothing until the press release is officially distributed next week. He wouldn't kill himself, Tan. No way."

Eli spoke calmly. "Take it easy, Murph. Where's the body?"

"Redcloud range. A jogger found him when he was runnin' this mornin'. It was that bitch he was snakin' who killed him, Tan. I'd bet my retirement. She shot him and made it look like it was suicide. It's the only explanation."

"Whoa, Murph. Are you saying you think he was murdered?"

"Tan, I'm tellin' ya he wouldn't kill himself like the MPs are sayin'. He had this E-7's wife he was sneakin' around with. Christ, I told him not to mess with her but it was like talkin' to the fuckin' wall. She's from El Salvador or Panama—someplace down south. He even had the husband assigned to FASO in Fort Leavenworth so he could play footsy with her on the sly. She's missin', Tan. She's not in her quarters and the neighbors ain't seen her since last night—and they got her kid! It's all horseshit, Tan, and these damn MPs ain't listenin' to me. Wait one. . . Word now is the MPs are changin' their minds. They think it was an accident. That's horseshit, too. The bitch killed him."

"Murph, I'm on the way. Where's Redcloud range?"

"Just as you enter the main post, across from the officer's golf course. Tan, I called Agent Sutton first; I didn't have a number for you. She gave me Jerome's number. Tell him I'm sorry I got him up, huh?"

"No sweat. I'll tell him, Murph."

"Hurry, Tan. I don't trust the damn MPs worth a shit."

"I'll be there in fifteen minutes, buddy. I'll talk to you later."

Eli tossed the phone to Jerome and swung out of bed.

"Got a homicide on post?" Jerome asked.

"Dan thinks so." Eli put on his pants. "The vic is the post sergeant major. MPs seem to be vacillating between suicide and accident."

"Rhodes? If it was, I can tell ya they'd *want* it to be an accident and keep a lid on it. Suicide doesn't look good for the Army's image."

"Dan says there might be a woman involved, a married woman."

"Then you'd better watch yourself. If it's messy, they damn sure don't want it aired. The brass will want this cleaned up quickly and with as little exposure as possible. I think the sergeant major was married. We attended a fund-raiser and he was there with what I thought was his wife. If he did have a wife, the commanding general will put the pressure on to keep the whole thing quiet."

Eli slipped into his shoes and picked up his shoulder holster from the nightstand. "Thanks, Jer. Sorry about the call waking you up. I should have thought of having new cards made with my cell phone number when I started work. I'll move out during the weekend so you and Millie can get back to your normal lives."

"Aw hell, don't do that, Elly. With you here, Mill is cookin' real meals for a change."

Eli patted his brother's slightly protruding stomach. "Like I said, I'd better move out pretty soon."

"Go get 'em, Br'er Rabbit," Jerome called as Eli headed for the door.

CHAPTER 9

The sun was just coming up over the pines when Eli pulled his pickup into the Redcloud range's huge gravel parking lot. He was immediately stopped by an MP guard.

"FBI," Eli said, showing his ID.

The guard stepped closer to the pickup. "Sir, all visitors are to report to Major Reeves, the officer in charge of the scene. Please park over there and stay within the taped-off area."

Eli counted five MP sedans and two Army camouflaged Humvee's as he parked beside Ashley's blue dodge van. She was leaning against the front of the vehicle with a scowl on her face.

He got out of his pickup and asked with his eyes.

She frowned. "Major Reeves told me his people didn't need our assistance."

"Have you seen the body?" he asked as he stepped closer.

"I was told very politely to stay out of the way."

Turning around, Eli walked back to his pickup and opened the passenger side door. A minute later he strode back to Ashley armed with a notebook and rubber gloves. He handed her a pair. "Take out your cell phone and hold it. When I tell ya, follow me. Keep one step behind and to my right. We're going to take a look."

Seeing the look in his eyes, she didn't argue, and quickly pulled her small folding phone from her purse. "You know something, don't you?"

He quickly told her what Murphy had told him, then turned

toward the knot of MPs clustered around a small building twenty-five yards away. "Here we go, Agent Sutton. Put on your best boo investigation look and follow me."

"What kind of look is that supposed to be?"

"Look at everybody like they owe you money."

They had covered only half the distance when Major Reeves stepped out of the cluster of officers and raised his hand. "Sir, I'm sorry, I don't recall your name, but like I told Agent Sutton, we've got this under control and don't need federal assistance."

Eli halted and began putting on his latex gloves. "The name is Tanner, Major. And may I remind you that the role of the resident office is to assist and advise your organization. We cannot advise or assist if we don't know what is going on. In the future please call us immediately when there is a shooting that results in a death. Now I have a few questions before we take a look at the sergeant major. Has anyone touched his body?"

The major shook his head. "I just told you, Agent Tanner, that we don't need—"

"Major, I was being polite before, now I'll give it to you straight. We are going to do our job here. Our job is to ensure the investigation is being handled properly. Now I ask you again. Has anyone touched the body?"

"I have to call the colonel and see what he says about this," the major said, elevating his chin.

"That's fine. Agent Sutton will let you borrow her cell phone. Now please answer my question."

"No, no one has touched the sergeant major. The captain who found him was running down the road and veered off into the parking lot to take a leak. He spotted the body and ran back to the road and flagged down the first car that passed."

"And who were the responding officers?"

"Look, Agent Tanner, let me call the colonel and—"

Ashley stepped forward, holding out her folding phone. Eli spoke evenly. "Call him. Agent Sutton and I will be taking a look. Oh, by the way, I understand you have a woman missing on post. Have your people found her, by any chance?"

The major grabbed the phone.

Eli nodded toward Ashley and they strode toward the taped barrier.

Seconds later Eli paused as he looked down at the dead man dressed in camouflage fatigues. The smell and ugliness of death were always the same. The sergeant major, who had occupied one of most respected positions in the Army, now lay on his side in the gravel with a bullet hole in the temple. Something odd caught Eli's eye and he squatted down to get a better look.

Ashley leaned over his shoulder. "Is that a gold chain in his mouth?"

"Part of it is. Can't see what the chain is holding. Coagulated blood has filled the bottom part of his mouth. Strange, huh?" Eli looked to his right, where a balding chief warrant officer with a salt and pepper mustache was standing. Eli remembered meeting him at the CID office. He was the senior investigator for the Criminal Investigation Division. Eli motioned the officer over. "Chief, give me a rundown on what you've got so far."

The middle-age investigator stepped forward and spoke almost in a whisper. "The major told us not to speak to you, sir. I'm sorry."

Eli glanced over his shoulder at Reeves, who was talking on the phone. "You know who's going to win this turf battle, Chief. What ya got?"

The chief sighed and squatted down. "Sergeant major has an M-9 Beretta in his right hand, and you can see the entry wound yourself. The weapon looks to be his personal weapon, the grips aren't issue. We're running a check now. Powder burns are consistent with the barrel being pressed against the skin. I figure he was on his knees when he pulled the trigger and fell forward. You can see the dust there on the right knee of his fatigues. When we roll him over we'll be able to confirm it.

Shell casing is over there with the plastic glass over it. Couple of things I don't like. The chain in his mouth is a mystery, and take a look at his legs—the fatigue pants are unbloused, and neither boot is laced or tied properly. The other thing is the large amount of blood in his mouth and the accumulation that drooled out onto the gravel."

"You're saying you think the angle of trajectory went down, not up?" Eli asked.

"Only explanation for the bullet to pass through the roof of his mouth like it obviously did . . . but that's speculation on my part. Bullets can travel funny sometimes. Need an autopsy to tell for sure, but it looks like that way to me."

Standing erect, Eli looked over to his left. "That the sergeant major's pickup over there?"

The chief nodded. "Yes, I haven't had a chance to take a look as yet. The major's boys checked it, though. Saw them inside the cab when I got here ten minutes ago."

Eli was about to ask another question when he felt a tap on his shoulder. He turned and faced the major, who motioned to an approaching staff car. "The colonel was on the way. He wants to talk to you."

Eli headed straight for the car. The left-rear door opened and out stepped a stocky officer wearing his dress green uniform. The colonel placed a gold-braided billed hat on his head and stepped forward, pointing an unlit cigar toward Eli's chest.

"Are you Agent Tanner?" he barked.

Eli extended his hand. "Yes, sir. I'm sorry we had to meet under these circumstances."

Ignoring the hand, the officer shook the cigar. "What in the hell do you think you're doing, ignoring my officers? This is our investigation and we don't need federal involvement."

"Again, I'm sorry, sir. But you're not quite right on that. I received a tip that this might be a possible homicide. And you are aware of our jurisdiction concerning homicide. It's a federal matter now."

"That's nonsense! It's certainly no homicide. Major Reeves

assures me the post sergeant major's death was suicide or possibly an accident. Where did this so-called tip come from?"

Eli stepped closer, keeping his eyes level with the colonel's hostile stare. "Sir, I've looked at the body, and there are grounds for ruling a suspicious death. I'm calling in the Georgia Bureau of Investigation and the state medical examiner on this. Right now a complete search of the area will need to be conducted. And I would appreciate your and your major's complete cooperation."

"Suspicious death? How the hell you come up with that? Calling in the GBI on this is ludicrous. And you still haven't answered my question about who tipped you."

Eli turned and looked toward the dead man's pickup. "Sir, I don't need to explain my actions to you, and right now I don't have time. I have to check that vehicle. Just pray I don't find what I'm looking for. If I do, we all have a bigger problem than you think. Excuse me."

Eli made a motion for Ashley to follow him, and he strode straight for the distant vehicle as the colonel growled, "What do you mean you don't have to explain your actions? The hell you don't!"

Out of the side of his mouth, Eli whispered, "Keep walkin', Agent Sutton, and don't look back."

His face flushed, Major Reeves quickly caught up and stepped in front of Eli. "The colonel is calling your superior in Atlanta. Just stay right where you are, Agent Tanner, until this is resolved."

Tanner motioned toward the two MPs standing by the pickup. "Is that the team that searched the vehicle?"

"Agent Tanner, I just told you wait until—"

Eli strode toward the two officers. "I'm Agent Tanner, FBI, what did you find in the cab?"

Both young specialists began to speak, but again the major stepped in front of Eli. "They found nothing of relevance to the shooting, Agent Tanner. I'm warning you for the last time that I will—"

Eli suddenly stepped forward and poked the shocked officer in the chest with his finger. "Listen to me very carefully. I am about to lose my patience with you. I am going to pretend I haven't heard you try to interfere with my duties as a federal officer. If you interfere with me one more time, I will charge you with tampering and concealment of evidence. I know what you are trying to do, but concealing evidence from me is not going to make the news any more palatable to the widow or to the citizens of Columbus. Now just back away and tell these two officers of yours to cooperate with me. Do it, now."

His face pale, the major stepped back and nodded toward the two MPs. "Tell him what you found."

The shorter of the two took a step forward. "Sir, we found a purse under the passenger seat. Inside, on top, was a pair of wadded up panty hose."

"ID in the purse?" Tanner asked.

"Yes, sir, billfold, checkbook, credit cards all there plus the usual pocketbook litter a lady would carry. The purse belongs to a dependent, Mrs. Rosa Hargrove, wife of Sergeant First Class Ronald Hargrove."

The other MP motioned toward the camper shell over the back of the truck. "I checked, sir. There's a mattress in back covered with a couple of poncho liners. Found a big earring and one lady's shoe. Sir, it looks like somebody did some huggy bear and kissy-facing in the back. The poncho liner was still wet in the center and the mattress was damp."

"Anything else?"

The first MP spoke again. "Yes, sir, in the cab was the sergeant major's LBE, helmet, and a rucksack. His holster was empty and the ammo pouch was missing one magazine. Nothing else unusual."

Eli pointed toward the range shed. "One of you go over and tell the CID chief warrant to come over here and see me. Did you both wear latex gloves during your search?"

"Yes, sir, and we touched as little as possible."

"Good, go on and get the chief," Eli said. He turned to the major with a cold glare. "You knew about this?"

The officer lowered his head. "The colonel told me to try and keep it quiet. Sergeant Major Rhodes's wife is very close to the commanding general's wife, and he felt it would serve no purpose to—"

Ashley watched Eli step forward and put his hand on the officer's shoulder as if consoling him. She moved closer to listen to him. "I understand what's going on. Honestly, I do. I was a sergeant and trained right here at Benning. But Major, it's time to forget about others' feelings and the Army's image. We've got a missing woman who is very probably involved in what happened to the sergeant major. I suggest you begin a postwide search immediately and put out an APB notifying all local and state authorities. Your colonel is wrong and you know it. Don't make the mistake he is. Do what's right and do it now. Go on."

The major nodded and strode toward the gaggle of waiting MPs.

Ashley raised an eyebrow. "You handled that very well. I'm impressed. So what's your theory? The woman shot him and made it look like a suicide?"

Eli walked to the truck and opened the camper shell back door. He glanced inside before facing Ashley. "You tell me, Agent Sutton. Would a woman leave her purse behind after she shot her lover, a lover, I might add, that she had just made it with?"

"The part about shooting him after making love doesn't bother me. He could have done something to hurt her or said something cruel. But leaving her purse with billfold, checks, and credit cards? No way. And there's something else. How is she going to make him kneel down and make him shoot himself? No, that doesn't make sense."

Eli looked back toward the range shack. "I agree. I think somebody caught them in the act. The boots being unbloused and not tied properly tells me the vic had to dress in a hurry."

"But why make it look like a suicide? And where is the woman?"

"Agent Tanner!" the colonel barked as he approached. He held out the cell phone. "I have your superior on the line and he wants a word with you."

Eli accepted the phone and lifted it to his ear. "Special Agent Tanner."

"Agent Tanner, this is Don Farrel, SAC Atlanta. This is a hell of a way for us to meet, over a damn telephone. What is going on? That colonel seems pretty angry. Give me a rundown."

"Sir, I'm ruling a suspicious death of the post sergeant major and am calling in the GBI. There's more, sir. A woman is missing. She appears to have been having an affair with the victim. It's messy, sir."

"The colonel is worried about image. That right?"

"Yes, sir. He's standing right here."

"I understand. In a sec put him back on the line and I'll explain he only has one option. Mine. Look, I don't know you and we haven't met so this is awkward. I don't know any other way to say it, but are you sure you can handle it? Be honest. I can have a team down there in a couple of hours."

"Sir, Agent Sutton and I will take care of it."

"Sutton? She's a wirehead! She's never worked a homicide. I'll send you a good man to help out, okay?"

"Thank you, sir, but that won't be necessary. We will take care of it. Sir, I'm passing the phone to the colonel now. Goodbye and thank you for your support."

"Well?" the colonel said smugly.

Eli handed him the phone. "The SAC will explain your options." Eli backed away, took Ashley's arm and walked her toward the van. "The colonel is not going to be a happy camper. Better get on that gee wiz computer of yours and notify GBI and the medical examiner. I'll talk to the chief about expanding the barrier and beginning a search of the area. Looks like we're going to be here awhile. That van of yours have a coffee machine by chance?"

She ignored his question, stopped and faced him with a glare. "What was that thing about walking a step behind you and to your right? The Japanese make their woman do that, and I hear the Saudis do it, but I'm telling you right now *I* don't do it."

"It's a battle formation, Agent Sutton. I was taking point and you were covering in the slackman position."

"We weren't going into a fight, Tanner."

"Yes, we were, and we won."

"It's not standard procedure and in no book I've ever read, Tanner."

Eli nodded. "It's in my book, I learned it from experience a long time ago. Oh, just so you know, the SAC sent his regards. Said he has complete confidence in our abilities and all that."

"Yeah, I'll bet. Okay, I'll defer to your experience on the formation thing. But the next time, tell me what's going on." She turned toward the van but stopped and looked over her shoulder. "The woman's probably dead, isn't she?"

Eli silently dipped his chin, then walked toward the range shack.

"It's a cross," said the Georgia Bureau of Investigation crime scene detective. He handed over a plastic bag. "Chain and cross are twenty-four karat gold, with no markings. Chain is eighteen inches when doubled and of unusual design."

Eli held the small bag up for a closer view. "Looks like a Baht chain, Ed."

"A what?"

Eli unbuttoned his shirt and pulled out a gold chain holding a tiny gold-encased Buddha. "See, the chain style is almost identical. They're called Baht chains. At least that's what they were called in 'seventy-two when I was in Nam. A lot of the locals over there wore them to hold their Buddhas—like this one, or other good luck charms. Same kind of clasp . . . but it's not really a clasp. You see how it's shaped kind of like a letter M, but rounded? The post exchange in Nam sold them. A lot of troopers bought them to send home to their girls or wives. Gold was cheap then."

Ed Faraday shrugged. "Makes sense, the Asian's are big into twenty-four karat jewelry. The cross has no special designs, it's your garden variety cross. Looks like ya made a good call on it being a suspicious death. M.E. found marks on the vic's chest; says the vic was hit with a taser or something like one. Took the fight out of him for sure. With one of those attached to you, all you can do is bulge your eyes and piss on yourself. He also says the trajectory of the bullet was definitely downward. Once he conducts the autopsy he'll know more, but he says he thinks the vic had to have held the weapon, muzzle down, at a sixty to seventy degree angle, which would make it hard to pull the trigger. My guess is he had help. When we run the residue test we'll know more, but I'll bet his trigger finger only has traces on the outsides. Somebody else's finger covered his. One more thing, the vic was moved once he'd been hit with the taser. When we turned him over, we saw that the toes of his boots were scuffed almost white. He was drug to the spot. The bad news is this damn gravel makes footprints and tire tracks a nonstarter. The other bad news is your killer is good at covering his or her tracks. Not a sign of a third person being here, and I'll bet the print boys come up with nada."

"And the truck?" Ashley asked.

The short detective faced her. "Very recent semen and vaginal secretions on the blanket along with smudges of makeup. That's experience talking, not lab results. But I'm pretty sure. We also collected hairs from two people from the blankets in the back; one of the people who was in back had very long black hair. It's almost a guarantee two people exchanged bodily fluids in the back of that pickup sometime last night. Found some change in the folds of the blanket near the tailgate. The vic probably sat on the edge of the tailgate to put on his pants. We'll have a lot more information once we get the body and samples processed."

"No blood in the pickup, then?" Eli asked.

"Nope. We've done about all we can for now. Like I said, we'll know more once the lab and autopsy results come back. M.E. gives us a rough time of death of between midnight and two A.M. That's based on the temp of the body and stage of rigor mortis."

Ashley handed the detective a card. "Give us a call if something else comes up. Thank you very much for your help."

The detective nodded and shifted his gaze to Eli. "Agent Tanner, I believe you can rule this out as a crime of passion. The taser, using suicide as a cover, and leaving nothing behind, means your killer had a well-thought-out plan and executed it almost perfectly."

Eli got up from the backseat of the FBI van, stepped down to the ground and extended his hand. "Thanks for coming so quickly, Detective. At least now we know."

Sitting in a newly erected tent beside the van, Major Reeves stood and walked over as the GBI detective departed. "Agent Tanner, I overheard the GBI detective. I'm sorry about this morning. What else can I do to help?"

Eli glanced up at the hot sun. "Since the search of the post hasn't turned up Mrs. Hargrove, I think you should go to Plan B."

"Plan B?"

"Start looking for her body. The killer will have dumped her. As I remember, Fort Benning is pretty much surrounded by water, the Chattahoochee River and the creeks that feed into it. I suggest you have divers check beneath the bridges where the roads lead off post, and I'd begin looking in places where a body could be dumped. Now that we know the cause of death for sure, it's time Agent Sutton and I talked to the sergeant major's wife."

The major grimaced. "Agent Tanner, I'm sorry about this, but the colonel and the commanding general had hoped that would not be necessary. The colonel has already notified Mrs. Rhodes of her husband's death."

Eli sat on the van's doorstep to get out of the sun. "We won't need to mention Mrs. Hargrove, but something like this can't be kept a secret for long. Your colonel is going to have to tell the widow the truth. Keep us posted, call us soon as you find something. We'll be at the widow's house."

Eli turned to Ashley. "Time to saddle up and ride. We're done here."

Ashley didn't move a muscle. "Tanner, I think it's time I told you I've never done anything like this before. I would understand and hold no grudge if you were to ask for help from a more experienced agent. I'm sure the SAC would be only too happy to provide one."

Eli walked around to the passenger door and opened it. "I know it's hot, but I didn't think real ice queens melted. You're not melting on me, are you, Agent Sutton?"

"What's that supposed to mean?"

"Good, I didn't think so; I was just checking. Drive this thing and get the air conditioner going."

Putting away her laptop and shutting the passenger-side sliding door, she finally looked at him. "I was serious, Tanner. I don't want to be a hindrance. I'm out of my field of expertise. I'm not comfortable with not knowing what I'm doing."

Eli motioned to the distant road. "The hardest part is coming up. Once we talk to the widow, it's all downhill. Trust me— you're doing great. Now come on, will ya? Get this thing on the road."

"Looks like a reception committee," Ashley said as she pulled to the curb in front of a huge white two-story stucco house.

Eli glanced out the window. "Yep, looks like the colonel wants to talk again. I don't recognize the others, but I imagine they're here to pay condolences. This is the Army civilians don't see. When you're in a while, the Army becomes family, and family takes care of one another. Don't be surprised to see women inside preparing food, cleaning, and whatever else they can to help. It's kind of a support-group thing, but it's a tradition to help those wives whose husbands have fallen."

"How are we going to handle this?" Ashley asked.

Eli grasped the door handle. "With sensitivity. Just follow my lead and step in anytime."

Both agents got out of the van and walked toward the house side by side.

"Agent Tanner," the colonel said, stepping forward, "Major Reeves informed me of the GBI's findings so far. I hope you understand our concerns in this matter."

"Yes, sir, I do, and Agent Sutton and I will certainly keep those concerns in mind. I understand you've told the widow?"

"Yes, and I just updated her on the death being a murder. I told her you two would be talking to her. She is not yet aware Mrs. Hargrove is . . . a part in this af—matter, but I'll tell her later this afternoon. . . . I thought I'd give her some time before I ripped her heart out. There was a time when all this wouldn't be necessary. Damn liberal press changed that, I can damn well tell you. They've got no feelings, the bastards, no feelings at all."

"Yes, sir. If it's all right we'll go in now," Eli said.

"Yes, of course, come on. I'll make the introductions and herd the other ladies out so you can talk to her privately. Just so you know, she was visiting a sick friend last night. We checked and confirmed it."

"Thank you, sir. That is helpful." Eli allowed Ashley to proceed him up the steps toward the front door.

Ann Rhodes held a fresh Kleenex as she sat on the couch facing the two FBI agents. She shook her head. "No, Agent Tanner, I'm sure Jerry hadn't received any threats; he would have told me. I wish I could help you, but I don't know who would want to—"

"We understand, Mrs. Rhodes," Ashley said. "Could you please give us the names of your husband's closest friends.

We'll talk to them and see if they might know someone he was having problems with."

Ann folded her hands in her lap and looked up at the ceiling. "Oh, God, let me think a moment. Jerry had many friends—but *close* ones? There weren't that many you would call close. Jerry didn't make friends very easily, Agent Sutton. He always said being a sergeant major was the loneliest job in the Army. Let me see. The first would be Sergeant Major Dan Murphy. He liked Dan, a lot. They went fishing together and told each other war stories, I think. Dan works in Building Four. There's First Sergeant David Gregory, but he just left for duty in Germany. . . . Let's see . . . oh, yes, Glenn Hoffman. He retired and lives in Columbus. Glenn and Jerry served together in the Special Forces in Vietnam. They were very close. Glenn works for the post office and lives near the river. I believe I have his address in my address book."

Eli gave Ashley a nod and stood. "Thank you very much for your help, Mrs. Rhodes. You have been most helpful. Again, I'm very sorry for your loss. We'll do our best to find the one who did this, I can assure you."

Ann Rhodes rose and dipped her chin to Ashley, but looked Eli in the eyes. "Did they find the woman Jerry was with?"

Eli held her gaze. "No, ma'am. She's still missing."

"Is she a suspect?" Ann asked.

"No, Mrs. Rhodes, she's not."

Ann broke her stare and nodded. "I'll get Glenn's address for you."

They heard footsteps, and seconds later Ann appeared and handed Eli a piece of paper. "I suppose you're wondering how I knew? Jerry was a very good soldier, Agent Tanner, but he wasn't smart. He would tell me he was going out to inspect training, but the next day I would smell perfume on the fatigues he'd left for me to wash. It was cheap perfume . . . like her, I imagine. I knew . . . I knew, but I also knew it wouldn't last. We were going to Washington, you see. He'd been selected by the Secretary of the Army to be the new sergeant major of the

Army. It was his dream . . . and mine. In Washington things would have been different."

Eli lowered his chin. "Yes, ma'am, I'm sure they would have been. We can see ourselves out. Good-bye."

In the van, Ashley glanced at her passenger as she turned on the ignition. "You men are really pathetic at times, you know?"

Eli nodded in silence.

"Like I told ya, Tan, I don't know a soul who'd want to kill Jerry. There's a bunch who would have liked to bust his nose, but kill him? No way."

Eli stood and extended his hand. "Thanks Murph; I had to ask. And thanks for the tip this morning."

"And yer sure it wasn't the bitch?"

"We're sure. Agent Sutton, do you have anything you want to ask Murph before we go?"

Ashley looked at her notepad. "You said you know Glenn Hoffman as well?"

"Sure, Huff—that's what we call him—went fishin' with Jerry and me a couple of times. Huff is retired S.F. He and Jerry go back a ways, served in the same team in da Nam. But I gotta tell ya, he's gonna tell ya the same thing I did. Jerry had enemies, but none that would have murdered him."

Eli patted his friend's back. "Thanks again, Murph. We've got to get to the office and start writing a report. I'll call ya when the dust settles on this and we'll go drink a beer."

Once outside, Eli slowed his steps and looked at his watch. "It's after five. I feel like I've been up thirty hours instead of only twelve."

Ashley sighed. "I'm beat, too. It doesn't look good, does it? Not a single lead, and they still haven't found Mrs. Hargrove."

"Something will turn up. The lab will find something that will help us . . . I hope. If you're up to it, we can go visit with Glenn Hoffman, or we can do it tomorrow when we're both rested."

"I vote for rest first."

"Good, that's my vote, too. Want to get a beer and wind down? You do drink beer, don't you?"

"You're learning, Tanner. You asked this time. No, I don't drink beer, but I'll have a gin and tonic. But Tanner, let's go to a place with some class. A place where I don't have to brush flies away and hold my breath when I visit the ladies' room. Oh yeah, and no country music."

Eli opened the van door and, expressionless, said, "Just drop me off at my truck."

"What happened to your offer of a drink?"

"I didn't know it was going to have so many qualifiers. I could agree to all but the last one. What's your hang-up with country music, anyway?"

"I prefer music that doesn't twang, okay? And I went with a guy once who . . . never mind, you'll just laugh and think it's silly."

"I wouldn't do that. Tell me."

"When I was in high school, I went out with this guy who played in a band. Yes, Tanner, it was a country western band. I had to sit for hours wearing a stupid grin like I loved the music he was making. Every time I hear the stuff it reminds me how dumb I was."

"What happened? I mean between you and Mr. Country and Western."

"He wanted me to tell him how great he was. He was okay but not great. I couldn't lie to him."

"Why, you liked him, didn't you?"

"Not enough to lie and feed his ego all the time. Anyway, he smoked. I didn't like walking around smelling like stale beer and Marlboros."

"All right, Agent Sutton, we'll go someplace nice. You pick the place. I need a beer and a chance to think."

Ashley gave him a side glance. "You've not giving up so easily, are you? I would have given in a little."

"No, you win. I was just sitting here trying to picture you at a table watchin' Mr. Country and Western with a grin. Can't seem to get that picture in focus. Did you wear boots, tight jeans, and a spade-front shirt?"

"That's enough, Tanner."

"You *did*, didn't you? How about a hat? Did you two-step and Cotton-eye Joe, too?"

"I'll drop you at your pickup."

"So I win after all?"

"I'll drop you off, and you meet me at the Bombay Bicycle Club. We'll call it a draw this time, okay?"

Eli sighed and leaned back in the seat, shutting his eyes. "What I'll do for a beer," he said in a stage whisper.

Eli rolled over in bed and slapped twice at the nightstand before finding the beeping cell phone. "Agent Tanner," he said, closing his eyes again.

"Tanner, it's me, Sutton. We've got another one."

"What time is it?" he asked, opening his eyes again. "Another what?"

"Wake up, Tanner. It's almost three A.M. A detective from the Columbus Police Department called me just minutes ago. The detective heard about our homicide on post and told me he was called to a house where an apparent suicide had taken place. Tanner, the victim had a gold chain in his mouth . . . the chain held a cross. The victim is Glenn Hoffman. . . . Did you hear me? Glenn Hoffman, the sergeant major's buddy."

Eli sat up. "Where's the body?"

"I'm on the way to pick you up. The detective is waiting at the scene and has already called GBI. I'll be at the house in five minutes."

"I'll be ready and standing out front."

CHAPTER 10

Eli bent over and shined the flashlight on the dead man's face. The victim was black.

Ashley leaned over. "It's the same type of gold chain, isn't it?"

Eli straightened up. "Yep, and same style cross."

A Columbus Police Department detective stood beside them and motioned to the body. "I gotta tell ya, if I hadn't read the National Crime Information Center's computer bulletin, I would have called it a suicide. The gold chain is what tipped us. The difference in M.O. is the weapon. This victim used a .22 on himself. I-talian job, semiauto, and expensive. We ran a check, and Hoffman didn't have the weapon registered and the wife says he didn't own a pistol. I pulled back the victim's shirt—taser marks on his chest. The killer must have kept the juice on him pretty high to keep him subdued. Those things can kill ya if ya use too much of an electrical charge."

Having seen enough, Eli panned his light to the small house twenty yards away. "Family find him?"

"Daughter did. She and Hoffman's wife live in the house. Daughter said her dad played cards on Sunday nights with friends down the street. He's off work on Mondays. When he wasn't home by one, she got worried. She called the friend's house and the man said Hoffman had left an hour earlier. She didn't wake her mom, just went out to look for him along with the friend. They found him here about one-thirty."

Headlights from an approaching car briefly bathed the crime

scene in a golden glow then went out. A short man stepped out of the car, Ed Faraday, the GBI detective Tanner had met the day before. Detective Faraday shut his door and shook his head. "Agent Tanner, looks like you've got yourself a serial killer."

Eli stepped closer. "Two homicides in two days with the same M.O. makes it appear so, Ed, but it's not a serial killer. Yesterday's victim and this one served together in Vietnam. We've got something else on our hands."

The detective shook his head again. "Well, whatever it is, you've got *three* homicides now. I got a call ten minutes ago on the way here. Seems the Fort Smith, Arkansas, Police Department read the bulletin we sent over the NCIC. They had a similar death three days ago, gold chain in the mouth. It was ruled suicide and of course wasn't entered on the NCIC. They hadn't buried the victim yet, and checked his body. They found taser marks. Like I said, three homicides. Your killer is gettin' around."

Eli turned to Ashley. "Better call the SAC and let him know. He'll want to declare an alert and bring in a behavioral scientist from Quantico. I'll call the Fort Smith police and get the facts."

The detective stepped back to his car and opened the door. "I called them from my phone while I was drivin'. I got some notes for ya. Their victim was a white male, fifty-four years of age. Retired from the Army as a sergeant major after twenty-eight years and worked for a trailer company as a—"

"Ed, was he in Special Forces by chance?"

The detective glanced at his notes then back up to Eli. "Yeah, I think so—says he had a Special Forces tattoo on his forearm. How did ya know he was a Green Beret?"

Eli exchanged looks with Ashley before lowering his head. "Ed, I think the killer must be going after the team."

"What team are you talking about?" Faraday asked, stepping closer.

Eli motioned behind him. "As I told you, Sergeant Major

Rhodes and this victim served together in Vietnam on the same Special Forces team. I bet the victim in Fort Smith was on the same team with them."

"Oh shit . . . how many are there on a team?"

"Twelve, if it was a full A-team, six if it was split. If it was a B-team, it's a lot more."

Ashley grasped Eli's arm. "How can we find out for sure if the victim in Fort Smith was on the team?"

Eli took in another breath to try to relax and think. "Victim's family would know, and we can contact the DOD. They'll have records, but it will take days, maybe weeks."

"DOD? What's that?"

"Department of Defense. I think I know a faster way. Go and talk to this victim's wife. Collect any pictures she may have of her husband in Nam. Also get all his Army records, especially his citations for awards or promotions. And the letters he sent to her. I'll visit the sergeant major's widow and do the same. We'll meet in the office and go over what we came up with. Ed, I'm leaving the scene in your hands. Please call the Fort Smith P.D. and have them talk to their victim's widow and do the same thing we're doing by collecting his Army pictures and records. They can fax the stuff to our office."

"Got it. I'll call 'em now." Faraday strode back toward his car.

Ashley still held Eli's arm. "Still want me to call the SAC?"

"Yes, fill him in and request DOD's help. Tell him we have to move quick. The killer has struck three times in five days, and most likely is going after the others."

It was ten o'clock in the morning when Regina set a full cup of coffee down in front of Ashley, who was going through one of the three boxes of photographs and memorabilia she'd gotten from Hoffman's widow. "I'll bet you haven't had a bite to eat this mornin', Agent Sutton. Want me to go get you somethin'?"

Ashley glanced up. "Thank you, Ms. Washington, but coffee is fine. You didn't have to make it, you know?"

Regina settled into a chair. "I know, but you and the boss being so busy and all. Can I help you in some way?"

Leaning back in her chair, Ashley wrinkled her brow as if frustrated. "I wish you could, but I'm not sure what I'm looking for. We'll just have to wait until Agent Tanner gets here with the sergeant major's things and tells us what it is we're looking for."

Regina smiled. "The boss is somethin', isn't he? He sure got a way about him."

"I guess I haven't noticed," Ashley said, picking up several pictures. "What kind of *way* does he have?"

"You know. A *way*—the way he walks and the way he talks but doesn't say a thing, his eyes and his look says it all for him. It's cool, definitely cool. GBI guys that were in yesterday usin' our copier told me he slam-dunked the military police major, big-time. Said the boss was cool as a cucumber and was right on ruling a suspicious death. I wish I'd been there to see it."

Ashley kept her eyes on the pictures. "Maybe you should start a fan club, Ms. Washington."

Regina got up and walked back to her desk. *Girl, see if I get you coffee again.*

The front door swung open and in stepped Eli, carrying a box and a smile. "Got it!" He strode straight to his desk, put down the box, and removed a framed picture from the top. "Take a look. It's a team photo. I got it from the sergeant major's study. There, in the middle standing by the captain, is Rhodes, and here on the end is Hoffman."

Ashley had moved beside him and was studying the picture. "I count eleven Americans. Are those South Vietnamese soldiers kneeling in front of them?"

"Nope, Cambodian Special Forces troops. Probably an A-team the team trained. I've got more." He reached in the box and took out a thin green plastic-covered book.

Eli opened it, and Ashley could see it was in fact a folder of some kind. "This is an award folder," he said. "We all got them along with the medals we received. See here, it's a citation. 'By Direction of the Secretary of the Army, the Army Commendation Medal is presented to Staff Sergeant Jerald D. Rhodes 110–65–2689, Infantry, United States Army. For exceptionally meritorious achievement in support of the United States objectives in the counterinsurgency effort in the Republic of Vietnam during the period four January 1972 to nine June 1972'."

Eli paused and removed the top paper from the folder. "This citation was standard verbiage, but at least we know the dates they served together. This paper here behind the citation is the orders published by their unit headquarters. It was published by Headquarters and Headquarters Company of the Second Battalion Fifth Special Forces Group. This is what we needed. See the names? There are eleven of them, starting with a Captain Robert E. Anderson.... Rhodes is the second name, Hoffman is the fifth, and our victim from Fort Smith, Edward D. McIntyre, is the tenth. We've got it. This gives us the names of the others. Agent Sutton, call the names into DOD. They should be able to run them through their computer and give us current home addresses on—"

Eli stopped in mid-sentence, seeing Detective Faraday walk in the front office door. The look the detective held told Eli he was bringing bad news.

Faraday motioned at the computer. "You read your e-mail from NCIC lately?"

Eli looked at Ashley, and she shook her head. "No, I've been going through victims' pictures."

Eli held out the paper in his hand. "Ed, here they are. We found the names of the other team members in a copy of orders."

"That's good work, Agent Tanner. By any chance is the name Edwin Turner on that list?"

Eli looked at the list of names and raised his head. "Third name on this list. Is he . . ."

"It's on your e-mail. Edwin Turner was found dead five days ago in San Antonio, Texas. His death was ruled suicide. Like the victim in Fort Smith, the cops didn't log it on the NCIC. They read our bulletin then sent us a report over the computer. Their victim had a gold chain and cross in his mouth. It matches the M.O. of your killer. And get this. They found a .22, Italian, semiautomatic. And the last digit of its serial number is only one number off from the one found at the scene this morning. It gets worse. The Junction City, Kansas, P.D. read our bulletin and sent us a report about an apparent suicide they had on the first of June. Victim's name was Duane H. Gosset. Same M.O. and the serial number of the .22 he used is one off from the one in San Antonio."

Eli looked down the column of names. "Gosset was the eleventh name on the list."

The detective frowned. "Looks like your killer is way ahead of us. How many does that make?"

"Six," Eli said. "That leaves only four to go. One of the team members has to be the killer—it's the only explanation unless it could be a team member's son or some other family member. . . . Regina, please get those e-mails printed in hard copies for me. But first get the SAC on the line."

Before Regina could pick up the phone, it rang. She picked it up.

"Columbus resident office. . . . Yes, sir, he just asked me to call the SAC." She held the phone out to Eli and whispered, "Boss, it's the ASAC, Agent Polous."

Eli took the phone. "This is Agent Tanner, sir, I'm putting you on the speaker so Agent Sutton and GBI Detective Faraday can listen to our conversation."

"Sure, go ahead, Agent Tanner. Have you seen the messages about the other victims?"

"Sir, we were just appraised of the others by the GBI, but I think I may have some good news for you. The killings aren't random. We now know that all the victims served together in the Special Forces on the same team in Vietnam in 1972. We also have the names of the other team members. With DOD's help we should be able to find the remaining five team members. It's our assumption one of the team members is the killer and will continue to go after the others. Our priority is to find the team members fast."

"I'll be damned, how did you make the connection?"

"Got lucky, sir. We got the names from an old set of orders from one of the victims. But we need to move fast and find the other team members. The killer is moving very quickly. Agent Sutton is faxing the names as we speak, and a picture of the team members."

"Right, good work. Look, Agent Tanner, the SAC feels you're in over your head on this. This office is taking the lead, effective immediately. We've got the manpower, experts, and assets to handle the case in a more expeditious manner. The SAC wants you and Sutton to come up tomorrow and bring our people up to speed. Bring everything you've got … Yeah, okay … Sorry, my secretary just brought in the fax of the names you sent. This is good work. Now if we just knew where to find these men. DOD is notorious for moving slow. We need to know where they live now."

"Sir, we'll work on it on this end. We just found the list of the names and will go back and talk to the victims' widows. Seeing the names may jog their memories. Maybe the men exchanged Christmas cards or something." Eli paused a moment and beads of perspiration suddenly broke out on his forehead. "Sir, I just thought of something, it's a long shot, but have one of your agents call the phone company in Fayetteville, North Carolina, and see if any of the five remaining team members lives there."

"Why Fayetteville?"

"It's the home of the Special Forces. Their headquarters is in Fort Bragg, just outside the city. Like I said, it's a long shot, but maybe one of them retired nearby to be close to his old buddies."

"Got it. I'll have someone check now. I'll see you and Agent

Sutton in the office tomorrow at nine sharp. In the meantime start faxing us what you have."

Eli hung up the phone and shrugged. "Well, you heard him. . . . Looks like we're out of it."

Her eyes burning, Ashley snapped, "In over our heads? What was that supposed to mean?"

The GBI detective cocked an eyebrow. "Ma'am, I'm not sure how you feds operate, but at state level it means this case has gotten too high profile to let the players play the game. The coaches and owners want in. I know it don't mean a hill of beans now, but I thought you two had a pretty good handle on things."

Eli gave the detective a small smile. "Thanks, Ed, but the SAC is right, we don't have the manpower or the experts. He made the right call."

"Well, I'm not doin' anything for a while. If you make me a copy of those names, I'll visit Hoffman's widow while you talk to Mrs. Rhodes. Cut your time in half."

Eli handed the page to Regina. "Would you please make Ed a copy of this." Facing the detective, he slapped him on the shoulder. "You know, Ed, you state boys ain't half as bad as I heard. In fact, how about this evening let's you and I go have some ribs and beer. I'll buy."

Ed shrugged his broad shoulders. "The boys will give me a ration of shit if they find out I ate with a fed . . . but hell, you ain't half bad yourself. It's a deal."

Taking the copy Regina handed him, Ed waved and walked out of the office.

Ashley cleared her throat to get her fellow agent's attention. "What do you want me to do with these things I got from Mrs. Hoffman?"

"I'd appreciate it if you'd read the letters he wrote to his wife from Nam. And Rhodes's letter, too, if you have time. We need to know what the team was doing, what was their mission. The Special Forces was involved in a lot of black operations over there, secret operations that the public and Congress didn't know about. Write down any names that come up of other units or people who were involved with the team. Our killer may be going after more than the team. And look for anything that indicates if any team member had problems with the others."

Ashley gave him a searching stare. "I thought we were off the case."

"We are, but we've got to bring the Atlanta office up to speed tomorrow. The more we know, the more we can help them."

"I don't like it, Tanner. Reading love letters of dead men is not my cup of tea."

"Okay, no problem. I'll do it when I get back."

"No, I'll do it, Tanner. You'll have to prepare to brief tomorrow. I'll back-brief you on what the letters say. . . . We could do it over dinner, but I see you already have a date with Mr. Good Ol' Boy. I'm sure he'll just love Bubba's ribs."

"I bet he likes the music, too. I'd invite you to go along but we both know what your answer would be. I'm headin' out to ask Mrs. Rhodes about these names, then going to see Murph to see if the sergeant major mentioned any of the names to him. I won't be back in. I'll see ya in the morning when you pick me up at six-thirty. We can discuss what the letters contained while we're drivin' to Atlanta. See ya then."

Ashley's eyes narrowed as she watched him walk toward the door and disappear from sight. Self-conscious of standing and staring, she glanced at Regina to see if she was caught.

Regina was looking at her with a smile. "I told ya he had a way."

Red-faced, Ashley turned in silence and walked to her desk.

Garth Brooks was singing the sad refrain of "The Last Dance" as Eli hummed along. On the last note, Eli finished his beer off and set the can on the table. He broke his distant gaze and shifted his eyes to his tablemate. "That's his best song."

Ed Faraday set down his beer can beside his empty plate. "I

don't know, Tan, 'I Got Friends in Low Places' was pretty darn good. Me and the wife do a mean two-step to it."

"You're right, Ed, that was a good one. I don't like his new stuff that much, but Clint Black seems to be gettin' better with every new—"

He stopped in mid-sentence, seeing a woman approach whom he hadn't expected to see.

Ashley pulled back a chair and sat down. "Congratulations, Tanner, your long shot hit pay dirt. Walter Schwark, number seven on the list, lives in Fayetteville. The resident office there sent the Atlanta office a confirmation message. Walter Schwark retired as a first sergeant five years ago. He works as chief of security for Sears in a mall in Fayetteville. The agents didn't make actual contact with him because he's in Florida on vacation with his wife. The Sears people said he was expected back in two days."

Eli raised his hand and spoke to a passing waitress. "Two more beers here and—" He looked at Ashley. "You going to stay long enough to have a drink?"

Ed scooted his chair back. "Cancel that beer for me, Tan. I gotta hit the road. Looks like you two gotta talk business anyway. Thanks for the dinner, the ribs were *de*licious. See ya, buddy. Agent Sutton, it was a pleasure."

"Thanks again, Ed. Let's do it again when you're in town again." Eli turned to the waitress. "Make that one beer and a gin and tonic with lime for the lady."

Ashley studied his face a moment. "I thought you'd be pleased with yourself, Tanner. Your long shot saved Walter Schwark's life."

"I am pleased, but I'd feel a lot more comfortable if our people could have talked to him today. He might know where the others are living or he might have an idea who on the team would have a reason to murder his old unit members."

"You're right, I'm sorry. This case is getting to me. I hate sitting here knowing that four men on the list are being hunted and the fifth is doing the hunting."

The waitress smiled as she set the tray of drinks on the table. "Sugar, ya want me ta play 'The Last Dance' again for ya? I just love that song."

Eli grinned and tossed a five dollar bill on her tray. "Would ya? I love it, too. Play it a couple of times. Thank you."

Ashley gave him a glare as the leggy waitress walked away. "You're just making all kinds of friends, aren't you?"

"She likes the same song I do, Agent Sutton. Give me a break. What did you find in the letters?"

Ashley sipped at her drink and set the glass down. "I made notes for you on the specifics, names of others, like you asked. In general you were right. The team was working a secret mission. They and several other teams were working in Cambodia fortifying a series of villages that were close to the South Vietnamese border. Seems some general deemed the villages vital for the security of Vietnam. The team worked in a village known simply as Camp 147. Hoffman's letters were the best on the subject. He was twenty-six years old in 1972 and had just married his wife, Imogene. She didn't know anything about the Army or the war, so Hoffman wrote trying to explain what he was doing. He was good at it. Even I understood what they were trying to do. Basically it was to train, arm, and equip the villagers to fight the North Vietnamese if they used the valley as an invasion route. Problem was, the war was winding down and Hoffman was getting worried that they were trying to do too much too late. His later letters betray depression and self-doubt. He obviously liked the people of the village very much and didn't want them to be put in serious danger. He thought that by fortifying the village the higher-ups were making the village a target. Hoffman turned out to be right.

"His last letters really tore at my heart. It was obvious to all the team the war was going badly and our government was trying to get out. It seems the entire team had promised the village chief in a ceremony of some kind that they would stay and fight alongside the people of the village and defeat the North Vietnamese. They also had promised the U.S. would provide air support and whatever else was needed to win. It didn't happen. In Hoffman's last letter he was crushed. The team had been ordered out of Camp 147 because of a change in policy about Americans' being in harm's way. The team was transferred to a place called Pleiku. A couple of days later the North Vietnamese attacked their old camp. Hoffman wrote that his captain, Robert Anderson, tried to mount a rescue operation, but the lieutenant colonel in charge of the unit stopped all his efforts. Hoffman told his wife he wanted to die when he heard over the radio the pleas for help from the Cambodian team they had left in the camp. He wrote that he cried like a baby when the voice on the radio said the camp was being overrun and that all was lost. He said the last thing the voice said was, 'Why did you do this to us?' "

Eli stared blankly at his beer can. Ashley waited for a response, but he didn't move a muscle. She waited another moment then touched his hand. "You okay?"

He broke his stare but didn't look at her as he spoke quietly. "Yeah, I was thinking of Sergeant Hoffman lying in his yard. After all he'd been through, to end up . . ." He finally raised his eyes to her.

"Guilt may be the motive. One of the team members couldn't take the guilt of leaving those people to die. In some twisted way he wants to erase it from his memory and the only way he can do it is get rid of those who were there."

"And the cross?"

Eli looked back at his can. "I had a Cambodian scout in my platoon. When things got dangerous he would—" Eli pulled out his gold chain from beneath his shirt."—put this Buddha in his mouth. It assured him protection or at least a better life in the next world. Our killer may want his teammates to find a better place when they're gone. A place where they wouldn't ever feel the guilt again."

Sighing, Eli put his chain back in his shirt and picked up his beer. He took a drink. "Any word yet from DOD on the others?"

"I don't know. Since the Atlanta office took over, the addresses would go to Atlanta, and *they* haven't answered my queries. It looks like we'll know tomorrow. Tanner, it's getting late. Don't you think you ought to call it a night and get some sleep?"

Eli lifted his beer again. "Go on, I'm going to finish this beer and listen to my song awhile. . . . See ya in the morning, and thanks for all your help and comin' over. I know you don't care for this place."

Ashley leaned back in her chair and glanced around. "I guess it's not that bad . . . flies aren't as bad tonight." She sneaked a quick glance to see if he was biting but saw he hadn't even heard her. His distant stare was directed at the far wall. She got up, gave him a last look, and walked out.

CHAPTER 11

Ashley felt like a leper as she stood beside Eli in the
crowded briefing room. The cold stares and distance the other
agents were keeping from them made her furious. She leaned
closer to Eli and whispered, "A great bunch of guys, huh?"

Eli lowered his head. "It's me they're giving the cold
shoulder. You'd better keep your distance or you'll be tainted
when you come up here to work."

"Forget that, we're in this together. All of this stinks,
Tanner. I don't like it that the ASAC took all our background
material from us. I thought *we* were supposed to brief the
background."

Eli whispered, "Stay cool. Just do what the ASAC said and
we'll be out of here and back in Columbus in a couple of
hours."

The briefing room door opened and the Assistant Special
Agent in Charge of the Atlanta office, George Polous, entered
the room and spoke loudly. "Please take your seats. You'll find
place cards on the table. The SAC will be coming in a minute."

"The way they're treating us, I thought they'd put us in the
next room and televise the meeting for our benefit. It stinks,
Tanner," whispered Ashley.

"Stead-dee. We'll just sit and keep our mouths shut, like
George here said."

140

Taking their seats, they both opened their briefcases and took out their briefing notes.

The ASAC took his seat next to two empty chairs at the head of the table. He cleared his throat, pushed his stylish tortoise-shell frames up on his nose, and motioned for his assistant to hand out the packets. "You're now receiving the background folders on the case. You'll find the investigation reports concerning the victims in Columbus and the reports sent in from the police departments that handled what they thought were suicides. Please note the killer's M.O. is laid out for you on the last page. In just a minute the SAC will be joining us as well as the behavioral scientist sent down from Quantico for the case. We are fortunate because Quantico sent their best, Dr. Ramona Valez.

"For you newer agents who might not have heard of her, Dr. Valez is the one who broke the Newton serial killings case, as well as the much publicized Hooper case. We can be—"

Behind the ASAC the door opened and Don Farrel, the SAC, entered the room, followed by a tall, striking, dark-haired, middle-age woman.

Ashley was shocked. She had assumed the famous Ph.D. was a dumpy gray-haired intellectual who wore thick glasses and figureless dresses. Ramona Valez was not even close to that image; she had the look and figure of a happy aerobics instructor, the kind one sees on early morning TV. She was wearing tight blue jeans, a white silk blouse, a single strand of pearls, and a five-hundred-dollar DKNY blue blazer. She didn't wear makeup and didn't need to; her olive skin was flawless. Her nose was a tad too big, but she was very attractive. But it was her high cheekbones and penetrating deep-set brown eyes that made her special. Ashley could almost feel the other agents undressing the stylish doctor in their minds. To her surprise, Eli's attention was focused on his briefing notes. He didn't even look up when the doctor took her seat at the corner of the table just two feet from where he was seated.

At the head of the table, Farrel smiled as he looked over to the doctor. "George has already introduced you, Ramona, but let me say for all of us here what a pleasure and honor it is to have you on the case."

Ramona Valez dipped her chin and looked down the table, panning the admiring faces. "I hope that I can be of assistance in some way." Her gaze lingered for a moment on Eli, then shifted to Farrel. "It's always nice to come to Atlanta and see old friends."

Ashley saw Eli's face reddening and almost poked him to ask what was going on, but Farrel was motioning to his left, at his number two man.

"I've appointed George as my case Agent in Charge of this one, folks. But before I turn over the meeting to him let me say a few things to get us started. As you all know by now, we've had six homicides spread over four states in the space of ten days. This case is unique in that so far the press has not gotten hold of it, and that's the way I want to keep it until it's closed. Security on this will be tight, *no* leaks. George and his team chiefs have worked hard since taking over the case and have connected the victims and already identified the killer's next probable targets. We—"

Eli winced when Ashley lifted her hand and said, "Excuse me."

Farrel leaned back in his chair with a scowl. "Agent Sutton, I was just going over my introductory remarks. I didn't ask for questions."

Ashley returned his glare. "Sir, I feel obligated to correct what you just said. Agent Tanner connected the victims, *not* the ASAC. And it was Agent Tanner who found the names of the team members, identifying the next possible targets."

Farrel nodded as if to a second grader. "Thank you, Agent Sutton. I'm fully aware of what the Columbus office has done. In the interest of time I felt specific laudatory remarks to individuals weren't necessary. Now may I continue?"

Ashley said nothing.

"As I was saying, George and his task force have already

done yeoman's work. In fact in light of recent information, this case may soon be closed. It is my good fortune to report that George has identified a suspect who is very probably our killer."

Ashley and Eli tensed with surprise. They had talked to Polous earlier in his office to give him a summary of their briefing packet information, and he hadn't mentioned a word to them about finding a suspect.

Farrel again motioned to Polous. "George, let's don't keep everybody in suspense. I'll turn over the meeting to you."

Special Agent George Polous nodded and picked up a stack of papers. "Our people have been working with DOD and more specifically the Finance and Accounting Office for military retired pay. A few hours ago the Washington office faxed us the addresses of the men who were teammates of the victims. We now have knowledge of the whereabouts of four of the five men in question. Only the whereabouts of one man, John A. Elder, is still unknown. Unlike the others, Mr. Elder was discharged from the military after his tour in Vietnam and does not receive retirement pay."

Polous passed half of the stack of papers to his left and the other to his right. "Please take a packet and pass on the rest. I'll go over it with you. As you can see on page one, the number of men who are possible targets has been reduced by two. DOD informed us Sergeant Barry Atkins was killed during the Desert One operation in 1974. You will recall the military's abortive rescue attempt of the embassy employees in Iran. Sergeant Atkins and others were tragically killed when one of the aircraft caught fire. Note also DOD informed us that Sergeant Frederick Woolshager died in a St. Paul, Minneapolis, V.A. Hospital in 1989 from heart disease. This reduces the list to three. I'll now discuss the newest information. Note the first name on the list. Captain Robert E. Anderson. He retired from the military four years ago as a colonel and was residing in Fairfax, Virginia. Agents were immediately dispatched to talk to him and to protect him. Our agents found instead that Robert

Anderson was missing and has been missing since May twenty-ninth. That is significant because the first victim was killed two days later in Kansas on the first of June. Mrs. Anderson reported her husband missing to local authorities when he did not return from his work as a sales manager for a computer graphics company. Let me move on to the other team members and we'll go back to Anderson later. The one remaining member of the team of whom we know the whereabouts is retired Sergeant Walter Schwark, who resides in Fayetteville, North Carolina. I said we know his whereabouts, but at present that's not exactly correct. We know where he lives, but Mr. Schwark is somewhere in Florida on vacation. He and his wife are due back tomorrow, and we are making every attempt to find him, but so far we've had no luck. John Elder is our current problem, but his residence and whereabouts should soon be known. Our people are working with the IRS and we expect soon to have his address."

Polous pushed his glasses farther back on his nose and pointed to an organization chart on the wall. "This is the breakout showing how my task force is organized. Team A, headed up by Agent John Hawks, is concentrating on the two team members who are possible targets. He has already dispatched a team to work with the Fayetteville resident office, and he has a team standing by to be sent out once Elder is found. Team A is responsible for ensuring the two men are protected and in setting the trap for the killer when he attempts to finish his business with either team member.

"Team B is headed up by Agent Josh Simmons. Josh's team is responsible for tracking down and finding our number one suspect, Robert Anderson. Josh is already running a computer search of airline manifests, credit card receipts, and car rental agencies. It's obvious our killer flew into or near cities close to the victims.

"I have taken the liberty of assigning each of you to a team based on your area of expertise. You'll find your names posted on the chart below the team headings. The room the team will work out of is also posted. Let me tell you all that the director has given us number-one priority on this case. You should have no problem securing any information you may need. If you run into problems, notify your team leader or me. I will be with Team B for the rest of the day. We'll all meet at ten A.M. and three P.M. daily to exchange information. If there are no questions, we'll take a ten-minute coffee break, then adjourn to the team rooms and begin work."

Dr. Ramona Valez lifted her hand. "I'm sorry, George, I don't have a question but I do feel before we break up I should mention some things for everyone's benefit. Don was kind enough to fax me the killer's M.O. last night, and the investigation reports. I have come up with a preliminary profile. It is obvious, of course, that the killer is very dangerous and very intelligent. He has planned these murders well in advance and has obviously watched each of his victims for some time before beginning his spree. I say this because of the timing of each victim's death. In most cases the victims were alone, which means our killer knew the victim's daily schedule and knew when to strike. Our killer is also methodical: he has left no sign of his presence, and it appears to me that he is on a schedule of some kind. I say this because of the instance where a woman was with a victim. The killer still went through with his execution despite her presence. This tells me the killer could not wait for a better time or until the victim was alone."

The doctor paused a moment and looked at notes. "Our killer is very intelligent and knows our procedures. He knows suicides are not logged on the NCIC, and he executes his victims and makes the murders appear to be suicides in the belief that their deaths will not be linked. It is obvious he believes this will give him time to finish off the whole team before a connection is made, if it ever would have been.

"Let me say also that the method of execution of the victims is purposeful. The use of the stun gun is most interesting. The killer immobilizes his victims, places them on their knees, and then lifts the victim's hand holding a pistol and helps the victim shoot himself. If my understanding of stun guns and tasers is correct, the victim is unable to move if the shock level is high enough. But the victim can see and he can hear. And that is exactly what the killer wants. I believe he wants the victim to know what is about to happen. At present the cross in the victim's mouth has me stumped. The religious aspect is of course obvious, but I don't believe our killer is a religious fanatic. I believe the cross has another meaning known to the killer and his victims."

Ashley lifted her head to speak, but Eli grabbed her leg under the table.

Ramona smiled at the SAC. "Don, I know you just mentioned Robert Anderson's being the primary suspect, and I hate to be a party pooper, but I would not get my hopes up. A retired colonel in his mid-fifties does not fit my profile. That does not mean to say my profile is infallible; it most certainly is not. But let me say I have serious reservations."

Farrel shook his head in frustration. "Ramona, are you saying we should look for another suspect?"

"Sorry, Don, but I'm afraid so. I believe you should proceed with your investigation of Anderson, of course, but I would also start from square one and begin looking into finding other possibles. George has his Team A and Team B, and I would be most happy to head a team of my own and begin looking into alternate theories of the killer's identity."

Polous's face tightened. "Sir, the doctor should work under my task force in Team B. An independent investigation will only cause communications problems."

Ramona canted her head and smiled. "No, George, I don't want to offend you, but you're too *organized* for me. I will report only to Don."

Don Farrel sighed and leaned back in his chair. "Okay, Ramona, you win this one, but I want you to attend the daily meetings and keep us all posted on what you come up with. It's settled. I suggest we take a coffee break then start work." He stood and nodded toward the seated agents, speaking in a solemn voice. "Folks, you're my first team and we're in the fourth quarter. We *will* score and break this case. . . . Two men's lives depend on it. Good hunting." He turned and walked out the door.

Polous gave the doctor a cold stare as the other agents began leaving. "You could have waited and voiced your concerns to me, Dr. Valez. This meeting was not the place to throw darts at me."

Valez stood and patted his shoulder. "You screwed up, George. You should have run the information about Anderson by me before telling the SAC you had your man. Think of it as a lesson. Go on, pout somewhere for a while, then come and apologize to me. I promise I'll accept."

Polous rose and hurried out the door, followed by his assistant. Ramona turned and looked at Eli, who still sat in his chair. She stepped closer and spoke huskily. "Where have you been all my life, good-looking?"

Eli shook his head and stood. "Don't start, Mona." His lips slowly crawled back in a smile as he stood and leaned forward to kiss her cheek. "I see you're still setting them up and knockin' 'em down. I don't think you'll get a Christmas card from the ASAC this year."

She shrugged. "He should have known better than try to keep secrets from me." Her eyes locked on Ashley. "And who is this?"

Eli motioned to his fellow agent, who was standing now, too. "Mona, meet Agent Ashley Sutton."

Ramona extended her hand with a pleasant smile. "Ashley, it is a real pleasure. After you interrupted Don during his opening remarks, I hoped we would meet. I am making a study of self-destructive behavior, and you seem to be the perfect candidate. Please don't worry, I'm kidding. But tell me, why did you feel compelled to correct Don?"

Ashley was still in shock that Eli had kissed the woman, and over the doctor's treatment of the ASAC. "It's a pleasure to meet you, Dr. Valez. I've heard quite a lot about you. To answer your question, I felt Agent Tanner deserved recognition for his efforts."

Ramona elbowed Eli in the ribs. "Eli, where did you find somebody willing to stand up for you? I thought I was the only one who still thought you were sane?"

"Come on, Mona, give her a break. She doesn't know you yet."

The doctor took Ashley by the arm. "Nonsense, Ashley and I are going to become close friends. So tell me, Eli, have you missed me?"

"Yeah, I miss getting humiliated on the tennis courts by you. Agent Sutton, you are in the presence of the best tennis player, man or woman, in Virginia. Mona, here, played in the pros in her younger years. Now she beats up on men who are dumb enough to play her."

Ramona batted her eyes. "Flattery never was your high suit. I've missed you, Eli. I still haven't found a doubles partner to take your place."

"I take it you two know each other from Quantico?"

Ramona nodded, keeping her eyes on Eli. "Eli and I are *very* old friends. I used tennis as an excuse to try and seduce him."

Embarrassed, Eli shook his head. "Mona, I told ya, don't start. Agent Sutton and I wanted to talk to you about the case."

"The cross, right? Don't look surprised. I saw Ashley wanted to speak up. What do you know?"

Eli motioned her to take a seat. "Mona, it bothered me the first time I saw the chain in the victim's mouth. It reminded me of Vietnam, when I had a Cambodian scout . . ."

Ramona listened without moving a muscle. When Eli finished, she looked at the far wall with a vacant stare and slowly nodded. "Yes, it makes sense now. The killer wants his victims to suffer, knowing they are going to die, yet respects them enough to want them to have a second chance in a better world. Interesting, very interesting."

Ashley took photocopies of the letters she'd read from her briefcase. "Dr. Valez, these are copies of letters the victims sent to their wives while in Vietnam. I read them and think they'll help you understand what the men were doing there. But it will also help you understand how close the team was and the incredible guilt they felt when their operation turned bad."

Ramona remained motionless a moment, and finally spoke. "Guilt? You say they felt guilt?"

"Yes, Doctor. You'll see when you read the letters."

Ramona stood. "Ashley, I see you need me. You have a bad case of formality. I'm Mona, not 'Dr. Valez.' I can see that you two will be perfect for my team. Wait here. I am going to tell Don to assign you both to me."

Eli quickly stood up and stuck his hand out, blocking her way. "Take Agent Sutton, Mona, but not me. I'm not what you call a very well-liked guy around here. It would only cause you grief."

"Eli, my dear, you were the only one in this room who served in Vietnam. You have the experience nobody else has, and I need you. The chain and cross are a perfect example. I would have wasted days and probably not found the missing piece."

"Mona, the SAC will never approve it. He doesn't trust me."

"He doesn't have to," Ramona said, pushing his arm down. "I trust you and that is what counts." She walked out and closed the briefing room door behind her.

Ashley looked at Eli with a glare. "You bruised my leg when you grabbed me. And what was that about 'take Agent Sutton but not me'?"

Eli sank into a chair and lowered his head. "Don't start on me too, okay? Mona was a great tennis partner, but working with her on this case is an entirely different matter. I would rather go back to Columbus and forget the whole thing."

Ashley raised an eyebrow. "You two had a thing going, didn't you? Don't deny it, I saw how she looked at you."

Eli slowly raised his chin, pinning her with a stare. "Mona is a good *friend*. She was one of very few who stood by me when things got rough over the Ruby Ridge report." His stare softened. "Thank you for standing up for me in the meeting. It was dumb, but I still appreciate it."

Ashley covered her embarrassment with a shrug. "You're right it was dumb. So, do you think the SAC will let us work for her?"

Eli allowed himself a smile. "Do you think you could tell Ramona Valez no?"

Charleston, South Carolina

Wearing blue jeans, cowboy boots, and black T-shirt, Kenny Chun leaned against the rental Mazda van, listening to Reba McEntire singing "The Heart Is a Lonely Hunter." He hummed along with the song and tapped his right boot to the beat of the music. His right hand held a Kool menthol cigarette, and he took a drag without missing a beat, then blew a small cloud of smoke toward the blazing sun.

Five hundred yards away, a sleek Learjet touched down smoothly and raced down the runway. A minute later the small white jet rolled down the tarmac past Charleston's international passenger terminal and continued on toward the cargo and private aircraft hangars.

Kenny flicked away his cigarette and pushed off the van. Time to go to work again. He opened the van's passenger door then walked toward the plane to meet his superior.

The aircraft's hinged steps were lowered to the ground as Kenny approached, and a solitary passenger walked down the steps. Kenny took his superior's athletic bag, motioned to the Mazda, and said in Cambodian, "Sir, Khek Penn is watching the target, and Hu Nim has everything prepared for you. His plan is a good one."

The passenger nodded. "Have our friends been supportive?"

Kenny smiled. "The contact has been very helpful but, like the others, he is worried."

"Nice boots," the passenger said. "Are they lizard skin?"

Kenny glanced down at them as he walked. "No, Texas rattlesnake. The famous bootmaker's store was in San Antonio. They are Tony Llama boots. These are just like a pair special made for Kenny Rogers."

The passenger glanced at his escort's brown, pox-scarred face and noticed the wisps of whiskers being cultivated below his lip. "So you are disguising yourself as the famous western singer?"

Kenny Chun grinned. "I have a cowboy hat in the van—it makes me seem taller."

The passenger nodded as he stepped up into the van. He sat in the front passenger seat and waited until Kenny had closed all the doors and slid in behind the wheel before saying, "I do see a certain resemblance. Take me to Hu Nim. It is time."

CHAPTER 12

10:36 A.M. Atlanta

Ramona Valez held Eli's arm as she walked with him down the hallway. Slowing her steps, she motioned toward an office door. "Here we are; this is where we'll be working."

Eli opened the door and held it open for the doctor and Ashley. Ramona set her briefcase on the table, opened it and pulled out an IBM laptop. She motioned her new team members toward chairs and leaned back in her chair. "All right, let's do some brainstorming. I'm going to tell you up front there are a lot of things bothering me about this case, but I want to hear your impressions first. Are you comfortable with the assumptions George and Don have made so far?"

Shaking his head, Eli sank into his chair. "Mona, I hardly slept last night thinking through the unanswered questions that were running through my mind. My biggest problem is I don't see how the killer could be so lucky. There's been no witnesses, no evidence left behind, no reports of strange cars parked in the victims' neighborhoods. No one heard the pistol shots or any conversations. Luck only goes so far. This killer is very lucky or very, very good. The problem I have is, I don't think he's that lucky, and nobody is that good."

"So what are you saying?" Ramona asked.

"I don't think one man could pull this off ... but two or more could. That would make more sense to me. Example: how does our killer know so much about the victims? You

152

mentioned in the meeting that it was obvious he had been watching them. I agree, but he had to watch each of them for an awfully long time to establish their schedules. The victim, Hoffman, playing cards on Monday nights, yes, that fits, but what about Rhodes meeting his honey? Was our killer so lucky that he just found Rhodes that night or did he *know* exactly where to find him? Has someone else been watching the victims and updating their whereabouts for the killer?"

Ashley rolled her eyes. "That's a little far out, isn't it, Tanner? If it's not Robert Anderson, what two people or group would have a motive for killing members of his Special Forces team? We're talking about cold-blooded executions here."

Ramona lifted her hand. "No, I like it. I agree that having more than one person involved would answer your questions and some of mine. But you are right, too, Ashley. Two or more people reaching a decision to execute human beings in this manner requires very strong motivation. Why would one or more assassins execute these men? It doesn't appear to be a routine hit; a paid killer would not have taken the pains our killer or killers have to make these murders appear to be suicides. And a professional would never take on so many in such a short time. Much too dangerous. Greed? No evidence to support it. Power? Who benefits if the team is dead? Love is out. And so is hate; if the motive was pure hate, the killer would have done more damage . . . made them linger in agony before killing them. Which leaves us with revenge. But revenge for what? What did these men do while in Vietnam that would cause others to go after them twenty-some years later?"

"Could be what the team *knew*," Ashley said. "In the letters the victims say that their mission was secret. It turned out to be a bust, and many innocent people paid with their lives. Maybe it's not revenge but rather a cover-up of some kind."

Ramona smiled as she reached in her blazer inside pocket. "I like it." She pulled out a thin flip phone and began pushing numbers. "You two have given me something to work on. . . ." She broke her gaze from Ashley and spoke into the phone. "Hi,

Simon, it's Mona . . . Yes, it's a difficult one. I need you and Mac to come to Atlanta and work with me . . . Simon, don't worry, I will clear it with Bryan later. Just bring your equipment and catch the first flight you can . . . The Atlanta office, that's correct. I'm staying in the downtown Marriott, so have Glenda book you rooms. And book two extra rooms for two others who will be helping me. My room number is 326, please try and get the rooms adjoining and close by . . . I said I would clear it, did I not? Now, please, no more questions and just do what I said. Good-bye."

Ramona folded the phone. "The two extra rooms will be for you two, but right now I would like both of you to fly to Washington on the first flight available. I want you to talk to Mrs. Robert Anderson. Find out everything you can about her husband. Had he visited any of the victims' cities prior to his disappearance? Did he have contact with team members? Did he withdraw money from the bank, cash in bonds, before he disappeared? You can think of many more questions, but those are starters."

Eli shook his head. "Come on, Mona. We can call the Washington office and get that information in ten minutes. You know they've already asked her those questions and checked out her and her husband. Why are you really sending us there?"

Ramona smiled as she reached over and patted Eli's shoulder. "Eli, dear, of course I have an ulterior motive. It's obvious Don and George believe Anderson is the number one suspect. We must therefore torpedo their theory before we can move ahead on *our* theory. Once we eliminate Anderson as a possible suspect, the SAC will have to listen to what we say with an open mind. Just now he and George wouldn't even consider the possibility of having more than one person involved in the murders. Please go and see Mrs. Anderson. Eli, talk to her as a veteran to a veteran's wife. And you Ashley, talk woman-to-woman with her. I trust your impressions and judgments about what she tells you. Go on, I am going to sit here, read the victims' letters, then start work on the new theory. Simon and

Mac should be here by this afternoon to help me. Here is my cell phone number. Call me as soon as you have something."

Eli took her card and stuffed it in his shirt pocket. "Better call the travel office and tell 'em we're on the way to pick up tickets. I suspect we'll make it to Washington before nightfall. We'll rent a car and drive straight to Fairfax. We'll have something for you by late this evening."

Ramona patted his back and winked at Ashley as she walked to the door. "Please keep your eye on him for me. He has a tendency to wander into trouble when not under adult supervision."

Ashley forced a smile. "Don't worry, Dr. Valez, I won't let him out of my sight. See you tomorrow when we return."

Once in the hallway, Ashley gave her partner a side glance. "Does that batting of the eyes and that touchy stuff she does always work with you men?"

Eli thought a moment before he nodded. "To be honest, yes. Something to do with our egos or testosterone, I can't remember which. Why are you asking?"

"Just wondering."

"Agent Sutton, don't even think about it. You're not the type that can get away with it."

"What type is that, Tanner?" she snapped.

"You know."

"No, I don't know. Enlighten me."

Eli slowed his steps and faced her. "Agent Sutton, you're different. You wear your emotions for everybody to see, and your eyes won't lie. Ramona can deceive anyone and make you believe anything she says. You're not a deceiver . . . you're a 'here I am, this is what you get' type of person."

"I'm not sure, but I believe that was a compliment, Agent Tanner."

"No, it was honesty, Agent Sutton," he said and began walking down the hall again. "I like the aisle seat," he said over his shoulder. "You want the window for the flight?"

"I like the aisle, too. You take the window."

Eli stopped, reached in his pocket and took out a quarter. "Heads I get the aisle. Tails you get the aisle." He flipped the coin, caught it and slapped it on the back of his hand. He looked at it. "Two out of three?"

4:30 P.M.

The SAC was about to leave for the evening when his deputy, George Polous, knocked and entered the office holding a piece of paper. "We've got it, boss, John Elder's address. It came in a few minutes ago from the IRS."

"Where is he?"

"It took so long because he's moved twice in the past year, but now he lives in Charleston, South Carolina. I contacted the resident office there and they're sending out a team to get him covered. Our people are leaving now and should be there tonight. That's it, sir, we'll soon have both team members protected and have traps set for our killer."

Farrel grinned. "Soon the good Dr. Valez will be eating crow. I want to see her face when our people nab Robert Anderson. I still can't believe she brought up the possibility of an assassination team as a theory at the three o'clock meeting. Keep me informed, George. I want this case closed by tomorrow."

"No problem, sir," Polous said confidently.

4:36 P.M. Charleston Bay, South Carolina

John Elder steered his small craft well clear of the wake made from the big tourist boat heading for Fort Sumter. He never could figure out why the tourists visited the place; the original fort was destroyed in the first battle of the Civil War, and what the tourists saw was nothing but a scaled-down version that wasn't even close to what the old fort looked like. Dumb, he thought, they're all dumb. He put the tourists out of his mind and looked out again, searching the bay. Seeing the blue-striped bayliner laying off to port, he nodded to himself as he steered toward the small cruiser. *Yep, that's her,* The Mackeral. *Dumb sonofabitch rents it but doesn't know a damn thing about how to run her. Dumb, they're all dumb.*

A minute later Elder cut the motor and glided alongside the sleek craft. "Ahoy on board, you radioed for help?" he barked loudly.

He heard a voice from the cabin. "Yes, please come on board. The engine died and won't start."

"Dumb bastard," Elder mumbled aloud. He quickly secured a line and picked up his toolbox. He climbed up the ladder, stepped onto the deck, and immediately felt as if he'd been stabbed in the chest with a red hot fork. Pain seemed to explode, sending searing lightning bolts from his chest to the rest of his body. He staggered and fell forward, knowing he was about to meet his maker.

His facial muscles involuntarily twitched and John Elder let out a moan. He opened his eyes and saw blue sky. Afraid to move and start the pain again, he lay perfectly still. He was overjoyed that he was alive, but fearful of what had happened to him. Was it a heart attack? Did I pass out? He wondered. He felt a gentle rocking motion and remembered he'd just stepped on board the cruiser and had thought he had seen a . . . Oh God! He moved his eyes right then left and froze, seeing a man seated on the pleasure deck's cushions. The man was holding a pistol and was looking at him with eyes totally absent of emotion. Elder knew then he had not suffered a horrible nightmare or a heart attack. In the instant before the pain had overcome him, he'd seen the man and seen something coming toward him in a blur. *No! This can't be happening. Sweet Jesus, no!*

Elder blinked. An ugly brown-skinned man was still there, holding his expressionless stare on him. A Cambodian, he thought. He had to be a Cambodian. Vietnamese were slightly lighter in color and their cheekbones more prominent. *The gold chain, yes, that tells me for sure he's a Cambodian. But why here? What is he doing here and why is he trying to kill me?*

"Very good. I see you have regained consciousness."

Elder shifted his eyes toward the voice and felt hope. He saw a handsome Eurasian man with dark brown hair, approaching him and holding two cans of Coke. Thank God, he thought, they made a mistake of some kind. They were druggies and thought he was the police or something.

Elder lifted his head and was about to try and sit up when he felt a quick stab of pain again. The man with the drinks shook his head. "No, Sergeant Elder, please remain still. My colleague, Hu Nim, will only increase the voltage and give you more distress if you try to move. Please, lie still. We have much to talk about."

Tears ran down the sides of Elder's face as the tremor subsided. He looked up at the good-looking man, whom he judged to be in his mid-thirties, and stammered, "Wh-what do you wa-want?"

The man handed a Coke to the Cambodian, brought up a deck chair and sat down. He looked into Elder's eyes and said, "I want you, of course. Do you not remember me, Sergeant Elder? You taught me how to fire a rifle and arm a claymore mine. You even allowed me to browse through your *Playboy* magazines. Come now, Sergeant, surely you remember Camp 147?"

Elder's eyes widened in disbelief. "No, you're . . ."

"Dead? No, Sergeant, as you can see for yourself, I am quite the contrary. Yes, most did perish, but I and sixteen others survived. An old friend of yours is also alive. You would recognize him, I am sure. Lieutenant Quan Tram. Yes, I see you remember him. He is the one responsible for my living, Sergeant Elder. He tended my wounds, and along with the others we made our way into Vietnam to seek refuge. We found instead only more suffering. The Vietnamese hated us, you see. They cast stones at us, and drove us away like dogs from every village we came upon. The three young children with us died, and four of the badly wounded. We had to return to our country, Sergeant. It was a very long journey and we lost more of us. Only seven reached Phnom Penh. We found no hope there, Sergeant, only more suffering. It is a sad story . . . very sad, and makes my heart heavy . . . very heavy."

Trembling, Elder spoke in a whisper. "I . . . I . . . didn't know. God, I swear I didn't know. We tried to reinforce the camp. We tried, but . . ."

"Yes, I know, Sergeant," the man said, nodding. "I have heard the story many times from the others. . . . I know about Colonel Stroud and the general who made the decisions."

"Oth-Others?"

"Yes, Sergeant, I have spoken to the others on the team, but circumstances did not allow me much time for conversation. You are different, you see, I owe you a debt of gratitude. You were the one who befriended me first and you gave me my name, remember? You called me Frenchy."

Elder nodded his head slightly and closed his tearing eyes. "Why are you doing this to me?"

"My name was Jean Paul Devoe, Sergeant. My father was French, remember? I lost my name and my grandfather and grandmother. I lost my uncles and aunts and nieces and nephews. I lost my village, Sergeant, because we believed in you and the others who pledged their word of honor that you would help us. You ask 'why,' Sergeant? You know the answer. You lied to us. I have waited for well over twenty years to fulfill my solemn duty to find you. And I have done so, Sergeant. I am here to ensure justice is done. I have come to help you . . . help you regain what you lost . . . your honor."

"I . . . I am so sorry, Mr. Devoe. I have . . ."

"Yes, I'm sure you are sorry, the guilt has been a heavy burden on you. I, too, carry guilt, Sergeant." Jean Paul stood. He turned and looked out over the bay with a vacant stare. "Lieutenant Tram led myself and the seven other survivors to a small village just outside Phnom Penh. . . . It was a very difficult time, Sergeant Elder. My country was at war and food was scarce. Tram taught me English during the nights, and during the day we fished to live. Then in April 1975 the Khmer Rouge came and the butchery began. Tram and I were at the river using fish nets when it began. We could hear the screams and gunshots. Once again we had no choice but to try and escape. We traveled to the coast and boarded a fishing trawler filled with others like us, human refuse cast out by war.

"Twenty-two days, Sergeant Elder. Twenty-two days and nights we fought to stay alive on that leaking boat. Half died of starvation. Thai pirates attacked twice, killing more, and the want of water killed others. When the Hong Kong patrol boat finally found us off shore, there were only nine of us left. Hu Nim here is one of those, and I will not tell you how we survived, Sergeant. But I can tell you the guilt I carry makes eating meat impossible for me.

"We three found Hong Kong no better than the Vietnamese villages that had cast stones. The people despised us, and we despised them, Sergeant Elder. There were large camps filled with refugees. Vietnamese and Cambodian, all of us were considered as nothing but refuse. We lived on the garbage of others—it was fitting, garbage for garbage. It was Lieutenant Tram who once again saved me. He and Hu Nim found others like ourselves who were willing to fight to stay alive. Tram organized a unit, and no longer did we starve. We took what we wanted and killed who got in our way. We rose from the garbage piles called camps and moved into the slums of Chow Won District and soon were competing with the Chinese gangs for dominance. We were better prepared than they, Sergeant; we were willing to die. We knew suffering far more than they and we struck faster and harder and gave no quarter. As a result of our fighting we gained the one thing we desired most—respect. Within six months Chinese gangs worked for us, and our services were in demand in other districts. We killed, Sergeant, we killed for money and respect. It is all the Chinese understand, you see. In order to survive, we did what we had to do and we became the best."

Jean Paul sighed and broke his distant stare. "Yes, I know

guilt, Sergeant, I know it very well. But it is not for those we have killed, it is for those who died fighting along our side. Thirty-nine men, Sergeant, thirty-nine men who left their homeland as we did, suffered as we did, and struggled as we did. *Them*, I feel guilt for. Their efforts and their sacrifice gave us the victory we thought not possible. They are the reason I am here, Sergeant Elder. They have given me the opportunity to fulfill my duty."

Jean Paul sat in his chair and looked into the former sergeant's eyes. "You understand little of what I am saying, I know. But know this, Sergeant. I am employed by very powerful men. It is not a government, but rather an old organization known only to a few. I have been in your country a year, providing services that benefit their businesses. They respect my work and have allowed me to use their intelligence assets to find you and all the others. My duty is almost done, Sergeant. Myself, Tram, Hu Nim, and ten others have traveled far, and finally our work is about to end. Once my duty is complete, we will leave your country and go our separate ways to find peace and happiness. Our suffering and our guilt will finally be over."

Jean Paul took a gold chain from his shirt pocket and leaned over. "And now, Sergeant, I give you your opportunity for peace. This is my gift to you. My grandfather gave a cross to Captain Anderson before the team departed our village for the last time. He gave it to the captain to ensure a safe journey to Pleiku. This cross is for your journey.... Perhaps your God is a forgiving God."

Elder looked into Devoe's eyes. "Are you going to kill me?"

Devoe placed the chain around Elder's neck. "Come, Sergeant, it is now time for you to rise. Nim will cause you much pain should you try anything foolish. Sit up slowly. Very good. Now I want you to get on your knees."

Elder clenched his jaw and hissed, "Fuck you."

Devoe dipped his chin toward Hu Nim.

Elder closed his eyes knowing what was going to happen, but was still not prepared for the sudden jolting pain that tore through his body. Urine seeped through his work trousers and blood poured from his lower lip where he had bitten through. The pain suddenly ended and he shook uncontrollably, his eyelids involuntarily twitching as Devoe leaned over again and spoke in a whisper.

"Get on your knees, Sergeant Elder, regain your honor. I will give you peace."

Sitting on the pier, Kenny Chun held a Kool cigarette in the corner of his mouth as he tried to rewind a cassette tape that somehow had become entangled in the heads of his Walkman. He ran his fingers down the thin brown tape and soon found a break and angrily tossed the tape into the water. As he looked up he saw the bayliner approaching and slowly got to his feet, took the cigarette from his lips, and tossed it to a watery grave. Exhaling a cloud of smoke, he put his hands in the back pockets of his blue jeans and rocked up and back in his rattlesnake boots until the cruiser nestled against the tires hanging from the pylons. Hu Nim stepped onto the pier first, then his superior, Jean Paul Devoe.

Giving a slight bow, Kenny removed one hand from his back pocket and motioned to the cell phone hanging from his wide leather western belt. "Sir, second squad leader called five minutes ago and reported number eight is located in a motel in Greenville. It is a city in this state, but to the north. The squad leader says number eight was visited only a short time ago by two men who drove a vehicle with government license plates."

Devoe exchanged glances with Hu Nim and nodded. "FBI, no doubt. They have finally made the connection. We will have to leave immediately."

Kenny grinned. "Sir, I took the liberty of notifying the air crew, and they are making flight plans now. By the time I drive you to the airport, they will be ready to depart. You will be in Greenville in a little more than an hour."

Devoe smiled and patted the young man's shoulder. "The cowboy hat not only makes you taller, it makes you smarter. Good thinking, little brother. Nim will drive me to the airport.

The sergeant's craft is secured to the aft cleat. Take the cruiser upriver to a secluded inlet and burn it. Use the small craft and return here and sink it farther down the bank. Nim will return and pick you up, and then the both of you will return to the airport and fly to our home base and begin phase two. Go now, and be careful not to get your boots wet."

Kenny gave a head bow and climbed aboard the cruiser. Jean Paul took Hu Nim by the arm and walked him toward the Mazda van parked at the end of the pier. "It is almost over, my friend. Once you return to base, check on the old one for me. Ensure the doctor is doing all he can to ease his pain. Tell him of your preparations for phase two. It will please him."

Hu Nim looked at his superior with concern. "It will be different with the authorities protecting the sergeant. Let me come with you, Jean Paul."

Devoe squeezed the Cambodian's arm. "They are not prepared for us. It will not be a problem. The FBI can be no better than the Triad's dragons we took out in 'eighty-six at that restaurant, remember?"

Hu Nim kept his concerned look. "Yes, but I was with you, Jean Paul. This time you have only the men of second squad, and they are young."

Smiling, Jean Paul motioned behind him toward the departing cruiser. "They are like Chun, wanting to please. Just as we tried to please the old one when we were young. Don't worry, my friend. It will be done quickly—I will see to it. Now, please, give me your cell phone, I have a call to make to an old friend."

5:35 P.M. Manassas, Virginia

In the basement of a renovated old stone farmhouse, Robert Anderson sat on the carpeted floor in a locked, unfurnished, windowless room. With ten days growth of beard and wearing only underwear, he slowly panned the room, as he had a thousand times, looking for a way out. A single light fixture hung from the plaster ceiling, and in the far corner attached to the ceiling, a security camera whirred as it panned back and forth. Several feet away from Anderson there was a mattress and blankets on the floor, and across from him, a toilet. The walls were wood paneled, and the locked steel door had a six-inch hinged opening through which food and bottled water were passed to him three times a day. Above the door a small speaker box suddenly clicked with static. A few seconds later the dreaded, computerized voice filled the room.

"Captain Anderson, Sergeant Elder remembered me—he was the first to do so. Perhaps because it was daylight? He is at rest now, he has finally found peace . . . There is another . . . one more, Captain Anderson. I am on the way to help him now. Sergeant Walter Schwark. You called him Shark, remember? Do you remember, Captain Anderson? Yes, I'm sure that you do. I must go now . . . but I will call you when it's done. Good-bye."

Anderson stood and screamed at the speaker box, "Noooo!"

8:39 P.M. Fairfax, Virginia

Eli opened the car door and sat in the passenger seat as Ashley scooted in behind the steering wheel. He took out his cell phone and looked at his partner. Ashley nodded. "Tell her and let's get some rest."

Eli pushed the number keys and only had to wait a few seconds. "Mona, it's Eli. We just finished talking with the colonel's wife. You have a pen and paper handy? Most of the stuff we got from the agents who already checked Anderson out, but there are some things we found in talking to her that help us. Here goes. Robert Anderson had not been out of the Washington area in over six months. He made no withdrawals from any source and his bank has not processed any checks since his disappearance. His car was found the night his wife reported him missing. It was found at a 7-Eleven where his wife says he got coffee before going to work in the mornings. The wife we just talked to is his second; the first, Anderson divorced after returning from Vietnam. Agent Sutton called her in Arizona, and it seems Anderson came home from the war despondent and depressed. He transferred out of Special Forces and changed his branch from Infantry to Signal Corps.

"The first wife said he was not the man she married, and they divorced because of irreconcilable differences. The second wife, Sandy, married Anderson in 'seventy-four. They've had two children, and it appears Anderson is a conscientious, loving husband and father. The eldest daughter is married now and told the colonel and Sandy a week before his disappearance that they would soon be grandparents. Sandy showed us the crib he was making in the garage.

"I also called Anderson's closest friends at work. All three said he was the happiest they had seen him since he'd begun work at the graphics company. Not one said he had any problems they were aware of. The Washington office also gave me a copy of his phone records from the house and office. No calls had been made to any of the victims' towns or cities. Bottom line, Mona, is we found nothing to support Anderson being the killer other than that he's missing. Anything new on your end?"

Eli held the phone away from his ear so Ashley could hear. Ramona Valez's voice sounded tired. "Afraid so, Eli. The IRS gave the office John Elder's address in Charleston. The resident office there went to the residence to make contact and found his wife almost hysterical. The marina he works for had sent him out to Charleston Bay this evening to fix a rental that radioed in with engine problems. Elder never returned, and the rental cruiser was found burning in an inlet on the Cooper River about two hours ago. No bodies have been found, but the local police are still looking. I do have some good news, though. The other missing team member, Walter Schwark, and his wife, have been found. They were on their way back from Florida on Interstate 85 and stopped four hours ago at a motel in Greenville to get a night's sleep. The motel manager had read the all-points on the Schwarks and notified the office. Resident agents from Greenville responded and are staying with the couple and will accompany them back to Fayetteville."

Eli tensed as he spoke into the phone. "Mona, have you told the SAC about the possibility of the killer having help?"

"Yes, at the three o'clock meeting. As expected, they don't buy it yet, Eli. The information you've just given me will give me another chance in the morning meeting."

"Mona, you've got to try again, now. If we're right and the victims are being watched, then our killer knows about the agents being with the Schwarks."

"Oh, God, you're right. I'll call the SAC right now." There was a click. She had hung up.

Ashley looked at Eli. "Are you thinking the killer will still go after Schwark?"

Eli sank back into the seat. "He has the advantage of surprise; the agents don't know they're being watched. Yeah, I think the bastards will try; nothing has stopped them so far."

8:48 P.M. Greenville, South Carolina

Walt Schwark took a beer out of the cooler and looked at the agent sitting on the bed. "You want one?"

The agent shook his head. "I'm on duty, sir."

Sitting on the other twin bed, with her back resting on the headboard, Sally Schwark lowered the book she was reading. "Tell him, Walter. This is silly. Staying in our room with us just isn't right. How am I going to sleep? Tell him to stay with his partner next door and we'll promise to keep the door locked."

Walt took a sip of beer and hunched his shoulders. "Jesus, Sal, he's sittin' right here, tell him yourself."

The agent shifted his gaze to Sally. "Mrs. Schwark, I'm truly sorry we can't tell you more, but as I explained before, one of us must stay with you at all times."

Sally ignored the agent and kept her eyes on her husband. "Walter, I don't mind them eating dinner with us, and I don't mind one of them riding with us in the car tomorrow, but I certainly do mind them *sleeping* with us."

Walter wrinkled his brow. "Sal, this is for our own good. Relax, will ya? Order one of them pay movies if it'll make ya feel better."

"Any one I want?"

"Yeah, but none of them kung fu kickin' flicks. Ya know I can't stand that fake crap."

Sally had already picked up the remote and hit the menu button. "Oh, good, they've got old ones. I wanna see *An Affair to Remember*. It makes me cry every time I see it."

"Sal, I don't think Agent Marks here wants to hear ya sobbin'."

"It'll make me tired, Walt. I'll be able to sleep."

"Fine, watch it. I'll sit over here by Agent Marks and shoot the breeze."

"Whisper, Walter, I want to hear my show."

"Fine, I'll whisp—"

The agent's cell phone began beeping and he reached for it in his jacket pocket, but the door suddenly flew open, sending splinters of wood and pieces of door hardware flying. Marks grabbed for his pistol but was flung back with the impact of a bullet in the forehead.

Having ducked down, Walter looked up, but was pushed to the floor by a man dressed in black. Another man strode past and raised his pistol, aiming at Sally, who had her hands up, waving them in front of her face as if trying to swat invisible flies. She cried out, "No please, no, pleaeeese!"

The man squeezed the trigger and Sally seemed to jump back in the bed as blood, brain, and skull fragments splattered the wall behind her head.

Walter was jerked to his feet and pushed toward the open door, but he still managed to look over his shoulder. He saw his wife, and swung at the man to try and get to her, but he was hit in the stomach so hard he sank to his knees. Again he looked at his wife, who was still sitting up in bed, but her head was slumped forward as if she'd fallen asleep. Unable to breathe, Walter gagged, but was jerked to his feet again and shoved out the door. Unable to keep his balance, he fell forward over a hedge just past the sidewalk. He hit the pavement of the parking lot and lay in a heap trying to breathe. Finally, air came. He looked up. A man was leaning over him.

"Do you remember me, Sergeant Schwark?" Jean Paul asked.

10:02 P.M. Manassas, Virginia

Robert Anderson was awakened by static coming from the speaker. He cringed, knowing a call was coming in. A second later he heard the computer-generated voice.

"Captain Anderson, Sergeant Schwark is resting now. He is finally at peace with himself for what he did. All of your team is resting now, Captain Anderson . . . all, but you. I'm coming, Captain Anderson . . . but first there is still unfinished business, quite close to you, actually. They are different, they deserve nothing but suffering for eternity . . . and they shall have it. . . . I am sorry, I must control myself. You will be last, Captain Anderson, as it should be. Your pain will soon end . . . I will help you. Sleep well. Good night."

Anderson threw back his blanket and shot up from the mattress to scream at the speaker box, but instead stiffly staggered back a step, gasping for air. Suddenly he jerked as if he'd been slapped and clutched his left breast. His eyes bulging, he staggered back again, hitting the wall. Unable to keep his feet, he slid to his buttocks as the security camera whirred, moving right, then lower, to keep him in view. Anderson's eyes rolled back and his arms fell limply to his sides as he toppled over onto his side.

Fifteen seconds later the steel door opened and a man

walked in holding a broom in one hand and a pistol in the other. Using the broom handle, the man poked Anderson in the rib cage, then in the groin. He got no response. His finger on the trigger, he looked into Anderson's vacant eyes, then cautiously moved closer.

"Is he dead, Chin?" asked a second man who came into the room.

Chin turned his head toward the speaker, and Anderson struck then. He kicked his foot up into Chin's groin, doubling him over, and grabbed for the gun.

The man standing in the doorway snatched the pistol from his shoulder holster and flicked off the safety with his thumb all in one motion, but as he raised his arm to fire, he was knocked back by a bullet slamming into his breast.

Anderson swung the pistol and fired again, this time at the gagging man rolling on the floor. The bullet blew through Chin's left ear. He fired again, missed, stepped closer and squeezed the trigger again. Chin's head slammed against the carpet with a dull thud.

Anderson ran out the doorway into a laundry area, where he forced himself to stop and listen. The man he'd shot in the chest was on his back in the doorway, making gurgling sounds as he rolled his head side to side. Then came another noise, a door being opened. Anderson crouched and faced the basement stairs with pistol ready. Hearing footsteps on the wooden steps, he ran toward the stairway firing.

Unprepared for the sudden attack, the man on the stairs ducked without raising his pistol. It was a fatal mistake. Anderson charged up the stairs, pulling the trigger. The man groaned, pitched sideways, hit the wall, bounced back, and fell head first. Anderson barely had time to flatten himself against the banister before the body tumbled past, leaving a trail of blood.

Listen! Anderson told himself as he stood frozen, peering at the open doorway at the top of the stairs. The *cha-link* of a round being chambered in an automatic pistol told him another one was waiting. Anderson still didn't move as he listened for more sounds or movement. Not hearing any, he spun around and looked for a way out. A long rectangular window above the washer and dryer was the closest. He backed down the stairway and picked up the pistol carried by the man he'd shot on the stairs. He backed up farther and threw the pistol he held in his right hand at the window. The shattered glass hitting the washer and dryer allowed him to quickly chamber a round and flick off the safety of the newly acquired weapon. He waited, knowing the remaining man had to make a decision, come down the stairs and hope he caught the escapee attempting to climb out the widow or run outside and around the house and shoot him coming out. Footsteps on the stairs told him what decision the man had made. Anderson raised his pistol, and as soon as he saw the man's feet, he fired.

Hit in the ankle, the man screamed in agony but didn't fall. He dropped to his knee and fired as fast as he could pull the trigger. Anderson was suddenly knocked backward. It felt as if he'd been hit in the thigh with a red-hot sledgehammer. The washer kept him from falling down, and he raised his pistol and fired again. Through watering eyes he saw that the man had toppled over but his foot had caught in the banister supports. He was looking at Anderson through unseeing eyes. A small hole above his right eye explained why.

Gritting his teeth, Anderson took a step forward to test his leg. He told himself he could endure the throbbing pain. He took another step and looked down at his wound. The perfectly round bullet hole was two inches above and to the left of his kneecap on his right leg. The exit wound was ugly; it looked like a small chunk of skin and muscle had been taken out of the back of his leg by a miniature backhoe. Worried that he would bleed to death, he bent over the body at the bottom of the stairs and removed the dead man's belt. Cinching it tight, above the wound, he was about to attempt to try the stairs when he heard a muffled voice. He grabbed for the pistol he had stuck in his underpants. Before ever touching the grip, he relaxed and let his arms fall to his side. He bent over again, felt beneath the dead body and touched what he was looking for. He pulled the small handheld Motorola from the man's belt just as the voice came over the radio again.

"House One, this is base, over. . . . House One, House One, this is base, report your situation again, over."

Anderson let the radio fall out of his hands and he clenched his teeth. Grabbing the rail, he began pulling himself up the stairs.

11:10 P.M. Days Inn Motel, Fairfax, Virginia

Eli was laying in bed but couldn't sleep. Thirty minutes earlier Ramona had called with the news that Walter Schwark was dead, as were his wife and two resident agents from Greenville. Eli stared up at the darkened ceiling seething in frustration, guilt, and anger. Ramona had told him witnesses at the motel heard doors being kicked in and shots being fired. Some had looked out their windows. A salesman had said he saw a man dressed in black stooping over another man in the parking lot and suddenly there was a flash and the sound of a gun going off. That scared him, and he'd backed away from the window. An elderly widow, on her way to visit her son, said she saw the same thing, but after hearing the shot she saw the man in black join two others and run to a gray van where yet another man was waiting in the driver's seat. The van had sped away.

The phone rang, startling Eli. He picked up the handset. "Agent Tanner."

Two minutes later, dressed only in jogging shorts and T-shirt, he was in the hallway and knocking on the door of the room beside his.

Ashley opened the door wearing a sweatshirt that went down to her knees. "More bad news?"

Eli headed back to his room while speaking over his shoulder. "The Washington office says the Manassas police just informed them they arrested a man who says he's Robert

Anderson. They're taking him to a hospital in Manassas. We can be there in ten minutes."

The Manassas deputy sheriff led the way along the hospital corridor. ". . . and there he was in his underwear, sittin' on the floor of McDonald's, holdin' a pistol, waitin' for us. The night crew was scared shitless. They said he came in and told them to call 911 and get out. He surrendered his weapon as soon as we entered and started tellin' us about his kidnappin'. We called you feds immediately. The guy refused to go, sayin' he had to show us where the house was. He said it was close by, but with him bleedin' like he was, I worried he wouldn't make it. We kinda forced him into the ambulance. He fought us like a damn wildcat, yellin' somethin' about a voice and men in his team being murdered. A nutcase, if you ask me."

Eli picked up his pace and drew alongside the deputy. "The Washington office agents arrive yet?"

"Yeah, one has. He told me to meet ya at the front entrance and bring ya up. Here we are, this is where they have him. Doctors in Emergency already worked on him."

Eli held the door open for Ashley, who had been trying to keep up. As soon as Eli entered the room and saw the patient lying in bed, he knew it was indeed Anderson. His face was bearded and he'd filled out and gotten gray, but he still had the blue eyes of the young captain standing in the center of his team in the old photograph.

A tall agent standing by the bed turned. "Agent Tanner?"

Eli nodded. "Yes, that's me. This is Agent Sutton, Atlanta. Thanks for calling."

"No sweat. Brad Brewer, Washington resident office. Agent Sweeney told me he talked to you about the colonel. He said you guys in Atlanta had the lead, so I gave you a call. Colonel Anderson, here, says he will take us to the house."

Anderson winced as he sat up. "We've got to go now. I have to prove to you I'm telling the truth. You've got to find him, he's not through . . . there are others he's going to kill."

Eli approached the bed. "Who is he, Colonel?"

Anderson shook his head. "I don't know, I just heard a voice generated by a computer, but he knows everything about the team and what happened at Camp 147. Please, get me out of here and let me show you."

The tall agent raised an eyebrow toward Eli. "The colonel says he doesn't know how to tell us how to get there. Says he was unconscious when he was taken into the house and he didn't know where he was. He only remembers what route he took out of the house and the road he followed until he saw the golden arches. It's your call, Tanner; Atlanta has the lead and you're the rep in town."

"Get me a doctor to monitor him, and let's get him into a wheelchair. We're going to check out his story."

The agent smiled. "I thought you'd say that. Everything's ready to roll. I've got a tac team coming and they'll meet us at McDonald's, where the colonel says he needs to go first to get his sense of direction."

Eli looked into Anderson's eyes. "Sir, while we're moving you, tell me everything you saw and heard. Keep focused, Colonel. I know you're in pain, but keep your attention only on me and listen to my questions and think before you respond. Got it?"

Anderson kept his eyes level with Eli's. "You have to stop him."

Minutes later, in the hospital parking lot, Ashley waited until the colonel and the doctor were in the resident office van before whispering to Eli, "What in the hell are you doing? We're not the SAC's reps here in Washington—he doesn't even know we're here."

Eli opened the van's sliding door and whispered, "They don't know that. Just be quiet and take my lead."

"Tanner, we're going to get in trouble for this."

"No, Agent Sutton, *I'm* going to get in trouble. What are they going to do, send me to Columbus, Georgia? Get in."

CHAPTER 13

Ashley hopped out of the van and followed Eli and Agent Brewer to the middle of the road, where they waved the FBI vehicles and Manassas police cruisers off to the shoulders. Eli spoke impatiently, "Brad, where in the hell is your AIC?"

Brewer shook his head. "He said he'd be here. I can run the op till he does, but I don't feel comfortable with it. I've never worked with a tac team."

Eli began taking off his blazer. "I've got experience so I'll take it till your AIC shows up." He tossed his jacket to Ashley and clapped Brewer's shoulder. "I need a look-see man, and you're it. You heard the colonel describe the house, so I need you to make a drive-by and confirm it's the place. Also look to see if there's any vehicles in the drive or next to the house. Remember, the colonel said there weren't any when he left the house."

Brewer handed Eli a handheld radio. "You take this one and I'll use my partner's. We'll take his car and call you when we pass the house." Brewer immediately faded into the darkness, leaving Eli to face the agents and Manassas Police Department officers gathering next to the tac team truck.

Ashley stepped closer to Eli and whispered, "Tanner, you'd better wait for their Agent in Charge. If anything goes wrong, you'll be blamed."

Eli handed her the radio. "Hold on to this while I at least get these people briefed on what's going on." He turned and raised his voice. "Okay, people, please give me your attention. I'm

174

Special Agent Tanner and I'm assuming the duties of Agent in Charge until the AIC arrives. I know many of you have not been briefed on the situation. First let me know who I've got here. Senior people please identify yourselves and tell me how many men you have under your control."

A thin police officer stepped forward. "Agent Tanner, I'm Deputy Colson from the Manassas P.D. I have six officers here and more on the way."

A stocky man stepped forward in full tactical equipment—dark blue fatigues, Kevlar vest, shoulder harness, and tactical radio headset. "Sir, I'm Agent Yates, ops officer for the resident office tac team. The commander and four members of the team haven't arrived yet but should be here within the next twenty minutes. I have eight team members present for duty."

Eli nodded. "Okay, so far so good. I'm making the tac team's truck the command post for the time being. Let me give everybody a quick update. Colonel Anderson says the house where he was held is down this street about a hundred yards and off to the right in some woods. Agent Brewer is now making a drive-by to confirm that it is in fact the house described by the colonel. For the present we will assume it is and begin planning. As you can see, there are no other houses around. According to the city map provided me by the police, the house is about thirty yards back from the road and the only entrance is a driveway. The map also shows the Manassas Battlefield Park backs up to the back of the house. The colonel says he popped four men in the house; all were armed. He says one was carrying a handheld—"

Ashley ran up to Eli, holding the radio. "Tanner, Agent Brewer just confirmed the house, and he saw a white Jeep or Blazer parked in the drive. Brewer is on the way back."

Eli raised his hands to quiet those who began talking after hearing the report. "Okay, people, we have to move fast so loosen up and listen. The situation has just changed. There are probable suspects at the house. Deputy Colson, establish a roadblock fifty yards back down the road and another one a quarter mile on past the house. No sirens, no bubble machines. Stop all traffic. Nobody, and I mean nobody, passes your road-blocks—and that includes your men. We don't want fratricide problems. Tell your people to be suspicious of everybody. Move. Agent Yates, you will assume the duties of the tac team commander since your boss isn't here. First priority is to secure the area around the house. Do you have gators and are your men all equipped with commo and NVGs?"

"Yes, sir, we have gators and each team member has tac headsets and night vision goggles," Yates said.

"Good, send a two-man team out now to snoop and poop to the driveway and lay out a gator. Once there, the team is to report and stop any person or vehicle from trying to leave. Send another two-man team to the back of the house to keep an eye on things till the rest of us go in. Before they go, brief all your people that suspects are considered armed and extremely dangerous. Verbal warning will be given, and if not heeded, shoot to maim is authorized. I say again *is* authorized. Go and brief your people and get those two teams out now. Meet me at the C.P. with the rest of your men in five minutes."

Ashley stepped closer to see Eli's face in the darkness. "What do you think you're doing? You don't have authoriza-tion to run this operation."

Eli ignored her and walked over to the driver of the tac team truck. "You have an extra vest and tac headset?"

"Yes, sir," the young agent said.

Eli patted his shoulder. "How about getting them for me and a pair of NVGs."

"Yes, sir. Are you going in with us?"

"Yep."

"Tanner, did your hear me?"Ashley said with a glare. "You can't do this. Wait for the AIC."

Eli faced her. "Look, Sutton, the killer might be in that house. We can't sit around here and wait. I'm making the deci-sion to go in because there's nobody else here to make it. You stay with the doctor and the colonel in the van. Agent Brewer will run the C.P. and coordinate all additional support that arrives."

"At least stay and run the C.P., Tanner. Let Brewer go in with the tac team."

Eli gave her a tight smile. "I'm going in. It's what I do. Call the Atlanta office and tell them what's going on, then call Ramona and tell her about Anderson—and Sutton, relax, this is what we get paid for. Go on, get back to the van and check on the colonel and make those calls. I'll see ya when it's over."

Ashley began to speak but the driver walked up holding a vest in one hand and the other equipment Eli had requested in the other. "Sir, here's your gear."

Eli took the vest. "Thanks, get me a commo check on the tac set and turn on those NVGs for me. You guys got the high speed stuff, I see."

Ashley backed away; he was in his element and beyond reasoning. She'd seen it before. She remembered all too well her mother trying to convince her dad he should retire from the department, but he had just shrugged and told her he couldn't, he needed to be good at something and he was good at being a detective.

Ashley stopped by the van and looked over her shoulder. In the headlights of a patrol car she saw Eli pull his pistol and chamber a round. He was going in just like her father had that night in August so many years ago. Buck Sutton went into the alley with his partner that night, but neither made it out alive. It had been just a kid that killed them, seventeen years old, scared, high, and armed with an Uzi. They said he was probably a lookout. Buck Sutton never saw it coming, they'd said; he died instantly.

Ashley closed her eyes a moment. Then, turning around, she was about to open the van door when Agent Brewer stepped up beside her.

"Sutton, where's Tanner?"

"Over there putting on equipment by the tac truck. He's

going in with the tac team. Talk to him, will you? Tell him to wait for the AIC."

Brewer immediately began walking toward the truck, and said over his shoulder, "He's right, we've got to go in now."

Seated in the van, a Motorola clenched tightly in her left hand, Ashley looked at her watch and nervously shifted in her seat. The last fifteen minutes had been the worst in her life. Anticipation, worry, and wondering had her constantly shifting around to find a comfortable position.

In the backseat the doctor leaned forward. "Agent Sutton, would you mind telling me what's going on?"

Ashley looked over her shoulder and saw that Anderson was asleep. "Is he all right?"

"Yes. I had to give him a painkiller and make him sleep. Are you going to answer my question?"

Ashley shifted back around to look out the window. "Sir, we're waiting for the tactical team to take down the house. I'm holding a radio on their frequency so we'll be able to monitor their transmissions. Please sit back and take it easy. I need to listen."

"I see," the doctor said, sitting back. "A 'house take-down' . . . yes, I think I understand . . . thank you."

A voice coming over the radio in Ashley's hand startled her.

"Lead, Road team. Over."

"Road team, this is Lead. Over."

"Lead, I'm in position and covering while sniper Bravo unrolls gator. Be advised: from my position I can see the house. I see a white Chevy Blazer in front of the garage, over."

"Roger, Road. We are in position and have visual of house and vehicle. Report when Bravo has joined you and you are set, over."

"Roger, Lead. He's back with me now. Gator is out and we are set. Over."

"Good copy, Road. We are deployed and moving in. Be advised: we have spotted one suspect moving in house. I say again, one suspect in the house. Team Four has visual on one male through telescope. He is moving from one unidentified ground floor room into another. Be alert. Out."

The doctor leaned up again. "What were they saying? I don't understand."

Ashley spoke in a whisper. "The whole team is on open mike, meaning we hear everything that's said. Road team is the team sent out to block the driveway with gator—it's a strip of metal teeth that, rolled out, will puncture the tires of any vehicle. Lead is the tactical team commander, and he just said he and the team were moving in. They have spotted a male suspect in the house."

"I can't believe this is happening, Agent Sutton. I mean, I've heard of things like this, but—but this is real, isn't it?"

"Yes, Doctor, it's too real."

Less than two hundred yards away Eli pushed his night vision goggles up on his forehead as he crept toward the house less than thirty yards away. The receiver in his ear buzzed with static, then an excited voice spoke in a rush. "Lead, this is Sniper Four. Suspect is moving toward back entrance. Light is on and I see him clearly. He has a handheld radio to his ear. Wait, he just hurried to the window and is looking out as if looking for something. He's bending over again . . . out of my sight . . . wait, there he is again, he's running to the back door. Door's opened. He's running toward the Blazer. You want me to stop him, over?"

The tactical commander spun around and whispered to Eli. "How in the hell did he make us? He knows we're here."

Eli quickly spoke into the small ball in front of his lips. "This is the AIC, negative, don't shoot. All teams get down and freeze. There is another suspect somewhere outside and he knows we're here. I say again, another suspect. Road team, are you ready? Over."

"Roger, AIC, we monitored Sniper Four's transmission and yours. Gator eats all, we'll snag him. We hear vehicle being started. Suspect is turning Blazer around . . . looks like he's going to come out nose first. Vehicle is moving down drive now. Twenty yards to gator, fifteen, ten, five . . ."

From where Eli was kneeling he could barely see the speeding vehicle in the darkness, but he heard the unmistakable sound of blowing tires.

"Gator got him! Suspect has lost control of—He hit a tree! Suspect's head is on steering wheel. Mike is moving in. Wait, suspect is getting out of vehicle. *Freeze!* FBI! We are armed! Move a muscle and you're history. Mike, be careful. Get those hands up where I can see them! Higher! Go ahead Mike, I got him covered. . . . Okay, bud, up against the vehicle, spread your legs. *I said, spread 'em!* . . . Lead, we have suspect cuffed. Mike is checking vehicle. Looks like firing wire on the front passenger seat . . . Shit, it is firing wire, and a box of blasting caps. I say again, blasting caps."

Eli was about to order everyone to remain in their positions when a shot rang out. The Road team leader's voice immediately came over the ear receiver.

"Shit! Suspect is down, shot fired. Oh, God, another shot. Mike? *Mike? Agent down! Agent down!*"

Eli was on his feet, panning the wood line to his right, when he saw the muzzle flash of the second shot. A third flash and crack confirmed all he needed to know. Lowering his night goggles, he broke into a run and yelled, "Shooter fifty yards to the northeast in wood line. Teams Two and Three deploy on line. Keep your distance!"

"This is Sniper Four. I got a visual, he's running deeper into the woods. Don't have a shot."

"I need a medic! Mike is hit!"

"Road, this is Lead, I'm on the way to you. Are you hit?"

"Negative, shooter's third shot missed."

"Road, stay down, house may blow any second. AIC in foot pursuit of shooter."

"AIC, this is Lead. Where are you?"

Eli dropped to his knee beside a fallen tree. "Lead, I'm in the wood line. Break. All members freeze and listen for shooter breaking brush."

Using his night vision goggles, Eli panned the woods in front of him and saw a glow to his left. He flattened himself and yelled into the mike, "Everybody down! He's got a night vision scope!"

A shot rang out and bark flew from the fallen tree only inches from Eli's face. He whispered into the mike, "Shooter is picking up our signature from the goggles. I'm taking mine off and going to rush him. Team Two, fire and keep his head down. Team Three, let me know if he comes up to shoot. I'm moving now."

Shots rang out on Eli's left and he was in instant motion. He jumped the log and ran to a large tree ten yards to his front. Flattening himself against the trunk, he tried to relax a moment and catch his breath. Taking two deep breaths, he peeked around the tree and whispered into the mike, "I'm moving forward again."

"Wait AIC! I see him moving back—no, he can't; Team Two's fire is hitting too close around him. Keep it up, guys! Go AIC, he's down again."

Eli pushed away from the tree trunk and sprinted forward ten yards before flinging himself behind a pile of dead branches. He was about to rise when the ground shook beneath him and the forest around him was suddenly bathed in golden light. A second later a thunderous roar rolled over him like a crashing wave. He popped up and saw the shooter only six yards away behind a fallen tree. Raising his pistol, Eli yelled, "Freeze! FBI!"

The shooter swung around to fire, but Eli fired first. The shooter jerked back, letting out a groan, but still tried to lift his rifle. Eli was already on him and lowered his pistol, aiming the barrel between the man's eyes. "Drop it or you're dead! . . . Lead, this is AIC. I have the shooter. Will need medic. Don't move, asshole, just lay there and bleed awhile. Lead, any of our people hurt in the blast? Over."

"Negative, AIC, everybody here okay. Bravo Two took a round through the shoulder and is mad as hell but okay. Suspect that drove vehicle wasn't so lucky. Hit in the forehead. How's your shooter?"

"Hurtin'. Bullet shattered his collarbone. Your boys are here to take him for me. Meet you at what's left of the house. Out."

Her hand shaking, Ashley dropped the Motorola on the seat beside her and lowered her head.

Behind her the doctor leaned back in his seat and let out a long sigh. "I'll never ever think badly of the FBI again. . . . I— I had no idea it was such dangerous work. The AIC or whatever he is should get a medal. I'd like to meet him sometime—he's got bal—guts, charging that guy."

Ashley lifted her chin and took the cell phone from her pocket. "Doctor, you rode with him here. The Agent in Charge is Agent Tanner."

"No! He didn't seem the type. Are you sure?"

"Oh yeah, I'm sure and you're wrong, he's exactly the type. Damn fool." Ashley pushed the number keys knowing she would have some explaining to do to Ramona Valez. Despite her promise to the doctor, she'd made the mistake of letting Eli Tanner out of her sight. Damn fool.

6 A.M. Leesburg, Virginia

The doctor shook his head. "He has become very weak since you have been gone. He needs to be placed in a hospital immediately. I have done all I can for him, but—"

Jean Paul Devoe raised his hand, cutting him off. "Yes, I'm sure you have. I want to see him."

The doctor looked at Devoe. "You have just returned from a long trip, don't you think you should rest?"

Jean Paul motioned to the door. "I must see him."

The doctor opened the door and stepped back. "I give him only a few weeks . . . if that," he whispered.

Jean Paul stepped into the dark room and walked toward the bed. A light came on, revealing a nurse who immediately stood. "He is sleeping, Mr. Devoe, and should not be—"

"Little one, is that you?" the man in the bed said.

Jean Paul motioned the nurse to leave as he stepped up to the bed. "It is me, old friend. It is almost finished."

Quan Tram sat up and hugged Devoe to him. "I . . . I am responsible for the captain's loss. . . . I should have—" He pushed Devoe back and began coughing. He brought a cloth to his mouth and coughed again and again. The cloth was stained with blood. Jean Paul patted his mentor's shoulder. "You never have to apologize to me, old friend. It was not your fault. It was mine. I should have given our people the duty and not the Chinese. Thankfully, their technical support is competent. They have already located Anderson in the Army hospital in Fort Belvoir."

Having finally stopped coughing, Tram leaned back against the headboard and rolled his eyes. "I must plan, then. You must finish the work and—"

Jean Paul again patted the older man's shoulder. "No, my friend. We will take care of the others first. Nim reports they will both be easy to pick up. We will follow your plan and they will be yours to teach suffering."

Tram nodded and looked into Devoe's eyes. "So it is done, little one . . . you have put them all to rest. . . . I should have been with you. I should have—"

"You were with me, old friend, and all the others were with me. I made them remember us all. I waited until I saw it in their eyes. . . . Each remembered, old friend. Rest now and regain your strength. In a few hours you will have your long-awaited opportunity to teach the lying devils how to suffer. You will make them remember as I did, old friend. Rest now."

Tram grasped Devoe's hand. "I cannot die now, little one. I feel death coming but I cannot die now. You must help me finish it."

Tears welled in Jean Paul's eyes as he tried to smile. "You

will finish it in only a few hours. Close your eyes and sleep. I will wake you soon and we will finish it together."

Patting Tram's hand a last time, Jean Paul backed away and turned for the door. His mentor was coughing again, but Devoe kept walking, afraid to look back. He did not want the old one to see more of his tears.

Days Inn Motel, Fairfax

The sun had been up for an hour when Ashley opened the motel room door for Eli, who was still talking to Brewer in the hallway. ". . . yeah, I'll just take a quick shower, change, and be right out. I'll see ya in ten minutes."

Eli stepped into the room and saw Ashley standing beside a cart covered with a white tablecloth. "What's this?" he asked tiredly.

Ashley pulled off the cover. "I called ahead and had them bring these things up to your room. It's supposed to be your wind-down kit—breakfast and a beer. I asked if they had a tape player and cassette of Garth Brooks singing 'The Last Dance,' but you know room service these days. I'm sorry you won't have time to eat. . . . When I called, I didn't know about the meeting."

Eli smiled as he pulled the bottle of beer from the tub of ice. "You know, Agent Sutton, behind that ice queen facade is a very understanding lady. Thanks. Meeting or not, I'm drinkin' this beer."

Ashley slowly backed toward the door. "Better enjoy that beer, Tanner, it might be the last good thing you get for a while. I got a call while you were in the debrief. The nine o'clock meeting they called is not just another debrief for the big boys. It's going to be held at Bureau headquarters. The SAC is flying up for it, and he's not happy. As I thought, he didn't know we were here in Washington. When he did find out, it was during the takedown. Ramona says the SAC told her he would never have given you authorization to take the lead for the Atlanta office. Seems the Washington office assumed you were the SAC's rep since you were here."

Eli took a long drink then lowered the bottle. "It's not our fault they made that assumption."

"You didn't try very hard to refuse the lead, Tanner. And as I remember, you volunteered to take over as AIC. You'd better be prepared, is all I'm saying. Might drink a cup of humility before seeing the SAC. And by the way, the deputy director of the Bureau is going to be at the meeting along with the Bureau's public affairs officer. The press broke the story this morning. They've got it wrong, but they have enough that it's headlines. It's gotten big, Tanner, real big."

Eli took another sip of beer and set the bottle down. He shook his head. "I have the feeling we'll be back in Columbus by nightfall. At least we tried—we had to try."

Ashley wanted to say she was sorry, but he was walking toward the bathroom as if in a stupor. She closed the door quietly behind her.

CHAPTER 14

8:20 A.M. Leesburg, Virginia

The driver of the white 560SL Mercedes slowed as he entered the outskirts of the small community of Leesburg. Seated behind the driver in the backseat, wearing a dark gray Armani suit, thirty-six-year-old Peter Wong put aside the copy of the *Wall Street Journal* and adjusted the knot of his silk tie. Turning slightly and raising his chin, he glanced at the passenger seated beside him.

"Does the knot look straight to you?"

Donna Chu, Wong's personal assistant, lifted her eyes from the laptop computer on her knees. "It looks fine, but I would have thought a former assistant U.S. district attorney would be beyond worrying how he looked when he met these two."

Peter smiled. "Worrying is what I do best. But it's not the knot I'm worrying about. Thankfully, within a year or two such meetings won't be necessary."

Donna folded down her laptop's screen and pinned him with a searching stare. "Do you really believe we can divest ourselves of the old ways?"

Peter Wong inspected his cuffs. "I would not have taken this position if I had not believed it possible. The men we are to meet are garbage. I detest dealing with such people."

"The stories about them are true?"

He looked at her. "What have you heard?"

"Peter, I've attended the same meetings you have. The

186

elders believe me deaf and dumb and speak among themselves as if I don't exist. I hear things."

"Be very careful. What is said by the elders is—"

"I'm family, Peter, don't tell me what I already know. I have lived with it all my life. I know what your meeting is about, and I know what these men do. Just tell me if the stories about them are true. I heard they are Cambodian and years ago came to Hong Kong in an old fishing trawler filled with refugees."

Peter Wong sighed and leaned back in his seat. "It seems you have listened too well. . . . Yes, they did arrive in a trawler, but most in the craft were dead from starvation or exposure."

"And it's true that they lived in a garbage dump?"

"Yes, but only for a short time. Like most refugees who were not deported, they had to find ways to survive . . . but these two made survival an art form. They organized scum like themselves, becoming thieves and, for a price, murderers. They became so successful they began to compete with a member of the family. Of course, the family member took action to eliminate his new competitors, but found them very formidable. Unlike others who had risen from the slums, these the family member had great difficulty in eradicating. So much so that his losses did not justify the expense. An elder stepped in with the solution. Rather than fight such tenacious foes, the elder brought them into the organization."

"I have heard they are the best at what they do," Donna said.

"Quite true. They have been providing services for the organization for a number of years wherever the organization's interests require them. As you know, a year ago they arrived in the States to work for your uncle. But they were also doing independent work on the side. That work has required us to bring others in they requested . . . more men of the same low sort. They also received technical assistance from us that could jeopardize all we have done to keep our intelligence capabilities unknown to the authorities."

Donna's eyes widened. "They threaten us?"

"Not as yet," Peter said, patting her hand. "Their work is

almost complete, I believe. They requested and received information just today from us that required extensive work on the part of our intelligence network. Today in the meeting I will make it clear we can no longer take such risks."

"It bothers me, Peter, that we have need of such men. And it bothers me that you are the one who must deal with them."

Peter forced a smile of reassurance. "Do not concern yourself. I've been told the old one is quite ill and the young one just returned from his work only last night. They should want to leave as soon as possible." He glanced out the window and saw they had already passed through the town. He patted her hand again. "We are almost there. Please call the estate and let them know we are approaching; security will need to open the gate. I remind you, you must stay in the car. If you were to see these men, it would violate security."

Donna Chu removed the phone handset from the console in front of her and began pressing the keys. She looked out the window just as the driver pulled off the highway onto a tarmac driveway flanked by rolling green pastureland framed by stands of majestic hundred-year-old trees. On a hill in the distance she saw a magnificent limestone mansion that had withstood northern Virginia's weather for over two hundred years. She wondered if the current tenants appreciated the beauty and history of the estate. She would have thought their kind would prefer a more modern building with all the latest gadgets and tacky appointments. The tenants were, after all, nothing but garbagemen.

On the ground-floor veranda, Jean Paul Devoe stood at the railing looking down the grassy slope toward the Potomac River. He lowered his head and pinched the bridge of his nose as if in pain.

From his chair, fifty-six-year-old Quan Tram spoke in a rasp.

"All is ready, little one. Our squads have the targets spotted for us."

A young man stepped out onto the veranda and bowed. "Sir, Mr. Peter Wong has arrived."

Jean Paul dipped his chin. "Escort him here, please."

The young Chinese servant bowed again and quickly departed.

Tram leaned back, resting his head on a pillow. "He has come to voice concerns. It would not be wise for you to mention our unfinished business with the others."

Jean Paul nodded and turned just as Peter Wong walked through the doorway and approached with a smile. "So good to see you again, Mr. Devoe. I trust you have recovered from your travels? Mr. Tram, I'm happy to see you as well. Are you feeling better?"

Jean Paul motioned to a chair. "We can dispense with the formalities and idle chat, Peter. Neither of us regards the old customs as practical. You asked for this meeting for a reason. What is it?"

Peter sighed as he took his seat. "Very well, I will get to the point. Since their arrival in this country, my superiors have taken great pains to stay in the shadows and not be exposed to the scrutiny of the authorities. Due to recent events brought on by your activities, the FBI is on a very ambitious manhunt. We know this, of course, because we have informants in their headquarters. The fact that four of our people are dead and one is under arrest and in a hospital is also of concern to us. Our agreement to support you in your independent work was based on your assurances that there would be no complications. That the FBI is conducting a search for you *does* constitute a complication. I understand that you believe you have a duty that requires accomplishment but such dedication cannot jeopardize the Organization. My superiors ask that you cease your work and leave as soon as possible for the benefit of us all."

Jean Paul's jaw tightened as he looked into the lawyer's eyes. "Peter, please remind your superiors the reason their businesses are legitimate and profitable is because our unit assisted in eliminating their major competitors. Remind them, too, I have an uncle, a very influential uncle who lifted Tram and I from the gutters of Hong Kong and brought us into his family. Tram and I have repaid my uncle with our services, from which the Organization has greatly benefited. My uncle knew of my sorrow and always understood that one day I would take my vengeance on those who dishonored themselves. You said a minute ago it was my 'duty.' No, Peter, it is not perceived, it *is* my duty. Tell *your* superiors *my uncle* understands my duty must be accomplished. He granted me permission to find them and I *will* finish my work and you and your superiors *will* continue to assist me."

Peter pursed his lips. "In this country we would say you're playing hardball. You know as well as I do your uncle is financing our operations. We can't refuse you, but at least understand our concerns. Your business is of no concern to us, but if you dirty us in the process you will dirty your uncle as well. I suggest you think about that. You are unquestionably a loyal servant and he regards you highly, but you are *not* family, Mr. Devoe. My superiors will voice their concerns to your uncle, I can assure you. Until we receive communication from him, we will continue to help you and in fact already have by finding where your escaped soldier was taken. I only ask that you finish your business and leave as quickly as possible."

Jean Paul dipped his chin. "I will finish my work within a week. Does that satisfy you?"

Peter Wong stood. "A week is acceptable."

Jean Paul inclined his head slightly. "The servants will see you out, Peter."

Quan Tram shook his head as soon as the lawyer departed. "I cannot stomach his kind. They smell of flowers and have never toiled under the sun. He sits here telling you not to complicate matters, and yet six months ago he thought nothing of asking us to eliminate the California scientist and his staff."

Devoe walked to the rail and once again looked out at the meandering river. "His kind have been very profitable to us, old friend. We who have been loyal and have been willing to

soil our hands have achieved what we have always wanted—
the opportunity to see justice done." Jean Paul walked to Tram
and helped him to his feet. "Come, it is time for you to teach
suffering."

9:10 A.M. FBI Headquarters, Washington, D.C.

Eli sat beside Ashley at the far end of a large table filled with
agents and staff. At the opposite end sat the deputy director, in
a dark blue pinstripe suit. Short and bald, the Bureau's number
two man looked to Eli like a well-dressed Yoda, of *Star Wars*.
Of course, he didn't have the funny ears, but otherwise he was
a dead ringer. Seated to Yoda's left was Don Farrel, the Atlanta
SAC. Eli had purposely avoided Farrel by arriving just before
the meeting started. The one surprise at the table was Ramona
Valez, who had flown in with the SAC and George Polous,
alongside whom she was seated.

Eli had tuned out the agent who was briefing, but tuned in
again as he asked for the next computer-generated slide, which
was projected up to a wall screen.

". . . and this, Deputy Director, is a summary list of on-going
areas of investigation concerning the case. I point out the last
one first. The bodies found in the ruins of the farmhouse, and
the body of the suspect shot by the sniper, were all of Asian
extraction, Chinese, to be exact, as was the apprehended suspect. Although the suspect has refused to speak, evidence
found in the debris and on their persons indicate all the men are
Cantonese Chinese.

"The Blazer at the farmhouse has been identified as a Hertz
rental from the National Airport. The vehicle was rented in the
name of a firm called the Jade Sun Company. It is a small computer software company whose main headquarters is in Hong
Kong. They have two sales offices here in the United States,
one in the Washington area, in Springfield, and one in Los
Angeles. Agents have talked to the president of the Springfield

office as well as the personnel manager. Both deny having any knowledge of the suspects, the Blazer, or the credit card used for renting the vehicle."

The deputy director shifted his eyes away from the screen. "Have you identified any of the suspects?"

"No, sir. All had identification in their billfolds, driver's licenses, credit cards, etcetera, but we found them to be bogus. We ran their fingerprints, but have come up with nothing so far. All we know for sure is that they are Cantonese Chinese and most likely from Hong Kong."

Running his hand over his bald head, the deputy leaned back in his chair and looked to Farrel. "What are you making of all this, Donny?"

Farrel signaled for the agent to go to the next slide. "Sir, it looks like this all must be tied to organized crime."

"Dead Chinese from Hong Kong says to me the Chinese syndicate," Yoda said.

Farrel nodded. "Yes sir, that's our theory based on the events of last night. There is a definite connection with the farmhouse and the killing of our agents and the Schwarks in Greenville. The gray van seen leaving the Greenville motel was found abandoned on a dirt road. The van was rented in Richmond at the airport in the name of the same Chinese firm, Jade Sun. The larger boat that burned in Charleston's Cooper River was rented to the same company. Agents have interviewed the car and boat rental employees, and we've come up with three who say the individuals who filled out the rental contracts were of Asian extraction. All used Virginia car or boat licenses and all used Visa credit cards. The license numbers have been checked and were bogus, but the Visa cards were real. Issued to the Jade Sun Company.

"Sir, the big question is why the Chinese syndicate is bent on eliminating a group of men who served together in the military. We're looking into the obvious connection, drugs, but so far haven't found evidence to support the theory. And the bad news, according to Colonel Anderson—who talked to our agents last night—is that he believes there are still other targets yet unidentified that this group is going after.

"Unfortunately, the colonel was in a great deal of pain due to a gunshot wound he received during his escape. After the colonel directed agents to the house, the attending doctor gave him drugs to reduce the pain and allow him to sleep. Agents took the precaution of sending him to the Army hospital at Belvoir, but have not been able to get more information from him. Dr. Valez, the case behavioral scientist, talked to the attending doctors on the phone this morning, and they assure her the effects of the drugs will have dissipated enough for him to be lucid later this morning. Dr. Valez will be talking to the colonel, trying to ID probable targets and obtain more information on the specific group within the Chinese syndicate. In the meantime we're working full speed with your organized crime experts and hoping forensics gives us something. We'll turn something up, I'm sure of it. Nobody is that good in covering their tracks."

The deputy leaned forward in his chair. "What can I do to help you, Donny?"

"Sir, keep the press off my back. Your staff has been providing everything and all the experts we've asked for, but the press needs to be handled by *your* staff, not mine. The demands are too big for my people. It's time your people dealt with them."

"Right. I agree, we'll take that one off you. Well, I don't see any need to keep you all from your business. However, I do want to commend Agent Tanner. Is he here?"

Eli cringed as he raised his hand. "I'm Agent Tanner, sir."

The deputy smiled as he looked down the long table. "I've read the report and been briefed on last night's operation. I commend you on you taking charge of the situation and going in. I also had a chance to talk to Dr. Valez before the meeting, and she tells me it was you who first connected the victims. Excellent work, Agent Tanner, excellent." The deputy's eyes shifted to Farrel. "You must be proud of your agent, Donny."

Farrel's face turned beet red, but he managed a nod. "Yes, sir."

Keeping his smile, the deputy rose, signaling everyone to stand. He went straight to Ramona Valez, offered his arm and walked her toward the door. "Dr. Valez, how can I convince you to come to Washington and work for . . ."

Ashley leaned over and whispered, "The SAC is coming up behind you."

Eli winced and waited.

"Tanner."

Eli turned. "Yes sir?"

Farrel stepped closer and lowered his voice to a hiss. "You're the luckiest son of a bitch alive. I wanted your ass on a silver platter for taking the lead and representing my office without my authority. You managed somehow to pull it off, but don't think I'll forget. You listen to me—you pull a stunt like that again and I'll have you drawn and quartered, you understand?"

"Perfectly, sir," Eli said, standing motionless, not showing a trace of emotion.

"Good. I don't like it, but you've placed me in an awkward position. I'm stuck with you representing our office here in Washington. Ramona is staying here to interview Colonel Anderson and the suspect you apprehended. I don't have a choice in this, but I can't have her running around loose up here when she's supposed to be working for me. You're it, Tanner. You're my lead up here, and Ramona will come under you. Just remember who's really running this damn case. George thinks he is, but you damn well know it's me that's under the gun. You report everything to me first. You get Ramona on board and make sure she understands that if she tries to one-up me on this, I'll make her life miserable for the rest of her short career. If anything breaks in this case, it will come out of my office and come from me, you understand?"

"Yes, sir," Eli answered softly.

"Good. Now that that's settled, you can go on and talk to

Ramona and get her squared away on the facts of life. Agent Sutton here will be returning with me. She'll be going back to Columbus."

Eli raised an eyebrow. "Sir, Agent Sutton and I are a team. I would like her to stay and assist me."

"Don't push this, Tanner," Farrel said with a glare. "She goes back to Columbus. The office has to be manned."

"Sir, I realize that, but temporary help will do until the case is closed. I need Agent Sutton's assistance if you want Ramona watched. Agent Sutton and Ramona seem to have hit it off—Ramona might not be as likely to try and pull an end run around her."

Farrel closed his eyes a moment and shook his head in obvious frustration. "Christ! Women. Ramona is the smartest damn woman I know, but I don't trust her as far as I can throw her. Point taken, Sutton stays."

Farrel turned and shook his finger in Ashley's face. "Watch her, damnit. She's a press hound and will do anything to make herself look good. It will be an all-Ramona show if she happens to break something. She doesn't understand the team concept. Make her understand. It will be *my* office, not Ramona Valez, who breaks any good news concerning this case. You understand?"

Ashley mimicked Eli's handling of the SAC, by standing still without showing any emotion. She dipped her chin and said quietly, "Perfectly, sir."

Farrel kept a hard look on Ashley, then shifted the same look to Eli. "Go on, both of you. And remember, either of you screw up and I'll have you both reassigned to embassy duty in Greenland."

Farrel marched away and Eli wrinkled his brow at Ashley. "Do we have an embassy in Greenland?"

Ashley sank into her chair. "Whatever possessed you to tell him you needed me? I would have been happy to go back to Columbus."

"I was being honest. I do need you to watch Ramona. Come on, let's find her and get started."

Ashley pinned him with a stare. "This case has become personal to you, hasn't it? I saw it last night in your eyes."

Eli slowly lowered his head. "When I saw Robert Anderson in that hospital bed yesterday, I saw me. I had thought of him before then as that young captain in the team photo, smiling and radiating confidence. That picture of him reminded me of me in 1972. I was young and confident just like him. And like him, I was confident because I knew I had good people around me who would lay their lives on the line for me. I cared for my men more than anything in this world, Agent Sutton. That picture told me Robert Anderson cared for his team the same way I cared for my squad. When he told us about having to sit in that cell and listen to some asshole tell him the men he had loved and respected were being murdered, I knew exactly what he'd felt. So yes, it's personal, very personal. . . . Those murdered men were fellow veterans . . . brothers of mine."

Ashley picked up her briefcase and stood. "Let's find Ramona and get started."

Eli finished telling Ramona Valez he would be the lead in Washington, and she immediately headed for the door, talking over her shoulder. "Come along, you two, we have interviews of Colonel Anderson and of the suspect to conduct." In the hallway, she waited, then stepped between Eli and Ashley, taking their arms in hers, and began walking them down the hall.

"Don told you both to keep your eye on me, didn't he? That's okay. I know Donny, he's worried I'll take too much credit when we break this. He's right, of course, I will, but he deserves that because of his archaic thinking. He's a dinosaur who doesn't appreciate or understand the cyberspace revolution. To him the Internet is something you catch fish indoors with. Now, don't worry, you two. I'll be good, for your benefit. However, there are rules. First, you may have been placed in charge of me, Eli Tanner, but 'charge' doesn't mean anything more than I report to you."

"Mona, I wouldn't dare think I could possibly be in charge of you. We're a team."

"Not exactly, Eli, and that brings us to rule two. I call the plays and decide game strategy. You carry the ball when I say."

"Okay, Mona, we're *not* a team, you're the coach, trainer, and quarterback. Agent Sutton and I are waterboys, or water people, or whatever."

"Yes, that's better. Now that we understand each other, I have to ask why in hell you two are so formal with each other. It drives me nuts—'Agent Tanner' this and 'Agent Sutton' that. What is it with you two?"

"That's the way I like it," Ashley said defensively.

Ramona gave her a sidelong glance. "Okay, for now we won't worry about the formal thing. Other than that, we'll all get along just fine. Oh, one more thing. I drive."

Eli rolled his eyes. "Why did I already know that?"

Ramona elbowed him. "I'm the psychologist here, Eli. Don't conclude that I'm a control freak just because I want to drive. I admit, I do like controlling my environment, but I'm driving because I've seen you drive. Remember?"

"Is he really that bad?" Ashley asked.

Ramona lowered her chin. "You're asking tells me you haven't ever ridden with him when he's behind the wheel. Do white knuckles and cold sweats convey a message to you? Oh, here we are, we're picking up a new member of our team in this office. He should be ready to go with us."

Ramona stepped ahead of Eli, opened an office door and barked. "Charlie, you ready?"

A young, portly Asian-American immediately appeared. He was carrying a computer case. "Yes. Dr. Valez. I've been waiting for you."

Ramona took hold of the young man's arm, marched him into the hall, motioned over her shoulder, and continued walking. "Charlie, meet Agent Eli Tanner and Agent Ashley Sutton. Gang, this is Charlie Lee, the FBI's leading expert on organized crime and, more specifically, the Chinese syndicates."

Eli clapped the young man on the shoulder. "Agent Lee and I met at this morning's scene. Good to see you again, Charlie."

"Same to you, Eli. A pleasure, Agent Sutton. Dr. Valez, would you mind telling me where I'm going in such a hurry? All I got was a call from the deputy director's office saying you would be picking me up and that I was to consider myself part of your team. Please remember I have been up all night at the scene and—"

Ramona didn't slow her blistering pace. "We'll explain all that once we're in the car."

"Dr. Valez, I respect your work greatly, but I must insist you tell me where we are going. I'm not particularly fond of surprises. And could you please slow down."

Ramona winked. "Charlie, I hope you'll still respect me in the morning. . . . Hey, lighten up, will you, that was a joke. We're going to interview Colonel Robert Anderson, and you'll meet the suspect Eli apprehended last night. Happy now?"

Charlie smiled and picked up his pace.

11:06 A.M. The Greens Country Club, Silver Spring, Maryland

Retired Major General Richard Stroud placed a golf bag in the trunk of his new Cadillac then lifted his right foot up to the bumper to untie a spiked golf shoe. He heard someone walking up behind him and turned his head to see who it was.

Jean Paul Devoe smiled and extended his hand. "General Stroud, I thought it was you. How nice to see you again."

Stroud lowered his foot to the pavement and seemed confused as he shook the good-looking stranger's hand. "Eh, yes, good to see you again, too—you'll have to excuse me but I don't recall when we met."

A red van pulled in beside the Cadillac and the driver's door opened. Stroud's eyes widened as the small brown-skinned driver in western clothing and snakeskin boots stepped out of the van holding a pistol and walked around to the passenger side. Then the van's side door slid back, revealing an emaciated man dressed in a Cambodian Special Forces uniform. He, too, was holding a pistol. And it was leveled at Stroud.

Jean Paul grabbed the startled general's arm. "Please get into the van. Do it now or my mentor will shoot you in the face."

Washington, D.C.

Seated in the front passenger seat, Eli turned and looked over his shoulder at Agent Charlie Lee. ". . . so you're saying we have no informants, or inside people in their organization?"

Charlie nodded. "That's what I'm saying. You can't think of their organization as you would the mafia, or Russian mafia, or even the drug cartels. The Triad organization's leaders and first two layers of high-level workers are from just three families. I mean that in the literal sense: they are all related by blood. Granted, it is a very extended family, but nevertheless it *is* a family. Penetration is impossible. Please understand: there are many Chinese syndicates in the United States, but most are localized in the major cities—New York, Seattle, and San Francisco. Most are nothing but glorified gangs led by thugs. The Triad organization, however, is very large, very old, very powerful, and very, very smart. The principal family leaders are in Hong Kong, but over the past ten years they have expanded by using promising young family members to run their new offices. Three years ago their U.S. corporate headquarters opened here in the Washington area, at Baileys Crossroads, to be exact. All legit. At least they appear to be legit. They act like a conglomerate, much like Proctor and Gamble. Except they don't sell soap, cereal, or food. They are into importing—toys, sporting goods, electronics, and computer parts, just to name a few of their products. Computer clones are their biggest seller. They now have offices throughout the major cities in the U.S. and Canada. Last count, they were out-right owners of nineteen companies, own majority stock in seventeen more, and have major stock holdings in twenty-odd others. We are talking major bucks."

Seated beside Charlie, Ashley leaned closer to him. "You said they *appear* to be legitimate. You found something on them?"

"Yes and no. *Yes*, in that more than several of their major competitors have in the past year experienced major catastro-phes. We're talking plant and office building fires, chemical explosions, and more than their fair share of key personnel dying or having terrible accidents. In one case just six months ago, a computer scientist and his entire staff were killed by CO_2 poisoning in their lab. *No*, in that we can't link a single incident to the Triad. I have been working on them for three years, and it wasn't until last night that I finally found something solid. The bodies of the four Chinese men are our first break."

Eli canted his head. "Break? In the meeting this morning there was no mention of a break."

Charlie nodded apologetically. "Yes, but for good reason. There's a leak within Bureau headquarters. You must under-stand that we're not dealing with get-rich-quick hoods. The Triad planned its move to the States many years ago and sent many of their young family members here to the States to school. Many are now American citizens, married, and have children. They look and act like John Q. Public, but their alle-giance is to the organization first. The director is aware of this infiltration not only in the FBI, but also in almost every depart-ment of the legal and criminal justice system. I head up a secret task force that for all intents and purposes is a genealogy unit. In cooperation with the British, I have been constructing a genealogy chart of the Hong Kong families."

"And the break you're talking about has something to do with your genealogy chart?" Ashley asked.

"Yes. Although you were told that the dead suspects had not been identified, in fact they have been—four of them, anyway. One was too badly disfigured in the explosion. You see, my task force has been constructing files on every Chinese employee who works for the organization. Agents have secretly taken pictures, collected basic background information, and surreptitiously collected fingerprints. We found out early it was not as large an undertaking as we thought: the number of family members here in the States is only between fifty and fifty-five people. Most of the people who work for the organization are Caucasian. Think of their business as Honda or Toyota here in the States. You don't see Japanese selling their cars, do you? The organization works the same way. The family stays in the corporate offices and makes all the major decisions. We did find, however, that the family brings in many workers from Hong Kong to be staff assistants, secretaries, maids, cooks, gardeners, etcetera. We expanded our files to include these people. INS helps us in this regard by reporting all Chinese who come into the States on work permits. Before they will accept and grant an application, the INS requires that each applicant have a sponsor company. It has actually been very simple. We have a list of Triad's companies, and cross-reference them with those people granted work visas. Once the workers arrive, we take their pictures and add them to our book. This morning the pictures paid off. We now know for sure that four of the five men in the morgue came here to work for the organization."

Ramona grinned and patted the steering wheel. "Hey, is Charlie something or what?"

Eli nodded as he turned farther in his seat and looked at Ashley. "This explains why the killer was able to move so fast and knew so much about the team members. Their organization provided the killer with people who watched the victims. My guess is the killer would fly in, be met by a surveillance team member who brought him up to speed then drove him to where he would find the victim. The team would play lookout.

When the killer was finished, they'd take him back to the airport. The killer could have used as few as two teams, who leapfrogged each other in advance of him from one city or town to the next. It would reduce the number who knew what he was doing."

Ramona bobbed her head as she watched the road. "Bingo! Eli, I think you're right. It all fits into place now. We now know *how* the killer accomplished his murders, and all we have to figure out is who and why. Maybe the colonel can help us. Charlie, can you show the colonel the pictures of the Chinese family and workers? Maybe he can ID one of them."

Charlie tapped his computer case. "Sure, I can let the colonel scroll through them on my laptop."

"We need to talk to the colonel about other possible targets first," Eli said. "Last night he wasn't all that coherent. He barely stayed conscious long enough to give directions to the house."

Ashley lifted her briefcase and took out a stack of papers. "I brought these along with me. Maybe they'll help him remember who else was involved with Camp 147. They're color copies of the pictures the two victims from Columbus took while in Vietnam. I also have a blow-up copy of the team photograph. . . . I thought he'd probably like to have it."

Eli leaned back in his seat and shook his head. "I don't want to see it again. It's sickening that they're all dead. Maybe it's not such a good idea to give him the picture, at least not until we're done with the interview. Seeing their faces is bound to upset him."

Charlie leaned over to look at the team picture. "Who are the people kneeling in front of the team?"

"Cambodian Special Forces," Ashley said. "Eli believes Anderson's team trained them."

"Cambodian? I thought Anderson and his team were in Vietnam?" Charlie said, his face flushing.

Ramona glanced in the rearview mirror. "Charlie, didn't you read the background folder?"

Lee shook his head as he hurriedly reached for his computer. "No, I just assumed the team was in Vietnam. Damnit, I should have read the damn thing. We might have your killer right there on that photograph."

Eli spun around in his seat. "What are you talking about? What in the hell are you doing?"

Charlie had already pulled his laptop from its case and set it on his knees. "Cambodians! Damnit! Cambodians are working for the organization. I think I have a breakdown on my hard drive . . . yes, here we go. Number of Cambodians working for the organization is five. At least that's all we're aware of."

Ramona pulled the car to the side of the road and turned in her seat. "Wait a minute. Let me get this straight. I thought you said the organization brought over Chinese workers from Hong Kong? What's this about Cambodians?"

Charlie motioned to his small screen. "I was talking in general terms. One hundred and forty-three work permits have been granted to Chinese workers associated with the organization, and there have also been four Thais, six Filipinos, one Indonesian, and five Cambodians."

Ramona threw up her hands. "Great, Charlie, next time, read the damn background material and don't talk in generalities. How many Cambodians are in that picture?"

"Twelve," Ashley said.

Ramona turned back around, dropped the gearshift into drive and stomped on the accelerator. "And the only person who knows those people is Colonel Anderson. Okay, let's stay calm and figure out the best way to approach this. Charlie, do you have pictures of the five Cambodians?"

"Yes. As soon as we arrive at the hospital I'll go straight to their administrative office and use their fax. I'll have the pictures in less than five minutes."

Ramona looked at Eli with a smile. "I smell a break here."

Mount Vernon, Virginia

Sixty-three-year-old, retired, Lieutenant General Douglas Gradd took a screwdriver out of his toolbox and leaned over to unscrew the air filter on his John Deere riding mower.

His wife stepped out the back door. "There you are. I was looking for you. You have a visitor, hon."

Gradd had placed the tip of the screwdriver on the head of the screw. He glanced up at his wife. "Who is it?"

"A Mr. Sary, he's a writer from Time-Life books. He says he wants to talk to you about an article he's writing about the Vietnam War."

"Shit," Gradd said, tossing down the screwdriver. "Bring him on out here, hon. We'll talk by the pool. Bring us out some cold drinks, will you, please?" Wiping his hands on the back of his work pants, he looked once more at the mower and kicked its rear tire. "Runs like a Deere, my ass. I'm tradin' you in on a Honda."

The back door opened again and Jean Paul Devoe stepped out wearing a Redskins baseball cap and aviator sunglasses. He smiled and extended his hand as he approached. "I'm very glad you have agreed to see me, General."

As soon as Gradd took his hand, Jean Paul spoke in a soft voice as he pulled back his shirt, exposing the pistol in his belt. "You will now walk in front of me to the side gate. If you yell or try to escape, I will shoot you dead and then I will also have to kill your wife. Move, General, I have a van waiting for us in the driveway."

Gradd looked at the pistol then raised his eyes to the younger man's face. "Is this a joke of some—"

"Follow my instructions. Now." Jean Paul pulled the pistol and leveled it at Gradd's wide midsection.

The general stepped back while lifting his hands and began to turn around, but suddenly spun, swinging his left arm toward Devoe's face.

Jean Paul stepped back to avoid the wild swing, lowered the barrel slightly and squeezed the trigger.

Wide-eyed, Gradd jerked back, grabbing his side, and fell to his knees groaning in agony.

The back door flew open two seconds later and his wife hurried out. "Douglas! My God, what hap—" From the corner of her eye she saw the sudden movement just before the pistol butt struck her temple. She fell to the brick patio floor in a heap.

Gradd screamed as Jean Paul walked toward him.

Fort Belvoir, Virginia

Ramona Valez sat by Colonel Anderson's bed looking into his blue eyes. "Can you think of anyone else who might have been involved with Camp 147?"

Anderson shook his head. "As I told you before, I've done nothing else but think about it since that damn voice told me they were close to me. The only possible people he could be talking about are Major General Stroud and Lieutenant General Gradd. Stroud was the operation commander and Gradd was the regional commander. I saw Stroud at the Pentagon several times before I retired. I made it my business to avoid the sonofabitch. I knew I'd get physically sick if I had to deal with him. Worse, I'd wring his goddamn neck ... sorry. Gradd was the vice chief of staff of the Army and retired two years before I did. I read in the *Army Times* that he retired in the area and was working as a consultant for one of the Beltway bandits. Stroud retired last year and did the same thing."

Ramona nodded. "Agent Sutton is checking on their whereabouts. I'm sorry we're asking you the same questions over and over again, but having a full understanding of what we are dealing with is very important. Now I want to show you a photograph. It was taken of you and your team, and there is also a team of Cambodians in the photograph. Would you please identify as many of the Cambodians as you can."

Anderson took the photograph from her hands but looked at it only a moment before his eyes began to well up. He took several breaths and wiped the tears from his cheeks with the back of his hand before setting the picture on his lap.

"I ... I'm sorry, seeing my guys is ... I remember only a few of the Cambodians' names ... but you're wasting your time; the North Vietnamese overran the camp. I saw pictures a recon bird took two days after the attack. Bodies were strewn everywhere. They're all dead."

Ramona pressed. "Colonel, you don't know that for a fact, do you? I mean it is possible some of these men could have escaped, isn't it?"

Anderson looked up at the ceiling for a long moment before nodding. "It is possible, but very unlikely.... I understand, Doctor, that you're trying to find who murdered my men, and I want to help you, but concluding that it could have been the Cambodian team is too much. Have you looked into the families of my team ... perhaps a son or brother of one of my men?"

"Sir, we have checked that angle and nothing panned out," Eli said, stepping closer to the bed. "Believe us when we tell you we think the murders are somehow linked to a Chinese organization known as Triad. Charlie has had the pictures of the five Cambodians who work for the organization faxed to us. Please take a look at these and tell us if you recognize any of them."

Eli handed Anderson the folder. The colonel opened it and looked at the first picture for a moment before setting it down. He did the same to the second and third, but when he saw the fourth picture he closed his eyes and bent forward as if stabbed in the stomach. "It's Tram, Lieutenant Quan Tram, the team commander."

Ashley stepped into the room and walked quickly to Eli.

"We're too late. Stroud and Gradd are missing. Mrs. Gradd is being rushed to the hospital, but it looks like she's not going to make it."

Charlie stood at the door and spoke as he grabbed the knob. "I'll get a picture and APB out on Quan Tram now. We'll get him."

Robert Anderson raised his head and looked into Eli's eyes. "He's paying us back for what we did. . . . I'm next."

Eli held the colonel's gaze. "He'll be the one who's hunted now, sir. There's no way he can get to you."

Anderson shifted his eyes to the window and looked out with a distant stare. "He was my friend. I . . . I don't blame him. . . . We left him to die."

Ramona patted the colonel's arm. "Robert, your wife is in the next room waiting to see you. We're finished here for a while and will tell the doctor to let her in, if it's all right with you."

Anderson looked back at Eli, fixing him with a stare. "I don't blame him . . . I would have done the same thing."

Eli took the colonel's hand in his own. "Sir, he murdered your men and has killed three women and two agents. It's not about honor anymore; he's forgotten what the word means. If your wife or your daughter were in the way, to get to you he would kill them without a second thought. Lieutenant Tram is not the man you knew . . . he's become a beast of prey. The war has been over a long time for most people, sir, but you and I know it will never be for us—we left too many friends behind to forget. Remember *them*, sir, not the guilt. There was nothing you could do. You tried . . . you tried, the way all of us veterans did. . . . We tried. Let it go, sir."

Tears trickled down the colonel's face as he lowered his head. "You'll find him, won't you?"

Eli squeezed Anderson's hand. "Yes, sir, we will."

Anderson nodded and wiped away his tears. "Let my wife in now, please."

George Washington Parkway,
Washington, D.C.

Less than two hundred yards from the busy parkway, hidden by dense vegetation, Richard Stroud sat nude on the ground with his arms and legs around a tree. His wrists and ankles were bound and duct tape covered his mouth. Eight feet away Douglas Gradd sat tied to another tree. Sweat trickled from every pore of their bodies, and their eyes bulged as the man standing between spoke with a rasp. "I am Lieutenant Quan Tram, team leader of Team Seven, Cambodian Special Forces. My mission was to assist United States Fifth Special Forces, Team Thirty-six, in their assigned mission to arm, equip, and train the people of village Pham du Nhai, known to you both as Camp 147."

Tram's eyes teared as he stepped closer to Stroud, who tried to scream but could only make muffled, animal-like noises behind the tape.

"My men did their duty . . . and the people of Pham du Nhai did their duty . . . and they all died. You and this one behind you gave us the mission . . . but you forsook us all. Did you think I was dead? No; you didn't know who I was . . . you did not know any of us. We were just 'indigenous support,' and the people were what you called an indigenous population . . . indigenous, a word as cold as your hearts. We had names, we had families, we had hopes and dreams, and we had faith, faith in your country."

Holding two syringes, Jean Paul stepped up next to Tram. He walked to General Gradd and jabbed one of the needles in the neck muscle above the clavicle. Gradd twisted and shook his head wildly side to side, all the while screaming in muffled squeals.

Turning, Jean Paul held the second syringe and walked toward Stroud, who began to jerk and twist, trying to break the plastic ties binding his wrists and ankles.

Tram pulled a silenced pistol from his belt and chambered a

round. "The drugs we are giving you will deaden your bodies from the neck down. You will feel no pain."

Stroud thrashed, jerked, and threw his head back as the needle entered his neck muscle.

Bringing the pistol up, Tram aimed and squeezed the trigger. Gradd's right kneecap exploded, splattering the tree with blood and bone fragments.

The gray-haired general beat his head against the tree trunk as Tram spoke in a monotone. "Yes, I lied. Of course you *can* feel the pain, but it is very dull and distant. It is the way I felt when I learned Captain Anderson and his team were being ordered out of Camp 147."

Tram turned and pointed his pistol at Stroud's kneecap. "My pain increased when the enemy was spotted and I called Pleiku for help. But help did not come. You two saw to that."

Tram fired, the knee shattered. Stroud's neck elongated as he arched his back in agony.

"The pain you feel now is nothing compared to my pain when I—" Tram suddenly coughed, buckled at the waist, and coughed again, spitting up blood. He tried to straighten up but lurched forward again, heaving up more blood.

Jean Paul hurried to his side, but Tram shook his head and pushed him away. Shaking and too weak to stand, he sank to his knees and lifted his head, gasping for air. Thirty seconds passed before he finally took a normal breath. He raised his pistol again and fired. Gradd's elbow slammed against the tree, shattered at the joint. Gradd threw his head back but managed only a catlike, high-pitched whine. Turning, Tram aimed and fired again. Stroud's upper arm blew inward, leaving blood and muscle tissue on the bark.

His hand shaking, Tram lowered the pistol and shook his head. "We broke their first attack but used all our claymore mines. . . . They attacked again after pounding us with their mortars. We held again but still they came. So many of them . . . Bunker Six went first, then Four . . . I knew then . . .

Bunker Two, then One. They were inside the wire using satchel charges. There was nothing we could do . . . nothing."

The old soldier broke his distant stare and motioned to the ground in front of him. "Look, the ants are already coming for you. Soon they will be feasting on your bodies. And like me in those last minutes, there is nothing you can do but wait and pray for a quick death." Tram shook his head slowly. "But it will not come . . . no, there is only more suffering. I left my bunker prepared to fight and die as a soldier. A soldier you were responsible for training . . . a soldier you promised you would support . . . But you did not come. You left me, my men, the people, to die." Trying to lift his pistol again, Tram began coughing and fell over to his hands and knees.

Jean Paul leaned over him. "It is over, old friend. I must take you to the doctor."

Tram coughed and heaved up blood for several minutes before finally being able to sit up on his knees again. He rolled his eyes to Jean Paul and lifted his hand. "Help me to my feet, little one. Let me rest over there, in the shade."

Jean Paul placed his hands under the emaciated former lieutenant's arms and pulled him to his feet. "We must go now."

"I must remain, little one," Tram said, lifting the pistol. "I will fight my last battle here. Take me to the shade and let me rest. I want to watch them suffer as we suffered for so long."

Jean Paul shook his head. "You have many years left, the doctor said if you—"

"No, little one. This is where it ends for me. Do as I ask . . . it is over for me, and you know this is true. Leave this old, sick one to die with honor. . . . I must die with honor."

Tears trickled down Jean Paul's cheeks as he walked Tram to a nearby tree and slowly lowered him to the ground. Tram leaned against the trunk and tried to unbutton his shirt.

Seeing the motion, Jean Paul kneeled, unbuttoned his mentor's shirt, and lifted the gold chain holding the ivory Buddha. He placed the figurine between Tram's lips then stood. "I wish you a good journey, old friend."

CHAPTER 15

Holding a black Magic Marker, Ramona backed up from her work and looked at the other pieces of illustration board taped to the wall of her room. She reread the points she'd written, thought a moment, and stepped up to add another sentence to her summary chart. Finished, she took a step back and nodded. "I think that's it. You guys agree?"

Ashley put her finger to her lips and whispered, "Not so loud, you'll wake him."

Ramona made a face and lowered her voice as she glanced at Eli, who was draped, asleep, across the bed. "Sorry. I forgot."

Seated in a chair, Charlie Lee rose and stretched his arms above his head. Lowering them, he spoke quietly. "Dr. Valez, we've all had it. We've been up for over twenty-four hours. I need to take a walk to clear my head. But to answer your question, yes, you've pretty well summed up what we know so far. Having said that, you'll have to pardon me, but isn't the work you're doing now purely an academic exercise? Those retired officers are as good as dead if Tram has them, and everything indicates he does. By now Tram's picture has been seen by every law enforcement officer in the state. He will be collared within days if not hours. What's the point of this? Once Tram is collared, the case is closed."

Ramona pointed to the third chart. "The organization, Charlie, that's who's behind all this. Sure we'll get Tram, but I want those bastards, too."

Charlie shook his head tiredly as he walked toward the door, then stopped and turned. "Doctor, I can tell you from experience, we can forget trying to connect Tram to the organization. There won't be a shred of evidence to support it. Yeah, he came to this country and worked for one of their companies; so what? The organization's lawyer will say the guy was moonlighting on the side and they had no idea what he was doing. And the chance of him talking and naming names is nil. Doctor, face it—this case is over. Congratulations. Now I'm going to take that walk. See you two in an hour or so."

Ramona turned to Ashley as Charlie walked out. "You think he's right?"

Ashley lowered her head. "I think I'm tired, and yes, I think Agent Lee is right. Once Tram is found, the case will be closed."

Ramona glanced again at Eli before walking over and sitting in the chair vacated by Charlie. She nodded slowly. "Yes, I suppose you all are right. All we can do now is wait." She looked at Ashley a moment and leaned forward. "What is it with you and Eli?"

Ashley raised her chin. "What do you mean?"

"Don't give me that look. I'm a trained psychologist who happens to believe I know people. It's a defensive mechanism, isn't it? It's the reason you always call him 'Agent Tanner.' You do it to keep him at a distance. Why?"

Ashley shifted her eyes to the charts. "What's this got to do with the case, Doctor? And what business is it of yours?" She looked at Ramona with a cold, questioning stare.

Ramona raised her hand. "Whoa! All I want to know is if you have a thing for Eli. If you do, I never asked the question."

Ashley felt her temperature rising, but managed not to show any emotion as she spoke. "Are you asking me if I have romantic intentions toward Tanner?"

"Simply put, yes. I'm a big girl, Ashley, and if you say yes, I'll back off. If you don't have feelings for him, then I'm going to give it another go. The guy needs me; he just doesn't know it."

Ashley forced herself to smile. "Dr. Valez, how could you possibly think that I—"

"Good, that's what I hoped. Thanks, Ashley. Now, why don't you do me a big favor and take a walk yourself. The air will do you some good."

Shifting nervously in her seat, Ashley wanted to pretend she didn't understand the request, but knew Ramona would see through her. She put on a plastic smile again and stood. "Yes, perhaps a walk would do me some—"

A phone beeped. Both Ashley and Ramona reached for their cell phones before they realized that the beeping was coming from Eli's cell phone. He rolled over and patted the nightstand twice before finding the device. His eyes still closed, he put the phone to his ear and said thickly, "Agent Tanner." As he listened, his eyes opened, then he shot upright in bed. Still listening, he swung off the bed and grabbed for his shoulder harness on the headboard. He suddenly became animated, stomping and waving as if very upset. He shook his head and kept shaking it as he slipped his feet into his shoes. Finally he spoke. "Got it, I'll be there in fifteen minutes."

He turned and tossed the phone to the bed so he could use both hands to put on his holster, then mumbled. "Idiots! Why couldn't they have just followed procedure. Damn, damn, damn!"

Ramona asked before Ashley could, "What's wrong?"

Getting his arms through the holster harness, Eli snatched up his blazer and picked up his cell phone. "That was Brewer. Damn park police got a tip that two nude men were tied to trees just off the GW parkway. A two-man team responded and walked into the woods without backup. Now, one is dead and the other is wounded. The wounded officer managed to crawl far enough away to radio in and say he and his partner were down. He also reported that just before the shots were fired he'd seen two old men tied to trees."

Ashley's eyes widened. "The missing generals."

"And Tram," Eli said. "He must have still been there and shot the park officers. Brad said the deputy ordered me to be the scene AIC. Well, which one of you is driving?"

"Me," Ramona said, heading for the door.

Brewer started talking as soon as Eli stepped out of the car. "The area is sealed and the shooter is still located by the two generals. We've got a sniper team close enough to see them through their scopes. . . . It doesn't look good. The sniper team says the two nude men are shot to hell and slumped over. They've spotted the shooter, but only catch glimpses. He's staying down, behind a mound of dirt, and they can't get a shot."

Eli already had his jacket off, and took a vest from a tac team member. "Your boys see anybody else?"

"No, it looks clear. The river is only twenty feet behind the shooter, and it's pretty open under the trees to the north and south of him. The team says he's alone."

"Vehicles?"

"Nope. Park police have checked up and down the parkway and all the off roads."

Eli shook his head. "I don't like it, Brad. How the hell did the shooter get them here? And why is he still here?"

"I don't like it, either. Ask the shooter when you take him, is all I can tell you. The tac team commander is waiting for you."

Ten feet way, the commander was easy to identify because he had scrambled eggs on his dark blue ball cap. Beside the commander, Eli saw a familiar face from the night before. He walked toward the two men.

The ops officer nodded. "Agent Tanner, good to see you again. This is Agent Rogers, my C.O."

Eli dipped his chin. "A pleasure. How you plan on doing it?"

The C.O. smiled. "The easy way. We'll pop a gas round, let him choke awhile, and see if he comes up for air."

"I need him alive," Eli said. "Shoot to maim only if he decides to play O.K. Corral. What about the hostages? You think the gas could harm them?"

"My team says they're beyond being harmed. No sign of life in either one nor in the park officer lying close to them."

Eli took in a breath and nodded. "Okay, do it. I'll follow in look-see mode only. Just remember I want him alive."

The commander turned and barked to the twelve men dressed in full tactical gear. "Move into position. It's a go."

The gas grenade exploded with a muffled *pop* and began spewing a cloud of thick white smoke. Kneeling by a tree only thirty yards away, Eli watched as the dirty white cloud began to drift upward. Suddenly, a thin, brown-faced man wearing odd camouflage fatigues stepped out of the smoke. He held a cloth to his face in one hand and in the other a pistol he swung left and right as if looking for a target. Hidden tac team agents called to the thin man to drop his pistol, but he fired in the direction of their voices. The *crack* of a rifle round erupted and echoed through the trees. The thin man jerked backward, caught his balance, and fired his pistol again. The tac sniper fired a second time. The small man spun and fell.

Eli stood and watched as blue-clad agents rushed toward the downed man. Suddenly, he sat up holding the pistol, but the barrel was pointed upward, just under his chin. Eli took a step forward and froze, holding his breath. The man's head jerked up. Eli heard the weapon's report and closed his eyes as the man toppled over.

"It's Tram, all right." Brewer was holding a photograph as he looked down at the dead man's body. "He messed his face up but there's enough to see it's him."

Eli nodded and turned to the tac commander. "Victims confirmed?"

"Yeah, the park police officer took a round through the head. Stroud and Gradd each took one in the knee, elbow, and stomach. Gradd had an extra one in the side. They died slow. . . . It was ugly. They were covered with ants. The looker, that lady shrink, took a look and pointed out to me that neither of them had a chain or cross in their mouth. Guess they didn't rate—or your killer ran out of jewelry."

Eli looked down at his feet for a moment to give himself a chance to think. He made up his mind and lifted his head, speaking loudly so all the agents and park police officers could hear him. "Okay, people, I want this scene locked down tight, now! Nobody comes in unless I approve. Absolutely no press! Brad, get a crime scene unit in here. Nobody walks around the area where the bodies were found until the lab boys give me an okay. Those that already have been in the area will remain until their shoes are tagged and okayed by the lab boys. Agent Rogers, work with the park police and search the area for footprints and vehicle tracks within the immediate vicinity, and work outward for a hundred yards in all directions. The shooter brought the victims into this spot somehow, and I want to know the how. C.P. will be over there by that big tree. Brad, I'm going to need a support unit in here complete with gas-generated light sets, the works. Let's go, people; I want answers. Find me some."

There was rapid movement away from him as Eli stooped down by the dead Cambodian. Taking out a pen from his shirt pocket, he leaned over and placed the pen under the gold chain dangling from the man's mangled jaw. He gave the chain a light pull.

"Is it a cross?" Ashley asked from behind him.

Eli scooted over a step so she could see. "No, it's half of an encased Buddha. . . . Bullet blew part of it up into the roof of his mouth, into his brain."

Ashley took one look and turned her head. "Oh, God . . . I . . . I think I'm going to be sick."

* * *

Holding a Pepsi, Eli walked into the shade of the large tree and handed Ashley the can. "You feeling better, pard?"

Seated on the ground, Ashley accepted the cold can and lifted her eyes to him. "I'm sorry, I should have handled that better."

"Don't worry about it. It happens to everybody," Eli said as he kneeled beside her.

"Even you, Tanner?"

He looked at her to see if she was goading him, but she seemed not to be. He canted his head. "Oh yeah ... more times than I want to remember. This damn heat doesn't help either ... makes it worse."

He reached over and popped the top of her can for her. "Charlie is here, he's making a tour of the scene. He congratulated me on closing the case. I didn't know what to say. My gut says this isn't right. What do you think?"

About to take a sip of the Pepsi, Ashley lowered the can and gave him a shrug. "What does Ramona think?"

"I haven't asked her yet. I want *your* opinion, you're my partner."

Ashley looked into his eyes a moment before taking the sip. Lowering the can, she shook her head. "I don't like it, either, Tanner. Tram staying here with his victims really bothers me. It's obvious he wanted them to suffer, but his staying so long doesn't make sense to me. I can't believe a man who planned so skillfully and traveled across the country killing for revenge wouldn't make another attempt on Anderson. The job wasn't done, it doesn't fit that he would just give up and wait to be caught."

Eli smiled and patted her shoulder as he stood. "Thanks, pard. I was wondering if I was getting paranoid or something."

Ashley lifted her can as if in a toast. "Anytime, pard. And thanks for asking for my opinion. Next time I promise I won't throw up all over your crime scene."

He was about to respond, but Agent Brewer walked up. "Eli, I just got a call. Local P.D. found an abandoned red Ford van in Springfield. They ran the license tag and it's a rental from National Airport. The doors were unlocked and they opened it to take a peek. Backseats had been removed, and they found blood on the carpeting . . . and they found our victims' clothes. Yeah—before you ask, the lab guys are on their way to the van."

Eli put his arm around the agent's shoulder and walked him toward the support truck parked fifty feet away. "I love it when you bring good news. Has the search team found tracks or footprints yet?"

Ramona walked into the shade of the big tree and sat down beside Ashley. She motioned with her head toward the departing agents. "I overheard Brewer tell Eli about the red van. At least now we can start closing the scene down—this heat is killing me."

Ashley looked at her new companion and motioned to herself with the Pepsi can. "Tell me something, Dr. Valez. Do you think I'm bitchy?"

Ramona lifted an eyebrow. "The heat must be getting to you, too."

"I'm serious, Doctor. This has nothing to do with the heat. I've noticed how agents keep their distance from me. I was just wondering if you thought I might come across as being testy."

Ramona lowered her head to hide her smile. "Ashley, let me put it this way. If I can see that chip on your shoulder, so does everybody else. It sits right up there and says in neon, 'I am a female who's taking no shit from anybody.' Let me put it another way by asking you some questions that don't require an answer. Have you had a real date in the last six months? And when was the last time a male colleague opened a door for you or asked your advice on anything? The answers to those questions, I think, answer *your* question."

Ashley took another sip from her can and looked toward the support truck. "Let's suppose I am a bit sensitive. What advice would you give me?"

Ramona leaned back against the tree. "Ashley, I've found

men are stupid about a lot of things, but when it comes to a woman's back-off attitude, they can smell it the way they can smell a cold can of beer in the fridge. If you did, let's say, have an attitude problem, I'd suggest altering your outlook. It's not that hard really. You laugh at their jokes, don't interrupt them when they're bragging, and smile even though you're bored to tears when they're still bragging. I've found men accept us professional women when they respect us. . . . Of course, that takes time, but if you do your job and do more smiling and less glaring, you'll do just fine."

"You don't think that's demeaning?"

Ramona smiled. "Demeaning is sitting around talking to a bunch of women and listening to them backstab and spread gossip about other women. Men aren't as petty, at least not until they get into high positions, then it's dog eat dog. No, I don't consider it demeaning on our part, I think of it as condescending because we put up with them. We control men, Ashley. The only question is how much control we use."

Ashley put her can down. "What about Tanner, do you control him?"

"Eli? Now we're talking about a different type of man. You can't put him in a box and say that's Eli Tanner. I know, I tried—it's what I do, label people. I found I couldn't do it with Eli. I guess that's why I tried so hard to get close, to learn what he was about. Problem was, the harder I tried, the more he kept me at a distance. It's funny how that happens. You think you've found the right man and you know you can make wonderful music together, but he doesn't want to listen to you play your song. I have to tell you, I resorted to all the cheap tricks . . . but like everything else I tried, they didn't work. So the answer to your question is, no. Eli has a way about him that I can't put my finger on. I'm working on it, though, believe me. I'm going to try a whole new approach. I'm not sure what it is yet, but the direct approach probably is going to be my choice. If it hadn't been for that damn call, I'd have had my chance when he was sleeping."

Ramona stood. "Talking about sleeping! I'd better call the deputy director and remind him that most of this crew has been on their feet for almost twenty-four hours. He needs to field a new crew so we can all take a good long rest."

Ashley rose, wiping the dead leaves from the back of her cotton slacks. "Do you think the case is over, Doctor?"

Ramona motioned to Tram's body, which was being photographed. "He was too old and too thin to manhandle his victims the way they were moved about. He might have been the planner. Maybe he even pulled the trigger. But there's no way that man didn't have some serious help."

"The Triad?"

Ramona pulled her cell phone from her pocket. "I'd bet on it."

9:00 P.M. Leesburg, Virginia

Jean Paul Devoe stood on the veranda looking toward the moonlit river. When he heard the footsteps behind him, he turned to face the eleven men he'd asked to join him. All were from his country and, like him, had been refugees in Hong Kong. Each man had served in the military and been with the unit for more than five years.

Jean Paul motioned the men to sit down in the patio chairs and looked at his small audience with a somber expression. "It has been confirmed by our Chinese friends that our old friend makes his journey with the enlightened one. We all grieve for his loss but know he will be blessed by those who have made the journey before him and cried out for justice to be done. Our old friend suffers no more."

Jean Paul paused and nodded as if to himself. "You have all been with me for many years, and we have achieved great respect. But no one respects you more than I. The past weeks, you have helped me fulfill my duty and we have accomplished every task ... except one. We now must begin planning to finish the work. Unlike the others, this will be very dangerous. The authorities have Anderson protected in the Fort Belvoir hospital. His extraction will be difficult, but we have the advantage of surprise. Tonight we will all pay our respects to our old friend, then sleep. Tomorrow we begin preparing and we move to our alternate base. I am sure the authorities know of our existence, and I do not trust our Chinese hosts any longer. From now on we will be on our own—as it should be. Remember, my friends, this will be our last mission together. As I promised, once the operation is over, you may go wherever you desire, to live the rest of your lives in comfort and peace. Good night, my friends . . . and may the enlightened one bless you."

In silence the men rose, bowed, and made their exit. Their leader was alone.

Jean Paul looked once more at the river and whispered, "Farewell, old friend."

CHAPTER 16

J. W. Marriott Hotel, Washington, D.C.

Ashley rolled over in bed. Slowly opening her eyes, she saw the curtains were pulled back, allowing in the morning sun. Confused, she sat up, saw her luggage beside the bed, and remembered. At Ramona's insistence they had moved from the Fairfax Day's Inn to the plusher Marriott, taking rooms next to the doctor's. Ashley glanced around at the beautiful suite; she'd had little time the night before to appreciate her new accommodations. She had walked in, dropped her luggage, and fallen into bed. The TV was concealed in a huge armoire, the refrigerator was stocked with goodies, and they even had mints on the beds. Getting up, she caught sight of herself in a mirror. "You look like the cat just dragged you in, dear," she said aloud. "And you smell like it, too."

Twenty minutes later, after showering and changing, she felt like a new person. She left the bathroom and only took three steps into the bedroom before coming to a dead halt. The digital clock on the nightstand read 6:10. Impossible, she thought, and lifted her wrist to look at her Casio. *My God, it is six-ten. Great! I thought it was around eight. Now what do I do? Coffee! Must have coffee.*

Picking up her purse, she walked out the door. She was about to turn right and follow the long hallway when the door opened one room down and Ramona stepped out in a robe. She was holding a tray. Bending over, she set it down by the wall then stepped back into the room, closing the door.

Ashley took a step forward, thinking she might be wrong. But she could already see she wasn't. The numbers were right there, 207. Eli's room. Ramona's room was 209. On the tray Ashley saw two plates with breakfast leftovers. Taking in two deep breaths, she set her shoulders and began to walk down the hallway.

Eli was at the elevator doors when they slid back, revealing Ashley. He smiled as she stepped out. "I was just on my way down to the café to look for you. I've been looking everywhere."

Her face said, If looks could kill, he would be dead and buried.

He held up his hands. "What did I do now?"

"What do you want, Tanner?"

Eli backed up a step. Clearly, she was upset about something, or *really* had a bad case of morning-person blahs. He spoke softly, hoping that might help. "We're working in my room and we need to run some ideas by you. We've ordered up coffee."

"I'll come by in a while," she said over her shoulder.

Eli shook his head and mumbled to himself, "I give up trying to figure her out."

Minutes later Ashley marched through the open doorway of Eli's room. Ramona's charts were taped to the walls, the TV cabinet, and even the mirror. The doctor was still in her robe, writing furiously on yet another piece of illustration board. Charlie stood beside her, nodding. Eli sat in a chair facing the wall and studying the charts. He motioned to a tray holding cups and a pot of coffee. "Grab a cup and take a look at this and tell me what you think."

Ashley looked at Eli, then to Ramona, then back to Eli again. "No thanks, I've had my coffee already. How long have you all been working?"

Eli rolled his eyes and motioned to Ramona. "She woke me

at five, came over with her pad, and has been Magic-Markering up a storm ever since."

Charlie sighed and shook his head. "She called my home at four-thirty and ordered me here as if she were my drill sergeant. Would you like some breakfast, Agent Sutton? Eli and I had ours brought up a while ago. I highly recommend you eat—it appears the good doctor is on a tear and we'll be here awhile."

"I heard that," Ramona said as she looked up from her work. "You like my option, don't you?"

Eli shrugged. "I want my pard to hear what you two have come up with and see what she thinks."

Ashley sank down in her chair as far as possible and managed to say, "What are you all working on?" She felt like digging a hole and falling into it; it was clear Ramona hadn't slept with Eli.

Eli set down his cup. "We've all been told to report to the deputy at ten this morning so he can congratulate us officially for breaking the case. The trouble is, none of us think the case is over. There's still the question of the other Cambodians who helped Tram with the executions. We know the deputy is going to tell us it's only a matter of time before they're caught since we have their pictures and prints. Ramona believes there's a way to do more than wait until they're caught. She and Charlie want to give the deputy another option."

Eli motioned to the first chart on the wall. "Ramona started from the beginning with the facts to see if we might have missed something. It appears we didn't. Colonel Anderson's story fits with why Tram committed the murders. It was pure revenge. Now, the question Ramona asks on the next chart is, why did Triad assist Tram in committing the murders? We all agree Tram could not have moved so fast without Triad's help. But they're business people whose bottom line is profits . . . so why were they involved in helping Tram with the murders? Their providing help doesn't make sense unless, A: they helped Tram because something was in it for them. Or, B: the organization owed Tram for services rendered."

Eli motioned to Charlie Lee. "Charlie thinks it's option B. Tell her why, Charlie."

Lee sat on the bed looking at Ashley. "Agent Sutton, as I told you, the organization's competitors have had more than their fair share of bad luck. What if it wasn't bad luck at all? What if the accidents were in fact acts of sabotage executed by a small group of highly trained specialists?"

Ashley leaned forward in her chair. "You're saying Tram was part of a commando squad?"

Lee picked up a piece of paper from the bed. "I called my counterpart in Hong Kong last night and had him fax me everything he had on Cambodians working for the family. He sent me this. Basically it says Triad has traditionally used outsiders to do its dirty work. It's safer that way—the hired guns never see their bosses, they deal and receive their instructions only through middlemen. The last paragraph of the fax is very interesting. It says that in Hong Kong it is common knowledge that a small group of highly trained Cambodians was brought into Triad twelve years or so ago to be, in their terms, 'garbagemen.' Our term is hit men."

Ramona pulled a piece of paper from her pad and placed it on the bed. "When Charlie called me last night and read me that fax, he basically ruined any chance I had for sleeping. It got the machinery whirring in my head. Charts three, four, five, and six are just one-liners, background on Triad here in the States. Look, however at chart seven—over there, the one taped to the mirror. The Cambodians came to the U.S. one year ago. Now look at the dates of the organization's major competitor's accidents. Isn't it odd that they all occurred in the past year? None the year before and only a small fire in a computer-parts plant a year before that. To me that implies a connection. Now to chart eight, the one on the minibar. I'm assuming the organization has a dirty-tricks squad in its employ. Assume Tram was the leader. Assume now that Tram is in the U.S.

carrying out commissions for the organization and he concludes it's payback time. He uses the organization's assets and tracks down the Special Forces team, surveils them, and when he's ready, he strikes. Everything goes well—except he hadn't counted on Colonel Anderson pulling a John Wayne on him. Now Tram has problems, because we've got bodies and a suspect. All of them are Chinese, and that could link them to the organization."

Ramona picked up the chart from the bed and held it up. "Tram is dead. But what if he wasn't? What if we collared him alive and he told us who his middleman was?"

Ashley smiled. "You want the organization to think he's alive and talking to us."

Charlie nodded and took over. "Exactamundo. We have my office leak that we have Tram, that despite the reports of his death he is very much alive and talking up a storm about his sabotage work for Triad. Any one of five Chinese Americans in Bureau headquarters could be the organization's informant. We leak the info and see which one bites. Monitoring their calls is no problem, and we'll rig an ether net up to their computers and slave it to another computer to watch everything that comes up on their screens if they try using the Internet to communicate with their cutout."

Ashley pulled on her chin. "What do we get out of this? I mean, sure, Charlie, you'll find out who the informant is, but we'll be no closer to finding anything on Triad than we have now. If they're half as smart as you say they are, the informant will notify a cutout who will pass on the information to the organization through some untraceable means."

"You're right," Ramona said. "But think of the repercussions within the organization. They'll know we think they're dirty. Now I ask you a question. What would you do if you were the head of the Washington office of Triad and you knew the FBI was sniffing around?"

Ashley shrugged. "I'd get rid of all possible evidence of my organization's involvement."

"Right," Ramona said. "And who are the only people who have been doing illegal activities for the organization who aren't family?"

"The Cambodians." Ashley nodded. "I see what you're doing. You're making sure the Cambodians are no longer a threat to anyone."

Ramona nodded. "And more. We'll be putting the organization on notice they'll be watched by us from now on. We might not be able to prosecute them for what they've done in the past, but at least they'll have to think twice before using sabotage to get ahead in the marketplace. We don't win, but we don't lose, either."

Ashley canted her head. "What about the Cambodians? Will they be killed by the organization or just disappear?"

"Money can buy anything," Charlie said. "If the deputy director signs off on this option, I would bet the Cambodians will be dead within twenty-four hours. The organization will hire locals through middlemen to do their dirty work. The Cambodians may be able to get away from us, but not from Triad."

Ashley looked at Eli, who had his head lowered. "What do you think about this?"

Eli wore a pained expression. "I know it sounds like a simple solution to our problems but, personally, I don't like it. Letting Triad kill them is not justice, it's murder. You know what gang justice is like—the people Triad will hire won't worry about civilians who may get in the way. It could be a bloodbath. I'm for *not* forcing Triad into this kind of action."

Ramona rolled her eyes and stepped closer to Ashley. "I'm afraid Eli is being a bit overdramatic. The possibility of the Cambodians being run to ground around civilians is very low. Besides, the organization may feel threatened by the deaths of their men and may already have let the contract. The option we are suggesting will at least give us the informant and put Triad on notice that we're watching them."

Ashley shifted her eyes back to Eli. "Tanner, I have to agree with Ramona and Charlie on this. We're talking about the lesser of two evils. This option may eliminate the Cambodians while putting the organization on notice."

Eli stood and forced a smile. "Okay, guys, I won't disagree with your logic on this. I just wanted to make sure we all understood and accepted the down side. When we see the deputy this morning, Mona and Charlie will present their plan and I'll explain the down side of it. The decision will be left up to him. Everybody agree?"

There were no objections. "All right, then," he said. "Let's rework these charts into briefing format and get ready to see the deputy."

10:30 A.M. FBI Headquarters

The deputy strode back into his office and approached the small conference table where three people waited. He nodded at Ramona. "The director agrees that we should adopt your option." His eyes shifted to Charlie. "Agent Lee, how long will it take for the technical support people to place the taps and rig the computers?"

"Sir, it can be done while they are away from their desks for lunch. I can leak the information at two."

"Do it. Have the technical support director give me a call immediately and let's get the ball rolling. Agent Tanner, we are officially closing the Tram case. Agent Lee will now take the lead on this other matter. It is unfortunate that we are unable to bring to justice those who assisted Tram in the Triad organization, but one day they will make a mistake and Agent Lee and his people will be there watching. On behalf of the director I want to thank you and Agent Sutton for your fine work in bringing the case to a close. I will notify Don Farrel of the good news and let him release the information to the press. We will of course leave out Triad's involvement, but it should nevertheless satisfy the public that the killer was stopped. You and

Agent Sutton will receive letters of commendation from me and the director. Now I want you two to take two days off, get caught up on your sleep, and sprawl out around a pool before writing your final reports. You both deserve the time off. I'll clear it with Donny and tell him you'll both be returning for duty on Monday."

Eli stood, dipped his chin and shook the proffered hand of the deputy. "Thank you, sir."

The deputy moved to Ashley with a smile. "Good work, young lady. I'm very proud of you."

Ashley shook his hand and spoke softly, "Thank you, sir."

Charlie held out the phone handset. "Sir, I have the Technical Support Division chief on the line for you."

The deputy strode toward Charlie and spoke to Dr. Valez. "Please stay, Ramona, I want you to help Charlie on this." He took the phone and began talking.

Eli whispered to Ashley, "Let's get out of here." He waved to Charlie and Ramona and whispered again, "See you two this evening." Once in the hallway, Eli said, "You bring any suntan lotion?"

Ashley extended her hand. "I want to congratulate you, Tanner. You're a very good agent and it was a pleasure working with you."

Eli shocked her when he ignored her hand and instead put his arm around her shoulder and began walking her down the hallway. "Come on, I know this *great* chili place in Old Town that has *the* best chili this side of Texas. You're goin' to love it."

"Aren't we going to wait for Dr. Valez?"

"Naw, she's not a chili person."

"They play country western music at this chili place?"

"Of course. But it's Washington, so they also have regular food, and even have a choice between red and white wine for the highbrows that go to the place to slum. Come on pard, I need a beer and—"

"I know, listen to Garth Brooks . . . wind-down time. Okay,

Tanner, but afterward it's straight to the hotel. I have to catch up on my sleep. And yes, I did happen to bring suntan lotion."

Eli laughed as he walked her down the hall. "That's my pard, always prepared."

2:45 P.M. Kwong Ling Corporate Headquarters, Baileys Crossroads

At his desk on the top floor of the ultramodern fifteen-story office building, Peter Wong set the phone back onto its cradle and pushed the button under the lip of his desk.

Seconds later Donna Chu entered the office. He motioned her to a nearby leather chair and spoke as if very tired. "I just received approval to terminate the garbagemen's contract. The elders agree they are a liability to us."

"Are you saying what I think you're saying?"

Peter looked into her eyes. "Ms. Chu, you were placed as my assistant by your uncle so that you would understand all the facets of our business. This is the unpleasant side. Yes, it means exactly what you think it does: contract workers in our employ are to be terminated before they become an embarrassment to us. You saw the message from our insider. The FBI will be probing our affairs, and the elders feel that warrants cleaning up *all* our loose ends. I asked you in here because you need to know how I handle such matters. When you are your uncle's chief assistant, you will have to know how such arrangements are made."

"I don't like it, Peter. I never thought I would have to be involved in something like this. I thought Uncle and the elders were through with that part of the old ways."

"It's business, Donna. I don't like it, either, but the decision has been made. As regrettable as it is, some good may come of it. I believe the elders may now realize that the utilization of such contractors is not worth the risk. Perhaps you will never have to be involved in such matters again."

Peter removed a manila envelope from his top drawer. "Precautions must always be taken when working with contractors. The Leesburg Mansion house staff has kept me informed of everything the garbagemen do and say while at the house. Under my direction the staff has also surreptitiously photographed every man. I know, for instance, that the contractors are at present moving to their alternate base in Woodbridge and very soon will be conducting an operation that entails the termination of the soldier we found for them."

Peter lifted the envelope. "I will give this envelope containing the photographs and location of the alternate base to one of our trusted employees, who will then pass it on to a gentleman who has many contacts in the Washington area. He will make arrangements and subcontract to a group that has the means of terminating our garbagemen. It is expensive, Ms. Chu. The price of such work will cost one million dollars plus an additional fifty thousand for the gentleman who made the arrangements for us. The work, however, is guaranteed. Should one group be incapable of fulfilling its obligation, another will be hired by the middleman, and if they, too, are unsuccessful, another will be employed until the work is complete. In matters such as this we demand complete satisfaction."

Donna nodded. "I understand. How long will it take for the work to be done?"

"Within twenty-four hours. It is important that the garbagemen be eliminated as quickly as possible. I authorized a higher payment for a speedy termination because in the past year the garbagemen requested and received a large quantity of weapons and destructive materials that were necessary for their work for us."

Donna shifted nervously in her seat. "What happens if they find out we have a contract out on them?"

Peter sighed and leaned back in his chair. "They would separate and flee the country, making the termination very difficult. Upon his arrival a year ago, Devoe insisted we provide each of his men three separate identities, complete with supporting documentation, including passports. So it is imperative they be eradicated while they are all still in their nest."

Donna slowly stood and slightly bowed her head. "Excuse me, Peter, but I am feeling ill. I will leave you to your work." Turning, she walked out of the office, shutting the door behind her.

His own stomach rumbling, Peter picked up the phone and began pushing the number keys, knowing he was sealing the fate of twelve men.

3:45 P.M. J. W. Marriott Hotel, Washington, D.C.

Unable to rest, Ashley got up from bed, put on her bathing suit and a robe, and left the room. Minutes later she walked through the doorway into the indoor pool area. Setting down her athletic bag and taking off her robe, she approached the deep end of the pool and dove in. Fifteen laps later she grabbed hold of the ladder and tiredly climbed out of the pool, hoping she would be able to sleep. Walking toward her things, she suddenly stopped. Just beyond the open glass doors Eli lay on a lounge chair on the outside sun deck. He raised his sunglasses and smiled.

"I give you a seven for style on the dive, but the difficulty factor was only point five. You shoulda done a can opener or a cannonball for more points."

Embarrassed at being caught in her practically invisible bathing suit, she continued toward her things. After putting on her robe and picking up her bag, she took in a breath, gathering her strength, and strode toward him.

Eli motioned to the lounge chair beside him and tossed her a towel. "Couldn't sleep, huh?"

She shook her head as she sat down. "Your *great* chili gave me heartburn. I see you couldn't sleep, either."

"I almost was, but Charlie called . . . the news wasn't good.

The taps didn't work. Seems one of the probables used a coworker's computer when he was away from his desk. Charlie suspects the probable sent the message through the Internet e-mail system but he can't prove it. Problem is, they can't prove the agent did anything wrong. She was on-line for only five minutes. She said she only accessed information on new cars. She said it was for a case she was working on—she had copies of the stuff she had printed up."

Ashley exhaled through her nose and leaned back in the chair. "Lie detector will get her. She can't refuse taking one."

"You're right, but Charlie said she told them to cram it. She resigned. They can't touch her."

"She's gone, Tanner, that's what counts. The organization lost their informer so we win even though she wasn't prosecuted."

Eli wrinkled his brow. "I wouldn't call it a win. I'd call it a draw. The Cambodians are the ones who lost. . . . Charlie told me the Jamaican dirty boys in town will probably get the contract. They're the ones the wise guys and druggies hire when they need a quick but efficient hit in the Washington area."

Sitting up, Ashley took a pair of sunglasses and a bottle of suntan lotion from her bag. She tossed the bottle over and it landed on his stomach. "All of this makes me glad we'll be back in Columbus on Monday. I am beginning to think dull is good."

Eli set the bottle of lotion aside and closed his eyes. "I learned that a long time ago."

Her eyes hidden by the dark glasses, she looked at the scar on his neck muscle just above the clavicle. He had a much bigger one on his right breast and almost an identical one four inches below that. She sat up again and picked up the bottle of lotion he'd set on the pavement between them.

"You'd better put some of this on those scars. They're getting awfully pink."

He didn't move. "It's all right, I'm going back to my room in a few minutes anyway; I need a good nap. Ramona is taking us out to dinner tonight to celebrate our closing the case.

Afterward I thought I'd go and visit with Colonel Anderson awhile and tell him what happened. Once he gets out of the hospital, he can get on with his life . . . I hope."

Ashley stole another long look at him and couldn't take it anymore. "Tanner, do you know Dr. Valez likes you quite a lot?"

Eli rolled his head toward her. "You've been around Millie too long, Agent Sutton. Mona likes all men . . . she likes manipulating us. We let her do it because she's nice to look at while she's doing it."

"No, Tanner, I mean it. She likes you."

Eli sighed and rolled his head back, facing the sun. "Give it a rest. I'm not interested. Mona isn't my type. I would always feel like I was one of her experiments and she was secretly trying to change my behavior or something."

"So, Tanner, you're saying you're a 'here I am, this is what you get guy,' huh?"

"Yep, Agent Sutton, that's it. I'm too old to change, and to tell you the truth, I don't want to. I'm getting it together again, and me suits me just fine . . . even my gut says so."

"Well, if Mr. Gut is involved I'm sure it's okay, then. If you don't mind, I want to go with you tonight when you visit the colonel. I'd like to talk to his wife. She's been through a lot and would probably like some assurances everything is going to be all right."

Eli smiled but didn't look at her. "I was going to ask you to drive anyway, *partner*."

"Nice to know I'm good for something, Tanner," Ashley snapped. Secretly, she was glad he was playing the game again. Leaning back in her chair, she decided it was time to change the rules a little. "Tanner, in the hotel in Columbus I told you I thought using our first names was unprofessional. . . . I was wrong. You are one of the most professional agents I've ever met. If it's all right with you I'd like to—"

Eli held up his hand as he rose up from his chair. "No, Agent Sutton. You weren't wrong. We should keep things just the way they are. We're going to meet Ramona and Charlie at seven in the lobby, so I'll knock on your door at about ten to. You'd better use that lotion on yourself. You've got an awful lot of skin to protect in that little suit of yours. See ya."

Eli picked up his bag and headed for the doorway. Ashley Sutton looked better than good in her bathing suit, and he couldn't take another second being around her without saying or doing something stupid. The ice queen was obviously melting, and he wasn't sure if he could handle the thawed-out version.

Woodbridge, Virginia

Jean Paul stepped into the living room where his men were seated. He lowered his head a moment as if in thought before looking into their expectant faces. "My friends, Nim informs me we were followed here by one of the house servants from the mansion. I believe it is now obvious our Chinese hosts believe us to be expendable. Each of you is family to me, so I cannot ask any of you to remain with me to finish my duty. You have done enough for me over the years, and I want each of you to have an opportunity to find happiness. The old one and I planned for this day, knowing it would eventually come. I am going to step outside for several minutes. Those who wish to leave, please do so with my blessing. Nim will provide you the documents and account numbers in each of your names so that you live the rest of your lives in comfort. To those who choose to remain, I promise only extreme danger and little chance of living long in this world. I leave you now to make your decision."

Jean Paul walked out on the front porch and stood for only a minute when Nim stepped out and joined him. "Jean Paul, none will leave you. The monks taught us life is suffering, and we shall all suffer together. If the Chinese want a war, so be it. Come and lead us."

Jean Paul wiped a single tear from his cheek and strode back into the house. He looked into each man's face and nodded. "The Chinese family is strong, but this family is stronger. The men who will come after us will be very good, but we are better. This night I will accomplish my duty with the first squad and half of the third squad. Nim and his second squad will teach the Chinese a lesson in humility, and the rest of the third squad will teach the assassins who come for us we are a family to reckon with. My plan for finishing Anderson remains the same, and the rendezvous point will now become our alternate base. Sary, take your squad and proceed with preparations. Be ready to leave within the hour for our staging location. Nim, I have a folder in my briefcase with a plan for our Chinese hosts. Get the folder and we will discuss it once the meeting is over. Penn, you and your squad will load the weapons and equipment in the truck to be taken to our new base, then begin planning for your reception of our visitors tonight. That is all for now, my friends. You must pack quickly and be ready to leave within two hours. Tonight will be an evening our enemies will never forget."

CHAPTER 17

10:30 P.M. Vienna, Virginia

Peter Wong turned off the television with his remote and collected his shoes from beneath the coffee table. His wife, Mey, walked toward the stairs leading up to their bedroom and spoke over her shoulder. "Don't forget to check the doors, Peter."

"Yes, dear." He made a detour into the kitchen to check the sliding glass door that led to the backyard and pool. He turned on the kitchen light and froze. Something hard pressed against his temple.

Hu Nim cocked back the hammer of his silenced pistol and smiled. "Mr. Wong, you underestimated us. Please yell up to your wife and say you forgot important documents at your office and you must go. I suggest you sound very convincing or my men will have to kill her."

Fort Belvoir, Virginia

Ashley turned off the rental car ignition and glanced at her passenger. "Are you sure he's going to be awake?"

Eli opened the car door and got out. He waited until she was out of the car and then patted the cell phone in his blazer pocket. "I called the hospital when you and Ramona were in the powder room. He said come on over. His wife is staying

237

with him in the room, and they're both late night people." He smiled and patted his other bulging pocket. "I brought him a present."

Ashley rolled her eyes and stepped up beside him. "You can't take liquor into a hospital, Tanner."

"Watch me, Agent Sutton. But I would feel better if you'd put these three cans of beer into your purse."

She shook her head and started walking toward the hospital's front entrance. "Forget it, Tanner. Rules are rules, and I don't have room, anyway. My weapon takes up all my beer can room."

He quickly caught up and nudged her shoulder with his. "Nice night, Agent Sutton. You ever see so many stars?"

She slowed her steps and looked up at the sparkling heavens. "It is nice . . . it was a good dinner, too. I don't think Ramona was too happy with you when you told her we had to go. I think she had plans of her own for you."

Eli shrugged and began walking again. "I like *my* plan better. I figure when we're finished here we can go over to the waterfront and watch the boats go by on the river at this neat little bar I know."

"It's a country western bar, isn't it, Tanner?"

"Kinda, but the beer is too expensive for it to really be considered what you call a real C and W place. It's just nice, and we can do a little winding down and do some comparing of notes before we have to write those reports tomorrow."

"I didn't bring any notes, Tanner."

Eli shrugged again. "I didn't, either, but it's still a better plan than just letting this night go by unappreciated. I guess I'm saying I would like your company, Agent Sutton. I happen to like your company, and I thought it might be nice for us to do our own celebrating . . . a partner thing."

Ashley slowed her steps again and looked at him with a smile. "I accept your offer, Agent Tanner. . . . I guess I have to drive us there, huh?"

Eli opened the front glass door and patted her back as she stepped through the doorway. "Of course."

Inside, they followed the signs and within seconds were standing in front of elevator doors. Eli shivered as he pressed the Up button. "I don't like these places. I spent more time in an Army hospital than I care to remember. It has its own smell, doesn't it? Smells like an Army hospital."

Ashley looked around and shrugged. "Looks pretty modern to me. I don't smell anything unusual."

The doors opened and they stepped in. Eli pushed the button for the fifth floor and leaned against the wall. "I can smell clean starched sheets and disinfectant."

Ashley was going to make fun of him until she saw the beads of perspiration on his forehead. She took his hand and gave it a gentle squeeze. "Thanks for asking me to share the stars with you this evening, Tanner. I happen to like your company, too."

Before Eli could respond, the elevator stopped and the doors opened. He let her hand go but patted her shoulder. "Hold that thought and we'll discuss it when we leave." They entered the dimly lit hallway. Across from them at the nurse's station stood a young female captain nurse updating a patient's file. A tall black MP sergeant was beside her. The soldier held up his hand. "Sorry, folks, but visiting hours are over," he said politely.

Eli motioned to himself. "I'm Special Agent Tanner, FBI, and this is Special Agent Sutton. We're here to talk to Colonel Anderson. He's expecting us."

The MP sergeant nodded. "I will need to see your IDs, please."

Eli got his out first, and the MP motioned to Ashley to stop looking in her purse. "That's all right, ma'am. The colonel's room is just two doors down and on the left."

Eli glanced in that direction and looked back at the black officer. "Are you his only security?"

They sergeant nodded again. "Yes, sir. There was an FBI

agent who stayed outside the door, but he left this afternoon saying the threat had been downgraded. We still have orders to watch him, though, until he's discharged. Is there a problem, sir?"

Eli gave the young soldier a smile. "No, I just wasn't aware they had already pulled our people, Sergeant. Thank you."

Seconds later Eli knocked on the door and stepped into the room. He was pleasantly surprised to see Anderson smiling and sitting up in bed with a bag of Chee•tos at his side. Sandy Anderson, too, smiled. She got up from a reclining chair and pushed the remote, turning off the television. Anderson extended his hand with a grin. "Agent Tanner, good to see you. I hear you're a fellow vet."

Eli stepped up and took his hand. "How did ya find out about that, sir?"

"The agent that was watching over me told me. He was quite a fan of yours. I didn't realize you were a pro when I met you the other day. I'm sorry. Hello, Agent Sutton, it's good to see you again, too. I'm afraid you caught Sandy and me watching 'Saturday Night Live' like a bunch of kids. I love these damn Chee•tos, and Sandy snuck them in for me."

Eli took a can of beer from his jacket pocket and held it out. "I thought maybe you'd like one, sir. It goes great with Chee•tos."

Anderson grinned again as he took the can. "You are a true vet, indeed! Thanks. I've been dreaming about a beer for weeks."

Eli took another one out from his inside jacket pocket and offered it to Sandy, who smiled and shook her head. "No thank you, I'll let him splurge tonight—he can have mine. Thank you, though. I think Agent Sutton and I will visit the coffee machine and let you two have a chance to talk a few minutes."

She took Ashley's arm and looked over her shoulder at her husband. "Hon, wipe your lips, they're orange."

As soon as the women stepped out and closed the door,

Anderson's smile dissolved and he pinned Eli with a stare. "You got him, didn't you?"

Eli nodded. "Yes, sir, we did. Actually, he killed himself when we were moving in on him, but he's no longer a threat to you."

Lowering his head, the retired colonel popped the top of his beer and stared at the can. "He was a good soldier, Agent Tanner . . . a damn good soldier. But so were my men . . . I guess he did what he thought he had to do."

Eli took the third can from his pocket and pulled back the tab. "Yes, sir, and he came awful close to making Sandy a widow. Remember that."

Only thirty yards from the two men, in the fire stairwell, Jean Paul Devoe raised his arm and looked at his wristwatch. "Two minutes," he said.

Standing beside him, Kheck Ly chambered a round in his 9mm pistol and looked through the small door window. "Roun and Tralay will take out the guard for you when they step out of the elevator, then it will be safe for you to enter the hallway. Anderson's room is number 514 on your right. I will follow fifteen paces to your rear to protect your back."

Wearing hospital pajamas and a robe, Jean Paul chambered a round into his Italian .22 and put it in the waistband of his pants. He reached up, patted the gold chain in the breast pocket of his robe and smiled. "You have done well, my friend. As always. Your reconnaissance of the hospital and of the target is commendable." He raised his wrist again and looked at his watch. "One minute."

Just ten steps from the fire exit doorway, in a vending machine canteen, Ashley set her coffee cup down on a table and made a face. "This stuff is terrible."

Sandy Anderson smiled. "You get used to it." She took a sip of her coffee and lowered her cup. "So you really think it's all over, Ashley? I miss my home and miss our lives."

Ashley nodded and patted the woman's shoulder. "It's all over, Sandy. Once your husband is released, he can finish that cradle and you can start thinking about how wonderful it will be to be called Grandmother."

"Oh God, don't remind me. That's one thing I'm not ready for. . . . That's not true, I really am. Bob is the one who is having a hard time accepting the fact he's going to be a grandfather . . . maybe not now, though."

Ashley began to respond but heard the elevator doors open down the hall. She didn't think anything of it but then heard a faint coughing sound followed by another, only slightly louder. She stepped toward the doorway and froze. To her right a very good-looking, small man stepped out of a fire exit doorway. She immediately stepped back and reached for the pistol in her purse, then turned to Sandy, putting her finger to her lips. It was the heavy gold chain around the handsome man's neck that worried her, and she told herself she wasn't going to take any chances. Motioning Sandy to get against the wall, she did the same and waited for him to pass the open doorway. A second passed, then another, and finally she saw him. She tried to move but couldn't. She took in a breath and suddenly stepped out and barked. "Freeze! FBI!" She glanced quickly down the long hallway and saw two men on both sides of the colonel's room door pressed against the wall, and just behind them she saw the form of the young black sergeant on the floor. She screamed, *"Eli, watch out! Men at the door!"*

One of the men stepped away from the wall and she saw a flash. Something zipped by her ear. She crouched, stepped back and yelled at the good-looking man. "Lay on the floor and don't move!"

Behind her, Ashley could hear Sandy sobbing. "Oh God, this isn't happening. This isn't happening."

Hearing Ashley's scream, Eli had pulled his pistol and chambered a round. He stood against the wall next to the door and heard a spitting sound. Backing up, he fired into the wall where he thought he heard the sound and grabbed the doorknob. He took in a breath, pulled back the door and fired to his right at a moving figure. Spinning, he was shocked to see a man's face only inches from his pistol barrel. The man's eyes widened and he brought his hand up, holding a gun. Eli fired. The back of the man's head exploded and showered the side of the wall and hallway with blood and brain matter. Spinning back to his left, Eli saw the other man was down, rolling on the floor and firing his pistol wildly, as if blinded. Eli raised his pistol, but a bullet slammed into the room's doorjamb and was followed by a thunderous cracking sound that echoed down the hallway. He ducked back inside the room knowing the bullet and gunshot had not come from the wounded man.

Two steps back inside the canteen, Ashley heard the booming report, too, and glanced to her right, where she'd heard the shot. She winced at seeing a small man running toward her with a pistol pointed at her face. She ducked just as she heard another report, and felt the air of the bullet pass by her ear and slam into the Coke machine behind her. Dropping to a knee, she began to fire, but it was too late, the man was already on her. Suddenly she felt as if she'd been hit in the head with a ball bat; everything became blurry and she was falling.

A fire alarm at the end of the hall began clanging as Jean Paul quickly rose up from the floor and pulled his pistol. He hurried into the canteen and joined Kheck Ly, who was peering around the door with his pistol ready. The woman lying at Ly's feet was rolling her head back and forth. Blood oozed from a wound in her forehead where Ly had slugged her with his 9mm Sig Sauer.

Jean Paul glanced at the other woman, sitting against the wall holding her hands against her ears, screaming hysterically. A shot rang out and Ly ducked back. He looked at Jean Paul and yelled to be heard over the clanging and screaming of the woman. "Roun and Tralay are dead! We must leave now before we're trapped."

Jean Paul's jaw muscles rippled in frustration and anger, but he knew he had to think of the others. He nodded, motioned to the bleeding woman at Ly's feet and yelled, "Use her as a shield. I'll take the other one!"

In Anderson's room, Eli was on his stomach. He quickly peeked down the hallway and ducked back. Behind him he could hear the colonel on the phone yelling, ". . . shots fired and at least one dead that I can see! Goddamnit, hurry!"

Eli readied his pistol and peeked again, but jerked back as bullets tore into the floor and ricocheted down the hall. He peeked again and, seeing movement, was about to pull the trigger, but jerked back and lowered his weapon. "Shitshit, shit! They've got the women! Colonel, tell them to seal all the post exits and that the shooters have two women as hostages!"

Eli stood, peeked around the corner of the doorjamb, then broke into a dead run down the hall, toward where he'd seen the fire door close.

Baileys Crossroads

The two guards at the front desk rose when the executive elevator opened and five men stepped out, led by Peter Wong. Peter smiled and motioned to the other men all carrying large athletic bags. "These gentlemen are with me. We'll be working on the twelfth floor, installing new equipment."

The shorter guard took a seat behind a computer. "Names, please?"

Hu Nim brought his hand from behind his back, holding the silenced .22, and shot the guard in the face. Nim turned slightly and shot the other guard in the chest, stepped forward and shot him again in the head just as he fell. Raising his pistol and aiming at Peter's forehead, he asked calmly, "Where is the security room?"

Peter lifted his shaking hand and pointed at a room only ten paces away. Bun Sani dropped his bag, pulled the silenced Mac 10 from beneath his jacket, and walked toward the door. He kicked it in and fired from the hip as he entered. The two startled men seated behind a panel of six TV security screens only had time to turn and face their killer before being riddled.

Nim lowered his pistol and again spoke calmly to Peter. "Are there any more guards anywhere in the building?"

Peter stammered. "A—A roving guard makes the rounds of the twelfth and thirtieth floors. Y-You should be able to see him on the security monitors."

Sani nodded as he looked at the screens. "He is on the twelfth, walking down the hallway."

Nim raised his pistol again, pointing it between Peter's eyes. "We don't need you anymore, Mr. Wong." He fired. Peter's head snapped back and he fell to the floor like a rag doll. Nim looked at his three men and spoke as he walked toward the elevator. "Sani, you will take out the guard then join us on the thirtieth and help us set the charges. We'll have your bag."

Inside the elevator he pushed the twelfth and fourteenth buttons and looked again at his men. "Remember, the night shift workers are on the fourteenth floor. No one should be on the thirtieth, but be ready when placing the charges to eliminate anyone you see. Bring all your firing wires back to me at the elevator lobby. You'll have exactly seven minutes once the doors open. Mainframe computers are first priority. I will blow my whistle at six minutes and thirty seconds. Anyone not at the elevators at seven minutes will be on his own. Once I push the detonator, we will have only six minutes to clear the building. Rendezvous at the rally point in the executive parking lot. Any questions?"

Hearing none, he raised his wrist and looked at his watch. "I have 10:55 hours and ten seconds."

Fort Belvoir, Virginia

Out of breath, Eli threw open the bottom floor fire exit door and crouched in a shooter's stance, spinning left then right, looking for a target. Seeing no threat or movement but hearing tires squeal, he stood erect as a new dark Ford van sped out of the parking lot and headed north toward the main road leading off post. "Shitshit *shit!*" he said aloud, and bent over to take in a breath. Above the clanging fire bells he could hear the sound of sirens.

Finally he took in enough air to straighten up again. Holstering his pistol, he walked toward the parking lot and took out his cell phone. He began pushing keys and put the small phone to his ear just as the FBI Emergency Operations Center operator answered. "This is Agent Eli Tanner, my location is Fort Belvoir Army Hospital. Four male assailants just made an attempt to kill Colonel Robert Anderson, patient at said hospital. Attempt failed. One assailant dead, one wounded. However, one MP sergeant is dead and one Army captain nurse is badly wounded. Agent Ashley Sutton and Colonel Anderson's wife taken hostage. I say again Special Agent Sutton and Colonel Anderson's wife taken hostage. Two, possibly more, assailants escaped heading north off post in black or dark blue new Ford van toward Highway One. Request immediate support. MPs are presently en route, but need local support and helicopter support ASAP. Assailants are Cambodian, I say again, Cambodian. They are dark-haired, brown or lightly brown-skinned males. They are armed and extremely dangerous. My cell phone number is 326–1560. My location is currently in parking lot north of hospital. Request notification of deputy director immediately and inform him of situation. MPs arriving at scene and I have to get off now to tell them direction assailants fled, out."

A light green MP car skidded to a halt beside Eli, who had his arm up and was holding his ID. He approached the car and tried to speak calmly. "I'm Agent Tanner, FBI. Two armed assailants just fled north in . . ."

Woodbridge, Virginia

On a ridge seventy yards from the house, Kaing Nay watched the approaching station wagon through his night vision scope attached to an M-16 rifle fitted with a sound suppressor. He brought a small Motorola to his mouth. "Soy, visitors approaching in car. They have their lights off. Car just stopped . . . four men getting out . . . wait, a fifth man just got out. All are carrying what look like Mac 10s. They are approximately fifty yards from house. Two men are leaving the others and are walking up the road. Begin the party. Over."

Inside the house, Soy Poc smiled as he pressed the sidebar on his Motorola. "Party beginning. Out." He walked two steps, pushed a cassette unit's Play button, and immediately the voices of the team filled the spacious living room from four corner speakers. Turning, he walked to the back door, where his scoped rifle was leaning against the wall. He picked it up, shut the door, and stepped into darkness.

A minute later he lay behind a mound of dirt where he had prepositioned the electrical detonator. Taking out his Motorola, he whispered, "I am in position. What is the situation, over?"

Kaing spoke into his radio. "Two men coming your way toward back of house. The other three are approaching front. One has stopped. The other two are heading for front entrance. You should see your two now."

"I have them both in my scope. One is raising a handheld radio. They are both moving toward back door. Give me an up when yours enter."

"Roger, one of mine has radio to his ear. They are by the door. One is backing up . . . he just kicked in the door. Both are in!"

Soy's two men disappeared inside the rear door. He lowered his head then depressed the detonator. For a millisecond, a brilliant flash of light turned the mound into instant daylight, which was followed by a horrific blast. Soy covered his head as pieces of brick, burning wood, and shingles plummeted to the ground around him like huge hailstones.

On the ridge, Kaing saw the house disappear in the explosion and saw the remaining man standing on the driveway blown twenty feet back onto the road. His mangled body was smoking. Standing and bringing his radio up, Kaing spoke in a normal tone of voice. "Soy, the party is over. All are finished. Meet me at vehicle. Over."

Baileys Crossroads

Hu Nim watched the last of his men climb into the van, then nodded to Kenny Chun. "Drive slowly and obey all traffic rules." Kenny was about to shift to Drive when a flash of light blinded him. An instant later a crack of thunder rolled over the huge parking lot.

As Hu Nim looked out his window, debris began to fall onto the pavement and the landscaped gardens at the base of the building. The sound of crashing glass was louder than the explosion as he rolled his window down and looked up at the structure. As expected, not a single pane of smoked glass remained and smoke poured out of the thirtieth floor's skeletal remains, completely hiding the upper floors that he knew would be an inferno.

Nim leaned back and rolled up the window. "They should have known better."

Kenny smiled as he drove to the parking lot exit.

Mount Vernon

Sobbing, Sandy Anderson brushed strands of brunette hair from her eyes and touched the woman beside her. "Ashley, wake up. Please wake up. Please don't die, don't die."

Ashley heard her mother calling above the strange ringing in her head. Her eyes moved behind her closed eyelids. Her mother was dead, she told herself. *Ohhh, God, my head hurts so bad. Why can't I open my eyes? Who's talking to me? It hurts, oh God, it hurts.*

Sandy leaned forward, seeing Ashley's blood-caked eyelids moving. "Ashley? Ashley, you have to wake up. Please, you have to wake up."

Ashley suddenly remembered the man in the hallway, a flash, another man coming toward her and swinging his gun hand and . . . her eyes opened and immediately a wave of pain made her grimace. She let the tremor pass and blinked despite the caked dried blood that irritated her eyes. Finally, the blurry figure leaning over her came into focus and she could hear Sandy's pleading voice plainly.

"Thank you, God. Ashley, we're on a boat of some kind. There are four men with guns. Oh, God, what are we going to do?"

Suddenly a man loomed over Sandy and she cowered. "Don't hurt us, please don't hurt us."

The man leaned over and Ashley recognized him immediately. Jean Paul handed Sandy a first aid kit. "Mrs. Anderson, please attend to the agent's head wound. We will not harm you. Soon we will be at our base and you both can rest comfortably."

He leaned down farther and inspected the gash on Ashley's forehead, then gently brushed back her hair. "Agent Sutton, I will butterfly your wound once we arrive. Please lie still and make no trouble for us. My colleagues are grieving over the loss of two of our family. . . . I suggest you give them no reason to quiet you."

Ashley spoke thickly. "Wh-Who are you?"

"Yes, of course, I am indeed sorry, Agent Sutton and Mrs. Anderson. I am Jean Paul Devoe. I inspected your purses and, of course, was very pleasantly surprised to find that I had you, Mrs. Anderson. Many years ago I considered your husband a friend. Please be assured no harm will come to either of you. But do nothing foolish or I will be forced to keep you in conditions that will be very uncomfortable. Mrs. Anderson, open the first aid kit and apply a bandage to her head and apply only light pressure. Mr. Sovan will be watching you both."

A small man materialized from the darkness of the cabin into the light of a single small reading light affixed to the wall.

Jean Paul patted Yos Sovan's shoulder. "He speaks and understands English very well, as do all my men, so say nothing that will disturb him. I will leave you ladies now. We will talk again soon."

11:30 P.M. Fort Belvoir

The hospital front-entrance waiting area had been turned into the temporary command post. The furniture was stacked along the lobby wall to make room for folding tables and chairs where three agents and an MP colonel manned portable phones. Street maps for all of Washington and its outlying communities were taped to the windows and the walls.

Brad Brewer, the designated AIC, walked up to a man seated in the middle of the room and handed him a cup of coffee. "You've had it, Eli. Why don't you go to your hotel and we'll call you if something comes up."

Eli accepted the cup and shook his head. "Thanks, Brad, but I wouldn't be able to sleep. I'd as soon stay."

Brewer pulled up a folding chair and sat down. "I just got word the wounded assailant died on the operating table. The good news is the nurse looks like she's going to pull through. Bullet collapsed both lungs, but the surgery went well. If she'd been hit anywhere but the hospital, she would be history."

Eli took a sip of coffee and lowered his head. "Someone said they found blood in the canteen and there was blood in the stairwell." Eli raised his eyes to the agent. "Do the lab boys think it was from one of the women?"

Brewer slowly nodded. "I didn't want to tell you till we knew something for sure. I'm sorry, Eli, but it appears that Sutton is the one who's injured. Based on what you told us, the crime scene tech says if she was the second one carried down the stairs, the blood was most likely hers. If she was first, then more drops on the steps would have been stepped on. They also found a piece of material snagged on the bottom of the Coke machine. You said she was wearing a blue suit, right?"

Eli closed his eyes and lowered his head again. Brewer leaned forward and patted Tanner's leg. "She's a tough little gal, Eli, she'll make it. Let me have a doc give you something, and I'll have one of the guys drive you to the hotel."

Eli began to shake his head but heard a familiar voice. "Eli! Thank God!" Ramona Valez blurted as she strode into the room. She wrapped her arms around his shoulders. "Charlie and I were worried sick when we heard. I'm so sorry about Ashley . . . but don't you worry, we'll find her. Come on, we have to talk."

Eli shook his head. "Mona, this is where I'm going to hear something first, and I—"

Charlie Lee walked up and took his arm. "Mona is right, Eli, we have to talk now. Come on outside and let me bring you up to date." He leaned closer and whispered in Eli's ear, "The Cambodians did more than make an attempt on Anderson tonight."

Eli stood and gave the Chinese American agent a questioning glare. "What are you talking about?"

"Outside," Ramona said, taking his arm.

Once in the parking lot, Eli spun around and faced Lee. "What's with all the secrecy, Charlie?"

Lee stepped closer and lowered his voice to just above a whisper. "Too many people in there, Eli. This can't get out to the press or they'll describe it as a ring of international terrorists on the loose. Look, Ramona and I just left Triad's headquarters. It was bombed about an hour ago. Over fifty night shift workers are believed to be dead, and that number could rise. You see, there is a twelve-hour difference in time zones between here and Hong Kong. The night shift was primarily made up of Chinese who sent reports and conducted business with the home office. So far there's been no survivors found."

Eli shook his head. "Charlie, all five of them were here. It couldn't have been."

"There are more of them than we thought," Ramona said. "There was an explosion in Woodbridge this evening. One body was found and the ID on him makes him Jamaican. Four more bodies were in the house but they're beyond identification. A station wagon found fifty yards from the house was registered to a Jamaican who is a known small-time leader of a group that contracts hits. So far four Mac 10s have been found in the debris, and boxes of ammunition and spare magazines were found in the car. Eli, this is too much of a coincidence. The Cambodians have to be responsible for all the action tonight."

"Jesus, what have we got ourselves into?" Eli said.

Charlie exchanged looks with Ramona and patted Eli's shoulder. "We're in a war, Eli—and right now the Cambodians are winning."

Agent Brewer yelled from the front door, "Eli, chopper just spotted the Ford van!"

Eli jogged inside and stopped by Brewer, who pointed at a map. "They've got it spotted here, in the sailboat marina just off the George Washington Parkway."

Ramona stepped up behind the two men and spoke in a monotone. "It matches the M.O. of the hit on the two generals. They changed vehicles."

CHAPTER 18

6:00 A.M. Washington, D.C.

Ashley felt her shoulder being shaken. She opened her eyes. Jean Paul set a steaming cup of coffee down on the small nightstand. "You look much better this morning, Agent Sutton. I would get up slowly if I were you. I am sure the wound will begin throbbing again. I have left aspirins for you there beside your cup."

Ashley lay still, looking up at him. "Where is Sandy?"

"She is having breakfast in the other room with Mr. Sovan. She is not as upset as she was last night. Please sit up, Agent Sutton; we must talk while she is occupied. Easy . . . yes, that is better. Now please tell me the name of the agent who was in the room with Anderson?"

"You can go to hell," Ashley hissed.

"No, Agent Sutton, we Buddhists don't believe in your Christian concept of hell. Please, no more dramatics. We both do not have the time. In a while I'm going to allow you to call the agent you called Eli. I must know if he is a man who can be trusted."

Ashley's glare diminished. "You're going to let me call him?"

"Yes, Agent Sutton. I want to demonstrate I am an honorable man, but I am also a man who has a duty to fulfill. I am going to make your Agent Eli a proposal for a trade. You and Mrs. Anderson for Robert. Now you understand why I am not talking to you in the presence of Mrs. Anderson. She would become distraught and perhaps hysterical if she knew of my proposal. I ask you not to tell her for both our sakes. Now please, answer the question. . . . What is the agent's full name?"

Ashley shook her head. "Mr. Devoe, you are wasting your time if you think Eli or any agent will deal with you. It is standard policy not to deal with people like yourself."

Jean Paul nodded without expression. "I understand your policies, Agent Sutton. Agent Eli will act only as a messenger to pass on my proposal to your superiors. And I can assure you they *will* accept. Is your Agent Eli like yourself . . . is he forthright?"

Lowering her head, Ashley spoke in a whisper. "Yes, Mr. Devoe. No man is more forthright than Eli Tanner."

Jean Paul backed away from her bed and motioned to the nightstand. "Drink your coffee, Agent Sutton, and please take the aspirin. I will be coming for you soon to talk to Agent Tanner." He turned and walked toward the door when Ashley spoke, almost in a whisper.

"You are the one they called Frenchy, aren't you?"

Jean Paul stopped and faced her. "How do you know of my old name?"

"I went through the pictures of Sergeants Hoffman and Rhodes. I saw your picture many times, Mr. Devoe. They both sent pictures of you to their wives and spoke of you in their letters. You were just a little—"

"I was a soldier, Agent Sutton. You were going to say 'boy,' but I assure you I was not. The war allowed no children their youth in my village. In your country boys play baseball and video games. In my village boys were made scouts and we patrolled the countryside. In your country mothers and their daughters go shopping in malls. In my village they loaded bullets into magazines and rolled bandages. We were all soldiers, Agent Sutton, because your country and Robert Anderson and his team made us into soldiers. The soldiers of my village are now only memories. . . . I am the last survivor. You asked me why, Agent Sutton? Do you dream? I do. Every night I see the faces of my people and I hear their anguished pleas for justice. I am still a soldier, Agent Sutton, and it is my duty to end those pleas. My people must rest in peace."

Ashley looked into Jean Paul's eyes, searching for a hint of remorse, but found only determination. She held his gaze as she spoke. "We won't rest until you are brought to justice, Mr. Devoe."

Jean Paul picked up the coffee cup and handed it to her. "Then, Agent Sutton, we are not so different, you and I. Your feelings about me are the same feelings I have carried for many years. . . . Yes, one day, perhaps, you will find your justice, and then you, too, will be able to sleep without the memories of the dead."

J. W. Marriott Hotel, Washington, D.C.

Fully clothed, Eli lay asleep across his bed. On the other bed, Charlie Lee opened his eyes and suddenly sat up, seeing Ramona sitting on the edge of the bed. She heard his movement, looked over her shoulder and winked. "You were wonderful, Charlie."

Lee's eyes began widening and she smiled. "Relax, I just sat down to put on my shoes. What time did you finally get Eli to leave Belvoir?"

Charlie looked at his watch and let out a tired sigh. "Three hours ago when they closed down the C.P. At the deputy's suggestion, they're running the show from headquarters."

Ramona stood and motioned to a tray on the dresser. "I had coffee and rolls brought up for you two. Looks like it's going to be another long day. The confirmed toll of the bombing is at thirty-two, and many more bodies are being recovered. They expect upward of sixty. Our Cambodians didn't mess around about signaling their distress at being put on contract, did they?"

Charlie stretched, then slowly rose from the bed. "I guess I'd better get over to the scene and see if anything of use has been found in the debris."

Ramona lowered her voice to a whisper. "How was Eli doing when you left the hospital? When I had to leave, he wasn't dealing all that well with it."

Charlie glanced at the sleeping agent. "He was doing better after the escape vehicle was found to be empty. I believe he expected Agent Sutton's body to be in it. I think he cares for her quite a lot, and not just in the professional sense."

Ramona slowly shook her head. "Knowing him, I bet he never told her. . . . Have some coffee and rolls before you go, Charlie. You're going to need—"

A phone beeped and Eli was instantly awake. He sat up, pulling the cell phone from his wrinkled blazer. "Agent Tanner . . . My God, Ashley, are you all right? Where are you?"

Charlie and Ramona hurried to him and he held the phone out slightly from his ear so they could hear. " . . . fine, Eli, and so is Mrs. Anderson. I have someone here with me who wants to talk to you."

"Hello, Agent Tanner. My name is Mr. Devoe. I want first to assure you the ladies will not be harmed. Agent Sutton suffered a slight injury to her forehead, but as you heard for yourself, she is doing quite well. Agent Tanner, I wish you to be the person I talk to from now on when I call. I want no trained hostage-rescue agents wasting my time. I have a proposal for you to pass on to your superiors. I desire to trade the two women for Anderson. I realize you are in no position to make such a deal, so I wish you to go to your superiors and I will call again in exactly one hour. Please inform them not to waste their energy in trying to trace the call. I believe you are aware I am not a fool. Agent Sutton assures me you are a man who can be trusted. Do not disappoint me. This matter is extremely important to me and I will not tolerate foolish games. I will now let you talk to your fellow agent to show you her earlier words were not taped. Please understand this is to demonstrate to you I do not play games, Agent Tanner. What I say, I mean."

"Eli, it's me again. I believe Mr. Devoe is telling you the truth about not playing games."

Eli spoke quickly. "Ashley, cooperate fully with him. You're sure Mrs. Anderson is okay?"

"Yes, Eli, she's in the next room. Mr. Devoe does not want her to know about the proposal. I have to go now. Good-bye."

Eli slowly lowered the phone and snapped his eyes to Ramona. "Did she sound all right to you?"

"Under the circumstances, yes. Mr. Devoe sounds like a very cool customer. I would have thought he'd have sounded more tense. I want us all to write down what we heard, word for word, and we'll compare notes on the way to headquarters."

Eli began pressing the phone keys. Ramona gave him a questioning stare. "What are you doing?"

"Calling the ops center. I've got to tell them what happened and have them make sure the deputy will see us when we get there."

Forty minutes after receiving the call, Eli, Charlie, and Ramona sat in the deputy director's office along with the division chiefs and the Bureau legal adviser. The deputy read aloud the phone conversation Ramona had written down, and when finished, he looked at the legal counsel. "Eric, I know we don't negotiate a man's life away, but are we bound by law to tell Anderson of this proposal?"

The lawyer shook his head. "No, sir. Federal law allows us to restrict access to any or all information to family members while the case is active. We can safely consider the proposal as information. Colonel Anderson does not need to be informed."

The deputy placed his elbows on the table and rested his chin on his cupped hands. "We're in a tight fix here. Bill, you spoke to me prior to the meeting about an idea. What is it?"

The Chief of Operations nodded. "Sir, this Devoe fellow

doesn't know what Anderson looks like. We could have an agent double for him and—"

"No tricks, sir," Eli said. "We don't know if Devoe knows what he looks like or not, and I'd bet Mrs. Anderson had a picture of him in her wallet. We have to play this straight with Devoe or we'll lose both women."

Ramona spoke toward the deputy. "Sir, I agree with Agent Tanner. It's obvious Mr. Devoe is very intelligent and has a great deal of knowledge about our operations. In going over the phone conversation, I believe Agent Sutton's one sentence to Agent Tanner was meant to be a warning to us when she said she believed Mr. Devoe was being truthful about our not playing games. She was giving us her evaluation of him as well as his capabilities from where she sits. In my opinion, she was saying that there is no way for her to escape and it appears to her Devoe means what he says. In light of last night's events, I would say she is correct. Mr. Devoe and his men did not run when they had the chance. Instead, they attacked. This tells me he has the manpower, equipment, money, and the confidence to do whatever he deems is necessary to achieve his goal. And sir, it is clear his goal is finishing his business with Anderson."

The operations officer wrinkled his brow and leaned back in his chair. "Dr. Valez, with all due respect to your professional qualifications, you're making an awful lot of just one comment by Agent Sutton. Devoe is a Cambodian, as are his men. Someone has seen them, and we'll find them within twenty-four hours. All we have to do is delay him with our decision until we locate where they are."

"Don't underestimate him, as Triad did, and the team of hit men that was sent to deal with him. He's been ahead of us all since day one, and as far as I can see, he still is ahead of us."

The legal counsel shook his head. "I think we're getting ahead of ourselves. He said he would call; let's hear what he has to say and take it from there."

The deputy stood and began pacing in front of the table. "No, Eric, I don't agree. Ramona is right, this Mr. Devoe has been ahead of us since the first murder. It's obvious we were wrong in assuming Tram was the leader of the Cambodians, and we were wrong when we thought there were only five of them, and we were wrong when we closed this case. I don't want to be wrong anymore. We can't afford any more bodies."

Charlie Lee lowered his eyes and spoke softly. "Sir, there is something else that we must consider. We won't be the only ones looking for Devoe and his men. Triad will have every hit man for hire in the country here within twenty-four hours to find and finish Devoe and his men. It's a matter of saving face."

The deputy stopped pacing and pointed at his Chief of Operations. "Bill, you're lead on this. Get additional help in here and form a task force with other agency and department involvement. I want a canvass of this town to find every Cambodian who lives here or has lived here in the past year. You were right, somebody has to have seen these people. I also want the airports, small and large, manned, and all known or suspected hitters picked up as they enter the city. Get a flash message out notifying all our people of our situation and have them track the hitters in their cities and keep us informed of their movements. People, this case *is* our first priority. Each of you division chiefs form a group of your best to work your field of expertise on this and send a rep to Bill's task force. Ramona, I want you working with our behavioral scientists, and I want to know who Mr. Devoe is. Get in his head and tell us how long we can safely delay our answer to his proposal."

The deputy looked at his watch and glanced at the table next to him, where two agents from the technical support office sat in front of recording equipment. "Devoe should be calling in a minute. Are you ready?"

The older agent nodded. "Yes, sir. We have the code for Agent Tanner's cell phone and have this phone coded identically. When Agent Tanner receives the call, we will receive it on this phone as well and the conversation will be recorded. It is also on a speaker so all of us will hear the conversation. In our offices we have an additional phone coded and we'll be trying to trace the call."

The deputy dipped his chin and turned to Eli. "Agent Tanner, have you been briefed on the techniques of hostage negotiations?"

Ramona spoke up. "Sir, the expert who talked to Agent Tanner didn't understand this situation. I told him to leave because he was wasting our time. Eli knows rapport must be established, and that's all that is necessary for now."

The deputy's face turned red and he was about to respond when Eli's phone began beeping.

The support agent turned on the recorder and nodded to Eli, who answered. "Agent Tanner."

"Agent Tanner, this is Mr. Devoe. Are your superiors with you?"

"Yes, they are, Mr. Devoe, and we have you on speaker phone. Are Agent Sutton and Mrs. Anderson doing okay?"

"They are quite comfortable, Agent Tanner. Please listen very carefully. I desire to make a trade of the two ladies for Mr. Anderson. I am fully aware such a trade is a difficult decision for your superiors, but I will make their decision easier for them. In exactly seventeen minutes the yellow line Metro train will make a stop at Pentagon Station. Your people will find a briefcase under the third seat of the second car. In the briefcase they will find car keys belonging to your rental car, Agent Tanner. Agent Sutton was worried that you did not have them. Please remind your superiors the briefcase could have held explosives. Also you will find that four colonels assigned to the Pentagon did not report for work this morning. We have them. I will release them in one hour unharmed. Again it is a reminder to your superiors of what I am capable of doing any-time and anywhere I choose. I promise to you the ladies will not be harmed. I make no promise for others. Make no mistake, I want Anderson. I doubt that you have told him of this pro-posal. I ask that you do so immediately. He will do the honor-able thing and sacrifice himself for his wife, Agent Sutton, and for others. You must help him regain his honor. . . . Tell him I am waiting. I will call back at six this evening for the decision. Warn your superiors I will not tolerate a delay on their part or tomorrow morning a lesson will be taught that will bring tears to many. Good-bye, Agent Tanner."

The line went dead and Eli slowly lowered the phone. The others at the table were frozen in their chairs in silence. The phone ringing by the support agents broke the foreboding quiet. The older agent answered, listened, and recradled the handset. "Sir, we weren't able to trace the call."

The deputy lowered his head for a long moment and finally raised his eyes. "I will brief the director personally on this. . . . He'll want the Attorney General in on the decision. The rest of you get started on my instructions. Bill, have your people confirm the briefcase and missing officers. I believe our Mr. Devoe has made his point. We'll meet again in two hours for an update from Bill on Devoe's surprises and on how his task force is going to be organized and manned. I expect each division chief to brief me on what you're planning. Expect the director and, most likely, the Attorney General in attendance at the meeting. Ramona, you and Agent Tanner remain a moment. The rest of you are excused."

Waiting until the office was cleared, the deputy sat down with a solemn expression and lowered his eyes to his hands. "We all know Devoe is capable of doing what he says if we delay our decision. We could play it tough and refuse his proposal and hope we'll be able to find him, but I'm convinced he will kill too many innocents before we do manage to locate him and his men. May God forgive me but I'm going to recommend to the director that we allow the colonel to decide if he wants to trade himself. That's going to be tough for the director and the Attorney General to allow, but they can't play hardball with Devoe, he's too dangerous."

Ramona nodded silently. Eli's jaw muscles rippled as he pushed away from the table and stood. "Sir, there's no question what Colonel Anderson will decide; we sure as hell can't wash our hands of this by simply letting him turn himself over to that killer."

The deputy wouldn't look at Eli as he slowly shook his head. "Agent Tanner, I understand your feelings, but if we do not approach the colonel, we are facing the worse of two evils—the deaths of many innocent people. It will be impossible to stop Devoe from carrying out his threats. If not a Metro station, he could bomb a bus station, airport, or even a fast food restaurant. He can strike anywhere, and we're completely powerless to stop him. I simply don't believe we can find him before he strikes."

Eli pinned the deputy with a stare. "We're not letting Anderson go alone, sir. He is incapable of driving himself to a handoff location for a trade, so I volunteer to assist him. But don't think for a minute I believe this to be a one-way trip. We've got to figure out how the colonel and I are going to beat Devoe."

Ramona shook her head. "Eli, even if Devoe allowed you to assist the colonel, he would just have you leave him somewhere."

Eli motioned to the recorder. "Devoe mentioned the word 'honor' twice. He would understand that it would be my duty not to leave the colonel someplace alone in his condition. I've thought about this since he first called and I have to believe there's a way for a reaction team to track us. Surely we're smarter than Devoe? Transmitters are awfully small these days, so all we have to do is figure out how I tell the reaction team to come in for the takedown once the women are safe."

Ramona began to respond, but the deputy said, "Ramona, Agent Tanner is right. We must try. I'll have our best technical support people work with him on this and get the special ops people up here, too." The deputy shifted his gaze to Eli. "In the meantime, Agent Tanner, talk to Colonel Anderson. You know him and so the information will be better coming from you. Tell him the truth and see what his decision is. I'll have a chopper on the roof in fifteen minutes to take you to him."

The deputy stood and placed his hand on Eli's shoulder. "It is a very difficult thing I've asked of you to do. You can refuse and I'll understand."

"Sir, I'll tell him . . . but I'm also telling him it's not a suicide mission for either of us. I'm telling him I believe we can beat Devoe."

The deputy walked to his desk and pushed his intercom. "Jill, notify operations I need a helicopter on the roof landing pad in fifteen minutes. And get Harold Johnson on the line for me." The deputy covered the mouthpiece of the phone and looked at Eli. "I'm going to get you the best there is for this type of mission. The CIA people have the latest high tech equipment, and you'll have it."

District of Columbia

Ten miles from FBI headquarters, Jean Paul sat in the dining room of a large house with a view of Anacostia Park and the Anacostia River. Pinned to the wall were large maps of Virginia and Maryland, and on the table were smaller topographical maps giving much more detail. Jean Paul finished writing on a yellow legal pad and stood. He walked to the Maryland map and inserted a red pin. "This spot is where I will meet Anderson again. . . . It is a fitting place for a soldier to die." He moved his finger and pointed to two green pins. "From here and here, Kaing and Soy will be able to see if he is being followed and also see any planes or helicopters they might try to use to track the vehicle. With the other precautions we have made, I see no problems for us."

Seated at the table, Hu Nim raised an eyebrow. "They will use transmitters, Jean Paul."

"We will ensure they do not use them. There is a device that can detect such things. Add it to our list of things that are needed. The mountains may cause communication problems with the handheld radios. We will need cell phones for everyone. We will leave tomorrow and make a reconnaissance, but you can begin briefing the men on their duties. Only minor modifications may be necessary once we see the actual terrain. Our plan is simple yet it ensures against trickery on the FBI's part."

Nim nodded and rose from his chair. "And the women?"

Jean Paul looked at the wall map again. "They will remain here under Sovan's watchful eye. I will call Agent Tanner and tell him where they can be found once I have Robert."

Hu Nim dipped his chin and walked out of the dining room, leaving his superior alone. Jean touched the red pin and whispered, "You will not be alone Robert, you will sleep with the ghosts of many who gave their lives for your country. . . ."

9:45 A.M. Fort Belvoir

Robert Anderson leaned back on his pillow and looked up at the ceiling. Slowly his eyes lowered to Eli. "I want my wife to live, Eli, but I don't want you to go with me . . . they'll kill you."

Eli forced a smile. "Sir, I know I'm gray and old, but I'm not stupid. I'm not volunteering for this duty because I have a death wish. I volunteered because I believe in us, you and me. Devoe has had everything his way and he thinks he'll keep it that way. I say you and I can beat him. We're two old Rangers past our prime, but we have a lot on our side. The high tech wizards of the Bureau and the CIA will be working with us, and we'll even have military support. Hell, sir, we have the whole U.S. of A. backing us up."

Anderson looked into Eli's eyes. "Eli, do you think we really have a chance?"

Eli's plastic smile dissolved as he held the colonel's gaze. "Sir, we have to try. . . . You and I aren't afraid of dying . . . we're afraid of losing again. And sir, I'm not planning on losing this one. Devoe is going down." Eli held his hand out to the colonel. "What'd'ya say, sir, are we going to be Rangers one more time and drive on?"

Anderson took Eli's hand. "I say, get me out of this damn hospital and let's drive on, Ranger."

District of Columbia

Kenny Chun walked down the carpeted basement steps with two plastic shopping bags. He strode to Sovan, who sat in an easy chair watching a small television. Chun took a can of Diet Coke from a bag and handed it to his friend. " 'General Hospital' on yet?" he asked.

Sovan accepted the can without taking his eyes from the screen. " 'Days of Our Lives'—Bo is helping Marlena so he can see Hope again."

Kenny motioned with his head toward the open doorway of the room ten feet away. "I have things for the ladies."

Still not taking his eyes from the small screen, Sovan waved his hand.

Ashley was sitting on her small bed thumbing through *Cosmopolitan* when the small man stepped through the doorway. He was wearing tight jeans, cowboy shirt, and sharply pointed rattlesnake-hide cowboy boots. She judged the young man to be no older than his mid-twenties. Glancing at Sandy Anderson, asleep on the bed beside Ashley, the young man tiptoed closer, whispering, "Miss, I brought you snacks and books to read. I didn't know what you would like so I bought all the top ten bestsellers in paper coverings." He set the bags on the floor beside the bed and motioned to the small television in the corner of the windowless room. " 'Days of Our Lives' is on. Would you like me to turn on the TV for you?"

Ashley shook her head and spoke softly. "No thank you . . . what is your name?"

"Kenny, miss. I am called Tep in my country, but I like Kenny here."

"Nice boots, Kenny," Ashley said.

Kenny smiled as if embarrassed. "They are like a pair Kenny Rogers wears. I saw him many times on TV in Hong Kong. He is very popular, you know. I have all his tapes and videos collected."

Ashley leaned over, took two Diet Cokes from the bag and handed the young man one. "You speak English very well, Kenny. Did you learn it in Hong Kong?"

"Yes, miss, the old one taught us. English is the second language, you see, and it was good business to learn. We watch all your TV programs on satellite in Hong Kong and learn new words all the time. I'm the best English speaker of us except for Jean Paul. He went to Hong Kong University and graduated with honors. The old one was very pleased."

Ashley took a sip of Coke, lowered her can and looked into the young man's eyes. "Kenny, you know you will probably die very soon working for Jean Paul, don't you?"

Kenny hunched his shoulders. "Life is suffering, miss. If the enlightened one chooses for me to die I will be reincarnated and be closer to Nirvana. I do not fear death; the enlightened one will bless my journey."

Ashley kept her gaze steady. "Buddha does not condone killing, Kenny, as my God doesn't condone the taking of another's life."

Kenny smiled. "Miss, I have seen all the movies and know you try to plant seeds in my head. Please don't waste your time. You know nothing of Buddha's blessings and know nothing of true suffering. Jean Paul understands and is driven to right the wrong done those like me and my family, who suffered greatly. Sovan, Penn, Sani—all of us have lost our families and our country. The French, you smiling Americans, the Vietnamese, our own Khmer Rouge, all have made us suffer in ways you will never know. The enlightened one knows, and we who seek justice know. . . . That is enough."

Kenny made a gesture as if touching the brim of a hat. "Good day to you, miss. I must see if Bo finds Marlena."

CHAPTER 19

On the top floor, in a small conference room, Eli concluded his background briefing and looked at the three men who were considered experts in their field by the FBI, CIA, and Special Operations Command of the Department of Defense. He motioned to Robert Anderson, seated in a wheelchair beside him. "The bottom line, gentlemen, is I'm asking for your support to keep the colonel and myself alive after the handoff, and at the same time to figure out a way to take down Mr. Devoe and his people. The problem is we don't have much time to come up with a plan. I'd like to turn over the meeting to Special Agent O'Malley, who will be Agent in Charge of the operation."

A ruddy faced middle-age agent nodded and pushed back his chair. "Call me J.C., guys. For the benefit of everyone, let me run down how we can expect this handoff to go down. Once we all see what we're up against, we can try and come up with solutions to the problems. First we have to assume Devoe will in fact allow Agent Tanner to accompany the colonel. Talking him into it will be Tanner's department. The second assumption is Devoe is smart and has the necessary equipment and people to do the handoff the right way."

O'Malley lifted his chin. "The scenario I'm about to give you is the worst case for us. The first thing Devoe will do is give us very little reaction time. He'll say it will start at one time but will call again and move up the time schedule. Tanner will be told to drive the colonel to location X, and Devoe will warn us he is not to be followed in any way. Once Tanner and the colonel arrive at X, it will be a place in the open, like a parking lot. Not far away will be a hotel or apartments, and somewhere in the building will be a lookout with glasses or a telescope. He'll call Tanner by cell phone and tell him that he and the colonel are to get out of the vehicle and leave everything in the car including the cell phone, watches, rings, etcetera. He'll then tell them to strip naked and walk to another vehicle Devoe's men will have prestaged. He'll have another cell phone in the car for Tanner and give him directions to location Y. He'll tell Tanner he will be watched and probably followed to ensure there is no tail. Tanner will get to location Y after traveling over long stretches of highway where lookouts will check for tails and aircraft. At location Y, Tanner and the colonel will be met by someone who will check every orifice of their bodies for transmitters. He will also have a wand and pass it over both of them to ensure they haven't swallowed a transmitter or placed one way up their behinds. Once satisfied they are clean, he will direct them to another location or possibly drive them to the last stop, where the handoff will take place. Once there, they will be searched again and business will be conducted. The spot will be in a remote place with limited access and be under the cover of trees or perhaps in a deserted building so that a passing plane or helicopter cannot observe the activity. The place will, however, have one, and most likely two, quick escape routes. Guards will be on the entry route into the spot and lookouts will be posted to cover all avenues of approach. Despite what you see in the movies, the hostages will *not* be at the final site. Their presence complicates things, so Devoe will have them somewhere else. Once he's satisfied we kept our end of the trade, he will tell Tanner where the women are located and hopefully let him call and have people confirm they are in good condition. Once they are confirmed safe, Devoe will expect Agent Tanner to leave the colonel with him."

Wrinkling his brow, O'Malley regarded Eli and Anderson. "That was the *worst* case scenario for us to deal with. It basically takes away any chance to track you both. Sounds gloomy, doesn't it?" O'Malley shook his head. "Don't worry, things are not as bad as they sound." He motioned to a balding man seated at the table.

"Chris Pullen, the Agency hostage expert, and I talked before you two arrived. We know we can defeat their attempts at keeping transmitters off you. It's just the last part we haven't figured out yet. I guarantee we'll have you tracked every inch of the way to the final handoff spot, but how we get the strike force in to protect you still isn't solved yet."

The third man at the table, wearing an Army green uniform with a silver star on each of his epaulets, raised an eyebrow. "Why is that a problem?"

It was the way he said it that made hope bubble up in Eli's chest. At the beginning of the meeting the brigadier had introduced himself simply as Walker and he had not said a word until asking the question.

O'Malley was caught off guard by the general's question and stammered, "Well, uh . . . General, a strike force just can't magically appear out of thin air."

Walker shook his head. "That's not quite true, Agent O'Malley. If you can track Agent Tanner and Colonel Anderson, we can have a reaction force mounted in our quiet Black Birds that can stay out of sight and follow at a safe distance until they reach the handoff site. They can be on top of the location, and the detachment can fast-rope out of the choppers and be on the ground in less than fifteen seconds. Tell me how you see the last part of the handoff. Run it down for me from when the colonel and Tanner arrive at the site."

O'Malley walked to the chalkboard and drew a circle and a line from the outside to the center. "Let's say the circle here is the site. The line is the entry road. A guard will be posted on the road as they enter the site. Others will probably be securing the site. The vehicle pulls in and is stopped by the guard to confirm it's Tanner and the colonel. The guard will then call Devoe and confirm both men have arrived. Remember, one of Devoe's men might be in the vehicle with them. Anyway, the vehicle will proceed into the circle until told to halt. Then both Tanner and the colonel will be told to exit the vehicle and move to a spot where they can be clearly seen. Devoe will now make his appearance. Tanner says he's done his part, now it's Devoe's turn to do his, free the women. Devoe tells Tanner where they are, and Tanner calls us and everybody waits until our people find the women and we confirm they are safe. We tell Tanner they're safe, and then Devoe will expect Tanner to depart. He'll be escorted back to the vehicle and leave."

General Walker sat in silence a moment and finally nodded. "Our problem is fifteen to twenty seconds, gentlemen. The way I see it, once Tanner receives confirmation that the women are safe, the clock starts ticking. My strike force will begin its attack run as soon as confirmation is given. The guards won't hear the choppers, but we have to assume they will see them coming and get off a warning. From the time they see the choppers and my first men hitting the ground, at most twenty seconds will pass. We need to make Tanner and the colonel somehow disappear during that time. We'll gain a few seconds because Devoe's people will be totally surprised and confused, but if Devoe is as good as everybody says, he'll recover first and begin popping at Tanner and the colonel."

Pullen, the CIA rep, lowered his head. "We have another problem. We have to ensure Devoe and his men are taken out quickly. If any of them call whoever they left in the Washington area, they may start blowing things up to make us pay."

The general shook his head. "No, we'll have an ECM bird overhead to jam everything within ten miles. The bird puts out white static, and believe me, nobody can communicate over any type of radio or telephone when the emitters are on."

O'Malley tapped the chalkboard. "That leaves us with the

twenty seconds to worry about. It's obvious they can't disappear, so we need a diversion of some kind. Something that will make Devoe and his men take their eyes off our people."

Pullen's chin came up. "We could tape bags of liquid to the abdomens and cover the flat bags with what we call 'second skin.' It's used in the film industry, and once makeup is applied, it will appear they are average American males who have a slight pouch. Tanner and the colonel can puncture the bags with their fingernails. As soon as the chemicals are exposed to air, it becomes a persistent gas that will severely affect anyone within ten to fifteen meters."

"What about Tanner and the colonel?" O'Malley asked.

Pullen nodded. "Yes, they would be affected as well, but at least they will be prepared for the effects mentally. Unfortunately, what we currently have also causes severe vomiting."

"Seems that one is too iffy," O'Malley said. "Devoe isn't going to be standing around with his thumb up his butt while these two are tearing at their stomachs. With that idea, he and his people are left with too much time to react. General, do you have a suggestion?"

Walker thought a moment and canted his head. "We need something that will scare them or confuse them. Maybe we can have a gunship fire rockets or missiles. . . . No, our weapons' killing radius is too great. I'm not sure we can modify our rockets or missiles in such a short time."

"What if they fired a smoke rocket?" Pullen said. "My people can handle the modifications to the rockets."

The general shook his head. "Still would have shrapnel effect when the body of the rocket broke up on impact. Tanner and the colonel could be wounded very badly. But that is an option to consider. I was thinking maybe we could make a low pass with a smoke chopper. The only problem is it takes time for the smoke to settle to the ground and obfuscate the site, plus it will cause problems for my people when they come in."

Eli decided to speak up. "If we need something that will scare them and shake them up, how about if . . ."

When Eli finished telling them his idea, O'Malley shot a look at General Walker. "Can you make that happen?"

The general allowed himself a small smile. "I can do better than that. I can improve on his idea. The only problem now is Tanner's." Walker shifted his expressionless eyes to Eli and pinned him with a stare. "You're going to have the advantage because you know it's coming. You'll have to pick your man beforehand and get close to him. When it happens, you'll have to make your move quick and focus on his weapon. Once you've got it, take out the biggest threat first and keep moving, don't stay in one place, keep shooting and moving."

Eli kept his eyes locked on the general. "I know what has to be done, sir."

Walker shifted his gaze to Anderson. "Colonel, when it happens hit the ground and stay there. With that leg wound of yours, you'll only be in Tanner's way if you stay on your feet. Tanner has to know everybody that's standing is the enemy. He won't have time to think, he has to react. You hit the ground and don't move. As soon as my people come in, roll over faceup and don't move. Tanner, that goes for you, too. When my people come in they'll come in quick. You hit the ground and stay faceup so they can ID you easily and move on to take out remaining targets."

O'Malley clapped his hands. "All right, looks like we've got a plan. Chris, tell the colonel and Agent Tanner how we're going to keep track of them."

Chris Pullen took a small metal disk from his pocket. "Gentlemen, this is the latest design of the smallest commercial transmitter on the market. The problem is, a security wand will pick it up because of the metal shell and the components inside. In this situation we'll have to use one that our people designed a year ago and recently turned into a reality. It is constructed entirely of plastics, ceramics, glues, and fiber optic wiring. It's bigger than we would like, but it works like a champ. Once it's swallowed, we'll be able to track you with no problem. Since you both will have them, we have redundancy and that makes it even better."

O'Malley stepped back to the table and picked up his notebook. "Gentlemen, it's time for us to prepare. Chris, I'll need your techs here as soon as possible with the transmitters. We'll have to settle on frequency compatibility and see what kind of work-arounds are going to be needed. General, I'll need your commo people ASAP to get me up to speed on the airborne command post's capability and also to talk to the Agency reps about their transmitters."

General Walker stood. "I'll have them over within an hour. I need to request the assets we'll need and begin staging aircraft and my detachment from Delta Force. I should be able to brief my people and be back to go over the plan again in three hours."

O'Malley raised his hand. "Okay, we'll all meet again at four and take a break to listen to Devoe's call at six in the deputy's office. Agent Tanner, you and the colonel will not need to be in attendance at the four o'clock. You two should get some rest. For now, you have all you need to know, and we'll fill you in on details much later. Okay, that's it."

Eli and Anderson remained in their chairs as the others departed. When the door shut, they looked at one another and Robert slowly lowered his head. "Eli, they're working hard for us, but we both know your idea is a long shot. I want Devoe just as much as you do, but my first priority is making sure my wife is safe. When I know she's out of harm's way, then I'll do anything you want."

"I understand, sir, and I feel the same about Agent Sutton. . . . I got kind of close to her. We'll still have surprise on our side, so it ups our odds."

Anderson reached over and patted Eli's arm. "Anything else got you worried?"

Eli raised an eyebrow. "To tell you the truth, yes, sir. The CIA DDO said we could swallow those big transmitters, but he didn't say how we were supposed to get 'em out. *That's* got me real worried."

Anderson grinned and pushed his wheelchair to the door. "That's good, Eli—you're thinking we're going to be alive after it's over. Come on, I need to find some real food, and I want to buy some Chee•tos for tomorrow's trip."

5:55 P.M. FBI Headquarters

Those seated around the large conference room table sat in silence listening to the Chief of Operations as he reported on efforts to find Devoe. ". . . and a check of the rental car agencies also came up negative. Sir, Devoe has covered his tracks well. We haven't developed a single lead. Even inside the Beltway most people can't distinguish a Cambodian from any other Southeast Asian, or even a Chinese or a Mexican, for that matter. I'm sorry, sir. We've done our best but we're still at square one."

The deputy nodded. "Bill, I know you and your task force have done your best." He looked at the faces of his other chiefs of divisions. "Do any of you have any good news to report?"

Silence and the lowering of heads told him his answer. The deputy turned to his left and looked at the director. "Sir, as you heard, despite our best efforts we have been unable to make any headway in finding Devoe or the location of the hostages. I ask your permission to allow Agent J. C. O'Malley to brief you on the second option we discussed earlier."

The director nodded in silence and steepled his hands under his chin as O'Malley stood. "Mr. Director, as we speak, final preparations for the Bureau, Agency, and Department of Defense joint operation called 'Sword' are almost complete. Agent Tanner and Colonel Anderson, 'Team Tan,' have been instructed on the use of their equipment and been briefed on possible scenarios. The strike force, aircraft, and support personnel are staged at Bolling Air Force Base and are on one-hour alert. If approval is given, Operation Sword will be ready to execute within an hour's notice."

The director lowered his hands to the table. "Agent O'Malley, if I approve option two, please tell me again how you'll be able to track the location of Agent Tanner and Colonel Anderson."

"Sir, Team Tan's internal transmitters emit a signal we will be able to monitor aboard a KC-135 military aircraft which will double as my command post. We would maintain a twenty thousand foot altitude and be able to track the location of Team Tan on a computerized, digitized map display within an accuracy of plus or minus five meters."

Turning and looking at Eli and Robert, seated to his right, Thomas spoke quietly. "Gentlemen, we speak of operational names and options, but it all really comes down to your willingness to try and stop these murderers. Before I make the decision, I must ask you if you still want to proceed with this."

Eli looked into the director's searching eyes and spoke without breaking eye contact. "Yes, sir."

Anderson nodded as he clenched his fists in determination. "Yes, sir."

The director exhaled slowly and turned to the deputy. "Larry, as I told you after the discussions with the Attorney General, we feel option two is our only recourse if your manhunt for Devoe and the hostages is unsuccessful. I approve option two with the understanding that your manhunt continues up till the time Devoe gives us for the handoff process to begin. So that everyone in the room is aware, the Attorney General has declared Devoe and his men a threat to national security. The Department of Defense has been authorized to provide us support, to include Delta Force and aviation assets from Special Operations Command. Agent O'Malley has overall operational command, and General Walker from SOCOM will have tactical command. This will be an historic joint operation made necessary by Devoe's proven capabilities. The President has been briefed and has authorized the

Secretary of Defense to allow military involvement. The President has given the Attorney General and myself the authority to approve the option, and as you just heard, I have done so. I will be in the ops center with the deputy during the operation and will monitor the operation in progress and—"

The cell phone in Eli's hand began beeping. Eli waited for the tech to turn on the recorder, then answered. "Agent Tanner."

"Agent Tanner, I'm sure you are with your superiors. Is that correct?"

"Yes, Mr. Devoe, but before I give you the decision, I need to know if the ladies are okay. May I speak to each of them, please."

"Of course, Agent Tanner. I expected no less. Here they are."

"Eli, this is Sandy, I'm doing fine under the circumstances, please tell Robert not to worry. Here is Ashley."

"Hi, Eli. I'm okay. Did you get the keys?"

Eli began to respond, but Devoe's voice came over the speakers again. "That should satisfy you, Agent Tanner. As I told you before, I would not harm them. They are not now here with me, so I await your superior's decision."

Eli let out a breath of air and closed his eyes as he spoke. "Mr. Devoe, my superiors accept your proposal, but there are two stipulations. As you know, Colonel Anderson sustained a major leg wound. He cannot move without assistance. The first stipulation, Mr. Devoe, is that I be with the colonel and assist him in reaching you. Like the colonel, I am a veteran of the Vietnam War, and the colonel and I have become friends. It is a matter of honor, sir, that I accompany him. I assure you I will follow your instructions to the letter and deliver him to you personally. The second stipulation is that the women be kept somewhere safe and not be taken to the handoff location. My superiors are concerned about the women's safety after the handoff is complete. My superiors request that you release the ladies upon the arrival of Colonel Anderson and myself, allow time for confirmation, and then the handoff of Colonel Anderson to you will be conducted. My superiors believe both stipulations are reasonable and actually benefit you."

With his eyes still closed, Eli held his breath and prayed as he waited for a response.

"Agent Tanner, what do you believe?" Devoe asked.

Eli spoke without hesitation. "Mr. Devoe, I agree that the stipulations benefit you and reduce potential complications. I do not believe Mrs. Anderson would want to leave her husband if she was at the site."

"Yes, Agent Tanner, you are correct. You, however, have again underestimated me. I fully expected someone to assist the colonel, and I am honored that it will be you. Your first stipulation is accepted. I also had no intention of causing Mrs. Anderson unnecessary anguish. Your second stipulation is also accepted. But please inform your superiors no tricks will be tolerated. Explosive devices have been placed in very heavily crowded locations that will cause a great many deaths. Should your superiors play games with me, a device will be activated as a lesson to stop such foolishness. Tomorrow morning at 0900 hours I will call with the first instructions for the delivery of Anderson to me. Position yourself and Colonel Anderson in a white van on the south side of the Springfield Mall and await further instruction by cell phone. Good-bye, Agent Tanner. I look forward to meeting you tomorrow."

Eli lowered the phone. Robert nodded and whispered, "Looks like we're a team, Ranger."

7:45 P.M. District of Columbia

Jean Paul folded the last map and placed it on the table before shifting his eyes to the nine men who stood waiting. "My good friends, within fifteen hours it will be over. You have all heard our plan and know what I expect of you. Soy, you will remain in position as observer on the hillside until the operation is complete, then rendezvous with us tomorrow night at our last base." Jean Paul turned to Nim. "Is everything prepared?"

Nim nodded. "All the equipment is packed in the vehicles and all checklists have been rechecked. We can depart when you are ready."

"And you have given Sovan his packet and instructions?"

Again Nim nodded. "He has everything and will depart only when you give him the orders to do so."

Jean Paul handed the folded map to Nim. "I must say my farewell to him, and will speak to Agent Sutton for a moment. You and the others can wait in the vehicles and I will join you in a few minutes." Turning, Jean Paul walked toward the kitchen and doorway leading to the basement.

Ashley was seated on her bed watching Oprah with Sandy when she heard a knock on the open door. Jean Paul stepped in and motioned for her to join him in the large open area outside the room. Sandy touched Ashley's arm. "Tell them we need more bags for the chemical toilet."

Ashley moved out into the well-lit room and saw Sovan wiping his eyes with a handkerchief. She looked at Jean Paul with a questioning stare. "Bad news?" she asked.

"No, Agent Sutton, good news. Tomorrow you and Mrs. Anderson will be free. The proposal was accepted. After tomorrow Sovan will depart your country, like the rest of us. I just bid him farewell for I will not see him again. Like the others, they are dear, trusted, friends."

Realizing the implications of his statement, Ashley lowered her head. "I won't tell Sandy about the trade until we're free—God, I hate you for this."

"Yes, Agent Sutton, I'm sure you do. Now please listen to me very carefully. Tonight your room will be locked, and will remain so until the authorities come to free you. Listen for them and stop them from opening the door until the simple detonation device is removed. This is simply a precaution that you do not try to open the door before they arrive. Please don't be alarmed. The device is harmless unless you do something very foolish. They will merely have to pull the two wires from the exposed charge to disarm the device. Sovan has been instructed to provide everything you need to be comfortable before locking the door."

Jean Paul reached out and gently raised her chin. "Agent Sutton, do you understand my instructions?"

She nodded silently. He nodded as he let his hand fall to his side. "I shall meet Agent Tanner tomorrow, and he will be the one who calls the authorities to set you—"

Ashley's face paled and her eyes widened. "What do you mean you'll meet him?"

Jean Paul took a step back, surprised at her sudden change. "He insisted on assisting Colonel Anderson. He no doubt believes there is still hope for the colonel, but I will quickly dispel those notions very early."

"You'll kill Eli, won't you?" Ashley was unable to hide her tears.

"No, Agent Sutton . . . Why are you crying? Ah . . . I see. You have feelings for Agent Tanner. No, please do not be concerned. My business is only with Anderson. I can assure you that as long as Agent Tanner is not foolish, he will be released unharmed." Seeing the look in Ashley's eyes, he stepped closer. "Your Eli is not prone to foolish things, is he, Agent Sutton?"

Ashley forced herself to keep her eyes on him and shook her head. "He is not a foolish man, Mr. Devoe."

Jean Paul allowed himself a slight smile. "Then there is nothing for you to concern yourself about, Agent Sutton. I must bid you farewell now. It has been a pleasure meeting you. Good-bye."

Ashley watched him until he disappeared up the stairs. Feeling weak, she had difficulty turning to face the door to the small room. She knew Eli would do whatever he could to save Anderson. He would be foolish for all the right reasons. He was going to go into the alley . . . she wiped the tears from her cheeks and took in a deep breath. Exhaling slowly, she rolled her shoulders back.

"Ashley, what's wrong?"

She opened her eyes and saw Sandy standing in the doorway with fear in her eyes. "Did he hurt you? Is he going to . . . ?"

"No, Sandy, I'm fine. I'm crying because I'm happy. Devoe told me we would be free tomorrow. He knows he can't stay any longer without being caught and is freeing us." Ashley took Sandy's arm and led her back into the room. "We're going to be fine. It's almost over for us all."

10:20 P.M. J. W. Marriott Hotel, Washington, D.C.

As Eli inserted the card to open his door, Ramona stepped out of her room and approached him. "Eli, I've been waiting on you—we have to talk."

Eli opened his door and shook his head. "Mona, I know what you want to talk about. Forget it, I'm going."

She followed him into his room and grabbed his arm. "Look at me, Eli. This isn't a game. Devoe will kill you. You can't talk or try to reason with him. He's fixated on killing Anderson, he won't let anything or anyone stand in his way. He will do it, Eli. He will kill Anderson just as he did the others, and he'll kill you for trying to stop him."

Eli looked into her eyes and spoke softly. "I know."

"Then why are you going, for God's sake!" She threw up her hands and turned away. "I don't understand you, Eli. You know if you try to save Anderson, Devoe will kill you, yet you're going to try. It means you're going to die, Eli. Don't you care?"

Eli took off his crumpled blazer and hung it up. "I care, Mona, and I don't happen to think I'm going to die. I think at this time tomorrow evening I'm going to be sitting by myself drinking a beer in a dark place, trying to unwind from the op."

Eli looked at her and pointed at his head. "I can see it, Mona, right here. I can see the bottle of beer in my hand and I can hear the music in the background. Do you think I'm crazy? I'm not crazy, Mona, I just don't feel it's time for me to go under for the last time. Wish me luck, or pat me on the back and say 'Kill the bastards for me,' but don't come in here telling me I'm going to die. I don't need that."

Her eyes welling, Ramona reached out and softly touched his cheek. "I'm sorry, Eli . . . you're right. I'm worried about you, that's all. I . . . I . . . care for you quite a lot and—" She began sobbing and covered her face with her hands.

Eli wrapped his arms around her and hugged her. "Jesus, Mona, don't cry on me. You're the toughest gal I know. Where's my old tennis partner, the one who gave no mercy to anybody?"

Ramona slowly backed away from him and looked into his eyes. "Stay with me tonight, Eli. Hold me and—"

Brad Brewer stepped into the doorway and came to an abrupt halt. "Oh . . . uh, I'm sorry. I was just—"

Eli motioned Brewer in. "Where's the colonel?" he asked.

Brewer motioned over his shoulder. "He's rolling himself down. He asked me to come ahead and make sure the door was open."

Eli looked at Ramona and wrinkled his brow. "The colonel is staying the night with me. We're a team now and we—"

Ramona lifted her hand. "I understand. I guess I'd better get to bed, it's going to be a long day tomorrow . . . but I guess you already know that, Eli. Take care, I want you to drink that beer you saw in your head." She took a step, kissed his cheek, then left.

Brewer raised an eyebrow once she was gone. "I messed somethin' up, didn't I?"

Eli smiled. "A G-man mess somethin' up?"

Anderson rolled through the doorway and whistled as he

looked over the room. "You FBI guys must get paid one helluva per diem. Look at that, they even turned down the beds and left mints. Eli, you want yours?"

Brewer patted Eli's back. "I'll pick you two up at six in the morning. Get some sleep, you're both going to need it." He walked out, shutting the door behind him.

Anderson unwrapped a mint and raised his eyes to Eli. "You think you'll be able to sleep?"

Eli sat on the bed, took the mint from Robert's hand and popped it into his mouth. "I think I'm going to try. It's settling in, and I'm getting used to it now, kind of like walking point. You know something is out there but you don't know where and when it's going to happen . . . you just know it is going to happen. It settles on you and you accept it." Eli quit chewing and looked into Anderson's eyes. "I've accepted it, Robert. It's out there and I'm ready for it when it comes."

Anderson nodded in silence.

CHAPTER 20

4:30 A.M. J. W. Marriott Hotel

Eli sat up in bed, fumbled with the light switch, and finally flicked it on. Mumbling, he got up and walked toward the door that someone was knocking on. He opened it and blinked. General Walker stood before him in camouflage fatigues.

"Morning, Tanner," the general said, then pushed the door all the way open and strode in, followed by two men and a waiter who was pushing a cart. The general clapped his hands together and barked, "Rise and shine, Team Tan, we're burning daylight, we've got work to do. Up, Colonel. First order of business is for you two to eat."

Eli let the departing waiter pass by him and turned to the officer. "General, we can't be burning daylight, it's still dark outside. My God, what time is it, anyway?"

Walker ignored the comment and question and motioned to the cart. "Eat, Tanner, you'll both need something in your stomachs. It will be your last meal for a while. It's only scrambled eggs, bacon, and toast, but you'll need it."

Walker motioned to the other men, who cleared off the table and set down their cases. "These are technical support people from the Agency. They'll be testing and helping you insert the transmitters. While you're eating I'll go over the schedule. You have eight minutes to finish your meal, then the transmitters will be inserted and we'll get a read from the command and control bird. O'Malley and Pullen are already airborne in the C and C, and we've tested the transmitters and they're reading them five by five. We want to test them again once they're inserted. Once that's done, we'll run another test outside and I'll brief you on the new accessories that O'Malley's tech people added to the van. Then we'll be escorted to Fort Myer to your staging area, where you will receive last minute instructions and await the call from Devoe to start the op."

Walker strode to the window and looked out at the dark sky. "Weather conditions are good for us. It's going to be a hot day, but there will be enough clouds to keep the airborne C and C out of sight. You'll be happy to know the Secretary of Defense approved all our requests for support and even upped the ante. We now have an additional strike detachment to allow more flexibility and quicker reaction time. We also acquired a special bird with infrared capability. Since the handoff site will probably be remote, the bird might be able to spot Devoe and his people from their body and vehicle heat signatures. Finding them before you arrive will give us plenty of time to position the strike force for a quick assault and also tell us where the targets are located and how many."

Eli raised his fork and spoke with his mouth full. "Sir, is there any chance we can take Devoe alive?"

Walker shook his head. "My people won't have time to read him and the others their rights, Tanner, or shout warnings. My people are trained to kill, and that's what they're going to do. I'm getting ahead of myself, but remember what I told you yesterday. When my people come in, they're coming in fast. You both must be on the ground faceup so they can ID you. Don't panic when you hear gunfire and explosions. Now, getting back to where I was . . ."

Eli exchanged looks of disbelief with Anderson and looked again at the one-inch-diameter capsule the technician held out to him. The tech made an apologetic shrugging motion. "We coated them with butter so they would go down easier."

Eli took the lightweight capsule from the man's hand and

held it up. "It looks like it's for a horse. What happens if this thing turns sideways when I try to pass it?"

"Swallow it, Tanner," Walker said impatiently. "You can worry about that after the op. The C and C is waiting for a read."

Eli placed the blue capsule on the back of his tongue, shut his eyes and gulped.

Seeing that his companion was still standing and breathing, Anderson mimicked his motions but immediately grabbed a glass of water to wash it down.

Putting on a headset and attaching a small device to his fatigue shirt, Walker spoke into the small ball in front of his lips. "Command, this is Delta Six, transmitters have been inserted, how's your read? Over. . . . Roger. Outstanding. I will tell them. Be advised we'll be moving outside in two mikes. Out."

Walker faced the two men. "Even from inside the hotel the transmitters are still reading five by five on their map displays. They're good to go. Let's move."

Minutes later Eli stepped out the rear entrance of the hotel into the service area and knew without a doubt it was past the point of no return. Six FBI vehicles were parked end-to-end, with two agents standing by each vehicle, and directly in front of him was a white Plymouth Voyager. Walker strode past Eli and looked up at the dark sky, speaking into his mike. "Command, this is Delta Six. We are outside and preparing to depart for staging area. Do you have a good read on Team Tan? . . . Roger. Outstanding. We'll be departing in one mike, out."

The general motioned to the van. "Let's move it. I'll ride with you to the Fort Myer staging area and explain how the radio works. The Agency installed an FM tac radio into the vehicle so you can communicate with the C and C bird."

Eli climbed in and sat behind the steering wheel as agents helped Robert into the front passenger seat. Walker sat in the back seat and leaned forward. "Transmitters are working fine and everything is good to go. Let three escorts proceed us, then pull in behind the third car. The rest will follow."

Eli shook his head as he started the engine. "General, I guess I should have told you, I'm not a very good city driver."

Walker leaned back in the seat and fastened his safety belt. "The police won't pull you over today, Tanner. Time to move."

Thirty minutes later Eli sat behind the steering wheel of the Voyager in the deserted Fort Myer post exchange parking lot. He glanced at his watch and saw it was almost six-fifteen as he listened to the general explain how the operation was being controlled from the airborne command post.

". . . and your transmitters are emitting a signal to the C and C that shows up as a small blinking yellow ball on their computer map displays. My scout birds will be directed by the C and C and keep a parallel course three miles away and out of sight while you two are on the move. They'll be flying low level and be alternated every hour with another bird so we can refuel and keep at least two birds in the air at—"

Eli's cell phone began beeping. He looked at the general, answered and held the phone slightly away from his ear so Walker and Anderson could hear.

"Agent Tanner, I am calling for Mr. Devoe. He apologizes but says you must collect Anderson and move to the following location. Be at Iwo Jima statue in no less than forty-five minutes. If you are followed, a bomb will go off in a Metro train station. Do you understand?"

Eli spoke slowly. "Yes, I understand. Colonel Anderson and I will be there." The line went dead, and Eli was about to speak when O'Malley's voice came over the van's radio speakers. "Team Tan, this is Command. We monitored the call. Looks like we were right about him moving the time up. He's smart. We are notifying Washington P.D. and park police to stay out of the area so there's no mistakes. Suggest you depart now to give yourself plenty of time in the traffic. Do you roger? Over."

Eli pressed the dimmer switch. "Roger, Command. And we will comply. Out."

Walker extended his hand to Eli. "Tanner, I won't wish you luck because you and I know in this business luck is made—make some, Tanner. Just remember, shoot and move. I'll see you when it's over."

The general patted Anderson's shoulder then got out of the van. He shut the door, gave it a rap, and barked, "Get movin'."

Eli backed into a space in the parking lot near the Iwo Jima statue and panned the other cars, wondering which one they would be told to switch to. Anderson eyed his companion and shook his head. "You weren't kidding, were you?"

"About what?"

"About being a bad driver. Eli, if you keep it up, we're not going to have to worry about Devoe killing us."

"Sir, give me a break. I'm just a little nervous here, and the damn traffic and shitbirds for drivers around here don't help. I'm sorry I ran over the curb leaving the fort. And I'm sorry I didn't see that car when we merged into that damn lane. Hell, that idiot must have been doin' fifty-five, sixty."

"That's right, Eli, he was; it's the speed limit. I'll keep an eye out next time and maybe we can get through this together. You want some Chee•tos?"

Eli reached in the bag, took out a handful and motioned with his head toward the bumper-to-bumper traffic only twenty-five yards away. "I hate traffic. I don't know how these people do it."

"It's called making a living, Eli. I have friends who work in the city and their commute is two hours in the morning and two and a half in the evening. They get home in time to eat, catch the news, and go to bed. . . . It's crazy here. It's no wonder the government is screwed up, everyone is a zombie."

Eli popped one of the Chee•tos into his mouth and was about to respond when his cell phone beeped. "Agent Tanner," he said.

"Agent, move immediately to Lady Bird Johnson Park. It is to your south and very close. Stay in right lane, there is only one exit. Drive into parking lot and park on east side. On the south side of lot you will see a blue trash can. You and Anderson exit your vehicle and leave everything behind including your cell phone. Take nothing from your vehicle. You will find envelope under trash can. Read instructions and follow to the letter. No tricks."

Eli spoke quickly. "Listen, bub, the colonel can't walk without crutches, so he'll be using them and—"

"My name is not Bub. I am called Sovan. No crutches. Carry him. Nothing is to be taken with you. No tricks, bub."

The line went dead. "I don't like that guy," Eli said.

The car speakers crackled and O'Malley's voice filled the van. "Team Tan, this is Command. We monitored the call. Be cool, Tanner, keep a rapport. The park is very close by, less than a mile. Looks like you'll be switching vehicles there. From here on out you two are on your own until it's over, but know we're close and got you on our screens. Over."

Eli started the van and pressed the dimmer. "Roger, Command, we are moving now. We appreciate your support. Will call when we arrive at the park. Out."

Eli shook his head as he slipped the gear into Drive. "Be cool, he says. He's not havin' to drive in this damn traffic. Rapport? Yeah, right."

Anderson filled his mouth with Chee•tos and rolled his eyes.

Eli pulled to the east curb, turned off the engine and pushed the dimmer switch. "Command, this is Team Tan. We have arrived and see a bunch of cars in the parking lot. There's a boat marina to our west. Any last minute instructions? Over."

"Negative, Team Tan. Good luck and good hunting. Over."

"Roger, Command. Team Tan exiting vehicle. Out."

Eli opened the door and walked around to help Anderson. "Okay, sir, easy does it to the ground . . . good. How do you want me to do this, carry you, or can you lean on me and hop on one foot?"

The colonel steadied himself and tested a small hop. "I can hop along if you just help me keep my balance . . . yeah, that's good."

At the blue trash can, Eli helped him sit on the curb before rolling the can back and finding the manila envelope. Inside were a single piece of paper and two keys on a ring. He began reading and his face flushed. He looked up at the morning sky and mumbled, "Damn, damn, damn."

Anderson worriedly looked up at him. "What's wrong?"

Eli's shoulders slumped forward. "We're not exchanging cars. We're going to get in a damn boat. Note says a bass boat at Slip Ten, on Pier Two just behind us. We're to drive the boat upriver toward Georgetown and stop once we pass under the Francis Scott Key Bridge. . . . Once there, we're supposed to strip naked. Everything is to go over the side, and then buddy boy will call us. Says our new phone is in the cooler on the boat. Damn, damn, damn, why a damn boat?"

"What's wrong with a boat?" Robert asked.

Eli helped him up and sighed. "It's a long story. Come on."

Airborne Command Post

Seated in a high-back swivel chair, Agent O'Malley leaned closer to the large color monitor where a map of a small portion of the Washington area was displayed. O'Malley canted his head and looked at the Air Force captain seated beside him, who sat behind an identical monitor. "What the hell is going on? My blinking dot has them in the middle of the Potomac River."

The captain nodded. "That's a roger, sir, they are in the middle of the Potomac. They are obviously traveling in a boat.

There! You can see they passed beneath the Memorial Bridge heading north toward Roosevelt Island."

Seated behind O'Malley, Chris Pullen rolled closer in his chair. "It's a good move on Devoe's part. Avoids the chance of any tail and Team Tan can easily be watched. Devoe is even better than I thought."

O'Malley didn't respond. He hadn't anticipated the move, either, and that worried him. Devoe had just surprised him, and that had rarely happened in his twenty-four years in the Bureau. He shut his eyes for a moment. He told himself the unexpected boat ride wouldn't make any difference, but instinct told him Devoe wasn't finished springing surprises just yet.

Naked, Eli unwrapped Anderson's leg bandage and tossed it over the side. He helped the colonel to his feet and raised his hands in the air. "Buddy boy's note said we were to turn around slowly three times then be ready for a call. Sir, please turn *real* slow so you don't rock the boat."

Anderson raised his hands, carefully balanced himself, and began moving around. "Eli, you're still wearing your gold necklace, you'd better lose it."

Eli kept slowly turning. "Can't, sir, it's a part of me. I haven't taken it off in over twenty years. It's my honest-to-goodness good luck charm. When we get to the guy that checks us, I'll tell him he can drill into the Buddha or do anything he wants to prove to himself it's not bugged but I'm not taking it off unless I absolutely have to."

Anderson hopped around again. "I understand."

The new cell phone began beeping and Eli answered. He listened for a full minute and finally said, "Got it, Mr. Sovan. We will comply."

Eli handed Anderson the phone and, speaking over his shoulder, walked very slowly toward the front of the bass boat. "Buddy boy says there's a built-in fish hold up here. Inside is a plastic bag with different sizes of shorts, T-shirts, and sandals.

At least we won't be meeting Devoe in our birthday suits. He says there's new bandages, too, and a cooler with drinks."

Anderson lowered himself to the deck. "Where do we go next?"

"I don't know. We're to proceed upriver just a ways to a boat dock on our right, where we'll see a green Impala parked in a lot just behind the dock. He wants us to take the car. Instructions and keys are in the glove compartment. Oh great, take a look at these iridescent green shorts. They're the same color as tennis balls."

Twenty minutes later Eli helped Anderson into the passenger seat and shut the Impala's door. Getting in behind the steering wheel, he looked at Robert, who had already opened the glove box and was reading the single page of instructions. Finished, he handed Eli the keys. "We're to get on MacArthur Boulevard, just behind us, and take it north to a small park in the small town of Glen Echo. Says we'll be meeting a person named Kenny there."

Eli started the engine and looked down at the iridescent yellow-green shorts and bright orange T-shirt. "All we need is a boom box—we could be rappers!"

Identically dressed, Anderson lifted his foot and admired his black and blue Nike sandals. "These are cool. That's the right word, isn't it, cool?"

Eli shrugged as he backed the car up to turn around. "If cool means ugly, then it's right on. All I know is we're easy targets in this getup."

Anderson set the piece of paper on his lap and studied Eli's face. "Do you think your idea will work?"

Eli kept his eyes straight ahead. "It has to."

General Walker sat inside the cavernous cabin of an Air Force PAVE Low III Special Operations helicopter that sat on a concrete pad at Bolling Air Force Base. With the general were seven men, seated behind sensor consoles and radio communications equipment. An Army major motioned to his monitor. "Sir, the C and C just downlinked to us. Take a look."

Wearing a headset, Walker looked at the map display on the monitor and saw the blinking yellow ball. "Command, this is Delta Six. We have a good downlink and have your picture. I have them on MacArthur Boulevard heading north, over."

"Roger, Delta Six, that's a good copy. When will your scout birds begin tailing, over?"

"Command, they are airborne now. I will keep them west of road. Be advised my scouts' transmitters will show up as blue balls on your screens. The strike unit and I will redeploy north in five mikes and laager vicinity Bethesda to keep us in general proximity to Team Tan, over."

"Roger, Delta Six. Good copy. Out."

Walker pointed at the screen and spoke to the major. "Keep the scout birds at least three miles to the west of Team Tan, but parallel. We won't need to keep the strike force airborne until Tan gets away from the urban sprawl."

The major nodded. "Roger, sir, I understand." He pushed his mike sidebar and spoke in a monotone. "Scout One, turn heading zero three zero and maintain course. I will direct you to recon area. Over."

Anacostia

Ashley wiped the white gypsum from her hands and shook her head as she backed up from the wall. "It's brick behind the Sheetrock. Looks like we're stuck here until help arrives."

Sandy stared at the door. "You think they're all gone?"

"Nobody responded when I yelled," Ashley said. "They must be. Just as a precaution, help me move my mattress to the door. I'm going to lay behind it and listen for our help at the door."

Sandy raised her eyes to Ashley. "Robert is giving himself to them, isn't he?"

Ashley knew she couldn't lie to her. She sat down on the bed and put her arm around Sandy's shoulder. "Yes, he is, Sandy, but Devoe told me Eli is going to be with Robert. I know Eli Tanner and I can tell you he won't give Robert up without a fight."

Tears streamed down Sandy's face as she rested her head on Ashley's shoulder.

Ashley felt her eyes water and lowered her head.

Kenny Chun lit a Kool and pushed away from the Ford Bronco he was leaning against. He put the lighter in his pocket and picked up the bag at his feet as the green Impala pulled into the park and rolled to a stop only a few feet away.

Inside the car, Eli turned off the ignition and looked at Anderson. "Remember to stay down when the action starts."

Anderson dipped his chin as the small brown-skinned man wearing a huge black cowboy hat approached.

Kenny took the cigarette out of his mouth, tapped on the window, and Eli rolled it down. "I'm Kenny, and I am not armed. Both of you step out of the car and stand by that picnic table. Keep your hands above your heads."

Eli got out slowly and looked down at Kenny's footwear. "Nice boots."

Seeing that the colonel was having difficulty, Kenny motioned to him. "You can help Anderson, G-man."

As Eli helped Robert walk to the table, Kenny opened the bag and took out a metal detector wand and stepped up to both men. "Take off the shirts and pull down your shorts, please."

As soon as Eli took off his shirt, Kenny's eyes narrowed and he pointed at the gold necklace. "You didn't listen, G-man."

Eli lifted the Buddha from his chest. "Kenny, check it, man. Break it in two if you want, but be careful so I can glue it back. I've worn it since 1972 and he blesses me."

Kenny lifted the Buddha from Eli's hand and eyed the wearer. "Are you a Buddhist?"

"I believe it's good luck. It belonged to my Cambodian scout who was killed in Vietnam."

With a pocketknife, Kenny scratched both sides of the worn ivory likeness, then ran his hand all the way around the thick gold chain. Satisfied, he raised his wand. "Lift your chain, G-man, so I can pass this over your chest and stomach. You may keep your charm. . . . Now turn around and bend over . . . stand erect and spread your feet apart." Kenny passed the wand beneath Eli's legs, and seemingly satisfied, commanded, "Help Anderson keep his balance."

After checking the colonel, he replaced the wand in his bag and took out a cell phone. Seconds after pushing keys, he spoke. "This is Kenny, they are clean . . . Yes, we will depart immediately." He lowered the phone, took car keys from his pocket and tossed them to Eli. "Mr. Devoe is pleased. Both of you get in the Bronco. Time for us to ride."

11:03 A.M. Airborne Command Post

O'Malley unconsciously spat out the end of an eraser he'd been chewing on as he watched the monitor. A small piece of the eraser struck his own hand, startling him, and he looked down. Seeing the eraser tip, he stared perplexedly at his pencil for a moment before realizing what he'd been doing. He turned. "How long have they been moving since they last stopped?"

Pullen looked at his watch, then his notes. "One hour and thirty minutes, J.C. Have they gotten off the Beltway yet?"

O'Malley exhaled slowly and motioned to the screen. "They've almost made the entire I-495 loop around the city. They're approaching Bethesda, where they got on. . . . I don't like it . . . they should have struck out by now for the final site. Why is Devoe delaying? How long will the transmitters work?"

Pullen smiled. "Over eighteen hours. My babies won't let us down."

The Air Force captain behind the monitor leaned forward in his chair, closer to the display. "They just exited onto I-270, heading north toward Frederick."

"Okay, now we're talking," O'Malley said. "They're making their move. Looks like the handoff will be somewhere to the north." He spoke into his mike as he unbuckled his safety belt. "Delta Six, this is Command. Appears the handoff will be to the north, over."

"Command, this is Delta Six. Roger. We are jumping our strike force to Frederick and will stand by. We are making map study of terrain to the north, but it's obvious the mountains west of Frederick would be the best for them. Provide visibility and yet cover of trees. We are sending our redbird over to make a run over the Catoctin range and Blue Ridge range west of Frederick and will have printout of hot spots within thirty mikes. We'll uplink the info to you as soon as we have it. Over."

O'Malley responded, "Roger, Delta Six. Out." He and Pullen walked to the lighted map boards on the far bulkhead.

Pullen pointed out, "The general's right, the mountains would be best. The valleys are too heavily populated. The Catoctin range has a lot of development . . . but look at the Blue Ridge, nothing to speak of. I'd bet it's somewhere along this portion of the Blue Ridge range."

O'Malley stepped closer to the map. "Not many roads going over them. . . . They'd want an entry road and at least one exit road, I would think. Circle all the areas with a grease pencil that fit this description: high ground with good observation, remote, and with a road very nearby. Once the infrared hot spot report comes back, we'll compare them to what we circled."

O'Malley stepped back and said aloud, "It's about time, we're finally getting ahead of Devoe."

* * *

Kenny leaned forward and tapped Eli's shoulder. "She's a good singer, huh?"

Eli hadn't been listening to the radio but nodded anyway. It was the first time the small Cambodian cowboy had talked to him except for giving directions. He listened for a moment and glanced in the rearview mirror. "I like Reba but I still think Patsy Cline will never be beat. That gal could wail."

Kenny lit a Kool and blew the smoke toward his partially opened window. "Yeah, she was good, but Reba is very beautiful, too. I saw her in the movie with Kenny Rogers . . . she was hot. You like my boots, huh?"

Eli looked back at the road and saw a sign saying they were only a few miles from Frederick. "Sure do. Rattlesnake, right?"

"Texas rattlesnake."

"Yeah, shoulda known. Tony Llama?"

"Of course; I got the best. Kenny Rogers has a pair like them. You will exit on Alternate 40 and head west toward the mountains. The exit is only two miles ahead."

Eli glanced at Anderson and nodded. "Got it, exit on Alternate 40 and head west. So, Kenny, do you two-step and do that line dance stuff?"

Kenny's face tightened and he blew another cloud toward the window. "Your American women don't like my brown skin. Even fat ones won't dance with me."

"Don't feel bad, Kenny, they won't dance with me, either. They don't like my gray hair and my age."

Kenny leaned forward. "Really?"

Eli raised a hand. "I swear, but a buddy told me the secret to success. He says country western bars are funny. You have to hang out awhile in one, let the regulars get to know you. You can't bar-hop and expect to do good. I'll bet you've been doin' a lot of traveling and haven't had time to hang in one place. That's your problem—you have to hang."

Kenny nodded as if to himself. "Yeah, hang. Yeah, that's probably it. I practice, you know? I have a video that shows all the steps. It's not so hard. Heel, toe, slide step, slide step, left step and . . ."

Seeing the yellow ball on the screen move toward the west, O'Malley clapped his hands. "It's the mountains!" he blurted, and spoke into the mike. "Delta Six, you monitor their turn off I-270? Over."

In his helicopter, General Walker responded immediately. "Command. Roger, we are moving strike force now to west side of Catoctin range and will go into hide position. We are keeping treetop level so we won't be spotted from Blue Ridge range, and there are plenty of small valleys to hide ourselves in. I have our Blue Flock on standby alert and will scramble them once Team Tan stops. Over."

Pullen wiped beads of sweat from his brow. "It won't be long now, J.C."

O'Malley's smile slowly faded and his jaw tightened. "I'll bet Tanner and the colonel are thinking the same thing—poor bastards."

CHAPTER 21

Operations Center, FBI Headquarters

The director strode into the conference room and took a seat at the head of the table. The deputy director stood and motioned toward the large-screen television to his right. "Sir, we have here the map display that the command and control aircraft is seeing on its monitors, and the speakers we've set up will allow us to hear all communications between Command and the tactical commander, General Walker. We believe the handoff will happen very soon. As you can see on the screen, Team Tan has crossed the Catoctin Mountains and is proceeding up the National Highway toward South Mountain, which is part of the Blue Ridge chain. The Air Force redbird has identified several hot spots in remote areas, meaning they've sensed infrared body and vehicle heat signatures here and here. We believe the handoff is this first location, inside the South Mountain Park on this access road. At this site the redbird has picked up the signatures of four vehicles and seven probable humans. We believe it is Devoe and his people. The blinking yellow dot on the screen is Team Tan, and you can see they're approximately three miles from the suspected handoff location. These blinking blue dots are the strike force helicopters. They've just moved into this position in a meadow a mile from the suspected site and are making final preparations for their assault. What you don't see on the screen is our diversion package known as Blue Flock. They will not be scrambled until Team Tan reaches the site."

The director studied the screen a moment before shifting his gaze back to his deputy. "How will the diversion and strike force insertion be coordinated?"

The deputy lowered his pointer and stepped closer to the table. "Sir, the timing is all based on the telephone calls. Let me explain. Once Devoe is assured we've lived up to our part of the bargain, he'll tell Agent Tanner where the hostages are located and allow him to call us. Tanner will in fact call the Airborne Command Post, which will act as though they are our operations, in case Devoe is monitoring. We'll hear the call and immediately begin the recovery operation of the women. We have six helicopters placed throughout the city area with tactical teams on board. Once we know where the hostages are located, we can have a chopper over them in less than three minutes. Our tac team people are prepared to rappel to the roof of the building if a suitable landing site is not available. Regardless, we'll have the hostages within four to five minutes. During that time Blue Flock will be scrambled and be on station. We will not tell Agent Tanner the women hostages are safe until Blue Flock is in position and ready to execute. Once they are and begin their approach and are only a mile from the handoff site, we'll confirm to Agent Tanner that the women are safe. When Command uses the phrase, 'The women are confirmed safe,' that will be the trigger to execute. The strike force will begin its attack approach perpendicular to Blue Flock so they don't interfere with one another. Once Blue Flock is clear of the target area, the strike force will come in and immediately drop the detachment by fast rope."

The director lowered his head a moment before raising his eyes again. "Are we sure Blue Flock will work?"

The deputy slowly shook his head. "Sir, to be quite honest, no. This has not been done before and we had no opportunity to rehearse the scenario using the assets. It was Agent Tanner's idea, and he said he knew the effect of this type of diversion and believed he still could stay focused enough to do what is necessary. It will all be up to him, sir. It will take fifteen to twenty seconds for the strike team to get on the ground. Agent Tanner will have to keep himself and Colonel Anderson alive until the strike force arrives."

Seated behind the director along the wall with the division chiefs, Ramona closed her eyes as the director nodded and spoke almost in a whisper. "It appears the safe outcome of the operation is in Agent Tanner's and God's hands now."

At Kenny's direction, Eli turned off the narrow National Highway onto a gravel road that continued uphill at a steep grade. Completely shaded by mammoth trees on both sides of the road, Eli knew the moment of judgment was close at hand. He reached out and patted Robert's shoulder as he kept his eyes on the road. Ahead, a small man stepped out onto the road raising his right hand. In his left he held a Mac 10.

A cigarette in his mouth, Kenny said, "Agent, stop by my friend, Kaing. Keep both hands on the steering wheel. Anderson, put both your hands on the dash."

Seconds later, Kenny opened the door and Kaing got in with Kenny and trained his weapon on Eli's back. "Drive slowly ahead," he said, and handed Kenny a Sig Sauer 9mm pistol.

Eli shifted to Drive, and looked to his left and right as he drove, realizing once again the subtle truth of Murphy's Law: something can always be counted on to go wrong. It was the trees. They were huge, and he knew there was no way the strike team's ropes would be long enough for the insertion. He would have to delay longer than twenty seconds.

Eli focused again on the road and accepted the calm that was settling over him. It was all right, he told himself, he would succeed, or die trying.

General Walker snatched off his headset and turned to face the young officer who had tapped his shoulder. "What, Captain?"

"Sir, I'm a Civil War buff and I've walked all the battlefields around here, including South Mountain Park. Sir, it's the trees.

They're over two hundred years old up there. The detachment's ropes are only fifty feet long. Those trees up on the ridges are at least seventy feet and probably higher."

Walker spun around and looked at the monitor. "Where's the closest open area?"

The captain pointed. "Here, sir, there are Civil War monuments located in this open grassy area."

"Christ, that's a good hundred and fifty meters away from where the redbird picked up the signatures," Walker blurted. He quickly put on his headset and spoke into the ball. "Strike leader, change of plans. You will land in open area one hundred and fifty meters north of original insertion point. Targets will be to your south one hundred and fifty meters on high ground. Do you roger, over."

"Delta Six. Roger. Will inform other birds and team leaders. Out."

In the airborne command post, O'Malley heard the radio message sent to the strike leader over the tactical frequency and turned to Pullen. "My God, we've just lost Team Tan. The strike force is landing one hundred and fifty meters away . . . there's no way they can get to Team Tan in time."

Pullen lowered his head in silence and closed his eyes.

Ahead just off road, four vehicles were parked side by side. Kenny said, "Stop here. Keep your hands on the wheel."

The rear doors opened and Kenny and Kaing stepped out. Kenny motioned up the road. "Both of you get out and walk ahead. Mr. Devoe is waiting."

Eli got out and walked around to assist Anderson. Two more men appeared from behind the parked four-wheel-drive Suburbans. One carried wood crutches and tossed them to the ground in front of the colonel. "You use those, Anderson. Agent Tanner, do not touch him again."

Eli stepped back and studied both new men as Robert picked up the crutches. They were both carrying short-barreled

Winchester riot shotguns and each had a Sig Sauer pistol in a shoulder holster.

The two men fell in beside Kenny, who commanded, "Walk up the road and stop when I tell you."

Anderson looked at Eli but saw he was looking ahead as if in a trance. Robert whispered anyway. "I . . . I . . . don't know about this, Eli."

"Stead-deee," Eli whispered.

In the FBI headquarters conference room, the deputy pinched the bridge of his nose as he heard about the change of plans.

The director leaned forward in his seat. "Larry, what does that mean, they've changed the insertion location?"

The deputy sighed and raised his head. "Sir, in effect it means it will take the Delta detachment at least several minutes to reach Agent Tanner and the colonel. It means that the chances of Team Tan just fell to almost zero."

The road petered out and became nothing but a wide trail as Eli continued walking up the incline. What looked like the top of the hill lay just ahead, and then he saw that the ground did finally flatten out. Suddenly, three men came into view thirty yards away. He ignored them and panned slowly to his right and his left. He saw immediately that he was actually coming up to the crest of a wide ridge top. To his right the ground rose sharply again, and all around, spaced twenty to thirty feet apart, were the majestic old oaks and maples whose distant branches and leaves high above blocked out most light. The persistent sun, not to be denied, had penetrated the thick canopy with small shafts of light that dappled the ground and formed golden pools all around him. Eli took it all in, and for a moment it reminded him of the trail in Vietnam where his platoon had been ambushed. But this time his enemy was in the open and already waiting for them.

He shifted his eyes to the three waiting men. The man in the center looked like a movie star rather than a killer. He was thin but broad-shouldered, and unlike the others, his eyes were round. But it was his high cheekbones and strong jaw that would have made him stand out in a crowd. Eli continued walking, looking into the man's eyes, and knew he'd been wrong—the man was a killer; it was in his eyes, locked on Robert Anderson.

"Stop here, both of you," Kenny said.

Anderson suddenly recognized the good-looking man. "My God . . . Frenchy?"

Jean Paul ignored Anderson and shifted his gaze to Eli. "It is a pleasure to finally meet you, Agent Tanner. You did not disappoint me. As a man of honor, I now keep my word to you." He lifted his left hand, holding a piece of paper. Standing to the right of Devoe, Hu Nim stepped forward, took the paper from Jean Paul's hand and walked toward Eli. Stopping six paces away, he leaned over, placed the page on the ground, and retraced his steps to his position beside his leader.

Jean Paul motioned to the paper. "It is the address to where the ladies are located. You may use your cell phone and instruct your colleagues of their whereabouts. Read only what is on the paper, Agent Tanner, nothing more."

Eli took the cell phone from his waistband and walked toward the paper, once again looking at the three men, noting the two men flanking Devoe were holding 9mm pistols in their right hands but Devoe had a military style Colt .45 stuck in the waistband of his tan slacks. Eli picked up the page and pressed the keys of the cell phone.

Special Agent O'Malley answered on the first beep. "FBI Operations."

Eli read slowly. "The missing FBI Agent Ashley Sutton and Mrs. Robert Anderson are located in a brick house in Anacostia. The address is 1861 River Lane. They will be found in a basement room. There is a simple detonation device affixed to their door that only requires the removal of the positive and negative wire leads. Call me back at the following number when the women are safe. The number is 227–1446."

Eli lowered the phone and nodded to Devoe. "Sir, you are a man of your word. When I receive the confirmation call, I will also prove I am a man of my word." *And my word is I'm going to kill you, ya sonofabitch.*

Devoe dipped his chin, accepting the compliment, and shifted his eyes to Anderson. "So, Robert, after all these years, you recognize me. . . . Most in your team did not . . . I had to help them remember."

"Why did you have to kill them, Frenchy?"

"It is a matter of honor, old friend. You made promises . . . we all believed you. I am sorry Lieutenant Tram will not witness the justice that is soon to be done. I have here his pistol. It is the one you gave him before you left us. It is fitting, don't you think?"

Ramona sat erect in her seat in the operations conference room listening to the voices of the tactical team, which had just rappeled from its helicopter down onto the back lawn of the house in Anacostia.

"Team One on the ground, moving to back door of the house. Team Two cover."

"Roger One. Got you. Go."

"Clear! Inside kitchen. Team Two and Three, go!"

"Roger. Moving in now . . . We'll go left, Team Three take the right rooms."

"Roger."

"C.P., this is Team One. We see steps leading down to basement. We're going down . . . cover me. . . . I see room and door. . . . Wait, I hear a woman's voice yelling about a bomb attached to door. . . . Agent Sutton, this is Agent Nolin, we know about the bomb. Get away from the door. Sam, you have it spotted?"

"Yeah, got it right here. . . . Okay, it's simple, only two leads attached to battery. I'm going to pull red lead first . . . good . . . now the white . . . good! We're clear. Agent Sutton, you can get up now. Mrs. Anderson, come with me, please."

"C.P., we have ladies with us. I say again we have the ladies with us."

The deputy pushed the switch on his console, switching back to the airborne command post radio frequency, and looked at the director. "Sir, Agent O'Malley was monitoring what we just heard from the airborne C.P. He will now wait until General Walker gives him the go ahead to call Agent Tanner and confirm the ladies are safe. General Walker is waiting for Blue Flock to arrive on station. Once they arrive and begin their approach, General Walker will have Agent O'Malley make the call to Agent Tanner."

The director took in a deep breath and exhaled slowly. Behind him, Ramona Valez squeezed the cross in her hand as she stared at the monitor. "Come on, Eli, I believe in you. . . . I believe."

General Walker spoke quickly into the mike. "Roger, Blue Flock Lead, I understand you and your flock are on station. Request you take up heading zero six zero and begin attack approach immediately. We have you on our screens and will vector you to target area. Target area is fourteen miles from your location and is ridge top, I say again ridge top. Please inform when ready to proceed, over."

"Delta Six, this is Flock Lead. I am banking now and taking up heading zero six zero. My flock is following. I am on course now. I am proceeding toward target, over."

"Roger, Lead. We will vector you, but right now you're looking good on our screens. My air controller will now take over for me."

Walker nodded to the Air Force controller seated in front of the monitor, who immediately switched to the command frequency and spoke into the mike. "Command, this is Delta Six. Make the call to Tanner, now. Flock inbound, over."

In the airborne C.P., O'Malley acknowledged the general and began pressing the cell phone keys.

* * *

Kenny Chun and Kaing had both moved past Eli and Robert and were standing beside Devoe and his two bodyguards. Eli turned slightly. Just three paces to his right rear a Cambodian was holding a shotgun on him. He was about to look for the other Cambodian but his cell phone beeped.

Anderson's eyes darted to him. Eli lifted the phone, turned, and saw the other shotgun-carrying Cambodian directly behind Robert with his weapon pointed at the colonel's back. Taking a breath, Eli answered. "Agent Tanner."

He listened for only five seconds and lowered the phone to his side as he took a step back and nodded to Jean Paul. "Mr. Devoe, the ladies are safe. Thank you." Eli screamed at himself: *Focus, focus, be ready, be ready!*

Jean Paul allowed himself a smile. "You may leave now, Agent Tanner, your duty is ov—"

Jean Paul heard a high-pitched scream like nothing he'd heard before, and suddenly the ground shook and his ears seemed to explode in pain.

Eli was in motion the instant he heard the jet's approach, but still wasn't prepared for the violent ear-shattering *cracking* sound as the jet fighter streaked overhead just above the treetops. He winced in pain but was already on the crouching Cambodian, who, like all the others, had instinctively ducked down. Grabbing the barrel, Eli jerked the weapon free from the stunned man, who still had his eyes closed in pain. He butt-stroked the man across the face just as another jet swooshed over just above the treetops at over five hundred miles per hour. Again the ground rumbled and the shattering, cracking sound reverberated in his head as Eli swung around, pointed the barrel at the crouching man behind Anderson, and fired. Half the man's head disappeared. Screaming to alleviate his pain, Eli jacked in another round, leveled the barrel at his next target and fired. He took another step as he pumped and fired, working right to left on the targets as yet another jet screamed over.

Having seen two of his men propelled backward by the

shotgun blasts, Hu Nim grabbed Devoe's arm and pulled him back. He fired his pistol as fast as he could pull the trigger.

Eli was spun around by the impact of a bullet that passed through his left bicep. He screamed as another jet streaked over, and spun back facing Kenny, who was running toward him with his pistol raised. Eli fired, and Kenny's eyes bulged and his big hat flew off as he doubled over in midair and was flung back four feet. Unable to lift his left arm, Eli dropped the shotgun and scooped up Kenny's dropped pistol, spun and fired at the man who was already firing his Mac 10 submachine gun at Anderson, who was trying to roll away from the small eruptions kicking up around him. Eli's bullet tore through the man's stomach, but the man kept his finger on the trigger as he staggered back. Eli charged forward, firing with each step, and finally the small Cambodian fell to the ground in a bloody heap.

Unable to hear, Eli felt the heat as the ground shook beneath his feet as yet another F-15 streaked over, causing another blizzard of falling leaves to swirl as if caught in a hurricane. He dropped to his knee, glanced over his shoulder and saw that Anderson had been stitched across the legs. The colonel's mouth was open but Eli couldn't hear what he was saying or yelling. He knew the look, however. It was fear. Eli threw himself forward and rolled just as bullets tore at the ground where he'd been. He came up in a shooter's crouch and saw Devoe and another man firing their pistols. He returned their fire and both men ducked behind the crest of the ridge. Something struck the back of Eli's foot and he glanced down. Another Sig Sauer was laying by his heel. He looked over his shoulder and saw Anderson lower his arm and fall back to the ground as if unconscious.

Eli rose up again, firing his entire magazine, then dropped down, picked up the pistol, jacked a round into the chamber, and broke into a run toward a nearby tree. Just as he'd thought they would, both men rose to fire again. Not seeing their target, they stepped forward. Eli stepped away from the tree, aimed and squeezed the trigger. The man beside Devoe jerked, staggered back, and fell to his knees. Eli moved the barrel to aim at Devoe, but Devoe fell to the ground and crawled back out of sight. Eli walked forward, leveled his pistol at the kneeling man, and fired. The bullet blew through the man's head and exited taking a portion of his skull. Devoe suddenly rose up covered in the man's blood and brain tissue and fired.

Eli jerked from the bullet's impact but remained on his feet and continued walking forward, pulling the trigger. "Die, die, die, die!" he screamed.

Jean Paul was thrown back against a tree trunk by the first bullet's blow to his chest and jerked spasmodically with each additional strike. He began sliding down the trunk, but his shirt collar caught on a knot.

Eli staggered forward, and the empty pistol dropped from his hand. Barely able to stand, he looked into Jean Paul's eyes. "You—You bastard, die."

Jean Paul's eyes lingered on Eli for a moment before shifting to Anderson's still body. Blood dribbled from his mouth as he spoke in a wheezing whisper. "It is over." He tried to lift his trembling hand to his blood-soaked shirt, but too weak, his hand fell back to his side.

Eli blinked to keep the blood running down his forehead out of his eyes. With a shaking hand he reached out, lifted the dying man's gold chain and placed the ivory Buddha between Devoe's trembling lips. His knees weakening, Eli sank to his knees and fell forward into a golden pool of light. Incredibly tired, he couldn't keep his eyes open any longer. The pain suddenly subsided as he sank further down into the cold darkness.

In the airborne command post O'Malley sat with his eyes closed, listening to the strike leader's heavy breathing as he ran from the helicopter with his detachment. "We're seventy five . . . meters clear of bird and . . . running toward ridge . . . We . . . we . . . are . . . receiving no fire. . . . We're entering tree line . . . going up ridge . . . still no incoming fire. . . . We're

almost . . . on top. . . . Jesus H. Christ . . . all targets are down . . .
I say again, all down . . . We're looking for . . . I see one friendly
down here. Need medic ASAP . . . We're looking for other
one . . . Found him . . . He's down too . . . everybody down . . .
need medic . . . I say again need medic, all targets and friendlies
are down."

FBI Headquarters

The helicopter settled onto the roof pad and the chopper's
door slid back. Ashley jumped down and ran straight to the
steps leading to the doorway. Four minutes later she pushed
open the operations conference room door and saw everyone
in the room sitting, staring at a large black speaker on a table
beside a huge television screen filled with a computerized map
display. She turned, saw a friendly face, and strode to Ramona,
who like the others was staring at the speaker. Suddenly, a
voice came over the speaker.

"Delta Six, this is the strike leader. Medics are working on
friendlies at this time. Preliminary report is as follows. Colonel
Anderson received multiple gunshot wounds to lower legs but
is stable. Agent Tanner received gunshot wound to left arm and
forehead. Head wound is not serious, I say again not serious, it
appears bullet grazed him. He is unconscious at this time but he
is stable. Report on terrorists is as follows: five dead, two
wounded. Both wounded are stable. Be advised an eighth terrorist was spotted by scout bird and neutralized on adjoining
ridge to our west. Terrorist is confirmed KIA. Strike force
casualties are one twisted ankle. We are moving wounded to
birds now, over."

Ashley stood frozen in place as the deputy flipped the switch
on his console and the static coming from the speaker ceased.
He stood and faced the director. "Sir, I believe this operation is
over. Devoe and his men are no longer a threat."

CHAPTER 22

Walter Reed U.S. Army Hospital, Washington, D.C.

With a shopping bag at her feet and a bandage around her forehead, Ashley leaned against the wall of the emergency room's waiting area. Brad Brewer pushed through the crowd of agents and reporters, entered the small room and walked straight up to her with a lopsided smile. "Agent Sutton, I have good news for you—he's fine, can't hear very well, but he was on his feet when I saw him ten minutes ago. I told him the good news about Anderson's condition not being life threatening. He asked about you."

Ashley's jaw muscles rippled. "The bastards held me at a debrief until just an hour ago. I should have been here when he arrived. Can you get me in to see him?"

Brewer looked around and lowered his voice. "They're moving him up to the fourth floor once they clean him up, Room 410. I came to get you. Nobody's supposed to see him until after his debrief, but I talked to the doc and he said if we made it quick you could see him. Look, I told the doc you two were engaged, so if you see the doc, play the game, will ya?"

Ashley patted Brewer's shoulder. "Thanks. Let's go."

Minutes later Brewer opened the door to Room 410 and allowed Ashley to step in first. He was about to follow her, but she turned around and was coming out, saying, "He's not here yet."

310

A doctor walked toward them and smiled at Ashley. "Well, he looks pretty good considering what he's been through, doesn't he?"

Ashley canted her head. "He's not here yet, sir."

The major's face paled. "That's impossible. I just left him ten minutes ago. He said he was going to the bathroom before he put on his gown. The nurse should have wheeled him up by now."

Brewer shrugged. "I'm sure the nurse is on the way with him," he said to Ashley.

She dipped her chin. "Please excuse me, gentlemen. I have to find a rest room myself." Bag in hand, she quickly walked down the hallway and went directly to the elevators.

Three minutes later she stepped out the doors of the hospital onto the lighted sidewalk. As she walked toward the small park across the street, she picked up her pace. He was seated on a bench, looking up at the stars. Seconds later she slowed her steps and forced herself to walk as if on a stroll. When she was within six feet of him, she saw that his left arm was in a sling and his head bandage was just like hers.

Eli broke his skyward gaze, sensing the presence of another, and lowered his eyes to the approaching woman.

Without a word, Ashley set the shopping bag on the bench and took out a bottle of Budweiser. She twisted off the cap and handed it to him. Reaching into the bag again, she took out a cassette player, set it down on the other side of him and pushed the Play button. Immediately, Garth Brooks's voice broke the silence with "The Last Dance." She leaned over and spoke into his ear. "Wind-down time, Tanner—you deserve it." She kissed his cheek, and giving him a last look, turned and began walking down the sidewalk. Tears rolled down her cheeks.

She was ten yards when he barked, "Hey, Sutton, ya wanna share my stars?"

She stopped and turned around. "I'd love to share your stars, Tanner, but Ramona told me what you saw in your head before the mission—that you were alone."

Eli took a sip of beer and raised the bottle. "Okay, now I've done what I saw. Come here and join me . . . please. I . . . I was worried about ya . . . real worried."

Ashley walked back, took a beer from the bag and sat down beside him. "Yeah, well I was worried about you, too, Tanner."

He leaned back again, looking up at the stars. "Garth can sure sing that song, can't he?"

She leaned back and rested her head on his shoulder. "He sure can. . . . You feeling all right?"

"I'm feeling a whole lot better now. Thanks for making it come true. . . . I had to get away for a while. It was the smell, ya know? I'll face it after I drink this beer and share my stars with you."

"I know, Eli. You don't have to explain to me; I know."

Closing his eyes, he put his arm around her shoulder and began humming along with Garth.

In Vietnam, the only way to really learn
about the enemy was to put small teams of
well-armed men down among the Viet Cong
and NVA to observe—
and survive any way they could.

SIX SILENT MEN:
BOOK ONE
by Reynel Martinez

Follow the bloody history of
the 101st LRP/Rangers by another soldier
who was there.

Published by Ivy Books.
Available in bookstores everywhere.

CENTAUR FLIGHTS
by Richard D. Spalding

**In this riveting firsthand account,
a Cobra pilot describes in devastating detail
life in the midst of fierce aerial warfare.
This is his story—bloody, graphic, and raw,
filled with all the danger and sacrifice
that comprised America's heroic hell in
Vietnam.**

**Published by Ivy Books.
Available in bookstores everywhere.**